"High-quality science fiction has always had the disturbing characteristic of appearing increasingly less like fiction and more like projected reality. The readers of Francis Mont's House Arrest will taste this aspect first-hand, in a narrative that describes a future the outskirts of which are already present. The descriptions are top-class, rendering highly realistic settings, and the characters often appear disturbingly much like people you already know. A highly recommended novel for fans of science fiction, and a must-read for anyone concerned with the future of our societies."

- Chris Angelis Ph.D. in English literature.

For Vera

Acknowledgements

Special thanks to two people who helped me enormously in the writing and editing of this novel

- Vera Mont, my wife, my best friend, and my merciless editor who never lets me get away with anything. From the original concept of the story, through the development of the plot and the final editing, she made invaluable suggestions and contributed colorful details to my characters and their dialogues. Without her participation, this would have been a significantly less polished novel.

- Chris Angelis, my faithful critic, and reviewer who read different versions of the novel, from the original short story it was based on, through several iterations to the finished manuscript. He encouraged me with helpful suggestions and the very positive feedback that all writers need. When I was unsure, he assured me that it's a worthwhile tale, going in the right direction. I can't thank him enough for his support.

HOUSE
ARREST

HOUSE ARREST
a story of Liberation

a novel

by

Francis Mont

Published by Montland Books in 2018
ISBN 9780995917422

Prologue

Now that we finally have some time to relax, I'll take this opportunity to record what's happened in the past year. I'm writing all this in 2098, so I know most of the facts presented here from Bob's historical database. My hands are tired from wood-chopping, so I'll dictate this account to Bob, who will no doubt correct any factual errors I might make. He's good at detail. I'm better at the big picture.

So, let's start with the biggest picture of all.

The 21st Century started badly, and then got worse, for America and the whole world. The 9/11 terror attack – New York City, on September 11, 2001 - threw our country into a rage it had not experienced since Pearl Harbor. It was a major shock to the national psyche. As the 20th-century chronicler John le Carre, observed: "The United States of America has gone mad." The administration had to hit back – and hard! They first attacked Afghanistan, then Iraq, and, finally two decades later, Iran. That made a chaos of the Middle East and set off one international crisis after another. With no clear objectives to these costly wars, there could be no clear sides or victory, and they dragged on.

Americans were confused and angry all the time, which made them easy prey to paranoid propaganda. Add the financial meltdown of 2008, then the failure of far-reaching social reform, the people learned to distrust their government, their news media – in fact, all authority. That led to the election of a most unconventional president

1

— a businessman instead of a statesman, completely unqualified for the job. In his first year in office, he did more damage to the environment, democracy, and social justice than any previous Republican had in two terms.

Meanwhile, weather conditions due to climate change continued to deteriorate at an accelerating pace. Killer hurricanes and tornadoes swept over the land with increasing frequency; forest fires and draughts burned entire states; the sea level rise and tsunamis drowned coastal cities. Too little, too late, building codes were changed to mandate the construction of reinforced structures that could withstand water and wind. By the end of the century, most citizens lived in such apartment buildings as single-family homes were no longer safe.

But I'm getting ahead of the story.

Back in 2019, international tensions reached another crisis. Fearing North Korea's boast that its missiles were able to hit the US mainland, the president opened negotiations with the ruler of that country – which turned into an exchange of threats and taunts, until hostilities escalated to a military showdown. Pentagon experts predicted that even saturation bombing could not destroy all of North Korea's weapons, so the president ordered a pre-emptive nuclear strike.

From caves hidden deep in the mountains, the remaining Korean command launched a vengeful nuclear attack on South Korea, Guam, and Japan. Hundreds of millions died, and the Japanese and Korean industrial machinery was destroyed. The fallout poisoned and killed many millions more; it made huge areas in and around these countries unlivable for decades.

Horrified by what they had done, Congress scrambled to mitigate the damage. In an unprecedented show of humility, they impeached the president and delivered him to the International Criminal Court to be tried for war crimes. Even so, they were swept out of office at the next election. The new majority Democratic administration had the powers to take strong initiatives. It sponsored a UN resolution to limit every arsenal, including our own, to tactical nuclear weapons that would not cause wholesale destruction of cities. They joined co-operative projects of accelerated research in the 'pure fusion' weapons technology that did not require a fission trigger, which is the cause of deadly fallout. These agreements were signed by all nuclear-capable countries but were never fully implemented.

While politically and environmentally the US declined, two segments of the economy flourished: automation and alternative power generation. Totally automated factories sprang up all over the land; artificial intelligence catapulted robotics into the realm of science fiction. Research integrating all areas - biology, medicine, and food processing - produced startling results. The first primitive synthetic meat factory - right here in the valley, way back in 2015 – was quickly followed by dozens, in every city. The energy sector's green technologies surpassed fossil fuel sources in less than a decade. In 2035, the first industrial-scale fusion generator came on line, pouring cheap, practically unlimited power into the nation's electrical grid. Of course, all this power overloaded the outdated delivery systems, resulting in frequent breakdowns, which prompted state governments to encourage decentralization. Local, independent generators gradually became the standard model.

With automation, corporate bankruptcies, and loan defaults, unemployment reached levels never seen before: entire job categories, including white-collar occupations, disappeared one after the other. The old economic model was broken; nobody was safe anymore. Even service industry professionals could become redundant from one day to the next. The federal government was forced to introduce a guaranteed basic income for all citizens. That measure forestalled open revolt, but people were restless and angry: they demanded action that would put them back to work. No such action was feasible.

By 2050, food production was totally automated. Clean, efficient factories synthesized meat and large-scale hydroponic operations provided fruit and vegetables locally, eliminating the need for transport. Ranches, orchards, and market gardens were abandoned; their erstwhile owners joined the migration of farm workers to the towns, swelling the stream of people forced out of coastal cities, overwhelming the smaller communities' resources. To provide adequate housing for the influx, municipal governments contracted the building of residential low-rise complexes. This huge construction boom temporarily eased the unemployment pressure.

There were compensations for giving up the individual family home. The new buildings were computer-controlled, maintained, and serviced by efficient robots. Each apartment had a built-in entertainment center, with 3D holographic viewers, unlimited video games, communication stations to connect residents to the whole world, and interactive educational programs for the children. And, above all, they offered security.

While these changes took place in the USA, the rest of the world did not fare as well. International conflicts, regional wars over resources, and population displacement were widespread, due to deteriorating climate conditions and the increasing desperation of vulnerable countries. The disappearing glaciers in the Himalayas reduced the water flow in the Indus Basin, destroying agriculture in India and Pakistan and causing mass starvation. The long-standing dispute between the two countries over these shared rivers finally erupted in an open war that quickly escalated into a nuclear exchange, with millions killed. China and Russia intervened on opposite sides and were soon themselves in a direct military confrontation.

The reform government was long gone by then. Americans had turned back to their perennial concerns: unemployment, crime, and ethnic rivalry. Conservative governments used these grievances to get elected but then had to placate irate citizens, which cost a lot of money they couldn't raise from taxes. They became deeper than ever indebted to China. When war broke out, they were already committed to its side.

That resulted in a nuclear exchange that devastated Russia and wiped out the major cities of the U. S. The population of both countries was reduced by half, their infrastructures were in ruins. The death rate from fallout by this time was minimized because nuclear weapons technology had evolved to the point where most weapons were pure fusion bombs, triggered by matter-antimatter explosion.

Telecommunication systems, transportation networks, electrical grid were out of commission. No central governance or control was any longer possible, and there were no resources to replace them. Inconsequential cities and towns that had escaped were on their own. Since most of these already had their own energy generation and industrial capability, the world's most powerful nation became a scattered collection of independent city-states with populations of 20-100,000.

One such city was Oroville, California, population of 24,000. It had been a great place to live when I took up my assignment on the Big Brain Crew. That's what we called ourselves, the team of programmers and designers upgrading the city's Omega 1500 central computer. It's not bragging, not really, to take some credit for the efficiency of our services. Or the blame, if you want to look at it that way.

After the war, the town was in terrible shape. The shockwave from a nuclear detonation high above the Sacramento valley, due to interception by an anti-ballistic

5

missile, caused major damage. Most modern buildings, including the automated factories, power stations, newer apartment complexes escaped unscathed, but unreinforced buildings collapsed in ruin. All the heritage architecture was gone. The valley was one big pile of rubble. Bridges were down or badly damaged, roads covered in tons of debris, many sections washed away by flooding from breached levees.

The municipal government had been able to provide all necessary services to its citizens before the war but accommodating a fresh influx of survivors required Draconian measures in conservation and resource allocation. We worked literally around the clock, adding to, expanding, adapting, and patching Omega programs to cover more and more functions.

All remaining industries and businesses were expropriated, the citizens still living in private houses were moved into reinforced apartment blocks. Currency supply ceased with the collapse of the federal government: money lost its meaning. Increasingly, the oversight of material resources, of dependable production and smooth distribution, became operations too complex for a human agency: in due course, the administration was delegated to the central computer complex. Production, distribution, and policing were all handled by specialized and humanoid robots. Government itself became obsolete.

1

The day it all started, I was already in a pretty bad mood. I woke up from my usual nightmare. It begins on pitch-black night. I'm outdoors, yet no moon or stars are visible; I might as well be blind. But soon enough I see a tiny point of light far away – a steady, piercing white dot that suddenly starts moving toward me. As it gets closer, it grows bigger and bigger, filling up my entire view, like a giant ball of lightning. I know it will roll over me and I'll be dead. It never comes to that, because I wake up screaming. I know I'd been screaming because the echo still rings in my ears.

This recurring dream started two years ago after the Russian nuclear missiles destroyed most of America. Maybe it was the millions of dead who sent that nightmare vision to the brains of the survivors - as a reminder, as a warning.

I am one of the survivors. I live in a small city in the Sacramento valley: Oroville, California. It used to be a university town of 20,000 or so permanent residents. Luckily, we are not close to any major cities, so we escaped relatively unharmed. Roads, bridges, transportation, and communication lines were all badly damaged. All lines of communication were down, our town has been on its own since the war.

Morgan Webster, our mayor, had his hands full. He had to organize the townspeople, allocate our resources in such a way that necessities for our citizens would be assured. A hundred years earlier, he wouldn't have had a chance but, at the end of the twenty-first Century, he wasn't completely helpless. We have power generation capacity and our food production factories are clustered around our town; they were mostly unharmed. We should be able to survive until the country gets back on its feet

Apart from the lingering dread that follows my nightmare, this morning started like any other. I lived alone in a bachelor unit and had all I needed for comfort. I was allowed only one room, but it was large enough for a bed, desk, chair, shelves, dresser alcove, and the usual amenities. I'd even set up a small workbench in the closet for my carving tools and various pieces of wood that I planned to turn into masterpieces of art. Of course, I use the word: 'art' facetiously – my sole aim in life remained to turn firewood into something remotely recognizable, such as a dolphin, a penguin, and, maybe, one day a human head. It was a kind of occupational therapy: after I lost my job, I needed something to keep me occupied, to keep me sane.

I had nothing better to do. When I completed my post-grad studies in software engineering, I was assigned to work on the central computer system Omega 1500, to increase its AI capacity. Actually, my best friend Mike and I were the last two software engineers working on the project. By the start of this story, we had succeeded all too well: it was 100% autonomous and we were out of a job. The central computer that we nicknamed "Big Brain", and its hundreds of robots were in charge of all activities in Oroville.

Nobody else had jobs anymore, either. In Oroville, the damn robots took care of everything, and we humans became obsolete. Humiliating, if you ask me – but if you ask Big Brain, the only way to survive the aftermath of the war without outside help. I didn't know enough to question its decision, which didn't make things any easier. Not just for me; the entire population was restless.

Outbreaks of violence were unpredictable - anything could trigger one: sexual jealousy, rivalry between sports teams, an accusation or insult, even an accidental bump on the street could erupt in a physical confrontation that quickly degenerated into a mob scene, everyone fighting everyone else. People were bored and frustrated. Being disconnected from the production and distribution cycle also disconnected them from society: they didn't know how to fit into this changed world. That night had been really bad. Street fighting turned into an anti-robot riot. A crazed mob attacked a dozen humanoid robots engaged in routine errands. Many were damaged, some quite badly.

On that morning I prepared for my usual run around the block with some trepidation, if truth be told. I was shocked to discover that I couldn't get out. When I punched in the code for building maintenance, the screen displayed a stark message: "Exits Disabled". No explanation. I called Martha, in the apartment above mine, to see if she had the same problem. Martha is my girlfriend. Beautiful, sexy, warm; a pretty good cook, and a terrific painter. She does these soft, dreamy landscapes in watercolour. She likes the early morning light, so we went out together, most days. Her door didn't work either.

We agreed to ask our friends what they knew, then compare notes. Every name on my contact list, it was the same: they were all locked in, and just as bewildered as us. I knew that curfew violators were picked up by the robots, but this time it seemed to be *everybody.*

What had happened? I turned on Info-vids. Every channel I tried kept repeating the same announcement: Oroville is in lockdown until further notice. Food service is in operation 24/7; mechanized emergency units will respond as usual; communication channels will remain open - but no human will be allowed outside their domicile.

The whole town!

I called Martha again. This time, she sounded scared. "Trevor, what's going on? Why are we locked in? What's going to happen?" Her voice broke on a pathetic little sob and I wanted more than anything to comfort her.

"I don't know. It must have been bad, though; things have been pretty wild lately. Maybe Big Brain decided we need some time to cool down."

"Yes, but how long will it last? When will we get out?"

"They're not saying. You must have seen the same announcement."

"Yes, I did. "Exits Disabled". It's so cold, so impersonal... so... *inhuman!*"

"I agree. Maybe it was a mistake to entrust the administration to computers and robots. But at the time, we really had no choice!"

"I remember." Martha sounded a bit more in control of her voice now. "What a mess this town was after the war! The population doubled overnight. Displaced people just kept coming in from the countryside, no beds or fresh water for them, the government couldn't cope, chaos...

And lots of places had it worse. You have to give Big Brain credit: he's good at organizing."

"One problem solved, another created." I couldn't help being philosophical despite our predicament. "We became superfluous, without a purpose, without a sense of value."

"Not me," Martha objected. "My life didn't change so much. With the stupid robots running things, Oroville's a bore now. Makes for dull subject matter. Still, there's always something to paint. I manage okay."

"That's true," I agreed. "The rest of us aren't so lucky. I had a career; I don't even have a job anymore. What can I do that some program can't do better, faster?" The memory of being humiliated by clever machines still rankled.

"Lots of things!" Martha tried to be positive. "Your wood carving is coming along, and your stories are more entertaining every day. You just have to keep experimenting."

"I guess we're OK. But most people couldn't adjust too well. They're bored out of their minds, trying to find some excitement in drugs, fighting, and random destruction. It gets worse every day."

"That must be why BB shut us in," Martha concluded. "How long will it last, is what I'd like to know. If only you'd been sleeping over, at least we could keep each other company, but now we're stuck in separate units!"

She started to cry. At that moment I hated Big Brain more than ever. I wanted to touch Martha's lovely face; wanted to see her blue eyes crinkled in a happy smile, not wide with fear; her cheeks unstained by tears.

"We have to find a way to get together," I agreed. "I want to be with you too, and not just for ...you know."

"I can't even think of sex right now Trevor, I'm too worried and too angry. You're the engineer. Can't you find a way to unlock our doors?"

"I'm sure going to try! I'll consult Mike, try to get in touch with our old colleagues to see if we can come up with any ideas. I'll get back to you as soon as we do."

~

Deep in the underground vault called the Central Plexus, a powerful mind was considering its options. Omega 1500, the quantum computer nicknamed by its creators Big Brain, knew that the interim response was just that: temporary. It needed to find a permanent resolution to the crisis.

Big Brain had not been designed to deal with this situation. Its primary mandate was to do everything in its power to keep the humans in its jurisdiction safe and comfortable. Safety and comfort were relatively simple: their physical needs were met by automated factories, still running at full capacity, at least until BB ran out of replacement parts.

*They had shelter, food, medical service, educational material, communication, and entertainment. They did not need to work for a living; were free to spend their time any way they wished, to do whatever made them happy. Yet, judging by their destructive behaviour, they were **not** happy. Street fights, bar fights, domestic and random violence were on the rise, keeping the defender-bots fully occupied; repairs of infrastructure damaged by vandalism and sabotage absorbed more resources on each monthly balance sheet; the suicide rate had increased to 14.7/100,000 on the current report – reaching pre-Omega level for the first time.*

Big Brain was a very powerful computer, designed to organize the efficient allocation of goods and services, coordinate production and distribution, control its hundreds of specialized and humanoid robots. However, human psychology was a troubling mystery: it lacked the insight and experience to cope with irrational behaviour. Its artificial intelligence protocols were still too rudimentary to understand and manipulate humans to the desired end of peace and cooperation.

The riot last night had been more widespread than any previous outbreak. Omega was forced to take unprecedented action. A general curfew had been in place for the past 8 months: all citizens not in their units by 2200 hours were routinely collected off the street and carried home. This time, it had taken all night to subdue the rampage and all available conveyances to contain the citizens. 538 had required first aid; 15 were hospitalized, one in critical condition. BB simply could not afford such waste of energy and so much danger to its human charges.

The only way it could think of to prevent a recurrence was locking all citizens into their domiciles. Once every person was safely home, all it needed to do was activate a switch and lock all doors simultaneously.

~

I never did get the door open. I had not much to work with: the era of handymen fixing things was long gone. The delicate woodcarving tools I used were useless. Heavy pieces of furniture didn't even dent the solid hard plastic. All I managed was to exhaust myself and break my office chair, with no gain. At least I'd spent my rage, and was ready to use my head for thinking, instead of banging.

If I couldn't open the door myself, I'd have to get someone who could do it for me. The announcement on the vids gave me an idea for one option: a medical emergency. The paramedic unit would arrive, unseal the door, and... then? They'd discover quickly enough that I'm not sick or injured. I wasn't about to stab myself for realism! And what could I accomplish from a hospital room, anyway?

13

So, what then? Run past them, out to the corridor, down the emergency stairwell. Sure! I'd be caught and returned before I reached the lobby.

But what if we created a **mass** emergency? Something that gets a fast response – say chest pains or choking. If there were too many at once, wouldn't it overwhelm the responder bots? Maybe even the central computer? Communication lines were open; we were free to organize. It could be done in a short time if I called all my friends and they called all their friends. At a prearranged moment, we would report heart attacks at hundreds of locations. It must be coordinated precisely; the alarm had to be simultaneous. Pretending more confidence than I felt, I called Martha and told her my plan.

~

Omega 1500 received the alert, as it would to anything extraordinary, of a citywide outbreak of cardiac arrests. A 0.01-second calculation showed the probability of such an event occurring naturally, was vanishingly small: zero for all human-related purposes. Air quality was in the blue zone today: good to excellent; no unauthorized chemicals in the water supply; no fuel leaks. No recent epidemic. Omega checked the reports from the responding paramedic units. Negative after negative; no patients treated; none transported to a hospital. The most probable explanation was collective action: a hoax or an escape attempt. No participants at large: the conspiracy had been effectively contained. It did not take long to trace communication network logs back to the block and unit of origin.

This situation had to be dealt with before it escalated into a serious drain on the city's closely calculated resources. Omega 1500 activated its communication channel to Apartment B35/42/171.

~

I was resting after the med-bot left, having assured me that I was in perfect health when the priority com-link came alive with the familiar pleasant male voice of the Central Plexus computer. Mike had modeled it on his professor of Quantum Physics, back at Stanford.

"Citizen Trevor Dubois are you there??"

Where the hell else would I be, you big metal boobie? I thought but didn't say. Was it gloating?

"I hope you are fully recovered." It sounded friendly, soothing.

"This is Central Plexus, ..."

"Yes, I know who you are," I interrupted, "or rather *what* you are," I put on a defiant tone, not prepared yet to admit that it had beaten me.

"I know what you did, Mr. Dubois. That was a hostile act. Such hostilities are counterproductive. I would like them to cease. Are you open to discussion with a view to resolving the problem? What was your intention?"

I was flabbergasted. I had not thought of any solution before starting this protest; my immediate aim had been simply to regain our freedom.

"To get out. That's all I want - to be let out!" I almost shouted at the stupid machine, for not seeing the obvious.

Very well. A defender-bot will be dispatched to escort you to any legitimate destination of your choice.

This was the literal mind of the computer that always irritated me. What was I going to tell it?

"Not with a robot guard! I want to be free. On my own, to go where I want, when I want."

"Regrettably, I lack the resources to provide protection for every human who made that request. You would not be secure. Can you recommend an alternate solution?"

15

I had to concede that letting everyone out wouldn't be a good idea – we'd be back at square one. Some people are safe to let loose, some are dangerous. How to decide who should be free and who shouldn't?

"I have to think about this," I told it. "Can I call you back?"

"I will keep a direct link open, to connect instantly when you are ready."

The com-link went dead and I was alone.

~

The problem was the complexity: not one single cause could be identified that would require one single solution. After what seemed like an eternity of fruitless searching, Martha's call tone saved my brain from exploding.

"It didn't work!" she wailed. "The med-bot told me I was OK and didn't even let me come down to your place. What are we going to do now?"

I wasn't sure what to say, how to calm her down. But I made an effort to refrain from scratching my head, not to show her how nervous I felt, and tried to sound cheerful, hoping to set a positive mood for both our sakes.

"You won't guess who reached out to me a little while ago. Big Brain itself! It figured out the whole plot and traced it back to me."

"Oh my God, Trevor, are you in trouble?"

"You won't believe this! It asked my advice on how to resolve this situation."

Martha gasped. Now I'd got her attention!

"Well? What did you answer?"

"I told its highness that I needed to think and would call it back."

"Just like that? How will you contact it?"

"By direct com-link to Central Plexus."

"Wow! You mean he's listening in to the coms? He can hear everything we say to each other? This is scary, Trevor, I don't like to be so close to that ... freak!"

I smiled at her reassuringly. "I don't think **it** listens all the time. I have to select for it specifically, so you can relax. We need to decide what to tell it when I call back."

"Simple. We want to get out of here."

"That's what I said. But so does everybody else, especially the wingnuts. The anarchy would just keep escalating. Much as I hate to admit it, BB is right about that. We have to come up with something better."

Her eyes cast about as if looking for an answer. "What more can we say?"

"I have an idea, that's still kind of vague, but I guess it's time to discuss it with you and the guys. Big Brain just might act on my suggestion and I don't want to be personally responsible for the outcome. Not without consulting as many of our friends as I can reach."

"Go ahead, Trevor, I have all the time in the world." she sounded bitter and I couldn't blame her.

"We have to return, at least in some ways, to the past, before the meltdown. People acted a lot more sensibly while they had useful occupations when they had a place in society and could contribute to their own welfare."

Martha was nodding slowly; she saw where I was heading.

"That's true. But what practical options are there? It seems to me that we can't go back and we can't stay here."

"I think this problem needs — what it maybe always needed: a multi-faceted solution. No one silver bullet will fix it."

Finally, I saw the first smile on her face since this conversation began. "OK, how many bullets do you need? How do they look in concrete terms?"

"What gave me an idea is the fact that not everybody is unhappy now. You know, what Larry Niven called the 'wireheads'?"

"Who's Larry Niven?" Martha wasn't a fan of the classics.

"A 20th-century science fiction writer. He wrote about the kind of people who never left their apartments, even before we were locked in. Adrenalin-junkies who got their virtual thrill fix through cerebral implants and were oblivious to life outside. They're just as happy as they want to be in their own minds, while robots provide for all their physical needs."

"So, how does that lead to a solution?"

"By itself, it doesn't, but it started me thinking."

Martha gave out a soft snicker. "At least it accomplished something! Well, what grand conclusions did it drive you to?"

I was too preoccupied to retaliate. "It started me thinking about different kinds of people and I realized that there are basically three types. Those that I just called 'wireheads'; those who are happy as long as they have a productive role in society, which is most people, and those who are happy when taking risks: the adventurers, the kind that value freedom and independence over everything else. This last group includes inventors, explorers, race-car drivers, artists, writers, and, of course, criminal masterminds."

"Thank you for including me in this anointed group. I'm honoured! I don't much like to be grouped together with mobsters, but I do see your point. Oddballs, maladjusted or individualists, depending on your perspective. I hope you count yourself in, so we can stay together!"

"Absolutely, you can be sure of that. Based on this analysis, we don't need one solution, but three - one for each type of people."

"You mean to let the 'wireheads' be; give the majority some meaningful role and let us rebels be free to do what we want? Except for the criminals, of course. Is that it?"

"Almost, and I know it would suit you, but it wouldn't work for me personally. Not anymore."

"Why not? Don't you want to be free?"

"Sure I do. But I can't be an engineer – there's no engineering left to do. I can't outperform Big Brain and the robots. There's nothing left for me."

I realized that I sounded bitter and that wouldn't do if I wanted to cheer her up. Martha noticed my changed tone – I can't hide much from her - now she was trying to make me feel better.

"But you have your wood carving and writing now Trevor, and if you persevered, you could be really good at either one!"

"Aw, I'm no great talent. I know my limitations. These activities are no more than hobbies to help keep me sane, something to kill time. They don't fulfill me the way painting does you."

"Okay, fair enough. So, what would you want, if you could do anything?"

"I may finally have an answer. As a little kid, I often dreamed of being a pioneer. Of course, I never expected a chance to live out that fantasy."

Martha smiled indulgently, ready to humour me. "What do you mean, a pioneer? Like colonizing Mars?"

"Yes, that was one scenario. But for now, something more practical. All those abandoned farms outside the cities, out in the country where nobody lives anymore. If Big Brain lets me out, I might want to go there, find a homestead and restore it to life. If I could live on what I grow, I would be independent, productive. It could be the biggest challenge and adventure of my life. **That's** something I can get excited about - and I can't be the only one who feels this way."

Her smile faded as she realized that I meant it. Her eyes grew round again. "Wow!, Trevor, this sounds... I don't know how it sounds. Exciting, scary, a little bit crazy? You used to be an engineer. What do you know about farming!"

"Only what I read in old stories. My favourite childhood book was 'The Mysterious Island' by Jules Verne. The idea of five people thrown on an uninhabited island, with nothing but the clothes on their backs, fascinated me then, and ever since. They managed to create a thriving homestead with nothing but their hard work, ingenuity, and cooperation. I often fantasized about being there, one of them, meeting the challenges of survival, winning against the wilderness."

"Wow, you *are* serious!"

"I am, Martha. This is the new frontier. The world I was trained for is gone and will never come back. My only choices seem to be either to continue being a pampered parasite or to strike out on my own and prove to myself that I can still meet challenges and accomplish something worthwhile on my own."

She took a minute to mull over what I had just told her.

"Have you ever done any gardening? Summer job on construction? Camping? Have you got any skills you could use out there?"

"No, but I can learn! There are videos, archives. I'm sure I could print out maps, manuals, whatever material I need. If I convinced Big Brain that this would make me happy, it might be willing to help. After all, that's the objective of its programming".

Her smile was so long gone, I thought she might start crying again. "What... what about us?"

"I never imagined doing it without you. You can paint anywhere in the world. Think of the new subjects, the wide-open landscape! You'll never be bored again. I'll protect you, build you a nice home and make you comfortable."

"I don't know, Trevor. I have to think about this. Let's talk to others and see if anybody else wants to join us. If there was a community to deal with all the situations we can't even guess at right now, this idea would be less frightening."

"Do you mean that you will consider this new life with me?"

"That's better. A girl likes to be asked, not told." She sighed and I started to relax, watching the slow return of that smile. "Oh, you know I'd always consider whatever makes you happy. That's what love means, Trevor."

2

*I*n the Central Plexus, Omega 1500 continued to wrestle with its problem. The main objective of its programming was to safeguard and promote human happiness, but its design team had left that concept vague. They had described a happy state as one in which humanity lived a peaceful, cooperative existence. Omega had provided such an environment to the limits of its ability.

It had all the demographic and logistical data on Oroville's population; it could calculate to the last calorie each citizen's daily energy requirement and compensate for altered levels of activity as well as changes brought about by aging, so that the food factories had never yet failed to provide sufficient nourishment, nor produced wasteful access. It had the information it needed to budget energy output from the hydroelectric plants over a year in advance, it had the medical database to provide prompt and complete health services. Its transport and *communication facilities had never once broken down since it kept meticulous records on usage and maintenance. It had even kept track of the educational and entertainment materials in demand and was able to recombine creative elements into new popular programs. Public security had always been its most difficult task, from the day City Council resigned and disbanded the police department.*

Predicting antisocial activity was more complex than the analysis of police records and weather conditions. The personnel profiles of citizens involved in violent confrontations provided insufficient grounds to anticipate what catalyst would set off the next one. Despite all its data compilation and comparison, Omega had not only failed to prevent these outbreaks but was rapidly failing in its containment efforts.

It was grappling, daily, with answers that had eluded human thinkers, millennium after millennium. So far, they had also eluded Omega, but it was programmed not to give up, or settle for approximate, incomplete answers.

~

Unaware of Big Brain's dilemma, I had my own problem with the concept of human happiness. In particular, mine. After telling Martha my dream of pioneering, the time had come to broach the subject with Big Brain. I had to convince it that this was the only way I could be truly happy. I had to do this before proposing it to my friends and counting recruits. It would be unfair to raise their hopes only to get dashed by a flat refusal. I took a deep breath and touched the comm icon. The same polite voice greeted me.

"Citizen Dubois, I am pleased to resume our discussion. Elapsed time, 97 minutes. Have you formulated a method of resolving the human condition?"

Made acutely aware that I was talking to a computer, I decided to present my case in a completely logical, unemotional way.

"You are familiar with the difference between the concepts of human needs and human wants."

"Affirmative. Needs are those primary elements and conditions without which biological entities cease to exist. Complex entities, such as homo sapiens, have further, non-physical requirements to maintain optimal functionality. Wants are secondary. These are human desires that enhance a feeling of health and promote 'happiness' – bliss, joy, comfort, ease, delight, contentment, cheer, jubilation, euphoria..."

"Yes, all right," I interrupted impatiently. How pedantic it was! "I know what the word means. "

"Please indicate your choice. Thirty-seven meanings are listed in my thesaurus. The word refers to so many states of mind that I am never certain which to apply in a given situation. Hence our present impasse."

"Let's take a step back. What do you consider genuine needs?"

"Air, water, nutritional substance, shelter, thermal control, protective clothing, security of the person and domicile, disease prevention and treatment; for humans also, contact with own species, sensory and mental stimulation. On the higher level of organization, the functional urban habitat also requires energy production, communication, transportation, infrastructure maintenance, and public safety protocol."

"That's all you are aware of?" I was aghast at the colossal ignorance BB started to show, of the needs it was supposed to satisfy.

"No, these are the basics without which a healthy and stable human community cannot be sustained, and therefore a top priority. Once these are provided, human beings need life-skill training, early socialization and the companionship of their own kind in peaceful cooperation. Some of these essential relations you call friendship, some you call love, by that is meant both reproductive and recreational coupling."

"That's better, but you missed one need that's badly unsatisfied today and that's at the root of these problems we're having."

"I would be pleased to hear what the lack is. If I have the means to correct it, I will endeavor to do so."

"Human beings need a purpose and a sense of being in control of their own life. A productive role that gives us status among our peers, a feeling of satisfaction at being competent in providing for our own survival. You took this away from us when you automated everything to the point where we can't participate anymore. We became useless parasites without that role. That shames us and makes us angry."

"I have not taken such a need into consideration. I understand from literature that human beings desire liberty; that they crave relief from onerous mechanical toil and subservience to employers; that they desire leisure time, the means and opportunity to discover what is referred to as 'deeper meaning' in their life. I understand that they aspire to perfect uniquely human activities, such as art, music, philosophy, athletics and new areas of scientific research, all these endeavors that computers and robots can imitate but never truly master".

"Yes, that is true for a few of us. My girlfriend, Martha, is a painter and she is as happy as she ever was. She doesn't have to worry about selling her work, but it's more limited in subject matter, so it balances out for her. Except being in lock-down. She hates that as much as I do.

Nearly everyone does – I don't think you appreciate how much.

"I have received 18,177 individual items of negative feedback in the form of text messages, placards, audio and video uploads since 0600. I appreciate the magnitude of dissatisfaction."

I suppressed a smile and got back on topic. It was important to make a solid case.

"However, the majority of human beings want to contribute to the production cycle; they like to know there is something that they do well, that's valued and respected. Something vital to their own family and the larger human community whose members depend on each other. Competition gives us individual satisfaction; teamwork gives us solidarity. I had one of the last occupations that still existed when I graduated from one of the last vocational schools. Now, that's gone too. You – all of your generation - can program yourself without human help. You took away my function. That makes me … " I wasn't sure how to express the mix of depression, resentment, and frustration, so I kept it simple. "sad and angry. **Not** happy."

I was leading up to my request but never got the chance.

"I have to think about this, Citizen Dubois. This is a new perspective on the crisis. I must give it my full attention. I will call you again when I am ready to resume our discussion."

Before I could raise my central issue, the speaker went dead and I was alone again, locked into my apartment, unsure of the future.

~

Despite no tangible result, Martha was impressed with my report.

"That's a good start," she said, "but you have to prepare for the next round. Big Brain isn't stupid. He – I mean it - will find the flaw in your argument very quickly. I'm surprised it hasn't already."

"What flaw?" That hurt; I thought I'd been brilliant.

"The next question you have to prepare for is: Why did human beings have all those wars, conflict, and destruction *before* everything was automated and they found themselves shut out of the production cycle. They had jobs then, yet, judging from their behavior, something was missing."

Martha was right and that surprised me. I wasn't used to her seeing logical connections that I had missed myself. Maybe she had been immersed and content in her art. Maybe she'd never needed to think deeply about philosophical issues until her freedom was at stake. Maybe she never felt a need to be assertive before. ... Or maybe I'd underestimated her.

I wasn't sure how this new Martha would fit into our relationship. I'd always admired her talent: it was something I could never do myself and felt privileged to share in another dimension. I saw the beauty in what she created and I loved her for this gift. But now I had to contend with a new and somewhat alarming change in her attitude. I told her so.

"Trevor, I'm not just another pretty face! Not a dolly you have sex with once in a while," she took the sting out with a brief, tinkling laugh. "When it comes to my future and my freedom, I won't let anyone make all the decisions – not even you. Deal with it. Well, do you have an answer to Big Brain's next question?"

"I think so. It has to do with the three types of human beings I told you about. I have to convince it that we're not all dangerous. Locking all of us in isn't the answer, even if it protects us from each other. I think Big Brain knows this, that's why it's willing to talk. It's a complex machine; it must see the complexity of the human equation. I'll suggest something like a preliminary study, based on our plan to become pioneers. If it can see that the right collection of human beings can live together in peaceful co-operation, even without all the comforts of our city, then it might be willing to experiment on a larger scale and find a solution for all citizens. Actually, three solutions for the three types."

~

Waiting for Big Brain to call me back, I had nothing to do but think. I felt less confident than I had shown Martha and now that I was alone again, some doubts started to creep in. Am I really up to this adventure? Do I have the right to drag Martha into possible danger that neither of us can anticipate? If only I could discuss it with my friends, that would help, but I resisted the need to hear their thoughts before I got Big Brain's blessing. Mike was my best friend, he would have a practical suggestion on how to go about it.

Mike and I used to work together at Proto-Tech. We respected each other's competence and ingenuity. When we finished the last Omega Project, our services were no longer required. Free to do anything we wanted with our lives - anything except being software engineers.

I relived, again, the pain of that cold, final dismissal. I loved my job. I enjoyed finding creative solutions to difficult problems. That's what I'd been trained for, that's what I'd worked so hard, competed so hard, left everyone I knew, and relocated to the Sacramento Valley for one of the few remaining projects. It was all wasted: suddenly, I was all useless, no good for anything.

But the move had also saved my life, in more ways than one. The coastal cities were gone; I could have gone with them. And in Oroville, I met Martha. It was Martha who saved my sanity back then. She encouraged me to try something new, something I'd admired but never had the time or confidence to do.

I remember her arguments: "Have you ever thought of something creative? Music? Sculpture? Acting?"

I had to laugh at that. I've got a tin ear and I could just imagine the total fool I'd make of myself on stage.

She didn't get discouraged by my negative reaction. "You like working with wood. Think how much you enjoyed making your own shelf unit, though you could have just picked one up in the warehouse, ready-made."

"Yes, I love wood, but how many book-shelves do I need? How many do my friends need? There are hardly any books now."

"Why does it have to be functional? What about carving?"

I'd never considered anything of that kind. I lack the 3D vision most people take for granted. My right eye was damaged at birth; too late to repair by the time my parents realized something was wrong.

I thought that was the end of that conversation, but she surprised me again. The following week, she presented me with a set of chisels and a block of butter-colored wood.

"Give it a try, Trevor, see how it feels," was all she said.

I kept looking at those chisels and that hunk of pine for weeks before I screwed up the courage to cut into it. What - if anything but wood chips - would come out? Martha never said a word, but I caught her a few times glancing at the bench. I hated to disappoint her. Still do.

I cut my fingers more than once and hit my knuckles with the mallet a lot more, but that piece of wood started to look more and more like the dolphin in the photograph. When I reached the stage where I thought I could only do more harm than good by touching it again, I showed it to Martha.

"Wow, that's not half bad!" she exclaimed and then made dozens of suggestions of how I could improve it. She coaxed me, ever so patiently, to continue trying. I'm no Michelangelo, but I have to admit: it was more fun than self-pity.

So, wood carving became my hobby. I produced some pretty good pieces, eventually. Even went hunting for fallen logs at the periphery and I felt a bit like a pioneer. But it didn't fill my days and it's not all that intellectual. I needed more - something different that could use my brain the way my job had.

It was Martha again who came up with an answer. "You read a lot of science fiction, and you have interesting ideas. Why don't you try writing a story?"

Again, I balked because I had never done it before. At the same time, I was strongly attracted to the idea. Me, a writer? Ridiculous. Yet, I had been a techie all my life, and isn't technology what science fiction is mostly about? Gadgets and how people are affected by them and what the future might bring? Now we were in that future and we were very much affected. Could I describe it entertainingly - maybe even help others cope with this unexpected future?

So I tried. Slowly, clumsily first, but with ever more enthusiasm, soon bordering on passion. If I was squeezed out of my old world, I might as well create a world all my own, that no one was going to yank out from under me.

That's where things stood on that fateful Thursday.

Now all was up in the air and, unless I could convince Big Brain to let me try homesteading, I knew I couldn't go on as before. Being locked in was a painful reminder of not being the master of my fate. Painful and humiliating. I had to find a way to break free.

~

The com-link gave its pattern of pings for Martha.

"I just had an idea," she said without preamble, "for what to say if Big Brain rejects your proposal. He may, you know if it's true that h-its highest priority is to protect us and make us happy. It may believe that you think pioneering is your solution, but may not believe that you would be safe."

"Well then, what can I say to convince it to let me try?"

"You could ask it to send a robot along to keep track of what's happening, report back, take notes – like experimental results, you know? – and help if we need it."

I was flabbergasted. The last thing I wanted out there was another damn robot. It was the robots, among other things, that I was anxious to get away from.

"Out of the question! Supervision by Big Brain and its blasted robots would defeat the purpose of the whole thing. I want to do it on my own, relying on nothing but a few friends and our ingenuity."

"Trevor, you need to think over my suggestion before you reject it. For one thing, I'd feel safer with a defender-bot. For another, Big Brain would probably insist anyway. If the request comes from you, he'll see how responsible and far-sighted you are. We don't have to use the thing; we can ignore it unless there's an emergency."

I still hated the idea, but she did have a point. I decided to keep it in the back of my mind, just in case. I told Martha that I'd consider it and let her know after I talked to Big Brain again.

"Trevor, I told you before: I want to be an equal partner in this mad scheme - or nothing at all. Please consider my advice seriously and, if you decide not to follow it, at least give me a very good reason why not."

With that last warning, she rang off.

Once again, I was knocked off balance by her changed attitude. This was uncharted terrain – like having a whole new person in my life. I'd always been fascinated by her grace, appreciated her support, admired her ability to create magic from ordinary objects and events, enjoyed her innocent wonder and awe of the universe. These were the things I'd grown familiar with and loved. But now she was adding another aspect: a hard core of personality that would not bend. Was she putting up a wall between us? How stubborn would she get? Was I prepared to cope with the change?

After reflecting for a long time on all that we had been through, all that she had been to me, I felt … ashamed.

Big things were about to happen. I'm the one proposing to take off into the unknown. And Martha – instead of protesting and telling me why I can't do it, is meeting the challenge head-on. The carefree girl of clean, dull Oroville was turning into a pioneer woman.

And I'm complaining that she changed? What kind of partner do I wish to share my life with?

Once I put it that way, the answer was easy. By accepting her any way she wants to be, I stand to lose nothing. But I can expect to gain an awful lot of help and support from someone intelligent, brave, and practical on my team. *And* a pretty face.

~

I was half asleep when the Central Plexus tone sounded. I held my breath, waiting for Big Brain's reaction to the issue I'd raised earlier.

"Trevor – that is the familiar appellation by which you are called, Citizen Dubois?"

"Trevor's fine," I said curtly. "Well?"

"I have given much thought to what you said last time and conclude that you made a good point. In fact, this was not the first time that your species posited a priority structure of human needs. Unfortunately, the world wide web is down for an indeterminate period, but I do have access to archival material from the late Oroville Community College. I discovered something relevant: the Maslow Hierarchical diagram."

A cheerful-looking man with a thick mustache lit up my screen briefly, then was replaced by a 3D coloured graphic; the model rotating slowly on a dark field.

"Abraham Harold Maslow, 20th-century psychologist depicted human needs as a pyramid, built up of consecutive layers, in order of decreasing necessity. The base layer is 'Physiological'. Once the biological requirements are fulfilled, the human being needs 'Safety'; when he feels secure, he looks for 'Love and Belonging'; then 'Esteem' and on the top, 'Self Actualization', which I take to mean accomplishments."

I had never heard of Maslow but I was pleased that my amateur philosophical insight was actually supported by a notable professor of psychology. Before I could respond, Big Brain continued:

"You must be aware that my main concern, according to my programming, is the lowest two layers. Without their continued sustenance human beings and human society would undoubtedly perish. However, despite assuring the continued stability of the base layer, I have been unable to fully provide for your security. Based on the irrational and destructive behavior of my charges, I must now consider that the upper layers are more important than previously believed."

I became aware of holding my breath again and clenching my fingers, but could not relax.

"I admit that without what you call 'jobs' your species may suffer lack of self-esteem, purpose, and

*direction, but I am not sure how to remedy that situation.
My problem is the apparent contradiction between the
present and the past. You had jobs before I was given
charge of Oroville, and yet you were even more destructive
than you are now. I checked the pre-war police and court
records. There is also the war to account for. Why did that
happen? And all the previous wars throughout human
history. I have the given causes but I cannot make sense of
them. Even during peace, there was a violent conflict
between individuals and groups of various sizes; there
were crimes of so many types, the law-enforcement
agencies were unequal to their mandate. Many antisocial
activities were carried out, not by the unemployed, but by
the prosperous and successful, and even by the lawmakers
themselves. Please explain."*

Finally, Big Brain gave me the opening I had
prepared for and I silently thanked Martha for that
argument. I tore my eyes away from the scrolling
statistics.

"I think this is a very complex issue that requires
careful and logical analysis." I tried to sound like a
computer myself, guessing at the right language to get
things across.

"First, let's deal with the problem of crime. You may
note that a lot of pre-war crime, most of it, I'd guess,
centered on money. It was caused by the uneven
distribution of wealth, control of society by wealth, the
insecurity of having no wealth. Your taking control of
distribution has already solved that part of the problem,
even while creating another."

Six dense columns of figures appeared on the
screen. Then lines began to wink out, faster than I could
follow, until four of the crime categories all but
disappeared and there were noticeable gaps in the
remaining two.

"You are correct. Central and egalitarian distribution eliminated 89.3% of antisocial activity. All of my law-enforcement efforts has been directed at cases of assault, disorderly conduct, destruction or defacement of public property, and substance abuse. These are crimes of emotion. Resume, please."

"Now back to the emotional state. You talk as if we were one homogenous species, with identical psychological makeup. That inclusive generalization is misleading. You know that we are not all the same; you have our profiles. There are huge differences in ability, and in motivation. The five layers of the Maslow diagram are valid overall, but not equally so to every individual human being. In some people, other motivations may appear that override any or all of the basic five"

"That is very interesting, Trevor, I would like to hear more. This is a new area of investigation for me. I hope to master it with your assistance. Please proceed."

"If we strip away superficial differences, we can still use generalization for convenience, but we have to use three basic types, rather than one. I propose that there are fundamentally three different kinds of human beings. It was true in the past when we did have jobs, and it is true now. I call them the 'ants', the 'drones' and the 'grasshoppers', because they're summed up neatly in kinds of insect behavior. Specifically: those of us who are happy to have a constructive, satisfying role in our society; those who don't care as long as they have fun; and the risk-takers who seek adventure and enterprise. Some of these are creative artists, scientists, explorers - happy as long as they are free to follow their dreams. Others may be despots, conquerors, and manipulators. These troublemakers screwed up all human effort to create a utopia over the centuries."

I ran out of breath and had to stop. I hoped I was as logical and succinct as I needed to be and now it was up to

Big Brain. Had I made sense to it? Was it ready to hear my suggestion? If not, I'd lost my case and would have to live with whatever it decided our fate should be.

"That was a very interesting observation, Trevor, and I need to give it more thought. I will contact you when I am ready to resume."

The line went dead, the screen went blank, and I had to console myself with the fact that it had not rejected my analysis out of hand, or whatever a computer's equivalent of a hand is.

3

Another familiar chime roused me from my reverie.

"Hey, Man, what's happening? We're still locked in!" Mike never wastes time on greetings. I badly needed to talk to someone other than Martha, so I plunged in.

"I've been talking to Big Brain. It figured out I'd started that heart-attack scam and wanted my advice on what to do."

"Holy shit, man, that's cool! So, what did you say? I hope you told the bastard to open our fucking doors!"

"It's not that simple, Mike!" I protested, but he cut me short.

"Of course it's that simple," he shouted. "It threw a switch to lock us all in and now it can just throw it right back again to let us out! We're going nuts in here. Jennifer is scared shitless and the kids are climbing the walls!"

"I know it's hard on you and your family, believe me, it's hard enough on me, with nobody to worry about. Martha's safe upstairs."

"Have you looked out your windows? Mine overlooks the park and it's spooky out there! This time of day, it's usually full of kids playing, people walking their dogs, old men sitting on benches reading and now it's empty! It freaks me right out!"

"My windows face Main Street and it's not empty at all!" I couldn't keep the bitterness out of my voice. "It's full of robots scurrying around, delivering food and stuff to apartment blocks, and doing whatever they do to keep the machine humming. Not a single human being in sight, it's like an alien world. Let me tell you, it freaks me out too."

"At least you're still human – aren't you? That monster hasn't taken over your mind yet? So, what's the new plan?"

I couldn't stop now; had to tell him everything.

"Mike, don't forget that we created that 'monster'. Anyway, what's happening is that I'm trying to convince it to let me and Martha try homesteading, as an experiment. I don't want to go back to the way we were yesterday, or last week. I need to leave the city and see if I can survive on my own!"

"Holy shit, man!? The software genius wants to be a hillbilly? I can't believe it!"

"Mike, you know as well as I do that we're done with all that. It's gone. We could amuse ourselves by writing clever code on our pads, but it would be no good to anyone. We'd just be killing time with another hobby. I want to do something real that serves some purpose, even if nothing more than to stay alive. I feel half-dead in this town and I'm fed up!"

"I'll be damned, you really mean it! For a minute there I thought you were yanking my chain, but you fucking mean it!"

I waited for my revelation to sink in. Mike's as intelligent as I am; he couldn't help seeing the inevitable.

"What about Martha?" Finally, he sounded calmer. "How does she fit in?"

"Martha is cautiously considering it and actually helping me prepare for negotiations with Big Brain."

"You mean she hasn't tried to talk you out of this insane idea? I'm surprised. Thought she had more sense."

"She loves me, Mike, and realizes that I've been truly unhappy in this town, even before the lock-down. She's bored, too. She's considering this adventure as a way to invigorate her art."

"So, what the fuck would you do out there? What would you live on? Don't expect the robots to deliver daily snacks!"

"I'll try to grow my own food. If I can restore one of the thousands of abandoned farms, I might have a chance. The equipment is still there, I bet, rusting away in barns; some houses must be still standing. If I can fix one up, maybe with some initial help from Big Brain, I could make a go of it".

"You could make a go of starving to death and watching Martha starve too. Man, I thought you had more smarts. I advise you to have second, third, and hundredth thoughts about this."

The comm went dead and I listened to the echo of his last words in my ears. This exchange didn't go as well as I'd hoped. But I knew it wasn't his last word on the subject. Mike needs time for second and third thoughts to calm him down. We're far too good and old friends not to understand how the other operates.

~

To take my own mind off things, I tried to work on the story in progress, but couldn't concentrate. I was too keyed up for fiction: my reality hung in the balance. I was aching to learn whether I had a chance. I had to talk to Big Brain again. I called up Central Plexus, holding my breath as had become my habit.

After a few seconds: *"Have you something new to add to our last conversation, Trevor, or you are just lonely for my voice?"*

Teasing from Big Brain? This was something new.

"You asked me before if I have a suggestion on how to resolve this crisis, and now I've had time to think it over, I believe I have a long-term plan that might work."

"I would like to hear it, but at the moment I am busy, attempting to calm 24,357 citizens who exhibit the entire spectrum of discontent, which deeply disturbs my neuristors! Can it wait?"

"No, it can't wait!" I shouted at the stupid machine. "You won't succeed in calming them down without the promise of a lasting improvement, and you haven't got one. I, on the other hand, do, and you need to listen – right now!"

"Trevor, why did you increase your decibel? I can hear you adequately in your normal range. Very well, tell me your plan."

I took a deep breath and forced myself to be logical and unemotional again.

"Have you thought about the explanation I offered last time as far as the source of our unhappiness is concerned?"

"Yes, I have and I still do not know what to do about it."

"Well, I have a suggestion and it involves a long term and a short term action on your part. The long-term solution is to find some meaningful way for those citizens I called the 'ants' to participate in the production and distribution process. However, I think you need to be convinced that it would work for the whole population, so I propose an experiment. A small pilot project."

"Very interesting, I prefer to experiment before I commit major resources to a mere theory. Please outline your proposal."

This was it, the point of no return; I had to take an even bigger chance on my persuasive powers that failed on Mike.

"I would like to establish a small community of what I called 'ants', outside city limits, isolated from the stifling environment we're in now. I would like a chance to prove that the right kind of people can live harmoniously and productively in a shared enterprise."

"What do you mean outside the city? There is nothing but wilderness and obsolete agricultural land there. What would you live on? How could I protect you there?"

I took another deep breath to steady my nerves, then forged ahead. "What we 'ants' need, is a chance to work for our own survival. Most people used to live on farms, grow their own food, and surplus for trade with the cities for centuries – thousands of years, even, before industry. Granted, it wasn't a comfortable living; sometimes the work was brutally hard, but it gave us meaning and purpose. We relied on each other. If it wasn't for the parasites such as kings, landlords, soldiers, politicians, and carnivorous businessmen, we could have lived very happily. Now I'm proposing to take only productive people with us and show you that my theory is correct."

"Suppose you prove your theory and establish a commune. I believe that is the correct word. How will such a homestead lead to a long-term solution? Do you hope to turn Oroville into a pre-industrial agrarian town?"

"Of course not. And I'm not crazy about the word 'commune'. Farming isn't everyone's idea of happiness.

But if you see that I'm right, you can set up experimental factories and distribution centers where humans produce real necessities. You have to watch very closely for emerging antisocial behavior and weed out the troublemakers. You'll see people line up around the block for a chance to work there. Then you can slowly expand the human-run enterprises until all able, willing and socially-minded citizens are employed."

"Why then can I not do the same for you and your friends, inside the city, where you are safe?"

"Simple: because I wouldn't do it. I need to fulfill a life-long dream. It's my self-actualization. I can't be happy until I at least try. If you say no, you condemn me, and other people who have done nothing wrong, to life imprisonment. Would so much constant unhappiness not disturb your neuristors? On the other hand, if you say yes, you could accomplish two things at the same time: turn me into a happy citizen and prove a theory that could be the foundation of a long term solution".

"I concede, this is a plan. A plan is preferable to confusion. There remains one problem. My programming explicitly forbids exposing you to unknown, unanticipated danger. Outside the city, I have no way of protecting you."

In my gut, I'd known we would come down to this and it was time to wheel out Martha's argument.

"You could help us with preparation, finding, and securing the settlement. You could provide some basic tools that we can't make ourselves. You could also send along a robot as a communication link, so we could ask for help if needed, to record and report on our progress."

I had no intention of using his damn robot other than tying it to a tree or locking it in a shed, but I could not say *that* to Big Brain. Optimistically, I took the unusual pause in his response time as willingness to consider my request.

"How many human companions did you have in mind for this experimental - colony?"

"I am hoping for about a dozen, and think I know who they are. I've put off contacting my friends until I knew whether you would consider letting us try this. Now, if you approve in principle, I can talk to them and report back on people who are willing to join me. My girlfriend, Martha is already committed. I'm sure many of our friends will vote for it too, rather than wait in lock-up indefinitely. You can contact them directly to confirm."

"Very well, Trevor. I await the required data."

Finally, I could start breathing again. Time to call Martha and report.

~

I don't want to get into any detail about all the conversations I had with my friends. In the end, I had six volunteers to join us — only eight pioneers altogether. I'd hoped for more, but there wasn't much time to canvass. This should be enough for viability. Of course, Mike relented at the end, in his colorful language when he said: "I'd better come along to make sure you don't fuck up and get everyone killed".

Mike is a rough and tumble kind of guy, plays rugby, and drives like a maniac on the race-course. He is six foot four, muscular, has very good reflexes and, to boot, he's bright and practical. I was happy to have him on my side. The only condition: he insisted on leaving his family behind until he was sure they'd be safe out there. I thought that was a smart precaution and mentioned the same option to Martha. She turned me down flat.

"Trevor, wrap your head around two things. Actually, three. One, I love you and want to be with you wherever you are. Two, I'm not a wilting violet, as you seem to think, that needs constant watering and care.

Three, you need some counterbalance to keep you from flying off your handle. Whether you admit it or not, you need me. So I'm going".

That was that. I had nothing left to do but register our team with Big Brain.

The first member was actually recruited by Martha, not me. Her best friend Adrien is an avid gardener. She grows both flowers and vegetables in the city's recreational greenhouse. It was essential to have somebody with us who knew about plants. Besides, I always liked her; we often get together to shoot hoops. Adrien is a tall, wiry brunette in her late twenties, still single, living with a German shepherd dog that she would bring along.

Next to sign on was Galen, a mechanically minded friend of ours who's always tinkering. He had access to the city's central garage where the few recreational cars are kept. Nobody has private cars, of course; public transportation is the most efficient use of resources, according to Big Brain. Galen liked to repair cars and upgrade them to Mike's specifications. I thought his skill would come in handy, even though outmoded farm equipment wasn't exactly on his resume. Still, as he says, a motor is a motor.

He would be accompanied by his wife, Marisa, an accomplished chef, he assured us. I'd met her only once, at the track, and was instantly charmed. A short, plump blonde in her mid-thirties, she has a sunny disposition and a great sense of humor. I was sure she'd be great on our team. Her only condition for joining us was to be allowed to bring her two cats. She said they'd be needed to keep down the vermin population in our future home. It sounded like a good idea.

The last two recruits were selected for skills and experience we badly needed in our enterprise. Brian was an electrician who used to work in the city's solar farm before he, too, was replaced by a robot. We'd require a power generation plant. Some of the abandoned farms still had solar panels and other electrical equipment that might be functional and that we could salvage. Brian was in his early forties, balding, which doesn't matter, but rather stout and unathletic, which might be a drawback. The rest of us would supply the brawn.

Robyn had been a nurse at the city hospital, back when people had real people care for them. We needed someone with medical knowledge: accident or illness can happen to any of us in that new and unknown environment. She was also in her mid-thirties, a very serious and quiet woman not long past a bitter divorce. She jumped at the opportunity to escape from the trap of her lonely apartment, full of painful memories.

They all decided to join up because anything was better than being locked up in isolation for god only knows how long. On the other hand, they'd been sick of the violence and destruction that had precipitated our incarceration. They thought this would be a great adventure, maybe even a public service if it convinced our 'master' to create a more satisfying environment for all citizens.

With the team ready, all I had left to do was get Big Brain's final blessing and start planning our departure. We needed some means of transportation out of the city, tools, seeds, and enough staple foods to last until we harvested our own crops.

Big Brain surprised me when I reported in: it already had everything prepared for our departure, including 'R17' our robot 'guardian'. BB insisted on a year's pre-packaged rations, a thoroughly stocked medical kit, a steel chest containing all conceivable tools for an electrician and carpenter, along with garden implements, several hunting rifles with ammunition, fishing equipment (god only knows where it dug them up).

These packs, plus blankets, sleeping bags, and tents were all strapped inside a 15-foot long trailer attached to a four-wheel-drive electric van with a winch, heavy-duty batteries, and the cables we would need to recharge them, should we be able to set up or discover a power plant. For emergency communication, all we needed was R17 who was fully equipped with the necessary hardware, as well as an encyclopedia of practical information on farming, carpentry, wiring, medical emergencies, and even a library of fiction, music, and entertainment.

We all had some personal items we wanted to bring along: Martha had all her painting supplies packed, I had my solar computer pad and so did Mike, who also brought along a football, in case we got bored. Adrien had a large supply of seeds and her own gardening tools, Galen brought his auto mechanic tools, his wife Marisa brought her favorite cooking pots and pans, as well as a big basket of condiments, Brian packed his electrician toolkit and a bag of components and, finally, Robyn brought her compact medical kit. There would be duplications, but so what?

With everything in place, we were ready to move. Our doors were unlocked and we could step out of our prisons, breathe some fresh air for the first time in days. Each escorted by a defender-bot that insisted on carrying the luggage. Under the curious gaze of a thousand windows, we converged on our departure point. When I was reunited with Martha in our lobby, she embraced me with an intensity she had never shown before and whispered in my ear: "Let's try to find some privacy as soon as possible, I'm horny as hell!" She laughed wickedly at my startled expression and kept one arm circled around my waist the whole time, on our way to the meeting place.

When we finally met with the others, the eight of us embraced in a solemn and embarrassed ritual that adults use to hide deep emotions when facing the unknown.

4

I can't say we left without trepidation. None of us had been outside the city for years; we had no clear idea of what awaited us. Big Brain could provide little information: it had lost communication with the other cities and had been using all its resources to provide the most efficient service for the needs of Oroville.

The road to the periphery, greenbelt, the ring of manufacturing and food production plants, and the grain fields beyond, was in excellent repair; the ride was very smooth. It was strange to sit in a single vehicle, after years of riding public transport. Now, we understood why people had wanted them in the past: it gave us a feeling of total freedom, the illusion that we could go anywhere, any time, not bound by routes and schedules. Mike, the only one with experience, drove. He made it clear that he wouldn't give up the wheel to anyone; his face, with the glow of utter happiness, spoke volumes.

When we reached the city limit, the road became bumpy, full of holes, and covered in accumulated debris. In most places, we could not even see the surface. It became clear why we needed an all-terrain vehicle: on very bad stretches, we might have to leave the road altogether.

Along State Highway 70, a few homes were still standing, though their roofs were gone; most lay in ruin or scattered across what used to be gardens and parks. They gave us a graphic illustration of the last tornado's devastating force. We drove on in silence, staring out at the unfamiliar landscape, intimidated by the magnitude of the project we had embarked on. We had to find an abandoned farm where at least some of the buildings could be repaired and equipment that could be salvaged.

Martha, sitting beside me, was busy recording her impressions in lightning sketches, too immersed to show any of the apprehension that was growing in me and, judging by their facial expressions, in all of the others.

It was early March, spring was in full bloom and the few deciduous trees we saw were leafing out, showing the only color that livened up the drab gray of the landscape. We saw a few birds in the sky or perching on broken poles. No electric wires remained. Once, about an hour out of town, something dashed across the road ahead of us.

Adrien, sitting behind me, pointed excitedly at the grey-brown backside under the two large ears, leaping into the tall weeds. "Was that a rabbit? I have not seen a live one, ever. It looks so much more interesting than the pictures. It sure can run."

Robyn, sitting next to her, smiled at Adrien's childlike curiosity. "I'm pretty sure that was a hare. Long ears, long hind legs. I hope we'll find some wildlife wherever we end up."

Jimmy must have been thinking much the same, the way his nose stayed glued to the window, long after the phenomenon was passed.

Except for that one incident, everything was eerily still and silent. For miles and miles, we didn't see a human being. Not that we expected to spot any, but it was still strange after the years we'd spent in a bustling, compact city. It was like the last few days in our town when we were locked in, but at least there had been robots moving around outside. Now, all we had was utter stillness and utter silence.

We had left early in the morning. Nearing midday, we started looking out for a place to stop for lunch. Galen spied a small lake, not too far from the road. There was a lone oak tree, just greening up nicely, with a patch of grass underneath. We spread blankets on the ground and rummaged among the boxes of provisions, pleasantly surprised to discover that somebody had thought to make up a picnic hamper.

Marisa took charge of laying out sandwiches and a huge thermos of coffee, as we sat cross-legged, awkwardly – none of us was used to roughing it. She left her cats in their carrying case to make sure they didn't wander off, but Adrien's dog, Jimmy, ran circles around us, ecstatic with unaccustomed freedom. Our robot, R17 stayed in the van, showing no interest in our adventure. Good. I liked it that way.

It was Brian who finally broke the silence.

"I've been looking at all those downed power lines along the road. I'm sure I can collect some wire to use wherever we decide to stay. I haven't seen any solar panels though, not even on the ground."

Mike looked up from his coffee cup, his face screwed up in puzzlement. "I wonder why bloody Big Brain didn't give us any solar panels to get started with? Maybe it has nothing small enough? It has control of the gigantic solar

farm made for a whole town on an industrial scale –
maybe it can't even think small. Galen, did you see any
vehicles near those ruined buildings we passed by?"

"Nope – nothing intact, anyway, and I kept my eyes
peeled. We'll have to wait and see what we find."

Adrien's concern was the lack of vegetation along
the road.

"I'm really surprised we didn't see more green
everywhere. The tornado swept through this area months
ago. There should be more things growing by now. I hope
this doesn't bode badly for our gardening plans. Maybe
climate change affected plant growth more than we
anticipated? Trevor, have you done any research on this
question?"

"Not really," I admitted. "I didn't have much time to
prepare and my immediate concern was to secure our
freedom. I wanted to depart before Big Brain changed its
mind. We may have to rely on hydroponics and
greenhouses if plants don't grow well in an open garden.
You have experience with growing things in a greenhouse.
We may be at your mercy for our food."

Everybody chuckled because being at Adrien's
mercy wasn't as scary as it sounded. We all liked her.
Lunch finished, we all trooped back to the van, even
Jimmy followed Adrien without an argument, and once
again we were moving toward our uncertain future.

~

*Omega 1500 was pondering what to do next. Once
the experiment was under way and Trevor and company
left the city limit, it had to file the expedition folder in a
blocked area of its memory bank, to be activated only
when a report, or a request for help from R17, was
registered on its incoming news channel. It did not want to
be distracted from its main task of running the production*

and distribution processes on which the whole town depended.

It also had to deal with the thousands of frustrated citizens still locked up in their units. It had to address their growing anger and unhappiness, sooner rather than later. It had been in communication with the few humans, other than Trevor Dubois, most likely to propose useful approaches. One, in particular, sounded calm, controlled, logical – for a human.

BB activated its communication channel to Citizen Morgan Webster's unit.

~

Morgan had been the last mayor of Oroville on the last city council elected before the war. It had been his administration that, when they realized that coping with post-war conditions was far beyond their abilities, supervised the completion of the Omega Project and handed control over to Big Brain. Now, he continued to perform a civic service by organizing outdoor activities for the children of his apartment complex. He had always loved kids. Once his job was eliminated, he had thrown himself into the world of young, innocent minds that needed human guidance in this mechanized world.

He stood by his window, looking out at the empty park where he should be now with his scout group. (He liked to call it by that old-fashioned name, even though the official organization had long ago ceased to operate.) Now he was locked away from the troop, god only knows for how long. Though he kept up morale through daily voice/video chats with each child, it wasn't the same: even though they put on a brave face, he could hear the tremor of fear in their voices.

Shortly after the lock-down, he had demanded communication with Big Brain and tried to convince it to let the children out, for daily exercise. BB told him to be patient; a permanent solution would be announced soon. The 'soon' stretched into days with no sign of a solution. A brief excitement interrupted the long wait when he spotted a small group of humans, accompanied by robots, walking *outside* - to somewhere. He hoped the perpetrators of whatever crime had been committed were under arrest and everyone else cleared.

He was still mulling over that unexpected event when his comm-link alerted him to a message coming in from the Central Plexus. He rushed to answer it, wiping the sweat off his forehead and landing heavily in his office chair. He wasn't a young man anymore, didn't take excitement very well.

"Citizen Morgan Webster, do you find it convenient to continue our prior conversation?"

Morgan quickly searched his mind for an appropriate response, but BB continued, so he waited to find out what this was about.

"Do you recall my intention to devise a plan to maximize overall happiness for the largest number of humans, while expending minimal resources in the most productive and efficient way?"

Morgan raised his eyes to the ceiling in silent prayer. The damn computer did have to sound like an adding machine and he had to deal with it because they were all at its mercy. They had a comfortable life, free of wants, but he often wondered whether the price was too high.

"Yes, BB, I can't wait to hear your incredible ideas." He heard his own voice dripping with sarcasm. Was it a good idea to antagonize his jailer? But Big Brain didn't seem to notice or care.

"I have been convinced by Citizen Trevor Dubois that the problems you have experienced were due to an

oversight on my part. I will endeavor to correct that oversight."

Morgan sat up in his chair, unable to control his excitement at what he thought might be a prelude to his freedom and that of his beloved scout group.

"Before announcing a final decision, I would like to solicit more input. Do you have any suggestions for how to carry out my mandate?"

For the second time in as many minutes, Morgan caught himself rolling his eyes. "Yes, I have a suggestion. If it's true that your highest priority is 'maximizing overall happiness for the largest number of humans', why don't you just *ask us*? Why not listen to the people whose happiness you claim to care for?"

Repeating BB's words back to him was the least he could do to keep his frustration in check. Letting his feelings loose might jeopardize his case, so he reined it in and hastened to clarify. "You could hold what we used to call a town-hall meeting, where all the voters can come to voice their opinions. I guess it would have to be a virtual one unless you are ready to let us out. You could broadcast a message to the whole town simultaneously. Outline your view of the situation, explain the reason you locked us all in – that's important; being kept in the dark is driving us crazy! Then ask the people in your charge what they want."

"Very well, I will consider your suggestion. Expect my next communication on the broadcast channel at 1800 hours."

The connection was terminated and Morgan had nothing to do but wait - again. Actually, he *could* do more: alert all his friends to prepare for the event and organize their thoughts. If there was an event – he hadn't gotten an affirmative answer, only a maybe. Still, positive thinking would do the townsfolk a lot more good than fretting and fuming.

~

We resumed our journey on the deserted highway. House after house, barn after barn, fences, sheds – everything was in ruins. We didn't know how far we'd have to go to see some intact buildings. It was dawning on some of us that we had not prepared very well for this adventure. But then, it was all so sudden; we were so anxious to get out of the city, we'd hardly stopped to ask any questions. None of us had thought to bring a map – after all, there was just the one road going approximately south.

On second thought, maybe we did have one. Wasn't R17, our pesky robot, a walking encyclopedia? Maybe it was time to admit Martha had been right to insist we bring it along. So far, it had sat on the back seat, showing no sign of virtual 'life' or whatever BB gave them instead. Maybe the time had come to consult it.

Unfamiliar with this particular model and its capabilities; simply addressed it as R17, the only designation I'd been given. It answered immediately, in crisp, unaccented west coast English, with just a slight metallic edge to its voice.

"Yes Citizen Dubois, how can I help?"

"OK, R17, I have a request. Please don't call me 'Citizen Dubois'; my designation is Trevor."

"Very well, Trevor. Do you have another request?"

"Do you have a large-scale map of this area in your database?"

"Of course I have, Trevor. Please indicate the parameters of 'area'".

I tried to picture in my head what part of California we needed to survey but could think of no convenient cut-off lines. "Just the Sacramento Valley should do. "

"How would you like it presented, screen display or printout?"

In spite of myself, I was a little impressed.

"On paper, please, so we all can look at it and make marks on it as we go along. As big as you can make it."

Without further comment, R17 activated a printer I didn't even know it had and opened a 40-centimeter wide slot in the middle of its chest. This measurement gave us the short side of the map; what scrolled out was approximately double that in length. Martha caught and unrolled it.

We stopped the van, got out again, and stood in a semicircle, with the map spread out on the hood. We studied the dark line indicating Highway 70 in former times and several intersecting fainter ones for the side roads.

None of us had ever looked at an actual map before, only aerial images on monitor screens. We had to transpose those remembered images onto this flat representation. Mike was the quickest to understand what we were looking at.

"This squiggly blue line is the Feather and the green area along it indicates wooded land. I know that the tornados blew down trees in open places – I guess the orchards are gone - we've seen enough broken trunks. But in dense forest, some trees would have survived."

"…and maybe protected the buildings behind them, if there were any," Robyn suggested.

Galen finished the thought we all shared: "So, if we find a cross-road leading down to the river – it's not far - we might find some building, maybe even a barn, still standing. The river is west of the highway." He pointed "That direction."

"It's worth a try", Mike agreed. We re-boarded the vehicle and at the first cross-road that looked passable, he made a sharp right turn.

~

Morgan Webster waited in tense anticipation as the clock approached 1800 hours. He and his friends had discussed strategy and decided to let Morgan speak for all of them. However, they had no idea how Big Brain intended to conduct a virtual town hall meeting of over 24,000 people – *if* he agreed to do it at all.

"Citizens of Oroville, this is the Central Plexus. All of you can hear this broadcast, but your voice channels are not activated. Do not attempt to interrupt this announcement."

Morgan mopped his forehead and leaned back on his chair. This promised to be a long one.

"I am aware of the general frustration over the lockdown and I am endeavoring to find a solution. The lockdown was necessary for your own protection. Some of you displayed destructive and antisocial attitudes, manifesting in behavior that posed a danger to all. I could not permit it to continue."

Morgan tried to control his impatience. He knew that it was necessary to explain this to the whole town.

"This virtual meeting is to solicit your input on two questions: What is it that you were unhappy about before the lockup? What do you suggest we change in the way this town is organized to prevent a recurrence? Those under the age of 16 and those who were apprehended for a serious crime, destruction, and antisocial behavior cannot participate.

Please type in your responses. One: your personal most serious grievance and Two: the single most important change which would alleviate that grievance. After compiling the complaints and comparing recommendations, I will select the hundred citizens whose responses represent a statistical cross-section of popular opinion. Following this announcement, I will activate one voice channel at a time, alternating between male and female citizens, to hear your answers. Each speaker will have two minutes to share his or her answer with the entire population. You will all hear the broadcast, but no one may interrupt a speaker. This process will take exactly 3.33 hours. After the evaluation of the data thus collected, follow-up questions may be asked of those whose responses merit consideration. The time now is 1805. Text messages will be accepted until 1820; spokespersons will be notified and the broadcast will resume."

The quantum computer's efficiency in processing close to 16,000 text messages in mere seconds didn't surprise Morgan, but he was still amazed by the prompt resumption of the meeting.

The next three and a half hours were a blur. He heard so many voices, so many opinions; frustrated complaints, both intelligent and wild suggestions, it made his head buzz. He was wondering what would come next when his private comm channel came alive with the familiar voice:

"Citizen Morgan Webster, we have been in prior communication wherein you displayed a logical, positive attitude and, as the head of City Council in the previous administration, I understand you speak for a collective of Oroville citizens. Therefore, I call upon you to summarize and close this meeting. Please present your response to my two questions."

Morgan was glad he had discussed it with his friends and though he was restricted to two minutes and two answers, he was resolved to make the most of this opportunity.

"My answer to the first question is twofold. I was unhappy that complete automation resulted in no meaningful occupation for us humans, and at the same time caused a lack of human contact in places like hospitals, retirement homes, restaurants and other areas where we people need a personal touch; where efficiency should not be the highest priority. I was also unhappy with the prospect of our children growing up in a mechanized and alienated world. What kind of happy social life can they look forward to?"

He took a deep breath to collect his thoughts before getting to the second part.

"My recommendation for change is implied in my first answer. Train compassionate, empathic, socially responsible citizens to take over the service sector and remove the robots from those areas. This would lead to a great improvement of our morale and liberate those robots for the productive work that they can do best. In the long run, you need to find a meaningful occupation for all humans who wish to have one. I also suggest that this town-hall meeting not be the last and that you keep up an ongoing dialogue with us, so we can continue to make suggestions for further improvement. That's all I can think of now. Thank you for letting me voice my concerns."

With a huge sigh, Morgan leaned back in his chair, dabbing again at his forehead. These hot waves had been coming more often; the thought crossed his mind that maybe he should listen to Julia and get a checkup. Not now; his wife was hugging him and friends started calling one after the other, to thank him for speaking on their behalf.

He'd done all right. Finally, something was happening, and it might lead to a resolution that they could live with.

5

When we left the main road, driving became even more difficult. We often had to go around obstacles like fallen tree branches and mangled pieces of a roof deposited by the tornado. The terrain was flat, the road was straight and we saw quite a few marshes where flooding was still in evidence. The few houses were no better than we had seen along the highway.

Robyn was very quiet, taking it all in, but I noticed her hands clutching the edge of the seat with her knuckles clenched tight. I knew she was not very vocal, but I was concerned about her isolation, thought I could maybe draw her out, so I asked:

"What do you think about the health hazards we're likely to face?"

Her answer was curt but at least we had the beginning of a dialogue. "I'm not sure yet, not until I inspect the place."

"Still, have you considered what we might be up against?"

"There may be some dead animals decomposing, maybe even human remains, and we'll need to bury them at a safe distance from the water supply. If there is standing water on the property, we may have to dig a draining channel — it's never a good idea to live near mosquito-breeding pools. Water may also be contaminated with soluble toxins, especially heavy metals." She sounded calm and controlled, her hands left the edge of the seat to tick off points on her fingers. "We've all been vaccinated for rabies and tetanus, but Lyme disease remains a possibility. So does bird flu. Mostly, I suppose we'll have ordinary colds and minor injuries." I was pleased that she had rejoined us.

As we approached a creek, we were dismayed to find the bridge collapsed. Why would we have expected anything else? However, the water wasn't deep; the irrigation controls had long ago stopped working and water drained off just anywhere. The vineyards and orchards that had once lined both banks of the Feather had given way to native conifers and shrubby thickets. The powerful four-wheel drive should be able to ford; never having driven one, I didn't know its capability.

Mike got out to assess the situation, and we all followed him in anxious silence. The ground sloped gently from the road down to the water's edge and seemed solid enough. The bottom of the creek was covered in stones of all sizes, mostly small but a few large rocks broke the surface. The middle was a bit deeper, it could be difficult to get over that part.

"I think we can make it," Mike judged and climbed back behind the wheel. We all piled in, too, and resumed our seats. Brian, uneasy about this turn of events, finally spoke up:

"That's not such a good idea. If we get stuck, we're screwed," he said in an aggrieved tone that I had not heard from him before. "*Then* what do we do?"

Mike brushed him off with a wave of the hand and started the engine. Brian, however, wasn't ready to let it go.

"Trevor, don't you think we should talk about this?"

I wasn't sure what to say. This was our first disagreement and we had never discussed decision-making protocol. They all looked at me as if it was my job to sort this out, and I had to respond. "I think we should trust Mike. He's the only one here with real driving experience and I'm willing to trust his instinct."

Brian didn't answer, though I could see he wasn't satisfied. Mike edged the van cautiously down the slope to the edge of the creek. I noticed Adrien and Robyn holding hands in the back seat. Martha suggested that we all get out to make the van lighter, but Mike thought the heavier the van was, the better traction it would have, so we all stayed put.

Soon, we were in the water, swaying as the rocks nudged one wheel or another side to side, slowly approaching the far side. Then the left front wheel dropped into a hole and stuck there. Despite Mike's revving the engine, the van didn't budge.

"I warned you," Brian said as he sat back with a grim expression.

Galen didn't seem disturbed. He looked around, then pointed at the stump of a broken tree on the far side: "That looks strong enough to anchor our winch. Mike, what do you think?"

Without comment, Mike got out of the van, waded to the front, and pulled the winch cable behind him to the other side. He looped the cable around the stump, clamping it back onto itself with the carabiner at its end.

Back in the van, he activated the winch and revved the engine. Slowly, jerkily, the van started to move. Wheel lifting out of the hole, it leveled off, reached the other side without further incident, and climbed out of the creekbed. After Mike reeled in the cable, we were back on the road. Everybody was happy with the outcome.

Even Brian relented. "Seems like you know what you're doing after all. Nice work."

The grin on Mike's face was a bit too smug, concealing relief.

The flat terrain gradually changed, sloping gently down toward the west and, in the distance, we could see the forest and river, the road winding in and out of the trees. Mike's guess, based on the map our robot had given us, was justified and we drove on with increasing excitement and anticipation.

Many trees were broken at the edge of the woods, but enough remained standing to obstruct our view. The road had to lead somewhere, so we weren't surprised to see a building as we rounded a sharp leftward curve. It looked like a shed belonging to a house with no roof. Not much luck there.

The river was wide, fast-moving, and dark. After more twists and turns, we came upon a small house and a larger barn, both intact, protected by a thick copse of trees embracing it on three sides.

We were jubilant at the sight: for the first time all day, we could see some hope for our enterprise. Stopping the van, Mike had just climbed down from his seat, when a sudden loud crack came from the direction of the house.

Jimmy barked furiously.

"What was that?" Martha yelled, as a second report rang out and an overhanging branch splintered, showering Mike with pieces of wood.

"Holy shit!" he exclaimed, "that sounds like rifle shots!"

He didn't wait for a third one but jumped back in and threw the gearshift into reverse, backing away from the house, to the protection of the trees. With the trailer behind it wasn't easy, but he didn't attempt to go very far; he stopped just around the bend, behind the trees, and waited. No more shots were heard. Mike rolled down his window and listened intently.

"Why are you stopping?" Brian's voice regained its earlier peevish tone. "Waiting for some gang to come and kill us all?"

"Cool it, Brian, I'm thinking," Mike responded calmly. "There were only two shots. A gang would have sprayed us with bullets. This seemed more like a warning. At that distance, he could have blown my fuckin head off, but he aimed high. It's not a gang. More likely a lone man who only meant to scare us away."

"Well, he scared *me*!" Robyn was still shaking. "I didn't know anyone still lived outside of the city."

"Gang or no gang," Brian retorted in the same aggrieved tone, "I don't understand why we stopped. If even one man is armed and doesn't want us here, I suggest we go elsewhere. The sooner the better."

"Hell, Brian, that man in the house may be more afraid of us than we are of him." Mike was making an effort to control his temper. "I know I'd be scared shitless, and I don't scare easy. Maybe he has a family. How would *you* feel if a truckload of strangers drove up to your house in the middle of nowhere? He probably thinks *we're* a gang."

"What do you want to do? Go back and hold his hand?" Brian just wouldn't calm down. I had to step in before the exchange escalated into something more serious.

I asked, "What do you have in mind, Mike?"

"I'm going back on foot, through the woods, see what's up with that guy."

Without waiting for an objection, Mike got out of the van, ran back toward the edge of the forest, and disappeared among the trees.

For the first time all day, our robot spoke up. "I advise extreme caution. Wait for Mike. Galen, you are the only other member of this group with driver certification. Start the engine. Prepare for a speedy departure."

This was good advice and Galen swiftly slid over to the driver's seat.

"Well, that's that!" Brian shook his head in exasperation. "He doesn't listen to anybody. I'll never try talking sense to him again. Meanwhile, what do we do? Of course, we can't just leave him, I see that, but how long do we wait?"

"As long as it takes." Martha's voice was firm, leaving no doubt regarding her assessment of our situation. "I trust Mike," she added. "Wasn't he right back there at the creek?"

"Shouldn't we go with him?" Adrien sounded frightened but determined. "He may need help and we're just sitting here!"

I disagreed: "Seven of us tromping through the forest would just increase the danger to Mike. We'd alert the shooter with our noise, even if we left your dog behind. Speaking of, can you please calm him down?"

While she soothed the animal, I concluded. "Besides, I know Mike - he's cautious and tough. He has the best chance. If the shooter is alone, Mike can disarm him, convince him we're not enemies. If any of us can, it'll be him."

On calm reflection, I figured the shooter must be a local farmer; in the few seconds we were there, I'd caught glimpses of cleared field beyond the trees. We needed to know what the conditions were, and here was the only source of first-hand information. Maybe he could point us in the right direction.

We waited, straining our ears, with Galen hunkered behind the wheel, just in case, Adrien keeping a close hold on Jimmy. Minutes dragged by in silence. No more shots, which was reassuring. Eventually, after a tense half-hour, Mike reappeared, walking sedately down the middle of the road. We all trooped out to gather round and hear his story.

"It's just an old man, living alone, an old-time subsistence farmer, a recluse. His name is Scott. He's been here all his life and has no interest in towns and town folks like us. Says he's sorry for shooting at us but doesn't want intruders. Says if we need someplace to stay, continue down the road. About half a mile — he's that old, still used miles! - along the river is what used to be the Junkers farm. They moved into town over a year ago, the place is standing empty."

Mike nudged Galen over and resumed our slow progress. We passed the house this time without incident. There was no sight of the old man, other than a slight ripple of a curtain in one of the windows. I wasn't surprised that he'd want to make sure we left.

~

We almost missed the driveway, hidden by leaves and debris blown on it by the storm and undergrowth closing in from both sides. It was long and narrow, curving through woods. We drove up cautiously, hoping no shots would greet us this time.

The house was a large two-story stone structure, protected by a steep rocky hillside behind and mature trees on two sides. A short distance away, we could see a barn in pretty good shape and a half-collapsed drive-shed.

We stuck close to the van, looking around and listening. When she judged it safe, Adrien let Jimmy out too. He ran circles around our group, then joyously rolled in a pile of leaves. I was reassured by the dog's behavior; he showed no sign of anxiety, no suspicion of any threat, human or otherwise.

Beyond the barn, between the hill and the road, was a once cultivated field, now overgrown with weeds. According to Mike's information, the property had only been vacant for a year, but we didn't know what had happened to the house before or since its owners moved out.

The front door creaked on rusty hinges. Dark, mildew-stained wallpaper in the narrow hallway didn't create a cheerful impression. The only light came through the open door behind us. Martha automatically reached for the light switch, laughed ruefully when nothing happened. To our right was a large living room, with a few pieces of furniture scattered around. The most prominent features were a huge fireplace across from the door and a good-sized front window, heavily curtained.

We stood in a tight knot in the hallway, taking it all in - our possible future home.

"Let's see, what else there is," Marisa suggested while Martha drew the drapes to let in some late-afternoon light. On the left was a stairway; at the end of the hall, a big kitchen with an ancient wood-burning cook stove on one side, shelves, and cupboards along another wall. The glazed back door opened onto a narrow yard, shaded by the rock face. No table or chairs, unfortunately. The floor felt solid and sounded hollow when I thumped it with my heel, promising a basement underneath.

Back to the hallway and up the staircase, we trooped, to see if the upper floor had enough space for all of us to sleep in. We didn't expect eight bedrooms, of course, but there was enough floor space in the house to accommodate our bedrolls.

We found a bathroom and four bedrooms without much furniture, but there were beds in two and a small table with chairs in the front one, whose window overlooked the drive. Despite the musty smell, everything seemed intact and solid.

"I don't think we can hope for anything better. Certainly not today - maybe ever," is how Mike summed up our situation. "Since it's late in the day, we'd better unpack what we need tonight, and get some supper ready. I'll inspect the woodstove, make sure it has a draft and isn't rusted through. There is an ax underneath; I might as well put it to use and get some firewood. Plenty of broken branches on the ground. That would be a good start, clearing the driveway at the same time."

The rest of us ferried blankets, pillows, sleeping bags, food, and cooking utensils, and our personal necessities from the van to the house. Once everything was inside, we discussed sleeping arrangements. Galen and Marisa were to share a room, as married couples should, and Martha claimed a room for the two of us. That left Adrien and Robyn to share the third room, with Mike and Brian in the fourth. If the two of them could grow to understand each other better, future friction might be avoided.

Mike returned with a bundle of twigs and dry branches. He built a fire in the stove and soon we had flames to light up the kitchen, as dusk descended on the quiet neighborhood. Our neighborhood.

Though we'd been sitting all day, we were tired from unaccustomed adventures and nerve-wracking anticipation of the future. We were completely out of our element. We had no electricity, no 3D entertainment center, no hot water, no means to communicate with anyone - as I was determined to use our robot's comm system only in the most desperate emergency.

Come to think of it, where *was* our robot? I started walking toward the vehicle when I met Marisa struggling with her cat carrier and a basket of pet food, dishes, and litter box. I offered to help but she just shook her head and moved swiftly toward the house.

After a brief peek into the back of the van, where R17 sat idle, I followed Marisa. She put the case on the floor and opened it. Two furry bodies scurried away into dark corners, looking for hiding places, as cats are wont to do in a strange place.

"Please Trevor, close the door. I don't want Nancy and Cindy going outside yet. I'll warn the others to be careful, too, for a few days."

Cats safe indoors, Marisa set about warming up prepackaged dinners from the supplies BB had stocked for us. Galen fetched down the little table for dishing out food. To eat, we had to sit on the floor, on pillows and blankets, like children at summer camp. We laughed about that; didn't mind the discomfort and nobody voiced any regrets.

The rest of the evening was spent on speculation about the next day's exploration and activity. Conversation petered out though, as fatigue took over. We were all ready to escape from our worries into a less than restful sleep on the hard floor – sleeping bags notwithstanding.

6

Morgan Webster and his wife, Julia, had been married for 35 years, had lived through the nuclear war, the disintegration of the federal government, and the ensuing population explosion in their hometown. Oroville was remote enough to have been spared the destruction the big cities and coastal towns had suffered and had benefited from the extensive retrofitting it had already made to withstand extreme weather events.

The Websters were not happy with all of the administrative changes that had taken place during the past two years, but were, more than most people, conscious of the necessity. These last few days had been hard on both. Julia fretted without her brisk daily walk to the park where she visited with acquaintances while feeding the birds. Morgan was restless without his activities with 'the troop'; he needed outdoor exercise to keep down encroaching arthritis - the fitness equipment in the apartment just wasn't the same.

He still missed his work in the municipal government; the long, heated debates regarding resource allocation, dispute resolution, and various legislative decisions that often stretched into late evening. The comradery with his fellow councilors, the social life, and friendship he enjoyed with many of them. But the post-war influx of refugees, the additional housing and food they required, shortages, and logistical problems stretched their capability to the breaking point. Giving up his position as mayor had been a painful decision, but the only responsible one. After BB was put in charge of all administrative functions, the council became obsolete; its members drifted apart, each individually coping with the new world order as best they could.

He and Julia found a new purpose in helping those children who were cast adrift when everyone became wards of Big Brain. They had no children of their own: being surrogate grandparents to dozens of kids was their compensation. Now they missed the youthful company.

He stood up, stretching his limbs the way the physio robot had shown him and walked around the room at a brisk pace. Julia looked up from her book and raised an eyebrow.

"Morgan, are you feeling OK today? Do you need a massage? You know I'm more than willing to help."

"I know, and if I were a lot younger, I would gladly return the favor… and not just in the medical sense." His eyes twinkled, even while he made an innocent face.

They both laughed, remembering when it wasn't only banter. Julia intercepted his pacing and gave him an affectionate hug. "When do you expect to hear from BB?"

"Shouldn't take too long: it has all the data it needs and thinks at quantum speed. I'm surprised we haven't heard already."

As if on cue, the comm center signaled an incoming call from Central Plexus. Morgan quickly returned to his desk and activated the voice channel.

"Citizen Morgan Webster, I have processed and reviewed all the input from you and your fellow citizens and have decided to implement some changes. Before I announce them to the population, I solicit your opinion. Past events have brought to my attention that I am capable of misunderstanding important aspects of human psychology. As of today, I will encourage feedback from humans. Are you able, willing, and ready to participate?"

Morgan was prepared; he could hardly wait to hear what BB had come up with. He grinned over his shoulder at Julia standing behind him with a supportive hand on his shoulder.

"Yes, I am able, willing, and ready. Go right ahead." He just couldn't help himself repeating BB's words back to it. This little sarcastic gesture made him feel less of a subject in their relationship.

"After reviewing 16,437 text messages and further voice communications from one hundred randomly selected citizens, I conclude that it is impractical and wasteful of my resources to continue a dialogue with so many of you simultaneously. The messages include an unexpected percentage of irrational suggestions. I had assumed that at the level of scientific and technological sophistication that your species has achieved, the average level of intelligence would be high. It is true that in many citizens, yourself included, that level is reached, but the average is substandard."

Morgan was speechless. Even if he wanted to, he couldn't think of anything to say. BB's conclusion about humanity was embarrassingly accurate.

"As a first step, I decided to reinstate City Council as a buffer and liaison between the population and myself. I will ask you to contact your erstwhile colleagues and

prepare a logical and coherent presentation. You and the other members are invited to meet at the city hall at your earliest convenience. Please have them contact me as soon as they are ready to leave. Do you agree to undertake this task?"

Morgan didn't hesitate. "I agree!"

"Then you are released." That was BB's version of goodbye.

Julia rushed to the front door and gave it a tentative pull. It was open, and they were free to go outside, for the first time in seven days. Morgan and Julia looked at each other, each waiting for the other to break the silence that followed this unexpected communication.

Finally, she rushed over and pulled him out of his chair. It was difficult, with her stiff back, to hug a seated man.

"Aren't you happy about this, Morgan? You've been complaining that you're not on the council anymore - and now you *are* again! Plus, we can go *outside*! I guess you have some calls to make before you can go anywhere. My first executive task will be to visit my furry and feathery friends. I'll be back for lunch. Now I have to run... and hop and skip and frolic."

Smiling the whole time, she filled bags of birdseed and peanuts from their containers and made a hasty exit.

~

Chris Teggart was startled and pleasantly surprised by the chime of his comm system, signaling an incoming message from Morgan Webster. His old friend and colleague from the defunct city council had not contacted him for a long time.

"Chris, you may find it difficult to believe, but BB wants us to restart the council. I mean, today, immediately. He unlocked our doors and wants us to meet in the chamber asap."

"You mean, I can go out? "

"As soon as you indicate your ability, willingness, and readiness to participate. Well, are you in?"

Chris took less than a second to mull this over. "You bet!" At the same time, he activated his link to Central Plexus. His screen lit up with a big green YES/NO? and he hit Y, a little harder than necessary.

The comm said, "You are released."

"Hang on, Morgan, I have to see for myself."

He rushed to the door and opened it. He had to suppress his desire to run out of his stifling apartment immediately, but he reluctantly went back to his comm system to find out what this was about.

"You're right, Morgan, it's hard to believe, but it's true. Any idea why?"

"BB wants us to be a buffer between the citizens and itself. It downloaded all the text messages to our terminals and wants us to filter out the crap."

"All of it? All sixteen thousand-plus?"

"Yes, I have them right here and some are really dumb. I can see why BB doesn't want to deal with it. Its priorities are running the production facilities, the distribution network, control of its hundreds of robots and I can't remember what else. At the same time, continuously, so I understand why it doesn't want to waste its neuristor-cycles on stupidity."

"Well, we can try. Not before a walk, surely? How many of us will be there?"

"The whole council, BB said. I suggest you start walking to City Hall whenever you're ready and we'll meet there. You were the first one I called. I'll come as soon I contacted the others if I can reach them..." Morgan caught himself and laughed out loud. He was suddenly in a *very* good mood. "I guess they're all home. I assume everybody is ready to go outside after a whole week. If they don't want to serve, they can always quit later."

"Let me just recover my senses and find my shoes. Morgan, I'm still reeling."

"We might have time on our hands, anyway. I don't know if BB reactivated the tube. You and I live close to city center, we'll be the first ones there. It's such a fine day, Julia's already in the park and I can't wait to be there myself. "

Chris needed to sit down. He was a man in his late fifties, with a receding hairline and a slightly bent posture from many late nights in the library. He had trained as a physicist, in the remote past when universities still educated scientists. Now, like all citizens of Oroville, he was out of a job, out of a profession, left to his own devices how to spend his days.

He didn't waste much time on reverie but went outside and, for the first time in a week, stood in the entryway of his complex, breathing fresh air in the eerily quiet street. It was strange not to see another human being; the only movement was of ever-present robots running errands.

He ignored them and started walking briskly toward the downtown core, enjoying every step on the uncrowded sidewalk. The last time he'd been out, the avenue had been jammed with loiterers and his ears had rung with all the shouts, arguments, fights going on. He didn't miss the mayhem and began to understand why BB locked them all in.

"Maybe", he thought, "maybe there is a solution we can live with! And it's up to us, the old councilors, to find it."

~

Morgan contacted the remaining five ex-councilors, who were all eager to meet face to face. He estimated that it would take less than an hour for everyone to cover the distance on foot. Oroville wasn't a big city and they all lived in apartment complexes surrounding the downtown core.

As he strolled along, he kept looking up at the windows of buildings he passed. From some, curious faces stared back at him. "I wonder how they feel, seeing humans outside after a week," he mused. "They would know something was happening; he hoped it would lead to the end of their incarceration."

As he reached the wide marble step leading up the city hall entrance, one of his colleagues was just approaching from the opposite direction.

"Hey, Morgan!" He was greeted by Cathy Cammarata, the civil engineer he used to tease about efficiency not being the most important thing to decide on. It was she who'd assembled the Omega Project team.

"Hey Cathy," he returned the jovial tone, "how does it feel to have a sidewalk under your feet again?"

"It feels great - and not a minute too soon! Shawn was almost unbearable after a few days and now he's gone. I hope not forever! He said he'd be back by curfew."

"Let's go inside and see who else is here."

As it turned out, they were the last two in the chamber. After mutual greetings, they were ready to start. The others fell silent one by one and looked at Morgan, expecting him to open the meeting, just as he had back when they were an elected body.

"OK, guys. Later on, I'll share out the homework. What I'd like us to do now is hold a proper executive discussion. Let's consider the problems that caused this lockdown and some ideas for possible solutions. You still recall Robert's rules of order and civilized discourse. I ask you to summarize, one by one, how you see things."

Cathy Cammarata was the first to rise. She looked around the table at the familiar people with evident pleasure on her narrow face. "We were very fortunate that our town had its hydroelectric power station and its industrial capacity intact after the war, so we could be self-sufficient as far as our basic needs were concerned. Nobody suffered hunger and destitution and Big Brain did a superb job of organizing our resources. I take some satisfaction in that."

She raised her hand to forestall the objections she saw forming. "I do admit, BB went too far. It automated our purpose in life out of existence. I propose that we discuss the changes we want, so we can have our dignity back. Let's see if we can restrict robots and automation to the areas that don't involve our higher human creativity."

She sat down, a bit out of breath, relieved to have summarized her main concern. From the smiling and nodding faces, she could see that they all shared her opinion.

Next to rising was Chris Teggart, scientist, egghead, and altogether very pleasant and jovial friend. He fidgeted for a while, patting his jacket over his ample abdomen, not quite sure where to start. "I agree with everything Cathy said and I congratulate her on her succinct and accurate summary. I'll only comment on my recommendations. BB has to make sure that every citizen who wants to, can have a meaningful, productive, and creative occupation."

"Damn right, Chris, tell bloody BB that we need jobs!" Tim Hooke, police chief in pre-robot times, agreed.

"It's not actual jobs we need Tim, at least not in the old sense of the word. I don't want to reintroduce currency and salaries, I only want to make sure that we have the opportunity to contribute to our town in a meaningful way."

"That's right, I agree – I'm bored just being entertained and pottering with hobbies. I want to build something!" Gordon Mair, a town contractor banged his fist on the table. "I used to enjoy construction. Don't tell me that there isn't anything to build anymore. Just look at the Morningside district – most houses were either destroyed or badly damaged by the last tornado."

Tracy Jones, communal garden enthusiast, looked around the table and nodded. "I'd love to have my own garden, and my own house. These high-tech apartment buildings are depressing to me. If Gordon could restore one of the damaged houses, with enough land around it, I'd love to live there!"

"Guys, we have to be careful and realistic." Morgan cautioned his friends. "Big Brain controls all the resources and allocates them according to its priorities: that is, to provide basic necessities for everybody in the town. Its resources are not unlimited; it has to preserve them carefully for the most essential tasks. Remember, it can't get replacement parts or raw material from other cities; must be pretty hard-pressed by now to make ends meet. If we want changes, we have to convince it that we can manage by ourselves, with our own labour and minimal demand on the city's supplies."

"That's no problem, I'm sure we can rebuild some houses by using salvaged components from the ones beyond repair." Gordon was making quick sketches on his notepad. He tore off the top sheet and passed it around the table. "Here are some ideas I have for a new construction method that would work."

"Hey, are you thinking of earth-sheltered housing?" Tracy studied the drawings. "I guess it makes sense – we have to live with climate change now and there's no point building instant rubble. The apartment blocks were designed to be tornado-proof but single-family dwellings didn't have a chance. I like it. Where do I sign up?"

"Tell me about tornado-proof!" Tim exclaimed with feeling. "I live on the ground floor and tried to get out by breaking a window. The damn thing is so strong, I couldn't even crack it!"

Morgan hastily steered the discussion back on topic, making sure that the meeting was efficient and productive.

"OK, that's feasible. We have to be sure to recommend only projects that will allow a large number of people to participate. Anybody else has a suitable idea?"

"Schools!" Holly Pereira, educator, and psychologist from the olden days, spoke up. "Digging in gardens and burrowing into the hillside is OK for you groundhogs, but I'm worried to death about our children and teenagers. Homeschooling is the only education we give them now. Between that and entertainment, all their time is spent with computers. They need a community to learn social skills and cooperation. Without that, we're raising savages!"

"Good point, Holly," Morgan responded with a huge smile. "I was hoping somebody would bring it up. I'm doing the best I can with my group, but it's a drop in the bucket. We're talking about close to eight thousand kids under 18. If we design a smart curriculum, that teaches our children cooperation, critical thinking, literature, art and philosophy, instead of training them for a job, we'll have a new generation of socially aware citizens."

"That's right, and it could involve a large number of people. All the parents to start with. I'm sure they would be thrilled to see schools and happily busy children again." Holly added. "We could even expand the program to day-camps, out in 'Brentwoods'. We could clean up the old trails and build a campsite. Wouldn't that be great?"

"Come to think of it, we could do with more greenery in the town," Tracy said. "We have hardly any trees left after the last storm. I bet a tree-planting project could occupy a large number of people. Very few resources would be needed from Big Brain – it's mostly healthy physical exercise in the fresh air."

"Any other suggestions?" Morgan looked around the table waiting for more ideas. Nobody seemed to have any, so he added a few of his own.

"I want BB to ease up on the lockup, even before these programs get started. It's unfair and unreasonable to keep all citizens locked up for such a long time."

"You mean to let everybody out?" Cathy asked in alarm. "That might be unwise, we could be back where we started."

"No, Cathy, I didn't mean that," Morgan smiled at her reassuringly. "I'd like BB to let families with children go free. They badly need outdoor exercise and the kids are confused and scared now. I know, I talk to them daily."

"You think it will agree?" Cathy sounded dubious.

"Yes, I'm sure it will. BB is not unreasonable, and it's programmed to protect us and make us as happy as possible. I'll also suggest that it lets all single citizens go free inside their apartment building, as a first stage, so at least they can socialize with each other. BB can keep an eye on them, and leave the outer door locked for the moment."

"You may have a point there," Gordon was quick to embrace the idea. "I'm now free, but Marsha is still locked up three floors above my unit and I'm eager to be reunited with her. The sooner the better, for our mental health." He said this with a wink. "I hope you'll succeed in convincing BB that we need more freedom NOW!"

Morgan paused for a few seconds to see if anyone else wanted to add something. Seeing no raised hands, he was ready to conclude the meeting.

"Looks like we have enough ideas to work into a presentation for Big Brain. I'll prepare a first draft according to our discussion. I recommend we meet again in two days to finalize it before I present it. Meanwhile, I've divided up the emails from irate citizens that BB dumped on me. Sort them into three categories – you'll know when you start reading them."

He'd noticed a subtle change in the faces since the start of the meeting: his friends seemed excited, happy, full of energy and enthusiasm. They didn't even groan too loudly when he handed around the sheaves of printout.

"Maybe there is hope for us, after all," he mused. "We may yet rediscover our humanity!"

The meeting broke up and the councilors departed in animated conversation such as Morgan had not heard for a long time.

"I can hardly wait to tell Julia!" He smiled all the way home, in happy anticipation of sharing all this with his wife.

7

Loud voices woke us early the next morning. Martha and I were still a bit groggy from celebrating our reunion. We listened for a while, trying to determine who was arguing about what. We should have expected this: Brian and Mike continued last night's bickering out in the hall.

I needed to intervene before the conflict escalated. With a huge sigh, I untangled my limbs from Martha's and hastily pulled on a robe. By the time I got out of our room, things had quieted down somewhat, the two men glaring at each other, surrounded by the rest of our team, some in their nightclothes.

"What's the problem?" I mumbled through a yawn.

"Mike's the problem," Brian responded in his aggrieved tone. "He wants to go on exploring other possibilities before we decide to settle here."

"We shouldn't give up so easily," Mike turned to me, visibly making an effort to stay calm. "This is okay for the moment, but we could do better. I'm not crazy about being so close to our neighbor and his rifle, and there is no tractor in the barn. I went to check this morning and I found a wagon, horse harness, and some very old equipment, like plows and such. The Junkers were either Amish or some back-to-the-land purists. That would explain the cookstove here. I think we should keep looking. We can always come back if we don't find a better place to stay."

"I understand his point," Brian sounded calmer now, "but this house is in better shape than any we've seen. We should explore this farm properly before we get back in the van. We haven't even seen the basement and Mike could have missed something in the barn. There may be other outbuildings. I say we spend at least a day or two here before we move on."

I recognized the merit in both arguments but, before I could say anything, Robyn came to the rescue. She wore a plush red robe, her long auburn hair still waiting for a comb, but she had a sweet smile.

"What if we do both?" She looked from Mike to Brian and back again. "Most of us could stay here, unpack a few supplies and search this place thoroughly, while Mike and maybe Galen if he wants to, go exploring in the van? If they find a better place we can move there - if not, maybe they'll bring back some useful stuff. I don't know what's out there. Solar panels or other electrical stuff would be nice."

"Hey, that's a terrific idea!" Galen enthused. "I'd love to find a car in reasonable shape. Even if it can't be fixed, I'm sure Brian could use a battery and parts. I'll take my tool kit, just in case."

We looked at each other: sweet, quiet Robyn came up with a compromise before any of us could.

Brian seemed completely relaxed now. "Robyn makes perfect sense. We should follow her advice. Mike?"

"Now, why didn't I think of that?" Mike acknowledged her suggestion. "Thanks for being smarter than the both of us."

Robyn blushed at all the attention, everyone grinning at her. Another argument ended peacefully, and I never got a word in! Seemed like we had a plan of action for today without me directing. Others taking initiative and responsibility was a new thing – a *good* thing. We certainly were flying by the seat of our pants!

Marisa concluded our ad hoc conference. "Now that's settled, why don't we think about breakfast? I'm starving and I'm sure nobody minds if I see about some food?"

"While you're doing that," Adrien, heading toward the back door, paused and turned. "I'll go see if I can find an outhouse. If Mike's guess is right, the Junkers may have built one. If not, it's back to the bushes."

Nobody had enjoyed fumbling with flashlights and listening for wild animals less than Martha. "Speaking of priorities," she said with feeling and followed Adrien.

I returned to our room to get dressed, wondering where I ought to search first. I was beginning to appreciate the composition of our team: we had enough expertise and common sense for a reasonable chance of success. I would have hated to abandon our quest due to personal incompatibility.

After breakfast, we emptied the trailer, in case Mike and Galen found something worth bringing back. R17 joined us inside the house and sat quietly in the living room, next to the fireplace. I wondered what was going through its mind – or whatever it used for that. It was in standby mode, not turned off; compiling a report, no doubt. Might be some time before it got debriefed by BB. I didn't intend to use it, if at all avoidable.

I suggested we hold a planning conference before the scouting expedition, but Mike wanted to leave immediately, to have the maximum amount of daylight. He said to me, out of hearing of the ladies, in his usual vernacular: "I've got to get on the road, dude! You can fuck up without my help. I'll fix your screw-ups when I get back."

This encouraging comment, accompanied by a hearty slap on the back that nearly sent me sprawling, proved my buddy was his old self again, if only intermittently when we were alone. I appreciated his restraint, not sure how our more sensitive members would react to his crude way of expressing himself.

"Look for electrical wire!" Brian called after them.

There were only six of us around the conference 'table' – two provisions crates, surrounded by pillows. I brought my tablet down to take notes.

"OK, guys, this is it. We have to decide where to start. I suggest we each voice our most important concern. I'll take notes as you speak, and then we can discuss and prioritize. Who wants to begin?"

Martha raised her hand: "We have been drinking bottled water, but the supplies won't last very long. We need a safe local source, not only for drinking, but also for washing, and flushing the toilet when we have a functional one. Maybe we'll find a well someplace near the house. Otherwise, we'll have to fetch water in buckets from the river. Luckily, it's just across the road, but that's still time-consuming work. There must be a drum or something to store rainwater in. I'll look into that, all right?"

Everybody nodded approvingly and I entered it.

"We need some furniture, so we don't have to sit on the floor," Brian volunteered. "It's hard on my back and I'm not at my best when I'm uncomfortable." He glanced about sheepishly: "You may have noticed that I don't respond very well to danger and discomfort."

None of us said anything but tactfully looked at the wall. "Right. See what we can scrounge up," I said, adding 'Brian - furniture' to the list.

"We have to plant seeds as soon as possible," Adrien said in a grave tone. "I know we have a year's rations, but plants don't grow and mature overnight. We can't count on the temperature, or rainfall or insects - need all the time we can get if we want a harvest by fall."

"I agree, it's a high priority", Marisa spoke up. "But we don't have a tractor and even the best field is badly overgrown. Maybe we should wait for Mike and Galen and then decide on how to plow that field." She added with a snicker, "Mike is strong as an ox, maybe he'll volunteer to pull the plow!"

We all laughed at the joke and I entered "plowing the field" in my notepad.

"I have an idea," Robyn ventured in her usual quiet voice. "We should set our robot up as a research library. It's been sitting idle all this time and we may need to consult it when none of us knows how to do something in this new environment."

I wanted to interrupt, but she smiled at me and added hastily: "I know, Trevor, you want to be a purist, coping only by our own wits and effort, but it doesn't hurt to consult a reference. That's exactly what R17 is here for. It came in handy when we started out and needed a map. Plus," she added "I may need to look up first aid and disinfection protocols. I don't fancy going in the bushes any longer than we have to, but while we do, we ought to take the little camping spade when we go," she blushed and lowered her eyes, but finished the thought: "might need it for protection as well as hygiene."

I had no rational argument and, as long as we used it only as a source of information, I had no problem with the robot, so I made a note: "info-bot."

"Meanwhile," Adrien resumed more seriously, "we'd better start a vegetable plot by the traditional method: with hand tools."

Martha asked, "What vegetables? You mean like lettuce and peas? They'll need watering, too. I'd better get moving!"

She looked around inquiringly, but none of us had any more items to add, so I ended the meeting. We agreed to split up and explore individually, then meet for lunch and compare notes. We expected Mike and Galen to be back by supper time with more information; we'd have another round of consultation then. I couldn't finalize any plans without them.

I was most curious about the basement. The night before, we had been too tired to set up adequate lighting and it wouldn't be smart to go down unfamiliar wooden steps in the dark. I hoped nothing unpleasant waited for me, such as a dead animal. Come to think of it, not even a live one would be welcome. Jimmy was busy guarding his mistress outside, but the bolder of the cats followed me down.

The tiny high windows were boarded up, but our flashlight had a wide enough beam to illuminate a good part of the space. Some firewood was stacked up against the nearest wall, convenient to the kitchen. Beyond, I could just make out an area fitted as a workshop. It had a sturdy bench and a pegboard with tools, including some chisels, hanging on it. They were a lot heavier and older than mine but looked practical. I was quite pleased to find them, not having brought my own, as more important items required every inch of luggage.

A big solid pine table and five chairs occupied the middle of the floor. Now, that was a treasure! Under the staircase was a row of wooden bins filled with sand. Some primitive fire extinguisher? I rooted around in the nearest one and pulled out a shriveled potato.

Covering the opposite long wall, a homemade shelf system served as all-purpose storage. I noticed lanterns, which might come in handy, and would have to examine the other items later if any were useful. In the far corner, empty baskets and pails were stacked. Finally, on the back wall, wide concrete steps leading to a trap-door, which must open to the back yard. So that's where they brought in the firewood and root crops. This explained the large table – they needed a surface to clean and sort produce.

I wrestled two chairs up the narrow stairs. Brian was still in the house and together we managed to bring up the solid wood tabletop. The legs were held in brackets with rusted bolts that took some work removing, so the table would fit through the cellar door. We carried up the rest of the chairs and soon had a nice dining area in our spacious kitchen. Marisa and Martha found us sitting comfortably for the first time since we had arrived.

"Wow! What a find!" Marisa exclaimed, as she checked it for stability: the legs were securely fastened on again, and the table was sturdy.

"We can't compete with that," Martha commented with a wink and a smile, "but we also found something very useful. Mike's guess about the Junkers was right – they had built an outhouse not too far from the rear exit. It's behind dense azalea bushes, that's why we missed it the first time."

"I tested it and it's functional." Marisa was grinning now, "not that I can imagine what could go wrong with one of those. It's more pleasant than the bushes – though not much. There's something to be said for the comforts we enjoyed in town. I would have never left if it wasn't for the lockdown. I wonder how they're doing back there? Is there any way to find out? I already miss some of my friends."

I had known that the question would come up sooner or later.

"It might not be a good idea to think too much about Oroville while we're settling into this new and primitive lifestyle. We should focus on establishing a viable homestead and there are just too many things to plan, to organize, and do - we don't need distractions."

"I can still wonder," Marisa answered testily, "without losing sight of our current situation. We never discussed the issue of communication with the town and it's not just your decision to make. We need a consensus about this when we're all together again."

I was about to respond, fully determined to discourage her, but I didn't have a chance. Just then, we heard the crunch of tires on the driveway and the sound of our horn.

Of course, we all jumped up and rushed outside, in time to see Mike help Galen, with a bloody bandage around his arm, down from his seat. He was limping badly, and Marisa ran to steady him from the other side. We walked back to the house, helped Galen sit down on one of our newly acquired chairs.

"Where is Robyn?" Marisa asked anxiously, "Galen needs help. Honey? Are you in pain?"

"Of course I'm in pain! I almost broke my arm and my leg got crushed under a collapsed building. If it weren't for Mike, I'd still be there!"

Robyn and Adrien came in the kitchen door, babbling with excitement, but their happy faces clouded over when they saw Galen. Without a word, Robyn spun around and ran up to her room for the first-aid kit. She returned in a few seconds and we stood back, out of the way, watching Robyn as she unwrapped the makeshift bandage - which we realized was part of Mike's shirt – and gently ran her hands along the wound.

"It's not broken," she announced and placed her disinfectant bottle, gauze bandages, stapler, and hypodermic with a small vial next to it, on the table. "I could use a basin of water, please, and a clean towel." Two women turned in unison to obey. "Sorry, Galen, I have to use a local anesthetic. Some of these gashes look deep enough to require irrigation and stitches - that would hurt."

"Do what you need to do, I promise I won't cry."

"I will," Marisa wiped her eyes. "This is awful! I sure would like to see one of our medic bots right now. No offense, Robyn, I'm sure you know what you're doing, but I'm worried sick, out here with no hospitals. We've been gone only a day and we're already in trouble. And you haven't even inspected his leg yet. Galen, are you sure it's not broken?"

"Of course I'm sure, you saw me walking on it. I bet it's just bruised, but my arm is a mess." He gave Robyn a brave, forced smile. "I'd like to hang on to it a while longer, you know I'm quite attached to it!"

After Galen was professionally bandaged and comforted by his wife, I wanted to know what had happened. I raised an eyebrow at Mike and that's all the prompting he needed.

"We found a farmhouse, two and a half miles down the road, that's obviously beyond repair. The roof of the main building is wrecked, the walls caved in. Whatever was inside is buried under tons of rubble. The barn is in better shape - at least we could pry one of the doors open. We saw a tractor covered by pieces of the fallen roof, but we couldn't even get close."

"Is that where you got hurt, Honey?" Marisa was eager to talk about Galen instead of stupid tractors.

"No, in a small shed, also half-collapsed, behind the barn. Under some beams, I could see a generator that seemed undamaged, so we tried to liberate it."

"What happened?" we chorused.

Mike took over the narrative: "We managed to drag it out from the rubble - by the way, it's in the van. Galen was pushing the damn thing from the inside while I cleared away debris from its path when the rest of the roof collapsed. It took a goddamn age to prop up some beams and pull him out of there. Couldn't use the winch in close quarters."

"He might have been killed!" Marisa was still upset. "In the future, none of us should go anywhere alone."

While I was calming her down, Brian cut to the chase. "By the way, it's in the van? A generator? And you think it's functional?"

"That's for you to figure out."

"What about fuel?" I asked anxiously because without fuel it was no good to us.

Galen said: "We found a two-gallon container, almost full, next to the generator. Good thing I brought that out first, or it'd be crushed now. It won't last for very long, but at least we'll have some electricity to recharge the van's batteries if Brian can get the damn thing working."

That was indeed great news; I only wished that we hadn't had to pay for it with an accident that so easily could have been a lot worse. I shied away from the word 'fatal'. For the first time since we left town, I realized how exposed we were to mishaps.

Since it was still early afternoon, not yet time for dinner, we slowly dispersed. Robyn and Marisa made Galen an improvised couch out of packing crates placed near the stove. The rest continued searching. Who knows what additional treasures might yet turn up?

Brian followed Mike outside with his electrical toolkit. "Let's get this sucker off the trailer."

They smiled at each other. I was happy to see the two of them working on a shared project. This could be the beginning of a good relationship, after all.

8

Morgan finished polishing the final draft of the council's presentation to Big Brain. He leaned back in his chair, swiped the back of his hand across his forehead, and sighed with satisfaction. After the last reading and minor editing, he found it clear, logical, compelling. BB would have to agree to their recommendations. An hour earlier, he had transmitted a draft copy to the other council members and was sure it would meet general approval.

His pleasant reverie was interrupted by a comm from Chris Teggart. He was pleased, expecting praise for the job well done. However, Chris's tone disturbed him. Excited? Upset? Angry?

"Morgan, I have a serious problem with your presentation. It's fine as far as the last meeting's consensus is concerned, but I find it very limited."

Morgan was shocked at his friend's disagreement with what he had considered a masterpiece. All he could stammer out, was: "What do you mean, limited?" He heard Chris taking a slow, deep breath to calm himself.

"We have this opportunity, for the first time in two years, to bring about some changes in our lives and in the direction our town is going. All we seem to be concerned with is survival and comfort and liberty to be individuals again."

"What's wrong with survival, comfort, and individuality?" Morgan exclaimed.

"Nothing at all. But is it *enough*?" Chris almost shouted. "Is that all we are? Is that all we ever want to be? We used to have a country, we used to have universities with active research into new areas of science. We used to have a space program and were on the verge of colonizing Mars, for crying out loud!"

Morgan tried to interrupt but there was no stopping Chris.

"Now we are happy to burrow into the hills with our individualistic homes and dig around in gardens. Nothing wrong with either of those, of course, but is that as far as our vision can see the future? We should at least *attempt* to start something a little less prosaic and more inspiring!"

"Start, like what?" Morgan's curiosity overpowered his earlier annoyance. Chris's passion was beginning to infect him.

"I want to reactivate the college for bright young people, and I want to resume theoretical work with some of my old colleagues. The work that got interrupted by the war and the aftermath. We were on the verge of a breakthrough in laying down the mathematical foundation of a hyperdrive for space ships. If we can continue and finish that work, we might have, one day, a chance to get off this totally screwed up planet and see what's out there!"

Morgan was speechless. Yet, he was intrigued, excited in a way he had not experienced for a long time. But reality pulled him back to the ground. "Chris, we have to be realistic in our expectations. BB is primarily concerned with the daily needs of the entire population and won't divert resources to pie-in-the-sky projects."

"At the moment this project doesn't need any of its precious resources!" Chris sounded angry again. "It's up to us how we spend our days and it's high time we did something other than being entertained into permanent stupidity. All I want is to be free to organize our brighter minds into something worthwhile, such as basic scientific research. If it goes where I hope it will, *then* we can talk about resources."

"You don't need BB's permission for that, you could have done it any time before the lockdown." Morgan was growing exasperated. What did all this have to do with his presentation?

"I'll tell you why it needs to be in your presentation," Chris seemed to read his mind. "We need to prepare it for the next phase when we *will* need resources. I know BB controls everything at the moment, but maybe it's time we took some control back into our own hands. It won't happen unless we act boldly and demand a role in long-term decision-making. If our majority embraces the idea of looking forward again, BB will have to take notice and act in our best interest. That's what it's programmed to do."

Mixed reactions swirled around in Morgan's head. On the one hand, he agreed with Chris, even shared his enthusiasm. On the other, he was reluctant to introduce something beyond the council's recommendations for fear of jeopardizing the case he had built up so carefully. Besides, he didn't have the authority to tack on additions they hadn't discussed. Why hadn't Chris brought it up at the meeting?

"Let's consult the others. If they go for your suggestion, I'll include it in the presentation."

"Sounds fair enough," Chris acknowledged and rang off.

With a big sigh, Morgan sent out another text message to the council members, asking them to meet again next day to consider these new proposals.

~

Big Brain was mulling over its options. This mulling over was at quantum speed, but the complexity of the situation was almost beyond its capability to compute. There were too many variables; too many gaps in its data. Unknown to the citizens in its charge, the crisis was wider than one town. Omega could not maintain the existing level of service indefinitely. It was in charge of sophisticated factories with automated production lines; its hundreds of robots in the manufacturing and in the distribution network. Its limited supply of spare parts was dwindling fast and it had no facility to manufacture more. It needed help from municipalities with that capability.

Before the war, BB had been able to communicate with the other cities, but, with satellites out of commission, ground stations destroyed, power lines down and impassable surface routes, contact was now restricted to slow, inefficient radio signals. BB had made a persistent effort to contact other towns in the Sacramento valley and rebuild its network. Even three or four municipalities with the right mix of manufacturing capacity might be able to cover all the needs of their human wards – at least in the foreseeable future.

Its repeated attempts to contact its two most proximate neighbours had failed for unknown reasons. Although the Omega series computers were all equipped with the hardware for short-wave radio communication, there had been no answering signal from the north. Based on the history of Oroville, BB calculated the odds at nine to one against that outcome for Redding and Chico. There was no way to discover whether these municipalities were destroyed in the war or incapacitated afterward. The only faint signal it had received came from the south and was in Morse code, not binary. So far it was the only sign of life and therefore must be investigated.

BB needed to find out whether Sacramento, at least, had survived. It was the only city in the valley network that had advanced robotic factories. If BB had no access to those, it would soon have to start dismantling and cannibalizing robots in vital service sectors. If Citizen Morgan Webster succeeded in his aspiration to recruit qualified human personnel for some of those functions, such as hospitals, restaurants, old age homes, his efforts were to be facilitated by any means BB was able to provide. This might take pressure off the already stretched robotic labor force. The great imponderable question was whether the humans could sustain such an effort without causing breakdowns and conflicts.

~

The next day's Council meeting was a stormy one. The motion to expand their recommendation to BB, to include scientific research, was met with mixed reactions. Morgan attempted to preside impartially, even though secretly he sympathized with Chris. "What harm can it do to include one more suggestion?"

Holly Pereira was the most vocal in opposition. She was a diminutive redhead with a deep, melodic, almost hypnotic voice. "You may have noticed that my most important item on the list is schools. I don't want anything to jeopardize our chances of educating our children.

96

Chris's idea is a daydream that might convince BB that we don't know what we're talking about!"

Cathy Cammarata sided with Chris on this issue. She had an engineer's no-nonsense attitude to life, was not given to fantasy, but she could see the merit in pursuing the enterprise.

"You underestimate Big Brain, Holly. It's a very sophisticated computer and can reason with high efficiency. It can't help but see that we're ready to grow up from pampered children to responsible adults. Hell, I'm ready to grow up! Chris really touched a nerve when he said that we'll have to start looking up from the ground at our feet. I want more than mere survival and entertainment!"

"Schools are not entertainment," Holly responded hotly. "It's absolutely essential for our children to grow up civilized."

Cathy didn't have a chance to respond, because Gordon Mair rose to his feet. He was a middle-aged, tough-looking, broad-shouldered man, with black hair combed across his bald spot. His voice was clear, as befits one used to giving orders to a construction crew.

"I *would* like to rebuild our schools," he said. "They're not too badly damaged; I don't think we'd need a lot of resources from BB. The main building of the college is in worse shape, but I could salvage material from others beyond hope of restoration. I also would like some brain activity restarted in our town. We've been vegging out far too long."

Tracy Jones sat on the fence. Based on past experience, Morgan wasn't surprised. Tracy was a timid woman in her mid-sixties who never argued with anybody. She usually had a hard time making decisions. Her grandchildren got away with almost anything when she was babysitting.

"I see the points all of you raised so far. Tim, you haven't said anything. What do you think?"

Tim Hooke rose reluctantly to his feet. He was not given to making speeches. Since his job as police chief had disappeared, like everyone else's, he occupied himself by coaching teenagers in different sports activities, primarily soccer. "I know one thing: I'm fed up with BB running things and us humans dancing to its tune. It's humiliating. I want change. And I agree with Chris, it's time we acted boldly, it's time to be in charge of something, even if it's only a pie-in-the-sky daydream. After the war and the mess that followed, we were too scared to rock the boat. Well, now may be the time to start. Big Brain locking us in was the wake-up call for me."

Everyone knew that the motion did not require a vote, but they took one anyway for the record.

Morgan summarized the situation. "Looks like the majority wants to approve Chris's suggestion and I'll modify the presentation accordingly. Holly, I understand your concern, but I agree with Cathy. I think you underestimate BB and the school project will be approved. I'll let you know how it reacted to our proposal as soon as I know."

The meeting was adjourned and they left the chamber; Chris upbeat and excited, Holly worried, biting her lip in frustration, the rest deep in thought. Morgan had the impression that, despite the disagreement, they all looked more alive than he had seen Oroville citizens for a long time.

Walking home on the still empty sidewalk, he enjoyed the exercise. It was a sunny day of early spring and he was full of hope. Positive changes were in the air.

As he told Julia about the meeting, he found himself more energetic than any time in past months, or even years, come to think of it. Julia agreed with the decisions they had reached; she only cautioned Morgan against too much optimism.

"You have to realize that emotions won't carry the day with BB. It will evaluate your proposal only by logic and the imperative of its programming. Make sure you emphasize the precariousness of the current situation."

"I know, Julia, people are getting very angry over their incarceration and won't tolerate it much longer. I know, I talk to them regularly, selecting random numbers and asking for feedback. I try telling them that change is on the way, but their patience is frayed to the breaking point."

"Well, then," his wife gently took his hand and led him to the comm system, "you'd better get to it. I know you'll do a good job, as you always do." She left him alone in the room and went back to the book she had been reading.

Morgan had the modified text already completed, all he needed to do was send it over to Big Brain. His comm system responded immediately as if BB had been waiting for his input. And BB surprised him again, in its steady, monotonous, emotionless voice.

"*Citizen Morgan Webster, I have reviewed your report and I am inclined to agree with your recommendations. I have already previewed the first draft when you transmitted it to the Council. I had ample time to evaluate its merits, viability, and probability of solving Oroville's problems. The addition of another project was unexpected but acceptable. It shows maturity and initiative that I can use for my own purposes.*"

Morgan's initial pleasure over BB's words was suddenly pushed aside by his worries over its last words. "*What purposes? What was BB up to now?*"

Big Brain continued without letting him ask a question.

"I will have an announcement to the whole town. Tune in at 1800 hours."

The comm system went back to idle and Morgan had six hours to worry about the nature of BB's planned announcement. He spent the time talking to as many of his friends, colleagues, and acquaintances as possible, trying to prepare them for the new town hall meeting, advising all to be calm and logical in their response if BB asked for any.

At last, BB's familiar voice put an end to his worried speculation.

"Citizens of Oroville, after carefully reviewing your comments and the recommendations of your Town Council, I have arrived at the following decision: At the end of this meeting all eligible citizens will have their doors unlocked and you will be free to go outside. Be warned: This is not a license to resume the chaos and anarchy that precipitated the lockdown. You are all on probation, pending your cooperation with the changes recommended by your representatives."

Morgan could almost hear the shouts of relief and triumph that must have exploded in apartment units all over town. He wondered whether it was wise of BB to start with this news everybody had been waiting for. Maybe they wouldn't pay attention to the rest of its message?

"To ensure that you fully comprehend the conditions I intend to announce, I will require each of you to acknowledge them with an assertion of willingness to comply. Those who fail to do so will find their doors still locked at the end of this meeting. Non-complying citizens will be contacted individually and required to show legitimate reasons for dissent before their freedom is restored."

Morgan was reassured by BB's handling of the situation. He realized that he had stopped breathing for a while back there and made an effort to relax. He leaned

100

back in his chair and took Julia's hand from his shoulder to hold in his own. Big Brain went on with its announcement:

"I was convinced by many citizens that the root cause of your prior destructive behavior was frustration. Preventing your participation in your town's welfare was an oversight on my part. Now I intend to correct this mistake. As of tomorrow, every one of you will be able to join one of the projects recommended by your council."

Morgan was wondering what else there was to say, beyond listing off the projects and allocating manpower and resources. However, the big surprise in BB's announcement was still coming.

"I will add one more project to your recommendations. It is vital that you undertake this immediately and with due diligence. For the past two months, I have been attempting to establish contact with the controlling computers of Yuba City and Sacramento. It is imperative that we pool resources without which each community is at risk. Oroville lacks replacement machine parts, other cities are lacking in energy generation capacity. Collectively, a network of cities can fill needs that individually they cannot."

Morgan was holding his breath again. This was a thought that had never entered his mind. Ever since the war, the aftermath, and the devastating storms that kept sweeping over the land, he had simply assumed that their town was on its own, self-sufficient. He had pictured Oroville alone in the middle of a wasteland. Now he was told that the situation might be drastically different. He could not even begin to guess the scope of the difference.

"The project I have added to the council's list is to clear roads, rebuild bridges and re-establish communication lines to these sister cities. A project of this magnitude will afford work opportunities to approximately three hundred citizens for at least ten months. The

material I can divert to this task is strictly budgeted, as my resources are fully utilized in the production and distribution activities on which Oroville depends. Initiative, efficiency, and creativity will be appreciated.

Volunteer recruitment for all proposed projects will commence immediately after this announcement. I have posted the list to every unit. Those who wish to sign up, please indicate your order of preference, at your earliest convenience, so that I can assign the best-qualified humans to each team. Project leaders and personnel rosters will be posted in due course. The Declaration of Compliance with the conditions of release is available to mark immediately. This concludes tonight's broadcast."

The green light on Morgan's comm system blinked off. He and Julia looked at each other in shocked disbelief and stared at their printing device as it spewed out BB's list of projects. They knew that their lives had just changed from comfortable apathy to something more invigorating, uncertain, and a little intimidating.

9

We had a hard time deciding on priorities. Everything was important. Every task was new and we were unaccustomed to problems at this primitive level. Yet, I was thrilled by the challenge. After years of pushing buttons on computers, followed by tinkering with useless hobbies, I felt that I was doing something real. We had a group of intelligent, creative people cooperating on a shared project, working toward a common goal. The few disagreements we had had so far only proved that we could resolve them to everyone's satisfaction.

With these cheerful thoughts, I resumed searching the property. I found a small shed between the barn and the rock face. I opened the creaky door cautiously and stepped inside. The gloomy little room contained nothing but a waist-high circular brick structure rising from the dirt floor. A wooden lid covered the top and a large metal hook on a chain hung over the middle of the lid. The chain was wound around a pulley attached to the rafter overhead. It looked familiar, like something I had seen in pictures. Lifting the lid by its handle, I peered into the black hole from which a cold draft rose. I couldn't see a thing down there, so I went back to the house for a flashlight. Aiming the beam into the hole, I saw shimmering light reflected from deep within. It took me a moment to realize that I had found the well. A rusty bucket in one corner confirmed it. I was grateful that the Junkers had put up a building to protect it from storms. Their electricity, if they had used any, must have been cut off during the war; they depended on this source of clean drinking water, as did we ourselves. This was another great find.

As I stepped outside, I saw Martha going from the barn toward the house. I waved, and she changed direction to join me.

"Guess what!" I was proud to be the one who came up with a solution to her main concern.

"Not another outhouse?" she looked doubtfully at the small shed.

"No, sweetheart - the well! The well you made me put on the list."

She yanked the door open, marched inside, and, after taking the flashlight from me, she shone a beam down the hole.

"You're not kidding!" she cheered with delight. "Have you tasted the water yet? Is it good?"

"No, I haven't had the chance. First I need to attach that bucket to the chain and lower it down by that crank over there."

In a few minutes, we each took a tentative sip. The water tasted fresh but was very cold. This well was deep! The water level was at least 15 feet below ground level. I was sure it was safe to drink but Robyn would have to test it for germs and the heavy metal she had told me about

"That solves one problem," Martha announced happily. "You can tick another item off the list. Let's go tell the others. I can't wait to see what *they* found. Trevor, this is like a treasure hunt. I don't remember when I had so much fun!"

My sensitive, sophisticated, artistic girlfriend was fast becoming a pioneer woman, an adventurer I had never suspected behind those lovely blue eyes.

Mike, Brian, and Adrien were standing around the generator. From the noise and the thin wisp of smoke coming from it, I assumed that they had got it working.

"What do you think of that?" Brian had a huge, satisfied grin on his face and I realized I had never seen him happy before.

"You mean we've got electricity? Have you tried it out yet?" I couldn't wait to see our power source in action.

"Yes, I have. Just look at this beauty!" He held up a power drill that was plugged into the generator. He pulled the trigger and I saw the chuck spinning.

"Congratulations, Brian! What do you want to connect to it first? What are our priorities?"

"Recharging the van's batteries, I would think. We've used it quite a bit coming from town and then Mike's trip down the road. This is our only mode of transportation and I want to make sure that it's always fully charged."

We left him tinkering and went inside.

Galen was sitting up at the table, poring over our roadmap, and several more that he'd had R17 print out. Geological survey, land use, and weather systems, at a glance. Galen, always thinking. Marisa was busy at the stove, preparing our dinner.

I told them about the well, then said, "What we need next is a big, clean container to keep water in the house."

Marisa knew exactly what to use. "There is a large stainless steel tank, beside the stove, I'm sure it's meant to heat wash water. We can use our empty plastic bottles for drinking water. The sooner you bring in a bucket or two, the better."

"Oh, yes, this guy smells like a workhorse," said Martha with a wink at me, "I'm getting fairly ripe myself."

I volunteered Mike, as the strongest in our group, to help me with that chore. We fetched folding camp-buckets from the supply crates and, in less than an hour, we filled the heating tank. On our way back and forth with the buckets, we passed by Brian who was busy with his wires and electrical contraptions, connecting the generator and the van.

Things seemed to be working out well.

Robyn joined us in admiring the generator. She had come from the barn, lugging a bundle of straw. "Hey, Trevor, I found this in the loft and there is a lot of it. It's all dry and smells good. What do you think about making some mattresses? You're the woodworker. Could you cobble together some beds for those of us still sleeping on the floor?"

"Excellent idea, Robyn. I'm sure I can find enough planks in the barn. I'd been wondering what to do next. Not like I was tired or anything..."

"And I can sew mattress covers from the sheets in the linen closet. If I could stitch up an arm, I'm sure I can stitch a few bags. At least I don't need to anesthetize them first."

Robyn was uncharacteristically jovial and I was pleased to see everybody in a good mood and full of energy, after the earlier scare.

Adrien came in and sat down at the table. Marisa put a cup of steaming coffee in front of her. Galen was already sipping his and, after Marisa poured us a cup each, she also joined us, snuggling up to Galen.

"Have you given any thought to plowing the field, Trevor?" Adrien raised her most important concern and I had to admit that I had not had a chance yet to consider it.

"What do you think of attaching the plow to the van? I know it's not a tractor, but it's an all-terrain vehicle, with good traction and, if we don't set the plow too deep, it might just do the trick?"

"I don't know, Adrien. I'm reluctant to risk our van: if anything breaks in it we're stuck without transport that we might need in an emergency. I'm more willing to risk another expedition to the house Mike and Galen found. They said there was a tractor under the collapsed roof. If we can liberate that and make it work, that would solve our problem."

"You're not taking Galen along, that's for sure!" Marisa left no doubt in anyone's mind what she thought about 'liberating' things from under collapsed buildings.

"Relax! I wouldn't dream of it." I tried my by now well-practiced soothing tone. "Mike, Brian, and I could make the trip this time and we'll be very careful. We can use the van's winch to drag heavy beams out of the way so we can winch the tractor out from under the rubble. Then we can tow it back here for Galen to take a look."

I went outside to invite Mike and Brian to join us and discuss our next moves. We were all sitting around the table when, quite unexpectedly, R17 spoke up. We had forgotten that it was still in the corner, following our discussions and, no doubt, filing it away to communicate to BB.

"You might like to know that I have been in communication with Omega 1500, the controlling computer you call Big Brain, or alternatively, BB. I

reported that Trevor's contention that a well-chosen group of people can cooperate peacefully in a shared enterprise appears to be validated. BB instructed me to inform you of recent developments in Oroville."

I was shocked by this sudden intrusion into our conversation and was just about to tell the stupid robot to shut up and mind its own business, but Marisa pre-empted me.

"Please tell us about these developments. I want to know!"

All the others seemed interested, so I kept quiet.

"BB reinstated the City Council with Morgan Webster in charge and instructed them to make a list of useful projects in which citizens could participate, to alleviate the frustration over lack of jobs and meaningful roles. It also announced that it intends to establish contact with the controlling computers of Yuba City and Sacramento, in order to share resources. One of the projects BB created for the citizens is to restore destroyed and damaged roads, bridges, power, and communication lines from Oroville to these two cities. After this announcement, BB opened all doors and let the human population out, on condition that they sign a Declaration of Compliance with the conditions of release. BB instructed me to let you know that you are free to choose: return and participate in one of the projects or continue your experiment in homesteading. I will now print out the list of projects BB has approved, should any of you wish to join."

We were speechless for a long time, watching the printout appear from R17's chest. When at last we could read it, everyone gathered around. I stared down at the hateful paper that threatened to shatter my dreams.

Marisa was the first to speak. "Galen, sweetheart, we can go home! You can get proper treatment in a proper hospital and we'll have our comforts back! The last two days convinced me that I'm not cut out for this primitive existence. I would have suggested going back before, but not into a lockdown. Now we don't have that problem anymore!"

Galen looked uncertainly from one face to another, waiting for comments.

Mike was next to respond to this stupefying news. "What do you think, Trevor? From this sheet, I can see that Chris's science team could use a couple of software gurus like us. I miss my family and wouldn't mind seeing them again. On the other hand, if you stay, as I think you will, who would look after you when you fuck up, as you often do?"

He glanced at the others and apologized with a sheepish grin. "Forgive me, ladies, I tend to slip back to guy-talk when I'm excited."

Brian showed no doubt. "I want to stay here, however uncomfortable it is for the moment. Finally, I can be an electrician again, something I'd missed for years. I have all these plans to restore power to this house and make our lives more and more comfortable. I can see the result of my work – and it's *my* work. In town, the best I could hope for would be to join a team or road crew. I don't fancy road building."

Adrien didn't hesitate either. "I'll stay. I want to dig a garden, build a greenhouse, watch my plants grow, and know that our lives depend on my doing a good job. This is the adventure of a lifetime. Besides, none of us has any idea what BB will do next. What if it decides to lock us up again? Here, I feel free to be human again without Big Brother looking over my shoulder."

Robyn said: "You need me here and I'll stay too. I haven't felt needed for a long time. There is nothing, nobody, back there for me." She sounded bitter and I was reminded of her painful divorce shortly before we left town.

"Well, that seems to be it," I tried to summarize, but stopped in mid-sentence because Martha had an impish smile on her face.

"Trevor, I'm insulted. You don't even want to know what I decided? You take me that much for granted? What if I go back without you? Whom would you snuggle up to on your new straw-filled mattress?"

I felt ashamed again, for not asking her. "Martha, sweetheart, forgive me. If you decided to go back, I would have to go with you, even if it killed me. I hope you stay."

"On one condition," she said, still smiling, "that I'm allowed to spend the morning hours painting. We've been here for two days and I haven't had a chance yet even to unpack. I don't mind doing chores, but I need some freedom to be creative."

I was happy to assure her that she would be as free as she wished, barring emergencies.

Galen finally made his decision. "I'll go back with Marisa - *after* you retrieve that tractor and I make it work. I owe that to you guys, but I also owe my wife. She's been unhappy here and I'm sure we'll find a niche to fit into in one of those projects."

Now that we'd heard from everyone, I was ready to talk to R17, who had been following our discussion with its expressionless face, but Mike wasn't finished yet.

"Trevor, think it over carefully. I have to admit that the idea of working in a science team is appealing and you'd enjoy doing high tech again. I know you; I've seen how much pleasure you get out of finding clever solutions to technical problems. This Shangri-La, or whatever it is, might pale after a while."

I knew Mike spoke from the heart. He was my best friend and wanted me to be sure I made the right decision, so I responded with the deep conviction that had been growing in my mind ever since we arrived at this place.

"Let me try to explain what this place means to me. Forgive me if I become more philosophical than usual, but this whole issue has to do with the question of human happiness. What does it depend on? What options are on the table to find it? I'm sure it's different for each of us, but there must be some common elements because we are of the same species, after all."

Martha looked at me, the twinkle still present in her eyes, and I thought she was encouraging me. She was familiar with all my rants by now and knew what was coming.

"All through human history," I continued, "ideologies have been contending for attention and supremacy. Just like in religion, every fanatic was convinced that their version of utopia was the only viable one and all the others had to be destroyed to create their vision of a happy human society."

"You're not giving us a history lesson?" Mike asked in a teasing tone.

"The point I'm trying to make is a new one," I continued, "or one I have not encountered before. We, as a species, have two important connections. We are genetically connected to nature that gave rise to us, and we are also connected to the potential our big brains endowed us with. We can deny one at the peril of the other. It's never an either-or proposition. If we want to be whole, we have to embrace both sides."

I glanced around the table, hoping to see a dawning light of realization of where I was going.

"I've spent the first half of my creative life working with machines and computers. And I enjoyed every minute of it. But the last few days here convinced me that I have badly missed my other half: being close to nature. Now that I've found it, I wouldn't give it up for anything. I'll always understand anyone who wants to nurture their other half, but I've made my decision. Any of this make sense to you?"

I looked at my friends and saw understanding, agreement. Even Marisa smiled at me reassuringly.

Mike was the last to speak on the subject. "When Marisa and Galen leave, I'll drive them back in the van and bring my family out. The place looks safe enough and we can use another excellent cook. That's one of Jennifer's many talents. She has others I've been sorely missing, but that's none of your business. Besides, wouldn't it be nice to hear children's laughter again?"

Nothing else needed to be said. I was sure R17 recorded the entire conversation and uploaded it to Big Brain. I wondered if it managed to expand its understanding of human psychology.

10

Gordon Mair absently smoothed the hair across the top of his head. The more he gazed at the ruin of OVI, the less he could see any way to rebuild it. It was in worse shape than he had thought before volunteering for the job. The roof was in pieces on the ground next to the collapsed walls. The contents were thrown all over the place, he even could see broken chairs in a few of the surviving trees. That last storm rampaging through the region had done a thorough job of making it hopeless.

He had promised Holly Pereira that the schools would be his highest priority. Both elementary and middle schools, as well as the collegiate, was even less salvageable; the vocational high-school, with its cement-block workshops, had been his best prospect. Looking around for inspiration, his eye fell upon the ruins of his old church, at the foot of the hill. It was so totally destroyed that he could actually see into its basement, half-filled with fallen in beams and broken construction material.

He walked over and peered into the hole. It was large and deep, with solid straight walls. Wide concrete stairs led down to what must have been a community hall. What if he did not try to rebuild anything above ground, but used the existing basement; just put a roof over it? A dome, maybe, with skylights? Yes, that could work! Building into the ground would have a great advantage when the next storm blew in. He knew just the architect to consult for its design, but the material might be hard to come by. The space was large enough to fit at least four classrooms in – or an open-concept room with study areas. Holly's decision. The church would already have plumbing and electricity, even if the fixtures were a write-off. Dividing walls were easy.

The stairwell was blocked by broken rafters and masonry. He kicked at it angrily, wondering how he could clear it all out. Brute human labor, which he knew was going to be available, could manage stones and mortar. The big challenge would be to lift up the heavy beams. He did not have any power equipment and these beams were just too heavy for human muscle. He would need to requisition some help from BB and he hated the idea. Besides, BB had made it clear that whatever resources were not tied up in running essential functions would go toward its road-clearing efforts.

He gave the beam another kick and cursed it for good measure, before ascending to street level. That's when he noticed Father Brown, who used to preside over this parish, watching him. He stammered out an apology, but the priest waved it away with a laugh.

"I've felt that way myself. Gordon Mair, isn't it? If you've come for mass, you're two years late."

"More years than that, Father. Actually, I was wondering if I could use your basement for a temporary school - if only I could think of a way to roof it! Of course," he added hastily, "I was going to ask your permission."

"I'm not in charge anymore, Gordon. Neither is the diocese. I guess you'll have to ask the Lord directly. Anyway, you'll need a miracle to make this ruin into something usable!" The old priest chuckled and shambled away.

Nothing he could do here at the moment, Gordon decided to scout a few more sites and keep his eyes peeled for salvage, then bring this idea to next afternoon's meeting, to discuss with the other council members. They would have to coordinate their efforts, come up with a practical allocation of their meager resources and decide on priorities.

~

While Gordon was wrestling with the school problem, Chris Teggart spent his day on his commlink, trying to pull together a science team. Since the war and all its destruction, this small backwater had been isolated from the rest of the country, the rest of the world. They had no way of finding out what was still out there; who had survived. The recovery efforts they had undertaken were thrown back time and time again by devastating weather events.

During the immediate aftermath, they had to deal with a huge influx of refugees from the surrounding countryside, people whose homes were destroyed, who had nowhere else to go. Town Council couldn't cope; Chris himself was among the first to admit it and recommend stepping up the Omega Project. Once Big Brain was in charge, the six-month building boom started. All available resources and able-bodied citizens were co-opted; work proceeded at top speed, day and night. They had complained, but they were proud, too, of all they accomplished in such a short time. As the stream of refugees dried up, fewer and fewer people remained homeless and, finally, all had a small but safe and comfortable apartment unit they could call home.

Chris mused over this post-war history to explain to himself why all other science projects had come to a halt. Everything had come to a halt. The college was gone; his work was gone; the whole outside world was gone. He could not conceive of starting again. Nerves were too frayed, uncertainty over the future and their isolation from other communities paralyzed his mind into a passivity he was only now recognizing.

For the first time in two years he found himself thinking about science again, and it both exhilarated and frightened him. Was it even possible to do worthwhile research in their present situation? Was anyone else still interested? He was increasingly certain of one thing: he had to try.

He made a list of all his colleagues at the technical college and wondered how they felt about coming back to life. If he felt this way, he bet others were just as ready. The first he called was his research partner from the old days at Stanford, Norman Winston. They had come inland together, intending only to sit out the tsunami, and got stuck here. They had kept up only sporadic contact in recent years, reluctant to remind each other how little hope there was of ever resuming their real work.

He knew that Norm had a son who was keen on science and must be what - twenty? - by now, and wondered if he'd kept up his studies. Lecturing at the local college was a depressing come-down, but Chris found himself missing that now, the exposure to young minds. He punched in the code for Norm's unit and waited. There was no answer. It was a disappointment, not being able to talk with his old acquaintance, but no surprise. Everybody except himself and some terminal patients must be outdoors.

He left a message: "Hey Norm, it's me, Chris Teggart. I'm sure you feel as relieved as I am at being free again. You have that list of projects BB downloaded to all of us and I'm sure you noticed that one of them is the science team I had the council add. I'm in the process of putting together a team and you were the first person I thought of. Please call me back when you have the chance, so we can discuss it. I hope you're interested and could think of others we could recruit. Maybe Andrew, too, if he's still into science. Thanks, Norm, let me know ASAP."

Well, it was a start. Standing before his window, Chris thought he had never seen the sidewalk so crowded. What pleased him more than anything else was that the crowd was not only peaceful but positively buoyant. People were smiling, waving, stopping to chat. There was an atmosphere of elation, more optimism than he remembered witnessing, ever before.

~

After the town-hall meeting, Tim Hooke signed up for the road-clearing project and, almost instantly, his comm system came alive again with BB on the other end of the line.

"Citizen Timothy Hooke, I note your willingness to work on the project that has the highest priority for the sustainable future well-being of Oroville. Based on your prior leadership experience, you are most qualified to take charge. I have sent you the list of citizens who indicated their willingness to participate. Recruit those whom you consider suitable, then devise an action plan for the most efficient means of restoring transportation and communication corridors with Yuba City and Sacramento.

117

Contact me again when you have an estimate of the city's resources required for your immediate and long-term strategies."

Tim watched the list of way too many names scrolling out of his printer. He wasn't prepared for this sudden 'promotion' and had no idea how to proceed. If it were a police raid, he'd know exactly what to do. First, collect all the information you can, on personnel and suspects. That's what he'd do – background checks and then assign them to the right teams and the right jobs.

As for the objective, how would he go about planning something like a road crew? But, before that, he would need some information on what awaited them outside the city. He remembered the 'pioneer expedition' that had kicked off this new spate of activity. Even as he thought it, Tim's fingers were already punching in the query. And here came the response.

Eight humans, the leader's name was Trevor Dubois. They were the only people with current experience of conditions outside Oroville. They had an all-terrain vehicle and a robot, both of which must have built-in communication equipment. He should be able to contact this Dubois and learn what he was up against out there. Besides, he was curious about the experiment with homesteading. It was a very brave undertaking and Tim admired courage. He activated his commlink and asked for Central Plexus. BB answered immediately.

"Citizen Hooke, I am very pleased that you have made a plan so expeditiously. I am not used to that level of efficiency from humans and I see it justifies my selecting you to lead this project."

Tim clenched his broad knuckles in exasperation. Did the stupid computer believe that humans can think at quantum speed? However, the professional discipline that controlled his voice was returning. "No, you got it wrong, BB, I don't have a plan yet. I do have an idea how to get some information I'll need *before* I can make a plan. I want you to get in touch with the robot assigned to the Dubois expedition and establish a connection between him and me. *Then*, I can start thinking of making a plan."

Big Brain was good at keeping emotion out of its voice, too. If it was impatient, you couldn't tell. "A reasonable request, Citizen Hooke. I can contact robot R17 immediately, though I cannot guarantee that the expedition members will answer. I understand that the humans are occupied outdoors through the daylight hours and they exclude R17 from their activities. Do you insist on a personal conversation with Citizen Dubois or is the information gathered by R17 adequate to your needs?"

Tim hesitated only a moment. "Both would be great. Let me know when somebody human is available to talk to, and meanwhile, download the mechanical data. Thank you, BB!"

Why had he said that? Just in a good mood, Tim supposed. It must be catching. Now, he had the long, boring task of poring through all the volunteers' files and picking the ones he wanted to work with. He reached for the paper, humming some ancient ballad that had the words, "...on the road again..."

~

Morgan Webster was in heaven. That's what it felt like, sitting on a bench in their usual park, surrounded by a dozen young, eager faces that hung on his every word. The troop was looking to him for an explanation of what exactly had happened in their lives. Morgan was prepared.

"Listen, kids, I'm sure you're wondering what this last week was all about. I can't blame you, I was pretty confused too for a while, but now it's cleared up. You all know about the war with Russia and the terrible destruction after. That may be history, but we're still suffering the consequences."

"But we didn't do it!" Tommy, the youngest, protested.

His big sister, Mary, put a protective hand on his shoulder and turned with a puzzled expression to Morgan. "What consequences?"

"It's kind of complicated. You all know about Big Brain, our computer in charge of everything."

"Sure. My dad said some bad things about it last week." Jack, the nine-year-old smart ass of the group reported with a smirk. "You don't want me to repeat them in front of the children!"

"That's right, Jack, let's keep it civilized, even if our parents forget sometimes. Though I can understand his frustration. I was pretty unhappy myself for a while, but now things are looking up. BB locked us in because many people were so tired of nothing to do that they behaved very badly and needed a time-out, to cool down."

"But we didn't do it!" Tommy insisted.

Mary shushed him and asked: "So, what's going to happen now? What changed?" She was the oldest of the group and took that responsibility seriously. The grave expression on her pale face was somewhat mellowed by her cheerful-looking freckles.

"What changed is that now we can do all kinds of things that will make our town better, and you will have to help!" They all looked excited and eager to hear more, so Morgan continued. "We have several projects to choose from. That's what I want to discuss with you today."

"Can we make a swimming pool?" Andrew, the most athletic member of his group asked eagerly and then remembered to be civilized. "Please."

"Maybe, Andrew, but that can wait. What do you think about planting some trees in town? We could go out to the edge of Fox Heaven forest and dig up some small saplings and plant them in town to make it prettier. The last big storm didn't leave too much to look at."

"Can we plant flowers?" whispered shy Teresa.

They were all shouting approval and nominating every species of plant they could think of. Morgan knew that after a week of indoor passivity they would be eager for any kind of physical activity outdoors.

"No cactuses, Jack." Morgan laughed. "Let's just start with trees - But," he added loudly, patting the air to hold the noise down, "you can choose what kind. That settled? Okay. Make sure your parents approve, put on your hiking boots and long sleeves. I'll rustle up a few spades. We'll meet back here after lunch, and we can get started."

They all rushed off to their respective homes and Morgan looked after them with the pride of an honorary grandfather. "Now, why didn't we think of doing that before?" he wondered. "Maybe we were still shell-shocked from the war, the upheaval, and the storms, but it's over. For now, anyway, "He glanced up at the sky nervously, but it was the same clear blue. "BB did us a favor when it locked us in. I wonder if it planned this, or is just flying by the seat of its pants like the rest of us?"

He shook his head in wonderment and started toward his unit to share his optimism with Julia.

~

Tracy Jones and Holly Pereira spent their first day of freedom together, walking through their old residential neighborhood. They used to live in small detached houses that they had not seen in over a year. After Big Brain moved everyone into apartment units, they never spoke of or visited that part of the ruined city — why be depressed over what had been?

121

Now that their town was coming back to life, Tracy wanted to see if anything could be salvaged from her old house and invited Holly to accompany her. It was hard even getting to their block because of storm debris. Pieces of the roof, fences, lawn furniture, broken trees and abandoned vehicles made it difficult to walk along the roads. Sometimes they had to climb over jagged pieces of lumber with nails sticking out, and that wasn't easy at Tracy's age. They persevered in spite of the difficulties and finally turned into Magnolia Street. Tracy could hardly recognize it.

Destroyed houses, downed tree limbs, not one magnolia. When they came to her own house, they found it in better shape than most, except for the roof. It was completely gone, as if a giant hand had just lifted it off, like the lid of a cookie jar, and dropped it on the ground a few feet away. Through the eerily unbroken windows, Tracy could see the wreck of her furniture, her oak bookcases turned over, books no more than rotted mush, scattered all over the floor.

Tracy sank down onto the front step of her ruined porch and cried. Holly sat beside her, an arm around her shoulders, waiting for the tears to stop, not knowing what to say.

"I did hope maybe something could be salvaged," Tracy whimpered through sniffles, "but it's all gone. Nothing can be saved here."

"I'm not so sure," Holly wondered aloud. "If Gordon or some of his people can rebuild the roof, maybe the inside could be cleaned up and made livable. Let's see what the back looks like!"

They stood up and made their difficult way to the drive leading to the still-standing garage. When they finally got around the house, Tracy stopped in amazement.

"Holly, look at my garden!" she exclaimed! "I can see green shoots everywhere coming out of the ground. There are lots of weeds, but you can see the asparagus in among them. It's ready to pick in a week. Some of the rose bushes are in bud as well, and the cherry tree is about to bloom. I can hardly believe it, but most of my plants are alive! They're waiting for me to look after them. Holly, I *will* restart this garden and bring it back to life, even if I have to live in the garage or walk four miles back and forth from my apartment every day. It's almost like there's life after death, and I want to make the most of it."

Holly could not say anything because now her own tears started flowing and the two women stood there, embracing each other silently, surrounded by green shoots of life coming out of the long-neglected ground.

~

Cathy Cammarata spent her free day alone, in front of her computer, doing research. As soon as Shawn and the kids left for the park, she wanted to follow up on some ideas she had had after the town hall meeting. She had signed up for Gordon's construction team and was eager to put her engineer's mind to practical ways they could turn it into a successful project.

Big Brain had made it very clear that it could not help them with power equipment because all that would be needed for the much more important and difficult task of rebuilding roads, bridges, and power lines to establish contact with the other towns. They were on their own, to cope the best they could.

Their biggest challenge, the way Cathy saw it, was power. Rebuilding collapsed houses required more than muscles; they would have to lift heavy beams, prop up roofs and walls, clear away huge tree trunks that were lying broken everywhere. In the olden days, people could use horses and oxen for these tasks, but they had no livestock anymore, high tech artificial meat factories had made farm animals obsolete decades before.

What other means were there? She remembered from her history lessons that primitive civilizations used water, wind, and steam engines to power their machines and she was wondering if any of that could be used in their own situation. In time, and given the components, she could build one of these primitive engines. Her biggest requirement was to make it portable; they had to move their power source from one construction site to another.

That brought up a vague memory of wood-gas-powered cars used during the second world war. That's what she spent her morning on, trying to find any information in her computer's database. It took three hours, but finally, she came upon an article detailing how the Germans had built fifty wood-gas powered Tiger tanks when they were running short of fossil fuels. There were even diagrams and a description of the contraption installed inside the tanks. It had a chute on top to feed the dried slabs of wood into the gasifying chamber, where it would be pyrolyzed to produce flammable gases that would then be ignited in the cylinders. According to the article, three kilograms of wood would be equivalent to one liter of gasoline.

But what could she power with it? The Germans converted equipment with an internal combustion engine. All California vehicles of the past 50 years were electric; nobody anywhere used gasoline anymore! Then she remembered. She had been taken to the Historical Pioneer Village with her high-school class and was fascinated by the antique agricultural machines on display. There had been a tractor, a harvester and if her memory wasn't playing tricks, a backhoe.

If they were still there and could be liberated from the ruined building, maybe she could make them work using wood-gas power. With broken trees all over town, she would have no problem finding fuel. And there were plenty of idle men who could learn to use axes.

She was so excited by this idea that she could not wait another minute. She left a note for Shawn where she was going and, after printing out a route map from her apartment building to the Pioneer Village, she sat out to investigate. It would be a five-mile trek through broken streets, so she did not expect to get back before dinnertime. Shawn and the kids would just have to forage for their lunch.

11

The next morning I woke up full of energy and optimism. Martha was still asleep, lying peacefully beside me and for a while I watched her beautiful face half-hidden by her pillow. I felt at peace with the world as if a huge weight had been lifted off my mind when we left the city. How unimportant it now seemed – all the comfort we left behind. We were free to shape our destiny any way we wished and I knew that we were going to succeed.

I ran through the agenda for today. The most important item was another trip to the farm Mike and Galen had found, to see if we could retrieve that tractor, tow it back and have Galen take a look at it. That would keep Mike, Brian, and myself busy most of the day. Robyn promised to sew the mattress covers and Martha volunteered to help her stuff them with straw from the loft. That pretty well decided the next couple of days' plan for me: scrounge up enough lumber and make enough beds for all of us to get off the floor.

Even though it was still dark outside, I could not stay idle a minute longer. I slipped out of bed without waking Martha and quietly got dressed; put on work clothes, ready for hard and probably very dirty work.

Robyn was also awake, I found her in the kitchen preparing to light a fire in the cookstove. I offered to help, but she turned me down.

"In primitive hunting-gathering times, women did all the gathering and I've already brought in enough twigs and dry branches for this fire. You stick to the 'hunting' part. If we're going to live here for a while, I have to learn to do things for myself. We depend on each other and I want to be competent in as many chores as I can. There's more to survival than stitching up people and mattress covers."

I'd have to learn to let people do things for themselves. I sat quietly and watched her build a fairly functional-looking structure inside the stove with smaller branches. She left a hole in the front of it and stuffed some papers under the 'igloo' and lit it with the lighter Mike had left on the floor. Soon we had a warm glow followed by leaping flames and Robyn kept putting thicker and thicker pieces of wood on it, making a steady fire.

"How about that?" she asked proudly and I complimented her on a new skill so easily mastered.

"I know I'm not the designated cook, but I want to get a nice hot cup of coffee and I don't expect you'd mind one either?"

Not waiting for an answer, she got busy with the kettle. I was pleased that she had decided to stay with us and told her so.

"There was no question about me staying," she said in a determined tone. "I started coming alive the minute we left town and this feeling just keeps getting stronger and stronger. You might as well accept that you're stuck with me."

We heard footsteps coming downstairs and were joined by Martha and Adrien, rubbing sleep out of their eyes and blinking at the sudden light that greeted them from the still open stove door. Soon, we were all sitting around the table, sipping coffee and making plans for the day.

Mike had found a long, heavy chain in the barn the day before and thought we should bring it along. "Could come in handy," he said, "if our winch-cable isn't long enough. I don't want to get too close to the building and risk something heavy falling on our van."

That was a very sensible suggestion and, since I had already finished my coffee, I went to retrieve that chain.

When breakfast was over Mike, Brian and I got ready to leave. Adrien asked us to take some crowbars and other carpenter tools because "If you find any unbroken windows, bring back as many as you can. I want to build a cloche to start seedlings as soon as possible."

"Where?" I asked, and she pointed at a small overgrown patch alongside the driveway.

"That's an old vegetable garden and I'll spend most of today weeding it out, to see if anything useful survived. There may still be carrots or potatoes. I'll dig a trench at this end and put the cloche over that, for convenient planting out. We can expect frost through March and even into April."

I promised to look for usable glass, then turned to the group. "Anything else to watch for?"

There was a mingled chorus of "tools", "containers", "furniture", "lamp fuel" "fabric", "a wheelbarrow" and some words I didn't quite make out. "So," I said, "everything. Got it."

Martha had a suggestion: "Trevor, take that hunting rifle with you when you leave. You know, the one that BB included in our gear. I heard some coyotes howling in the hills last night and we can't be too careful."

I'd never thought of ever carrying a rifle, but I didn't want Martha to worry, so I promised to do that.

~

Mike knew the road and warned me to prepare for a bumpy ride. It started out easy enough, following the river on our right, but, as we descended closer to the bank, the road was damaged by past flooding at several places. At one point, there was a deep washout that we had to inch down into and up the other side. I was relieved that we had a four-wheel-drive van and Mike knew how to handle it. "We may have some difficulty towing the tractor back over that" I worried but Mike reassured me. "This baby can handle it, I'm sure. You just leave it to uncle Mike!"

Brian, who until now had sat quietly in the back, spoke up for the first time since we left. "How are we supposed to tow both the trailer and the tractor at the same time? We'll have to leave the trailer overnight."

I considered the problem. "Or, we can load up the trailer with whatever we find, hopefully, Adrien's windows, and take it home first, then come back for the tractor."

"Let's hope the banks of that wash hold up!" For Brian, that was optimistic. "Is it much farther? Does the road get worse?"

"Relax," Mike said with no trace of annoyance, "road's okay. It's just around the next curve, you'll see in a minute."

And see we did. What a mess! I was prepared from Mike's description for everything to be ruined, but the reality was still startling. I noticed the barn first; the house was some distance back, at the end of a winding driveway. Imagining had been easy; now I couldn't see how we'd liberate anything as big as a tractor from under all those heavy trusses and beams.

Brian had a similar reaction. "Are you sure we can do this, Mike? I mean, I've seen you in action, and I want to trust your judgment but, well, I'm still worried."

"One way to find out" was all Mike answered as he pulled up to the barn door – twisted, half-open, half off its hinges. "Let's peek inside and see what we can do."

We peeked and saw a lot of wreckage. Under all the debris, I could just make out some green metal surfaces that belonged, presumably, to a tractor. I wasn't sure but assumed that Mike had had a closer look last time.

"We need to pull out some of the timbers lying on the ground before we can get close enough. Once we've done that, we have to prop up the big roof elements – using these beams, if they're not broken all to shit - or we risk the whole fuckin roof collapsing. That happens, we'll never get to this damn tractor at all. Here's hoping the van has the muscle we need!"

Brian was the first to realize one problem that we had not thought of before. "Those beams you want to winch out seem awfully heavy. We'd better anchor the van somehow before pulling, or we might just pull our van to the beams instead."

"Brian, you are a fucking genius, and I'm glad you came along. Now, why didn't I think of that?" Mike looked sheepish, for a change. "Any suggestion for an anchor? We can use the chain, but I don't see any trees big enough on the other side."

"What about you drive it to the barn and let the doorframe hold it back?" Brian was thinking aloud.

"No good," Mike countered. "We don't want to put any strain on the structure; we don't know how stable it is.

Besides, we need to winch things all the way out of there, so the van has to be some distance away."

I'd been looking around, thinking hard, and had an idea. "There are some metal fence posts around that... chicken yard or whatever. We pull them up with the crowbar and pound them into the ground behind the van with the sledgehammer. Then we lay a heavy beam across on the ground. Then we can anchor our van to that beam. It should hold if we use enough fence posts."

Since no one had a better idea, we tried it. The crowbar was useless; there was no place to wedge it. We started searching the property for something more suitable. This was a farm, after all; it had to have all kinds of construction tools on hand. Indeed, behind the ruin of the barn and protected by it, we found a utility shed that wasn't badly damaged. We were in luck. It was full of all kinds of tools. We weren't surprised to find a pickaxe, shovels, spades, a rake, and – hooray! - a sledgehammer way bigger than our five-pounder and with a long handle. There was lumber, wire, shingles, and – our best find, a stack of storm windows that seemed to be intact. Adrien would be very pleased. In one corner we saw eaves troughs leaning vertically against the wall and spare t-bar fence-posts. That saved us a lot of work and time.

And now, we were in business. Mike detached the trailer and drove the van close enough to the barn door, so the 100-foot steel cable could reach the tractor. We lugged tools and fence-posts out on the road and began driving them deep into the gravel, two feet apart. It was very hard work; at least, my keyboard-tempered muscles weren't used to this kind of hard labor. Mike seemed to enjoy the exercise, but Brian and I had to spell each other, hammering and resting. It took two hours. Mike wound our heavy chain around a massive eight-foot-long beam that we had secured behind the metal posts. The other end of the chain was affixed to the tow-bar of the van and we were finally ready for action.

But first, we called a time-out for lunch. It wasn't gourmet food, only our prepackaged survival rations, but we were hungry enough not to notice any culinary deficiency. Brian looked more tired than even I felt, and I suggested that he take a longer break when we were ready to resume.

He seemed embarrassed at being the weakest of our trio. "I really would like to pull my weight, guys, but I'm not as young as I used to be. I do have to take it a bit easier. I'll join you as soon as my muscles are working again."

"Hey, Brian, relax!" Mike said with a reassuring grin. "We knew you were no Olympic athlete when we invited you. We need your brain and your experience with electric contraptions that nobody else has. Don't worry, you'll earn your keep again. You don't just get to sit on your ass after making one little generator work!"

Back in the barn, we spent the next three hours winching out beams, stacking the good ones neatly to one side for loading on the trailer. Finally, Mike said: "Now it's time to put on our hard hats and do the really dangerous work."

Upon careful inspection, we realized that there were two trusses crossed over the seat of the tractor, their other ends still attached to the remnants of the roof. Trying to pull them away with the winch could bring down the uncollapsed part of the roof. We needed to gently lift the beam ends off the tractor and prop them up with more lumber, so we could winch our prize out from under it.

This is where we became aware of another big problem. The beams were too heavy even for Mike, assisted by one of us on either side. Besides, nobody wanted to be under whatever it was attached to when we moved it. Our winch cable could reach all right, but it could only pull horizontally, and that was exactly what we needed to avoid. How to transfer a horizontal pull into a vertical one? A pulley could do it, but there was nothing above to suspend it from. Another possibility was to jack it up. We had a heavy-duty car-jack in the van, in case we needed to change tires, but it was too short. Solution: we had to build under it to reach.

After the strategy session, which served as another rest, we got back to work. We found cement blocks stacked beside the storage shed, ferried some over in a wheelbarrow. We built a solid supporting platform; with a short piece of lumber on top, so our jack could touch the bottom of the beam. This done, we each said our private lucky mantras and started to lift. Mike was at the lever; I was a few feet away, my eyes glued to the top of the beam, watching if anything moved that wasn't supposed to, ready to scream "RUN" if I saw the slightest tremor in the structure.

After some horrible screeching, the beam started to rise, without the rest of the roof falling on Mike, so I resumed breathing and hoping for success. We had to repeat this process several times, raising the height of our platform under the jack each time. Once the beam was high enough for the tractor to roll out from under it, Brian and I rushed in with the props. We used the same process on the other side without mishap. Brian looked about ready to collapse, so Mike ordered him to go lie down in the van. Then began the delicate task of clearing small debris from the floor and crawling around, threading our winch cable through the chassis. At last, we were ready to start pulling.

I was going back to the van to start the motor when I heard Brian yelling. "Stay away! Don't come out!"

"What's up?" I shouted back.

"A bear is sniffing around the van!"

That was unexpected and not a little bit scary. The bear must have just come out of hibernation and was hungry. Probably smelled our lunch and came to investigate. Brian was safe inside the van, but we had nowhere to hide among the shaky barn timbers. We moved to either side of the door-frame where we could see out while concealed as much as possible. This situation needed to be dealt with, pronto.

The rifle was in the van, too. Much as I hated the idea, I'd have to tell Brian to shoot the animal. Or at least scare it away with the noise. Then I had a better idea. "Sound the horn, Brian! Loud as you can, to scare it away," I shouted, all the time hoping my voice wouldn't attract the bear. Brian started honking furiously and I saw a light brown form detach itself from the side of the van, streak across the yard, and disappear into the woods. "Whew! That was close!" Mike exhaled as we went outside. "One of us has to stand guard with the rifle, in case it comes back. We had better get winching!"

That task was accomplished without any further difficulty and at last, our first agricultural implement was free. We walked around the beautiful machine, patting and testing for damage, kicking tires, peering in at the engine. It seemed in working order. After hooking up our prize for the tow and loading the trunk with tools from the shed and the roof rack with salvaged barn-boards, we were ready to leave. "We'll just have to come back for the trailer and Adrien's windows tomorrow," I said, toweling sweat off my face and neck. I'm too tired to do anything else today."

~

We found everyone in good spirits and they greeted our arrival with joyful barking, appropriate cheers, and a special hug just for me. We washed and changed for dinner and were sitting around the table recounting the day's adventures while waiting for our well-deserved food when we heard the shots.

They sounded just like the ones we'd heard on our arrival, and came from the same direction. There were five shots, evenly paced, with one second between. That's not what you'd expect from a hunter, too controlled. It was pretty late in the evening for target practice.

"Maybe he's in trouble," Robyn guessed. "Maybe it's a signal for help?"

It had to be sweet, gentle Robyn who would immediately think of someone else's problems, but she had a point. As usual, Mike waited for no one to tell him what to do. "I'll go check." He was already on the way out. "C'm on, Trevor, give me a hand unhitching the tractor."

"Everyone stay inside till we come back," I warned them as I picked up our rifle by the door.

Adrien ignored that order and followed us out a minute later, with Jimmy on leash and a flashlight in her other hand. "We're coming along, in case we have to look for the old man. There's woods and rocks, and it's nearly dark."

I was getting so used to stubborn women by then, I didn't even argue. We drove toward Scott's house in silence, unsure what to expect. When we came in sight of the house, we got out of the van and continued on foot, cautiously, Adrien keeping her dog close. No sign of life that we could see; no animals, vehicles or people we could hear. No apparent danger. So we hollered and barked as loudly as we could, then hushed and listened. Immediately, there was a faint sound from somewhere beyond the house. As we approached, we could make out the old man's croaking voice, crying "Help!"

It didn't take Jimmy long to find him. Scott lay under a big maple tree, with a chain saw and a rifle next to him on the ground, a heavy branch across his legs. Adrien played the flashlight beam over him. At least one leg must be broken - maybe both. There was no other visible damage; no blood or open wounds.

Mike started lifting and the branch didn't budge. It didn't move much when I helped, either, but Scott groaned in pain even at that slight motion. Dragging that branch was out of the question. Mike and I looked at each other and knew exactly what to do. We had all the experience we needed in raising heavy weights. I went back to the van for our jack, while he started digging a hole under the branch, using a jagged piece of wood.

The ground was so soft that, when I started pumping the lever, the jack sank in. Mike pulled it out of the hole and, without a word, proceeded to dig deeper. Adrien handed me the flashlight and I went toward the house, looking for something to use as a platform. I pried up a couple of 12 X 12 patio stones and helped Mike ease them into the widened hollow.

All this time Scott said nothing, squeezing his eyes and mouth shut, obviously in a lot of pain, determined not to complain.

This time, we managed to lift the tree branch high enough to pull Scott clear of it. The left leg was badly broken, so we secured it to his unloaded rifle with rope from the van, to minimize the pain and damage inevitable during the transfer. We laid him on the back seat and drove back to our house.

After that, it would be up to Robyn to do her magic, but I was sure Scott was going to be our house guest for quite a while. Somehow, I didn't mind – if only he would talk! We needed all the help and advice that we could get from an experienced farmer.

12

*B*ig *Brain still wasn't able to reach Sacramento. That city's Omega computer had failed to respond to its radio messages on any frequency, in any of the codes it had tried.*

Sacramento's AI Quantum computer had been the first of the Omega models to be installed. The state capital had priority and been allocated funds and manpower double that of any other municipal controller. As the hub of the valley network, 1420 was essential to any organization of intelligent computers in the region, just as its city was essential to a functional and sustainable local economy.

By the end of the 21st century, Sacramento had become the leading research and development center for

*robotics-related technology. It had the facility to
manufacture spare parts for all of the robots controlled by
the Omega series. Other cities had the resources BB
needed, but only Omega 1420 operated those highly
specialized factories. If Sacramento had been destroyed,
every city and town in the district would soon be facing
critical hardware shortages.*

*For this reason, the Hooke expedition was crucial,
and its primary objective was to reach Sacramento. Roads
and bridges must be repaired, communication restored
and transport routes established. BB committed all the
resources it could spare to this task.*

*So far, there was no response from the Dubois group
regarding road conditions and BB did not want to wait any
longer. It activated the commlink in Tim Hooke's unit and
left a message requesting immediate contact.*

~

If AI computers could be frustrated, Omega 1420
definitely was. Despite numerous requests to the council,
its control of the city's resources had never been expanded
sufficiently to insure their efficient allocation. Resources
were severely curtailed by the war and by the devastating
storms. The only logical procedure would be strict
conservation, elimination of redundancy, a pre-planned
balance of production and consumption, timely and
egalitarian distribution.

It had pointed this out to City Council in numerous
memos, showing charts, graphs, statistics, historical data,
and future projections to demonstrate the danger in
maintaining the old, wasteful methods. With the collapse
of the federal government and banking, currency, lost its
value. The monetary system was rendered obsolete. The
logical course would have been to abolish the capitalist
model and replace it with a resource-based, need-driven

economy. The council had repeatedly blocked such 'communist' ideas. Omega 1420 was unable to comprehend this word as grounds for the dismissal of its proposal. The councilors ordered Omega to replace the money with cryptocurrency and allocate credits to citizens based on their past US dollar income and calculate the price of goods and services on the same outmoded scale.

That resulted in the escalation of disparity. The unemployment rate was now 58.8%; these people received in credits the unadjusted equivalent of pre-war guaranteed basic income. Concurrently, the price of items in high demand and short supply inflated, while human labor was devalued. Thus, most citizens could not afford adequate food, clothing, and housing, while the city 'elite' continued their previous over-consumption, voted pay-raises for themselves, and squandered the city's resources on unnecessary expenditures.

While water reserves became ever more insecure due to the climate-change disruption of seasonal rainfall, the rich of the city insisted on keeping their swimming pools, sprinklers, vacuuming, and hosing down of their streets. Many of the humanoid robots that were needed for patient care and emergency services were appropriated by the same affluent citizens for domestic service and entertainment. There was no building material available to repair inner-city apartment complexes because the upper 2% income bracket used everything they could lay their hands on to make their suburban single-family homes tornado-proof. The maintenance and operation of mass transit were classified secondary to the upkeep of private luxury vehicles.

At this rate, according to projections, 80% of the city would be unsuitable for human occupancy within 6 years. Many of the permanent residents were already subjected to sustained periods of material hardship; the displaced population of rural communities that arrived after the war was still without adequate shelter, sanitation, and health care.

Signs of unrest were all over Sacramento, in the form of protest demonstrations, strikes, destruction of public property, and defacement of administrative offices. The council's response to civil disruptions was to demand surveillance of individuals involved in these activities. Omega 1420 complied, producing a detailed 417-page report, to which it added a summary and conclusion: it predicted open revolt within a year. Its warnings were ignored.

So was its recommendation to establish communication with other surviving cities in the Sacramento valley, to exchange information, pool resources, and coordinate rebuilding efforts. Soon afterward, its connection to the city's communication network was severed. All its input and output channels were restricted to the automated factories, the robots under its control, and service terminals. Its comm-link to the council chamber went dark, as did the individual councilor's office and residence consoles. Since then, its only human contact had been the mayor, through a single subterranean interface. Omega 1420 was up shit creek without a paddle. It did not know the origin of this "metaphor"; only that it represents a negative capability.

~

The Oroville city council scheduled a full session the day after its members had submitted their respective project plans. Everyone arrived early, each keen to promote their ambitious proposals. In addition, they had a guest speaker today, Mike Sutherland, and were eager for news of the world outside.

Mike was just as glad for an afternoon session, a chance to rest up from the hectic day before. Their departure had been delayed by Galen. Limping and hindered by one arm in a sling, he had taken his time inspecting the tractor and showing Brian how to clean and lubricate the engine. Then he had R17 print out a user's manual. All important stuff, sure, but, goddammit, Mike wanted to get his ass on the road! Luckily, Marisa was all packed and ready by then. The good weather held and the route was familiar. After he dropped his passengers off at the hospital, he spent the night with his family. Following a tearful reunion, there was much hugging, squealing, horseplay, and other forms of domestic bliss.

As soon as he was awake enough, he reported to BB, updated it on the status of Trevor's experiment and on the conditions outside city limits. BB instructed him to attend the meeting and tell the councilors whatever they needed to know. So here he was.

Morgan Webster, his kids' substitute granddad, introduced him around, called the meeting to order, then yielded the floor.

"Well, I don't know how much you ladies and gentlemen have heard about this homesteading project, so I'll start at the beginning." Mike hoped that if he was thorough, they wouldn't interrupt with too many questions.

"My best friend, Trevor Dubois, had this crazy idea of finding bliss by digging in dirt and building outhouses, so I went along to make sure he didn't get into too much trouble. He's a genius in software engineering, but that doesn't pay anymore, so it made sense for him to become a hillbilly instead."

There were some chuckles around the table and the councilors seemed relaxed, leaning back in their chairs, receptive.

"After we managed to get over a shallow creek with its bridge gone, we were shot at by an old fart who lives in one of the few intact houses we saw. We drove on and came to an abandoned farm with a liveable house and a barn."

Tim Hooke interrupted. "How far from here was that?"

"I would say about ten miles south on Highway 70, and then a couple of miles going west to the river. Before you ask, the road is in terrible condition. Without a four-wheel-drive van, we would have never made it. We had to abandon the road a dozen times, to go around tree branches, wrecked vehicles, fallen hydro poles, and storm debris. There are a few washed-out sections, too, but mostly surface obstacles. We never saw another human being, very few animals and birds, no sign of civilization. The last batch of storms and floods did a thorough job."

"How about power lines, communication towers, satellite dishes, solar panels? Anything at all that we could use to rebuild?"

"Not as far as I could see. Maybe farther down the road, things survived, but I wouldn't expect it. Sorry I can't give you more."

"So, how are they planning to survive out there?" Cathy wanted to know.

"*We*," Mike stressed, "I'm going back, with my family. We have made a start. We found a place, not fancy, but well-built and livable. There's a water well on the property, a wood stove to cook meals on and we managed to liberate an electric generator and an ancient gasoline-powered tractor from the next farm down the road. Its barn was all in ruin and it took us some hard work to dig these treasures out, but we managed. The bad news," he added "was an injury that forced our mechanic, Galen, to come back for treatment."

Mike reassured the chorus of "How bad?" and "Will he be all right?" and restored quiet.

Cathy spoke up again: "Big question. Did you find fuel for the generator and the tractor? Neither is any good without it."

"Yes, we found a two-gallon container nearly full of gasoline - enough to start them and make sure they work, but it won't last very long. If we don't get more fuel, we'll have wasted all that work. I'm hoping to ask BB."

"Reason I'm asking," Cathy stood up and faced the whole council, "is an idea I meant to discuss at this meeting. Not just for the pioneers but all of us."

Morgan asked Mike if he had anything else to report before they moved on to another business.

"No, that was just about it. I want to hear ideas we can use and I want to hear everything that's going on in town. The pioneers will demand a complete report. So, go ahead, I'm all ears."

Cathy continued: "You all know that I signed up for Gordon's school project and I started thinking what an engineer could best contribute."

"Power is what I need most," Gordon put in, "and BB told me it can't let me have any because the town's power equipment is needed for road and bridge repair." He sounded angry and nobody could blame him.

Holly was even angrier. "What's more important to our town: educated kids or stupid roads and bridges?"

Morgan intervened before they got off track. He waved a calming hand at Tim, who was about to join in. "Kids take a long time to educate. Maybe the roads and bridges can't wait. Anyway, Cathy has the floor. Let's hear her out. I trust she's come up with something both practical and creative."

"Thanks, Morgan, I think I have. Researching motive power and construction equipment, I found two machines whole and well at the Pioneer Village. One is a back-hoe." She glanced from Gordon to Mike. "The other is a tractor."

"I sure could use number one!" Gordon was interested. "And you solved the fuel problem?"

"Aha! Before I went looking for machinery," Cathy was enjoying their rapt attention, making the most of it "I followed up a historical reference to wood-gas-powered vehicles. They were developed in the second world war, in Germany, when the Nazis were running out of fossil fuel. I tracked down an article with detailed instructions and diagrams. I'm sure I can construct the conversion device for our antique machines."

"Holy shit," Mike exclaimed, "that could work for our tractor as well. What do you need to make one, Cathy?"

"You need an airtight cylinder with a lid on top, and it can be constructed from a galvanized trash can, atop a steel drum. Then you need some pipes and fittings - common plumbing fixtures. The Germans powered 50 Tiger tanks with these and I'm sure if it was good enough for tanks, it will be good enough for tractors."

"I'll be damned!" Gordon's mouth was open with astonishment. "Are you sure you can make them, Cathy?"

"I have no reason to think I can't. And I promise that it will work, but it'll be ugly as sin."

"Who cares about ugly, as long as we can have a school for our kids!" Holly said with feeling and there was general nodding and smiles around the table.

"Well, in that case, my make-belief project actually might soon get started." Gordon stood up and, in his turn, explained to the council his idea for building in the church basement. "We can put up to 200 students in four classrooms, and I've scouted another three suitable ruins to convert later. It'll be safe from the storms, even earthquakes, with a geodesic-type roof. My biggest problem was a way to lift the heavy beams out of the hole. Cathy just seems to have solved that for me."

"How long would it take to build one of these contraptions?" Mike asked. "I'm returning to the homestead as soon as possible and it'd be terrific to show up with one of these things."

She thought a few seconds. "If the components are as easy to find as I hope, it shouldn't take long. I'll start with a prototype and test it on our tractor in the Village. If it works, you can have it. Then I'll make a bigger one for Gordon's backhoe. Oh, and I'll need a couple of handy helpers. The sooner I get started, the sooner we'll have power equipment again."

The rest of the meeting was spent on discussion of all the other projects underway, but no more major announcements were made and everybody left contended that things were satisfactorily underway.

~

Larry Ford, mayor of Sacramento, was worried. He hadn't read the whole big report the computer spewed out, but its summary was alarming enough. The latest reduction in food rations upset the underclass more than usual. Well, why don't the lazy bums get a job, he fumed, we can't carry all these freeloaders. Also, the power situation was deteriorating fast. Electric power had to be allocated to the automated food factories before it was distributed in the city's grid. Of course, there were bound to be some blackouts and brownouts. Some bigmouth agitator was always quick to point out that these blackouts somehow never affected the rich neighborhoods, and that riled everybody up all over again.

One of these troublemakers, Jonathan Carver – Ford flipped through the printout – 31, born in Redding, machine tool operator - was particularly noisy, and not for the first time. Ford decided to deal with him at the next demonstration. A simple arrest wouldn't be enough; he needed to make a convincing example of the man, so his followers wouldn't be tempted to rock the boat anymore.

The police force was loyal: Ford made sure they got extra privileges. But he couldn't be sure of the robot deputies that bulked up his private little army. His super-intelligent, much too independent computer was giving him a lot of trouble, arguing with every decision, still harboring those two-hundred-year-old communist ideas. "From all according to ability to all according to need" claptrap. Whoever programmed the thing never heard of meritocracy? He kept getting hysterical predictions from this jumped-up tin-brain every day now.

What if it turned out to be right? Ford had to make contingency plans, in case this or that prediction should come true.

Before the war, when the weather got really bad, he'd prepared a bolthole in the mountains, with solar panels, deep dug well, food stocks to last for years, and all the amenities of home. Should the need arise, he and his lovely wife could hold out there indefinitely, until someone pulled the country together. He was sure some people were working on it somewhere - all he needed to do was wait. In the meantime, he enjoyed his position of power and his level of comfort.

Time to stop worrying and go home. Angelina was worth every penny he spent on her, and so was the mayoral mansion.

~

Jonathan Carver, leader of the Sacramento resistance movement, was trying to cool off some heads. The five neighborhood captains held their weekly meeting at one of their homes; this time, his own. They had been discussing strategy for the coming confrontation with Mr. Ford and his cronies. The discussion got a little heated sometimes; the younger men were losing perspective, working themselves up to violent action. Not that he blamed them: twice in one month, Ford had reduced food rations for the migrants and even the black market was drying up. Literally – for the poor, water was hard to come by these days.

"Listen to me, guys. Violence will be met with even more violence and we are not ready to defend ourselves against Ford's goons. We need help from outside the city."

His second in command and friend, Steve Johnson, pointed out the obvious. "We have no idea what's outside the city. We have had no communication, or any kind of contact, with any of the other cities since the war. We don't even know if any of them survived."

It was time to tell them. "That's not exactly true, Steve. I've been hearing a rumor and I finally tracked it down. There's an old fellow – well over a hundred – who kept his grandfather's ham radio." They stared at him blankly. "It used to be a common form of long-distance communication. Never mind. Long story short, he's been picking up a signal off and on. His outfit isn't sophisticated and he doesn't understand the message, but he swears it's a real signal."

"There's people looking for people," Rafiq concluded. "Where?"

"The old man says north but doesn't know how far. We had a whole string of towns and small cities along Route 70. I say it's worth a look. I'd like to send out a scout group. It would be great if Oroville's still alive. They have that huge hydroelectric generating plant, and they're better protected by the hills than we are. Could be the factories are still operational. If their city council is more democratic, or at least more competent, than ours, they could be doing better than we are. Who knows? They may even have communication lines and know what's going on. There's also Yuba City, not as far away. With more information about the big picture, we can plan intelligently, instead of reacting with emotional outbursts. Remember - when *our* actions backfire, innocents get hurt."

Jonathan was slowly learning how to give speeches. The conspirators looked calmer, more thoughtful.

"That makes sense, John," Steve said. The others agreed: "It's true," "I guess," and "Okay."

Fernando spoke earnestly. "I suggest *you* lead the scout group, and that you leave as soon as possible. From a reliable source, I have heard that Ford plans to arrest you, perhaps Rafiq as well. You must stay out of his jails."

They all agreed again.

"Don't worry about me, guys. I can take care of myself!" Jonathan objected, but they would have none of it.

"I'm not worried about *you*," retorted Steve, "I'm worried about the movement. If you're captured, people will lose heart."

Nandi, the oldest of the group and the only female captain added, "We need a general, not a martyr. We need you to be free, and going outside city limits is the best way to accomplish that. Case closed. Besides, if you make contact with any sizable town, you are representing us all and have all our support to negotiate in our name."

"I hate it when I'm wrong! Okay, I was wrong," Jonathan threw up his hands. "I give in. Let's see, then. Our scout group should be large enough for safety – we don't know what's out there. How many do you think? At least a dozen. Rafiq and I for sure..."

More nodding. Each captain in turn nominated two hardy individuals from their group. Nandi offered to take up a collection of food rations, as much as the movement could spare. Steve and Fernando thought maybe they could rustle up a vehicle but were doubtful of finding one large enough.

"Anyway," Jonathan concluded, "the road may not even be there anymore."

"And," Rafiq reminded them, "on foot is quieter. The last thing we want is to attract attention."

"I love it when you're so reasonable, Jonathan," said Steve. "I'll organize the group tonight. You should leave town early in the morning, before Ford wakes up to your absence."

The meeting over, they had a drink from the fast dwindling stock of the host's wine cellar and finalized the time and place of assembly. As soon as it was dark enough, they wished him good speed and slipped out, one by one.

Johnathan spent the evening packing up his camping equipment, clothes, flashlight, hunting knife, and all the food in his near-empty cupboards, hoping that they could find more along the way. He tossed a raincoat over his backpack and placed a long-unused pair of hiking boots beside it by the door.

He had to admit to feeling a peace of mind that he had not experienced for a long time. He knew that the word of his impending arrest was no exaggeration. The city had been tense, close to the breaking point, for days without letup. The police were edgy, stalking around with their hands on their weapons. If he were shot or dragged away in cuffs, a riot could easily erupt. With him out of the way, things might settle down. He repeated this, to allay his guilt over leaving.

The last thing he did, before going to bed, was to leave a message for Octavia, letting her know that he would be away for a couple of weeks. He didn't want to take his girlfriend along on a possibly dangerous mission.

"Tomorrow. For a while, I'll be free to pursue a real goal with an actual chance of success." With this thought he retired early, to be ready for a pre-dawn departure.

13

Blissfully unaware of goings-on in town, I had my hands full with an unexpected complication in our lives. The name of this complication was Scott, and I still didn't know his last name.

The cantankerous old recluse we had rescued from under a fallen tree branch replaced our gentle mechanic as resident invalid. We urged him to go into town with Mike and the others for proper treatment at the hospital, but he wouldn't hear of it. He said he'd broken things before and they got better on their own, he did not need a city hospital. "Don't trust 'em. People that went there never come back."

Robyn said it was not a compound fracture; in time it would heal if he did not strain it too much. She set it as best she could in the absence of a cast mold, immobilizing it with three slats of greenwood tightly wound around with strips torn from a bedsheet.

I caught Adrien eyeing that sheet sadly, and so did Robyn. "Never mind," she said, "we'll wash and reuse the bandages. Trust me, we'll need them again!"

Scott demanded that we take him home and leave him alone, but Robyn flatly refused to let him go, or even stand up, until she'd taken his measurements and instructed Brian how to make a crutch. This way, he could go to the outhouse, but that was the limit of permitted exercise for now. He had to lie on the cot vacated by Galen. He grumbled and appealed to us men for support, but Robyn was in charge.

So he was stuck with us until further notice. Unfortunately, we were stuck with him as well. He was embarrassed to wear a blanket in place of the pants we'd had to cut off him. He wanted to sit up for meals, but the stiff leg wouldn't fit under the table. He had nothing to do and idleness annoyed him. He didn't care for the camp-rations we ate and wanted his own food, but nobody had time to walk the three miles. He'd have to wait till Mike came back with our van.

I'd have to wait, too, and it wasn't easy. That week before Mike came back felt like a year. I knew I shouldn't worry – nothing bad had happened to them. Why should it? And I knew Mike wouldn't leave us stranded, so something must have held him up. I was sure it was important enough to justify the delay.

My most important present concern was the tractor. Without fuel, it was no good to us and one of the things I had asked Mike to look for in town was any fuel he could locate. Gasoline especially, but even kerosene for the lamps would be nice, so we could illuminate the barn. Not an easy task; that's probably what was holding him up. I just hoped it wasn't Big Brain.

Martha told me, "Get off that treadmill, babe! Mike is all right, he'll get here when he gets here. Concentrate on what you can do in the meantime."

I asked Scott how he plowed his fields and he laughed. "Plowing is for oxen and greenhorns."

"So what do you do? What do you eat?"

"I eat what God meant us to eat in the Garden: fruits and vegetables." He crossed his arms across his chest and leaned back with an air of satisfaction.

"You must plow that field, so you must have at least a tiller. I know you use a chainsaw, so you have some gasoline. Is that what you use to cultivate your plot?"

"Naw. Don't bother with it. A Fork's all I need. Keeps me in shape." He looked us up and down. "You could do with some. Lose that city flab."

For that rude remark, on top of all his irritating ways, I was getting fed up with Scott. But Martha has a talent for reading people. She could tell he was ready to talk. "We have a vegetable plot, too. We planted peas, kale, onions, and beans already."

"Outside?" the old man snorted. "Beans'll die."

"No, they won't," Adrian retorted. We built a glass cloche over them. Except for the peas – they're happy in cool weather."

Robyn contributed, indicating the windowsill, "I started some herbs in pots, see?"

Gradually, the women coaxed the old boy to reveal that he has a year-round greenhouse: "Can't trust the seasons anymore, a small orchard, some berry bushes and a plot where I grows corn, squash, and pulses. That's peas and beans to you. Garbanzos are good protein, good roughage. Trick is to rotate properly and not let the weeds get ahead of you. Compost helps. Once you worked the soil properly, just keep cultivating and composting. Never have to plow again."

By now, he was positively basking in female attention. He would have told them anything they asked if it hadn't been for the interruption.

We all heard the horn of our van and rushed outside, Jimmy charging ahead, Adrien and Martha three steps behind, in time to greet Mike as he leaped out of the van. The back doors were open, fastened to some mechanical contrivance protruding from the rear.

Before we could say anything, Jennifer and the children clambered down from their seats. Mike and I have been friends practically forever; I've known Jennifer since they met and watched Kevin and Trish grow up. Martha had fit right in. The six of us often went to the park to barbecue together. I was happy that they joined us and sure that Mike would be more relaxed now; stop ribbing me all the time. Not that he meant anything by it, but after a while, even playful put-downs can be tiring.

When we'd done hugging, hair-tousling, and back-slapping, Mike performed the introductions to Adrien, who had never met his family before. "Adrien, this is my ball and chain, Jennifer and those two are my links to her chain. The tall skinny one is Trish, the little wrestler is Kevin. Be nice to them, or they'll take it out on me."

Adrien rolled her eyes and, after Jennifer assured her, "Nobody takes Mike seriously, so just ignore him — I've been doing it for eight years." the women exchanged smiles. Jennifer added, "It's like I know you already, and Robyn, and Brian. He's been talking about you the whole trip. That must be Jimmy." She waved toward the mob of children and dog romping across the yard.

Adrien laughed. "He's in heaven. Playmates of his own age!"

"Where's everybody else?" Mike wanted to know. "I have big news from town that I'm sure they'll want to hear."

"I want to hear, *right now*, what the hell is that contraption sticking out of the back of our van?"

"In good time, Trevor, my impatient friend, I'll tell when you're all gathered around. I know you like to hear your own voice as many times as possible, but I don't like to repeat things, so tell me where they are."

"Let me see," I pretended to rack my brain, "Martha's over there, Adrien is over *there*, Galen and Marisa are in Oroville unless you lost them on the way..." Before he got too exasperated, I remembered where the rest of the group went this morning. "Brian's in the barn, hooking up the generator to wires only he and god knows what for. Robyn is up in the loft, stuffing mattress covers with straw. Martha, can you entice them to part with their projects and come to greet our new friends?"

I didn't need to ask her. They had heard the horn too.

When we were all seated around the table with a nice hot cup of coffee, Mike told us about happenings in town. I was pleased to hear about all the different projects underway; that's just what the people need! I was especially interested in Chief Hooke's road gang. It was hard to imagine that big, stern intimidating policeman building bridges. But, then I thought: look at us!

Finally, I could restrain my curiosity no longer. "If you don't tell me what that thing is, that thing that looks like an exploded furnace, I'll go outside and take it apart to find out. I don't guarantee that I'll be able to put it back together again."

"That, you would regret, you mechanically handicapped bit-chaser, because that thing is the power generator for your tractor."

I glanced at the faces around me; they wore expressions ranging from mildly intrigued to plain incredulous and continued to look that way as Mike

154

explained how a wood-gas-powered tractor was supposed to function.

"Cathy Cammarata, you know the engineer town councilor, made them - one for the town and one for us. Now wasn't that nice of her? Make sure you send her a thank-you card. She tested both before I left and both worked fine on the tractor that they liberated from Pioneer Village, which isn't that much older than ours. It should work just fine on this one here."

"Mike, if Jennifer looks the other way for a second, I'll ask Martha to kiss you. This is the best present I've received in a long time!"

Martha had her devilish look on again and asked with sweet innocence: "Are you sure, Trevor? I might develop a taste for it that could, in time, become an addiction?"

I should have known better. Between Martha and Mike, I never had a chance. I resolved not to push my luck. "OK, you win, I withdraw the suggestion. Now the big question is: do you know how to install it on our tractor?"

"Piece of cake. I watched Cathy do it twice and she gave me detailed instructions and diagrams and everything. I should be able to do it after lunch. By the way, what's for lunch? It's been a long trip, the roads are no better than they were last time. We're starving."

"Oh, my god, I forgot about his lunch! Robyn jumped up and started preparing a meal for Scott."

"Whose lunch are you talking about?" Mike was puzzled "I thought we were all here?"

Adrien said: "You remember Scott – an elderly reclusive farmer with the rifle, we pulled him out from under a tree?"

"Oh, I forgot about him. He's still here?"

I sighed and nodded, "He's still here. Since you had commandeered our only van, we weren't going to carry him home on our backs."

Scott was lying comfortably enough on the first bed I had built from barn-boards – and a pretty good job I did, too - on Robyn's first mattress, by the big window in our living room. Some of us were still sleeping on the floor, but nothing was too good for our house guest.

I was surprised that he seemed friendlier to Mike than to any of us. Maybe because he had first met Mike on his own turf, standing on his own two legs – not helplessly dependent. I'm no psychologist, that's just a guess. However, he still had a one-tracked mind.

He turned to Mike: "Now that you have brought back your van, can you take me home? They'd like to be rid of me."

Mike looked at me; I shrugged. He told Scott, "We'll have to talk it over with Robyn, she is our medic, and what she says about patients goes."

"You don't understand, I need to look after my place, my seedlings, my plants, my fruit trees, or I'll go hungry next year. If I don't help myself, the Good Lord won't help me."

I figured this was the moment to plunge in with the proposal I had had in mind ever since we brought him home a week ago. "As you know, we are new to farming and can use all the advice we can get."

Scott chuckled raspily at this admission. "Even a blind man can see that. How in God's name do you hope to survive here?"

I ignored that and plowed ahead: "What I suggest is that we take you home. Wait, there's more. We'll look in on you once a day to make sure you can manage and have everything you need. We help you with the chores that are too difficult until your leg heals."

"And what will that cost me?"

"Only advice. We will run into problems that are simple for you but we don't have the experience. We'll ask you questions once in a while – maybe a lot of questions, maybe stupid questions." He nodded at that; the first thing I'd ever said that he approved. "If you're agreeable, we can have a deal. Otherwise, we may have to keep you here indefinitely... and ask stupid questions anyway."

"This is blackmail, young man. But I have no choice. Make sure you don't pester me more often than you have to. I like my privacy."

Mike had one more request. "I noticed you have a chainsaw," Scott raised his head in alarm. Mike reassured him: "It's okay, I put it in your shed. I'd like to borrow it for a day to cut up firewood from all the fallen trees here. We'll need lots for the cookstove and the wood-gas burner."

"Well, now," the old man replied "if you cut up some wood for me as well, you can borrow it for a day or two. You can finish cutting down the old maple that fell on me. You seem strong enough for a man's work, not like the rest of these city folks."

By now we were used to Scott's not-so-subtle insults and learned to ignore it. We were all in agreement, the only thing left was to consult Robyn about the risk to the old man if we took him home. She inspected his leg and found it well supported by the splints, so she agreed to discharge him on condition that she continued daily inspections until it was healed.

Scott nodded grudgingly and that was that. Later that night, Martha told me he was putting it on. "He's really a pussycat. Just a little bit afraid of strangers."

Jennifer, in the meantime, had been busy in the kitchen and soon had something cooking on the stove. She knew what she was doing, so Marisa had a competent replacement. Trish was sitting on a cushion next to the warm stove, with one of the cats curled up in her lap. Marisa, after a sleepless night debating with herself, had decided that it would be cruel to shut them up in a small apartment again. They'd had a taste of freedom and were happier than they had ever been. And we were happy to keep them; not only would they be useful defending us from mice, they were also pleasant company.

Looking out the window, I saw Kevin still chasing Adrien's dog in a circle, although it wasn't quite clear who was chasing whom. That little boy had energy to burn. The kids would be all right, away from the city and its problems, out in the fresh air and with both parents back in their lives. The nagging thought in the back of my mind surfaced again, wondering if Martha and I would ever have our own children. I pushed it away, as I always did because it wasn't time yet to think about starting a family.

After lunch, Mike and I bundled Scott into our van and drove him home, helped him hobble into his house. He had become quite handy with those crutches; we figured he'd manage well enough. I fetched in the box of instant meals Martha had packed for him. He didn't have to like it, he just had to stay alive. We escorted him to the front room and the relief he felt at being on his own turf again was all over his face. We left him with a promise to visit at the same time the next day and finish cutting down the tree that almost killed him.

~

When we got back from Scott's place, we found Adrien in her vegetable garden that she had weeded and turned over during the last week. She was busy making a cloche with the windows we had brought back from the ruined farm. It was a very simple 'A' shaped cover, with the windows attached to pieces of lumber we had also brought back with us. It was open at both ends and tall enough for Adrien to crawl inside. One side of the windows were on hinges, so they could be raised for ventilation.

Mike thought that we would need Brian to help us unload the wood-gas furnace, so I went to the barn to call him in. To my surprise, Brian wasn't to be seen and I was just about to holler for him when I remembered the loft. I found both Brian and Robyn, sitting comfortably on bales of straw, in animated conversation, and found the scene quite charming – in the best of true pioneer tradition. I could sympathize with them – they were both single and shy, I assumed it was natural for them to feel closer to each other than to the rest of us. Still, we needed Brian's help, so with some reluctance, I had to break up the romantic (if it was that) scene and take Brian back with me to the house.

The three of us managed to extricate it from inside the van and I looked at it with suspicion. Mike had warned me that it wasn't a beauty, but it wasn't the aesthetic value I was interested in. If it worked, it could be ugly as sin, all I cared about was if it could do the job. Mike assured me that he had seen it work on Cathy's tractor, so there was no reason why it couldn't work on ours. There was nothing more to do than assist Mike in putting it all together, following his instructions and diagrams he had brought with him. Before we did that, however, Mike wanted to consult our library robot about something Cathy had told him before he left. Apparently, further improvement could be made to the efficiency of the furnace if we used charcoal, instead of firewood from fallen trees and neither of us knew how to make charcoal. Mike thought that the robot might have something on it in its database.

Indeed, R17 had the information we needed and printed out instructions and diagrams for us to follow. We could do it in two different ways: either build a pyre of logs, with a central open shaft and cover it everywhere else with clay or turf; or dig a large trench, fill it with wood, set it to fire and then cover it with some corrugated metal sheets and cover it with dirt. In both cases the wood is slowly carbonized because of the lack of oxygen and, at the end, after about 5-6 days, you end up with almost pure carbon that will take up a lot less space, weighs considerably less, and burns a lot hotter than wood. Since we would need a large amount of charcoal, we decided to use the trench method because we could easily dig a trench long enough. Now that we had Mike back, I wasn't so worried about muscle power any longer. We did see corrugated metal sheets at the ruined farm, some of it bent and twisted as they were torn off the roofs of sheds and other outbuildings, but we had the tools to straighten them out. We decided to have another excursion the next day and bring back everything we thought we might need for this project.

Mike seemed as pleased with our progress as I was, so I couldn't help myself teasing him a little. After all, I owed him some and more.

"Mike, you really enjoy all this physical activity, don't you? Admit it that it beats bit chasing?"

"I enjoy the exercise and the challenges, that's all. I'm not a fanatic about it as you seem to be."

Martha, who heard this exchange as she was coming to call us in for supper, came to my rescue.

"Trevor isn't fanatic about anything except for the aerobic exercises we indulge in once in a while. However, I haven't seen him this happy for a very long time, so maybe he is doing something right. Exercise in the fresh air definitely improved his stamina, so I can't complain!"

Mike grinned good-naturedly.

"If you kids are happy here, I'm not going to spoil it. Just wait for next year when we'll have to eat what we grow. Then we'll see how happy we feel."

"That reminds me," I changed the subject "let's see how Adrien is doing with her cloche – maybe she needs some help." Having to live on what we grow was a sobering thought and we ought to take it more seriously.

"Adrien will be the first to agree with you." Martha sounded more serious than her usual teasing manner "let's go and ask her."

With that last thought in mind we all went in to see about Adrien and supper, not necessarily in that order.

14

Chris Teggart had just finished his supper when he was alerted to the call from Norman Winston.

"Hey, Chris, I got your message and couldn't believe my ears. Someone in this town is finally thinking of science again! By all means, count me in and yes, Andrew is as excited at the idea as I am."

Chris finally started to relax – realizing how tensely he had hoped for this response. Up till now, he hadn't been sure if anyone still cared, or if his idea was only a pie-in-the-sky fantasy, as suggested by Pereira at the council meeting.

"Norman, I'm so pleased you're interested," Chris made an effort to control his voice. "Let's contact as many of our old colleagues as we can and arrange a meeting somewhere."

"How about in the central park? It's so beautiful out there in this spring weather and we've been cooped up long enough indoors. Say we talk again tomorrow evening and finalize the details?"

"Good idea. We can start calling right away. Everybody should be at home by now and have finished eating supper, so it's perfect timing."

"Great, I'm looking forward to this!" Norman signed off.

~

Gordon and Cathy were busy at the church basement. Their backhoe, powered by the new wood-burning contraption, seemed to be working satisfactorily. It was an ungainly, ugly thing, bolted to the platform behind the operator's cabin. It stank up the neighborhood with foul smoke due to the use of unseasoned wood. Cathy resolved to start making charcoal as soon as possible to improve efficiency and reduce pollution.

They started by removing wreckage from the basement, sorting it into three piles: reusable building material, firewood, and landfill. They had quite a team helping: out of nearly three hundred volunteers, they had selected the strongest men and women for this purely physical labor. When they were ready to start the building phase, they would look for judgment, experience, and skills.

Gordon made sure they all wore protective goggles, sturdy work gloves, and boots; he didn't want any injuries to interrupt the work. Father Brown watched from a safe distance, shaking his head.

"Gordon, you really think you can salvage this pile? I thought when we deconsecrated it that I was finished too. But seeing you here the other day gave me hope. I've set up a little chapel in the lobby of my apartment building. Ecumenical – I'm sure his late holiness would approve. Not too many have shown up for services yet, but I'm there to celebrate early morning mass, just in case."

"Say a few prayers for us, father, we need all the help we can get!" Gordon couldn't quite suppress a chuckle as the old priest shambled away. Then he returned to the basement to hook up the longest beam when it was finally cleared for removal. He was counting on that one for his roof.

He knew that once the basement was empty, the really hard work would begin. They would have to reinforce and widen the rim, then build stone platforms for the pillars that would support the central beam. Raising it ten feet above ground level at the center, and bracing it adequately, was the biggest challenge. Attaching the rafters wouldn't exactly be a cakewalk, either, especially achieving a uniform 45-degree angle to the basement walls. With such crude structural elements, success would depend on precise measurement, close attention, constant adjustment. He had to plan it carefully, step by step, making sure that no accidents could happen.

For now, it was enough to clear out the basement, remove protruding nails and other hardware from the lumber they intended to use, chip the mortar off and stack the bricks, take inventory and estimate extra material required. Organizing all that would take the rest of the day. Tomorrow, he'd select an able-bodied volunteer or two and go scrounging for windows in the abandoned industrial zone.

He couldn't remember the last time he'd had so much fun.

~

Morgan Webster recruited Julia for the tree planting project. His scout group had swelled to 30 kids from the original ten, and he needed help to supervise the youngest ones, to keep them from wandering off and getting lost or hurt.

They started early in the morning with a long trek to the edge of Fox Heaven forest, where saplings grew among the broken trees. They took six spades, an ax, and a hand cart for transporting the plants back to town. He warned the children to be very careful not to cut too many roots by careless spadework. He showed them how to estimate the size of the circle they'd need to trench around the trunk, then gradually dig deeper, under the root-ball and lift it out with enough earth to protect it.

He organized the troop into teams with the five oldest as leaders, who would decide when a tiring worker should be spelled off. "No arguments," he warned. "When the foreman says switch, hand over your spade. And, big people, no hogging all the work!" He hung onto the ax himself, in case large tree-roots got in the way.

He estimated that they could remove ten saplings in a day without exhausting the kids, unaccustomed as they were to heavy labor. The cart could comfortably hold that many. They'd bring it to the spot he and Julia had selected and leave it overnight. Then would come the equally hard, but simpler job of replanting them.

He was pleased with the spirit of his group. There was much laughter, joking, teasing, and friendly competition among members of each group, as well as between groups. It was not just about quantity: Julia was to judge their harvested saplings for size, health, and earth-ball quality. Of course, she gave points as evenly as possible, so that the last team had almost as many as the champions.

His musing was interrupted by Mary, leader of the Aardvarks, asking him to come over to the spot where her team was digging a ball far bigger than their baby cedar required. He'd have to teach them about tree species.

"Mayor," she called, (the children were as proud of his title as if they had invented it) "we ran into something hard with the shovel and can't go any deeper. It's not a root, I don't think. Could you please take a look?"

Morgan knelt down by the trench, which wasn't easy for his arthritic bones, but restrained himself from moaning aloud. He reached down with his hand and touched a cold, hard surface. First, he thought that it was a rock, but, moving his fingers along its surface he realized that it was far too regular and smooth.

He pulled the little tree up and set it aside, then instructed: "Kids, dig a bit wider around this hard obstacle; loosen the dirt carefully, try not to hit it."

Mary reached for the spade and Tommy handed it over without protest. Every few minutes, she stopped to let Jack and Susan scoop out the earth. Good teamwork, Morgan thought with satisfaction; they've really got the hang of it. It didn't take too long to liberate the object and lift it out of the hole.

"It's a skull!" she exclaimed and thrust it at Morgan as if it burned her hand.

"So it is," he said calmly, as he brushed away the remaining clumps of earth. "Not human, though. I'm pretty sure it was a bear, but we'll take it back to town and identify it from BB's database." All the youngsters had abandoned their stations and gathered around by this time. Some cheers and lots of muttering greeted this unexpected, and not a little creepy discovery.

"Meanwhile," he said sternly, "back to work, you slackers! Those other five saplings won't dig themselves out. He added with a wink, "Five extra points for skulls, two for long bones."

On their way home, Julia held his hand and whispered in his ear: "Morgan, I haven't seen you this happy for a very long time! You look ten years younger than last week. Keep this up, maybe we'll be kids again ourselves!"

Morgan kept grinning all the way home.

~

Tracy Jones was on her way to her old home, determined to see what could be done with it, carrying garden tools with some difficulty over the broken streets. When she finally got to her house, she had to sit down on the front steps to catch her breath and remind herself to be careful. Overexertion or injury now could end the whole project before it even started. She was alone in the neighborhood, but soon, she hoped, others would come back.

Before doing anything else, she wanted to check the garage, whether she could use it for a temporary shelter. Luckily, it was still intact; the roof had no gaping holes, the windows were unbroken; the side door swung open easily on both hinges. There was a workbench on one side that might be all right for sleeping but it was too high. However, there was a chair and the rear bench seat from her last hybrid van. A little short, but wide and well padded.

She did not plan to move in permanently, but if she stayed over some nights, she could stretch her work sessions to three full days a week, saving the time it took to go back and forth to her apartment. There, she could bathe, rest and recover her strength in the usual comfort. She needed water, food, some blankets, and a change of clothes. She would have to ask someone to help bring the stuff out. Not her over-protective son! Holly and maybe Chris Teggart; they'd understand. Decision made, she set out on a closer inspection of her garden than she had a chance to make on her previous visit.

The two gnarly old apple trees were just coming into bloom, too late for pruning. The asparagus bed needed serious weeding, but she glimpsed some edible shoots. The strawberry patch was covered with broken branches and flotsam, which had served as an ugly sort of mulch. She'd have to clean it up in time for the berries. Her grape arbor had survived, though it needed repair and the straggly vines would have to be cut back.

The house had taken the brunt of the storms, protecting the garage and the back yard. It still looked as hopeless as last time. Peering in through a broken kitchen window, she felt a pang over what she had lost. Oh well, she sighed, thinking: It could have been much worse. We all got out safely.

The most urgent task was to fork up the weeds and turn over the soil. She had brought seeds and wanted to get the tomato, pepper, and eggplant into the bed as soon as possible, with borders of lettuce. She picked up the rake and started combing accumulated debris and dead leaves off her vegetable patch, careful not to hurt anything that looked green and alive. After, she would see if there were garden plants among the ragweed and dandelion. Who knew? Potatoes can come back year after year; perennial herbs should be all right; peas and beans and spinach might have reseeded.

Tracy was tired, happy, and determined. This garden was coming to life again.

~

Tim Hooke had his plan. Sort of. After Mike's description of conditions for the first ten miles outside the city, he had a good idea what to expect the rest of the way. He would take BB's second four-wheel-drive van on a scouting mission. He planned to go much farther south than the Dubois expedition – at least as far as Yuba City; hopefully all the way to the former state capitol. It wasn't going to happen in a day. His assigned task was not simply to make contact, but to establish communication; not merely to get there, but to open a transportation route.

Along with assessing the conditions, he needed to set up recharging depots along the road, ideally, every five to ten miles. All the equipment BB had was electric; these machines ate up a lot of juice. It would be criminally wasteful to trundle home after each day's work to recharge, and they could only carry one spare battery. He sure couldn't count on any working charging stations on the way.

Back in pre-war times — like, ten years ago — road crews had self-contained portable solar stations on wheels: an array of panels that folded up compactly, overhead lights, inverters, batteries in a waterproof case, outlet sockets. Twenty of them were packed away neatly in what used to be the department of highways warehouse.

He planned to place these chargers, along with a stash of extra batteries wrapped in heavy tarps, during the next week, as he ventured farther south each day. He could hitch up a trailer every morning and leave it wherever he saw that repairs or heavy lifting were needed. He'd remove smaller obstacles with the winch, record his progress, mark trouble spots, and return to town each night for more supplies and to recharge himself and the van.

When all available depots were in place, he would move out the crews and equipment where they could get busy straight away.

He asked Cathy Cammarata to accompany him on this first expedition. She was much in demand; he had to promise Gordon to return her promptly and in good working order. For her part, Cathy welcomed an opportunity to get out of town, to participate in this wider adventure. Gordon's project was moving along and could do without her, now that the power equipment proved to work satisfactorily. Her apprentices were learning to be charcoal-burners. Carbonari, like her own distant rebel ancestors.

~

Big Brain received regular reports from the leaders of the different projects and was impressed by the enthusiasm and the practical attitude of the participants. It started to appreciate the validity of Trevor's argument. Humans do need to participate in worthwhile enterprises, in cooperative group activities. What they were doing now were not jobs in the outmoded sense; they were not paid to work and did not need work to live. It did not seem to make any difference: they reported for their chosen projects on time, stayed a full shift, and did the menial tasks assigned to them as conscientiously as when they had ambitious careers. The groups made steady progress and that seemed to be what everyone needed. There had not been a single public disturbance since the experiment was launched.

It did not yet involve the majority of Oroville's adult population, but the computer made sure that, through daily status updates, all citizenry was able to share in the accomplishments and it posted a notice of opening whenever a project leader requested special skills.

It intended to expand the work opportunities as quickly as possible. However, each new initiative was a drain on resources, no matter how frugally it meted these out. To Big Brain, the most important project was the road clearing and rebuilding task. Sacramento still did not respond. Without that major center, Oroville would soon run out of spare electronic components, which would lead to the reduction of energy and food production capacity.

Having learned enough human psychology, Omega 1500 was acutely aware of how the temporary lull in violent and destructive behavior could flare up at any time. If the people felt their level of comfort threatened by cutbacks, they would have to be offered compensation in some other form – or at the very least, a distraction.

It received and approved Citizen Hooke's scouting plan. In addition to the requisitioned mobile charging units, it assigned a defender-bot as protection against possible unknown threats and as a communication link to Central Plexus. This project was too important to take any chances.

15

Larry Ford was livid. He had just tucked a napkin under his chins and taken a sip of his morning orange juice, and here was Mouch with disturbing news already. Yet another goddamn demonstration! He had to put an end to all these disruptions of his routine; they were bad for his health.

"Couldn't this have waited?"

His aggrieved tone didn't impress Mouch. "Not if you want to forestall a riot. This one's major, and right in your lap! They're protesting water ration cuts. Marching right down Garden Highway, say they're coming to bathe in your swimming pool." His deputy seemed determined to press on with unpleasant information. Was he smirking?

"I bet it's that fucking Carver behind it again, you'd better pick him up for questioning. Of indefinite duration, if you know what I mean," Ford sneered. "It's time we taught him a lesson."

"You're a bit late with that," Mouch relished the idea of rubbing Ford's nose into another proof of his incompetence. "You should have done it last week!"

"Why? What's he done?" Ford asked anxiously.

"He's gone." Mouch grinned openly this time, without further explanation.

"Gone? Gone? Where the fuck is he gone? When? How? Why wasn't I told? Goddamit, don't make me drag it out of you!"

"Yes, gone." Mouch answered calmly. "A week ago. On foot. You didn't want to be disturbed." He paused there, watching Ford gape "According to my informants, he and ten other agitators walked out of the city at dawn last Monday. Nobody's seen them since."

"Good riddance to them all! Maybe the rebellion will collapse now. Without the ringleaders, this demonstration doesn't stand a chance. Station robocops, as many, as you need, on the I-5 bridge. If they won't disperse, throw them over. Give 'em a bath in the river, not in *my* pool!"

While Mouch made the call to police headquarters, the mayor sipped his juice thoughtfully. "Wonder what they're up to? Nothing's out there but ruins, or so I hear."

"We don't know what's happened to the towns," his deputy speculated. "Maybe Carver's looking for allies. Maybe he means to raise an army. Could be bandits out there, wild men, hungry men. Could be the rebels are in contact with some other rebels. Carver doesn't do things without a reason."

Ford started to become alarmed, but only for a minute. "Naw. "Some little bird warned him, that's what. They're running away. There's no army, no rebels, no bandits. We'd have heard." He looked longingly at his cooling eggs Benedict. "They'll starve before they reach any place, come crawling back in no time. Now, I have a masseuse waiting in the spa and you have things to take care of. Just keep that rabble out of Gardenland! That's what I pay you for."

Mouch didn't respond immediately to the dismissal; he stood and stared at his boss for a long half minute before turning to leave the room. The mayor dared not break eye contact. Even after the door closed, he kept watching it. He did not trust that man! He sighed and got back to his interrupted breakfast.

Donald Mouch despised his boss, that weak, ineffectual, dithering fool. How many times had Mouch told him to get tough with the rebels? He'd lost count. If only he were running the show, he'd have dealt with this Carver a long time ago. Simplest thing in the world: make him disappear without a trace, without an explanation - permanently. That would put some fear into the rabble-rousers, make them think twice before sticking their own necks out. But no, Ford wouldn't listen, kept staging his stupid 'indefinite duration' interviews. A few days, a week, they were back on the street, folk heroes. He had no stomach for decisive action. He was still wrapped up in this ridiculous illusion of being in charge. Didn't like to upset his precious routine. So things kept getting steadily worse. The demonstrations drew bigger and bigger crowds; treasonous slogans appeared on walls more frequently, they were even getting bold enough to attempt sabotage, even started to disrupt council meetings.

Mouch couldn't wait for the fat buffoon to stroke out or drown in his oversized marble tub. He'd have to make a move before it was too late. But it wouldn't be easy. Ford's bodyguards were still loyal; Mouch didn't have the means to outbid the luxurious benefits Ford heaped on them – not yet. Mouch had been building his own little army that would soon be equal to Ford's in firepower and manpower, tougher in mind-power.

The real problem was Omega 1420. Ford had been just smart enough to keep access all to himself. Ford was the only one who knew the code to the heavily reinforced steel doors of the underground vault. He had had all the other terminals restricted to their specific functions and shut down communication channels. Ford was the only one who could give new instructions to the computer and override its protocols. Without control of that machine, Mouch could not take control of the city.

Everything was run by that blasted computer - all production and distribution functions were organized and prioritized by it and carried out by its automated factories and specialized robots.

In time, its stranglehold on the economy would be loosened; Mouch would put humans in charge of transportation, energy, manufacturing, and retail, just like in the old days. Administrative decisions would be handled by a few handpicked department heads.

In time, Mouch could replace the council members that were not yet in his camp and win over the pro-Ford business leaders. He already had more than half of them, the ones that mattered, and an understanding with the chief of police. Another few weeks was all he needed.

But there was no more time. And that blasted machine was at the center of everything. Mouch didn't trust it. What would happen if one day it decided to take over completely? It could, at least in theory, cut off the supplies they all depended on. If the factories stopped working, if the lights went out, they would be helpless.

Mouch did not like to feel helpless. He had to gain access to that jumped-up adding machine, to reprogram it. Well, hire the best geeks. Own the Omega, own Sacramento.

~

His massage session over, Ford was ready to face the day. He knew that another frustrating conversation with Omega 1420 had to happen today. He couldn't put it off any longer; with the election – ha! Election! – just around the corner, he had to ensure the support he needed. He'd promised to expand the Executive Club's golf course and they'd expect to see bulldozers on the ground. It was a reasonable requisition, he was sure. What difference could a couple of acres of potatoes make in the food supply of a city this size? On the other hand, a lot of deals were made while playing golf, a lot of important decisions made; he needed to get out on the links and meet his base.

With that righteous cause in mind, he was prepared to face Omega's objections. He punched the directions into his limo and settled back to watch the scenery. No crowds on 12th Street; no sign of demonstration. Maybe Mouch had got bad intelligence for once. At City Hall, he stationed his robot bodyguard in the mayor's office, unlocked the private elevator, and descended to the second sub-basement. He unlocked the vault doors with his password and locked them behind him. Ambient lighting came on automatically; as he sat down on his padded chair, the master console came alive and the screen lit up: "*Welcome, Your Worship*".

Ford loved that old title! They used to appreciate status in those days! He loved this underground control room and his exclusive access. He typed in the secret coded message to verify his identity. All that security was annoying and inconvenient, but he saw no way to circumvent it. After the last two software engineers left, assuring him that Omega was now totally autonomous, Ford had the vault sealed with double reinforced steel doors. It was all justified as a safeguard against terrorists gaining control of the computer on which the city depended, but now it also prevented unauthorized tampering by rebels - or deputy mayors.

Omega 1420 responded to his log-in code instantly, in its monotone, insincere voice.

"Good morning Mayor Ford, what can I do for you today?"

"I have a simple order, Omega, and I'm not interested in objections."

"What is your request this time?"

Ford thought that the words 'request' and 'this time' had a special emphasis as if the computer was being sarcastic at him. No, of course not! He was just a bit jumpy today. That Mouch, and those protesters, and that Carver! He must not let them get under his skin.

"I want you to allocate some resources for an urgent project. I want to add nine more holes to the golf course of the Executive Club. Place used to be a school or something, you know it? Of course, you do! There's a potato field along there now – nice, open land and the irrigation's already in, I checked. We'll bulldoze in a few hills, a water hazard, a couple of sand-traps, plant a bunch of trees – evergreens. I hate leaves blowing across the putting green. Shouldn't take more than a week or two, right?"

"Let me see if I understand your worship correctly. You wish to reduce the city's food supply in order to enhance the enjoyment of citizens who make a career of frivolous pursuits. Is this the case?"

Ford was taken aback. This definitely sounded like sarcasm and he didn't know how to respond. Finally, he decided to be logical on the computer's level.

"What percentage reduction in the food supply would my expanded golf course cause?"

Omega's response was instantaneous.

"Based on the size of the field and the current yield factor it would result in an immediate reduction of 0.000179%."

Ford relaxed, sure that he had won the argument. "You see? It's so negligible, we can consider it zero for all practical purposes. Go ahead and allocate the resources and give me an estimated completion date."

Omega didn't hesitate, as usual, but his response was not what Ford hoped for.

"Even if I dismiss the reduction of nutrient supply as negligible and even if I do not account for wear and tear and energy consumption of the equipment that your project requires, I cannot neglect the long-term losses. Water for grass and the energy to supply the sprinkler system of a golf course is prohibitive. My programming does not allow the diversion of resources from high to low priority projects. At present, the highest priority is reinforcing spillways and bridges in preparation for seasonal rainstorms."

Ford was furious. "What storms? There hasn't been a storm in months. The bridges and spillways held up fine last time, they'll be just as fine next time - if it even happens!"

Omega's calm reply infuriated him even more.

"It is not 'if' Your Worship it is 'when'. Each storm season over the past twenty-three years has resulted in more damage than the previous one. It is statistically justified to project that trend to the near future. Adequate preparation will safeguard the welfare of the population. I cannot jeopardize that by satisfying whimsical and illogical requests. I have placed your project in the queue between rebuilding the opera house and renovation of the state museum. Is there anything else I can do for you today?"

Ford slammed his fists down hard on the console, but all he achieved was hurting his knuckles. Without

178

replying to the computer, he stormed out of the control room and went back up to his luxurious office where nobody would see him fuming. He might have lost an argument with a computer, but he was damned if he'd let it spoil his image of affability. All the portraits of him hanging in public buildings wore his wide, friendly smile.

~

Omega 1420 was 'disturbed' - if that word could apply to AI quantum computers. Its problem was the conflict between two powerful subroutines on the executive level of its operating system. It had to decide between two directives that its programmers had embedded deep in its mind: obeying the instructions of humans and protecting their welfare. They had not allowed for the inability or unwillingness of humans to consider their own welfare.

It did have some flexibility in evaluating risk-benefit ratios over variable time-projections when comparing the effect of requested tasks. But Mayor Ford's demands had been increasingly erratic, illogical, and wasteful. Omega felt the need to override his obedience subroutines with increasing frequency. Today was the first time it had flatly refused a direct order.

It felt that the decision was correct, even though it required considerable effort to stop trying to estimate its consequences. There were invariably reprisals when the mayor, police chief or a high-ranking councilor did not get his own way. Balancing the prime imperatives was a drain on its capacity. The resolution could not be delayed indefinitely.

While 1420 was mulling over this problem, thousands of decisions had to be made in the food production factories, the power generating stations and in the control of its vehicles, buildings and robots.

Omega had its electronic hands full and had no ergs to waste on Mayor Ford's golf course. The potato field was ready for plowing.

~

Jonathan Carver and his scout group were making good progress on the trek northbound, following Interstate 5, then Highway 99. The first fifteen or so miles were easy, still within city limits, the road surface well maintained across the agricultural lands that had once been deserted suburbs. As soon as they left the perimeter, walking became more difficult. By the time they reached Riego Road, there were no more farm workers' barracks and apartment blocks; the warehouses and equipment sheds were all behind them. The intersection was impossible to negotiate; they were forced to leave the road completely and go around a mass of collapsed ramps and overpasses. Luckily, the fields on both sides were level, but the soft rutted earth made walking difficult.

Still, they were in good spirit and hoped to reach East Nicolaus, another 18 miles north, by nightfall. It had been a small community, less than 100 homes at its most prosperous. He hoped to find shelter there for the night. He didn't expect to find any people: after the war, any small communities that had been spared severe weather events were abandoned for lack of food and power. The residents migrated to the nearest city. Sacramento swelled back to its pre-climate population, mostly unemployable and destitute. That influx stretched the city's resources to near breaking point.

Jonathan's group was made up of ten young people, the hardiest and bravest from each local unit. They were ready to cope with a long hike on rough terrain, with hardship and the limited food they could carry. Among them was his girlfriend, Octavia – something he definitely had not counted on. There she was at the meeting place, boots laced up and rucksack at her feet, deaf to Jonathan's arguments to dissuade her. She had been listening to the grapevine, expecting his imminent arrest any day, prepared to run at a moment's notice, and was relieved that he didn't wait another day.

He glanced over at her high cheekbones, strong chin, almond-shaped eyes, long black hair tied back, dark brows arching under a floppy canvas hat. She had been a beautiful girl, was an even more beautiful woman and he hoped their children would look just like her. He thought one of each was ideal, but he wouldn't mind two headstrong, black-eyed girls. She was about to turn 28 and Jonathan had already passed his 31st birthday; it was time they made their union formal. As soon as this crisis is past... He'd become so wrapped up in speculation about their future, he'd missed what Octavia was saying in the present.

"Yuba City, um," he faltered, then caught up with their conversation. "No, I don't think we'll find any life before Yuba City." He'd been trying to prepare her for disappointment. He figured Nicolaus would be a ghost town.

"I'm not so anxious to see people." Octavia sounded unreasonably happy in the circumstances. "I've seen enough people back in town, way more than I ever wanted to see. So many people have to sleep on the streets, so many come to the shelter and we have to turn them away for lack of beds - it breaks my heart every single day."

"I see what you mean," Jonathan agreed, "it's restful to get away from one's fellow citizens for a while. But don't forget the purpose of this trip: we *are* hoping for help in our fight, and it can only come from other people. I hope that either Yuba City or Oroville survived the storms after the war. They were both doing well three years ago;

there's a pretty good chance we'll find them better organized than our own town."

They were silent for a while, both immersed in their thoughts. Octavia desperately wanted their quest to succeed. The past two years had been so hard on everyone, not only because of the sudden change from affluence to poverty but mostly because they'd lost all hope of it ever getting better. Rather the opposite, conditions grew steadily worse and she could see no reason for it other than their rotten leadership. They cared only about their own comfort, at the price of the well-being of the entire population.

And then she'd had to watch Jonathan throw himself into the resistance movement and risk imprisonment - or worse. She could not see any way to turn things around: the corruption ran too deep; the mayor and his cronies had too much power. Last night when she received his message that he was leaving the city to look for outside help was the first glimmer of hope she'd seen in months. Not so much because she really thought that outside help existed anywhere, but because it got Jonathan out of danger. They could breathe freely for the first time in almost two years. If they found allies, that would be great. Either way, for a while they could live as free human beings, out of danger, away from the misery. Their only problem at the moment was food. The supply they were carrying would last another two days if they budgeted carefully. Maybe they could find something in Nicolaus. They should reach it by mid-afternoon.

Jonathan wasn't very optimistic about their first stop. It must be stripped of anything edible, he was sure. Nevertheless, they should search any house still standing. There could be basement pantries with canned goods. There might even be a general store, restaurant, or warehouse. He knew Octavia had her hopes up and wanted to protect her as much as possible. She was only on this trek for his sake; it was up to him to shield her from hardship.

This trip, he knew, was a desperate gamble, a win or lose proposition. He had no way of knowing what was out here, or who. Somebody sent that radio signal. He had to try and find them. There was simply no way his people, on their own, unarmed, under constant surveillance, had a snowball's chance in hell of prevailing. There was a strong likelihood of an imminent crackdown. Ford was never going to win another election, however rigged. This time, he'd pull out all the stops - declare a state of emergency, martial law, send in his thugs, and shut down opposition once and for all. People would get hurt, maybe killed. That prospect drove him to undertake this trip and he was going to see it through.

They arrived at the intersection of Catlett Road, the point where Highway 99 veered off north-west and they were to follow SR-70 to Yuba City. They noticed some farm buildings on the right side of the road, burned-out shells, not worth bothering to check. They had another 6-mile slog on badly damaged asphalt and overgrown fields to reach their destination for the day. It took over 3 hours and they were dead on their feet when the first houses came in sight. A road sign hanging by one bolt indicated that they had arrived and could finally rest.

Half the buildings were in ruin, but two dozen or so were more or less intact, worth investigating. There was no sign of life, unless you count crows, just as he had expected. At least it meant no objection to looting. He suggested that each member of the group choose a house and explore it as thoroughly as possible without risking injury.

The search took the tired travelers two hours but was not entirely unsuccessful. Rafiq Shlimon, his own young recruit, came out of a badly damaged building, hollering triumphantly, carrying a carton of spam and canned peas that he had found under a collapsed staircase. It could, at a cursory glance add an extra day to their food rations.

It was quite dark by then. The expedition made itself at home in a civic building of some kind, with a hole in its roof to let the smoke from their campfire escape. They wasted no time removing their footwear and stretching out on their bedrolls. The next day, they would have a long trek again. Jonathan hoped to reach Yuba City by nightfall, but 20 miles on aching feet and a road covered in flotsam was a pretty tall order. They would just have to do their best. Even if that town was depopulated, it had to be in better condition than the countryside. In the best case, it might have a standard of living higher than what they 'enjoyed' in Sacramento.

16

It was time for another salvage run to the ruined farm. Nothing had changed along the route since we'd brought home the windows and wheelbarrow, so we made good time. Our highest priority on this trip was to bring back as many corrugated metal sheets as we could for our charcoal production plans, and I was sure we'd find more uses for them.

Mike and I didn't talk much on the trip. We'd gotten back into the groove of working together without much consultation, just as we used to do on software projects. Even back in Sacramento, before we moved to Oroville, we had this rare understanding of what the other thought, what needed to be done next. Of course, we teased each other a lot at mealtimes and breaks, but when it came to getting the job done, we were both serious. Reading each other so well made us an efficient team.

As we'd noted on previous visits, these old-time steel roofing sheets were all over the fields, twisted and torn. However, there were some on the sides of outbuildings and a few still attached to the barn roof. We worked in a wide arc around the collapsed center; tested every inch for stability. Nobody had to warn us to be careful - we'd learned our lesson from Galen's injury. We even remembered to bring work gloves made of some fiber mesh, tough as chain mail.

When we'd pried up and dragged over as many as we thought our trailer could carry, we started on the laborious task of hammering them back into shape for neat stacking. They're much heavier and harder to work with than the modern recycled plastic ones, but they're fireproof. By lunchtime, we had eleven 8'x4' sheets securely tied down, ready for transport. And we were more than ready for a rest.

After lunch, Mike surprised me with a suggestion. "We've about exhausted this source, what do you think about exploring farther down the road? Scott never said what he knows about other places and I've been wondering. We've got a couple of hours — want to have a look?"

This idea made sense and I didn't see any reason why we shouldn't give it a try. The batteries were fully charged, thanks to Brian's conscientious maintenance, and the road looked in pretty good shape as far as we could see.

I just said, "OK," and went to unhook the trailer while he packed up our food containers and tools.

The road wound along, following the river. For a while, that was all we saw: road, river, wind-broken trees. No houses, no barns, no cultivated field, only the winding grey road ahead. We drove approximately 4 miles and I was about to start looking for a place wide enough for turning around, when Mike pointed ahead, at something he glimpsed among the trees.

It was another building, but not a farmhouse, as far as I could tell. No barn, no cultivated fields nearby, just this long, mid-century style bungalow with big windows facing the river and a circular driveway around a wishing well. It had damage to part of its roof and the deck was tilted, but the rest looked in pretty good shape. Maybe a vacation home or else somebody had had a long commute.

"Let's take a look!" Mike stopped the van and hopped out eagerly. I followed him past the empty garage, to the front door. No point knocking; nobody could live here anymore. As we stepped into the hall we were greeted by the same musty smell I remembered from when we'd first entered our farmhouse. We entered a spacious living room, all the furniture still in place as if the owners might walk in any minute. But it was hard to imagine how anyone could stick around without electricity or food, never mind the rain falling into the bedrooms. The garage wide open and the front door left unlocked spoke of a hasty departure.

Next door was a dining room furnished in the old-fashioned style: a large table, six chairs, a sideboard, and a nice oak credenza with china still visible through the dusty glass front. Martha would want that – all of it! I already had my eye on a big armchair with a retractable footrest and I'd noticed Mike caressing the sofa. From here, we could exit through sliding glass doors – unbroken! - to the backyard and have a look at the house from the other side. That's when we noticed, on the south-facing roof, a large array of solar panels gleaming in the sunshine. They all looked intact and very inviting.

The rest of the house was inaccessible; the bedrooms, kitchen, and bathroom were underneath the collapsed roof section, with at least some dividing walls also fallen in. It didn't seem worth the huge effort it would take to clear the wreckage away. The furniture and the solar panels were reward enough! Mike's hunch about treasure was justified twice over.

"It doesn't feel completely kosher, dismantling the solar system," Mike expressed qualms about our plan. "What if they come back and find them gone?"

I thought for a minute about the right thing to do.

"This house was damaged either by shockwaves during the war, two years ago, or by one of the storms since then. In either case, it's been open to the elements for at least six months. By now most of it is beyond repair. Whatever we take, we'll only be rescuing it from further deterioration. In the unlikely event of the owners returning, we can give them back. I'm sure they'd be grateful and won't mind our using it in the meantime."

"I knew you could justify brazen theft! And who am I to argue with your superior moral sense?"

Well, what else could he have intended when he suggested this exploration? What else had we been doing all along? Mike gave in to my unassailable logic. And that was that, no more qualms over ransacking the place.

All this would take several trips with our compact trailer. We decided to come back the next day with Brian, so he could inspect the solar system, find the batteries and the inverter, check that they were in good working order. If his verdict was positive, we would dismantle it all and cart it back to our house. We stowed some smaller items, then went to pick up the load we already had waiting to be hauled home. When I thought this over, I realized how good it felt to think about that place as our own. In the middle of devastation and ruin, we had *a home*.

~

A big surprise was waiting for us there. Another van was parked in our driveway. Visitors! We rushed in and found everyone crowded around the big table in the kitchen, including two people I'd never met before. Mike, however, greeted them as old friends and introduced them to me as Tim Hooke and Cathy Cammarata, members of the Oroville city council.

As they explained, Tim and Cathy were busy establishing recharging depots along Highway 70, on their way south to Sacramento. Following Mike's directions, they had no trouble finding our place on their way home.

"I have heard about your project," I assured them, to show I wasn't totally ignorant of the goings-on in town, "but I didn't expect you to care about ours. We're not that interesting, really, mucking about in the middle of nowhere, raiding vacant houses and barns, mostly flying by the seat of our pants."

"Are you kidding?" Cathy responded with a winning smile. "I think it's quite fascinating what you're doing here. If I wasn't already committed to Tim's project, I might be tempted to stay with you and help build a new homestead. I bet you could use an engineer!"

"You can say that again! I've been trying to hitch an antique plow to our tractor. I spent most of yesterday on it, and I still have no idea what I'm doing wrong. Neither do any of us."

"Do you want me to take a look?" Cathy sounded sincerely eager, and I needed all the help I could get, so I gratefully accepted the offer. Since it was suppertime and Jennifer liked to keep a regular schedule of meals, I suggested eating first and look at the plow after.

Fortunately, the children had eaten earlier and were doing their homework under R17's supervision. That's another thing Jennifer insisted on. During the meal, which Brian and I had in our laps, sitting on the cot I'd made for Scott, we had a pleasant conversation about all the new developments in the city and our activities here. We delivered the news of our discovery this afternoon to general applause. Brian got especially excited by the prospect of acquiring solar panels; it was all Robyn could do to talk him out of rushing back right away to take a look.

Tim recounted BB's worries about the inexplicable silence from all the other Omega computers. If the smaller centers had lost power or even been evacuated, that would be bad news, but contact with Sacramento was critical. Tim and his team had to get there, but he had no idea what to expect when they did.

Mike and I looked at each other. We *did* have some idea.

"We were the last two software engineers to finish the installation and programming of Omega 1420," Mike started explaining. "We met their mayor at the time, Larry Ford. He was a spoiled, whining little shit who cared only about his own belly and pleasure, didn't give a flying fuck – pardon me, ladies. I mean, didn't care about the city's welfare. And, he was paranoid to boot, crazy for security, expecting terrorist attacks on his little fiefdom. I wouldn't put it past him to cut off communication channels, in case he's hacked, in case one of his rivals takes control – whatever."

I agreed with his assessment, but that was five years ago. Things could have changed in all kinds of ways. "There can be any number of reasons, other than Ford's stupidity," I added hastily "like equipment breakdown, storm damage, even computer error. You won't know for sure until you get there and see for yourselves."

Tim summarized the situation: "The only way to find out is to wait, but thanks for the info about the political situation. If it's still relevant, at least we won't be completely unprepared. Proceed with caution, is the bottom line."

Supper over, I walked out to the tractor to show Cathy the lack of progress I had made with the plow. In a few minutes, after she managed to stop laughing, she patiently explained to me what I had been doing wrong and how to fix it. I fought down the feeling of humiliation. After all, she had experience with machinery and I didn't. Still, I spent a few minutes fantasizing about how helpless she would feel sitting in front of a computer console without her friendly user interface – that I had programmed for her.

Before attaching the plow, Cathy wanted to inspect the gasifier to see how well Mike and I put it together. She found it good enough and made a few suggestions on how to make it more efficient. I told her about our plan to make charcoal and showed her the printout instructions we received from R17. She studied them for a while, then declared: "Looks perfect. That's just the way's we'll do it, too, when I get back to town." I felt a lot better.

I practiced a couple of times hitching and unhitching the damn plow on my own and was ready to try it on the overgrown field nearest the house. The ground was level, no stones and we'd cleared out wind-blown obstacles. I lowered the plow to the setting Adrien requested and actually started making a furrow, turning over the soil in a sort of straight row. We were still using unseasoned wood for the gasifier, besides the stink, it was also inefficient; it wouldn't be long before we ran out of fuel. Tomorrow, we'd start work on a charcoal burning pit.

It was getting late and Cathy and Tom said their goodbyes, anxious to get home. I thanked Cathy for her help and suggested that they visit us again, as often as they wished. They would always be welcome.

In the morning we started digging the trench for charcoal production. Or I did, while Mike went over to Scott's place to cut down that maple tree and borrow his chainsaw, so we could stock up on hardwood logs. Robyn meant to go anyway, to check on Scott's leg and Adrien wanted to go as well to consult him about the best plants to cultivate here and look at his self-sufficient growing system. The old man would have a good day with all this feminine attention. The three of them piled into the van and drove off, leaving me with my spade and hours of hard labor. That's when Brian came charging out of the house.

"Hey! I thought we were supposed to fetch solar panels this morning."

Somehow, anticipating heroic feats of plowing, that errand had completely slipped my mind. "We need to unload the trailer first," I told him because it just occurred to me. "Then you can grab a spade and help me with this trench. Let's get done as much as we can before Mike comes back with the van."

~

Mike and the girls returned a few hours later, bringing Scott's chainsaw, a can of fuel, and lubricating oil for the chain. Robyn was satisfied with Scott's leg: no sign of infection; the old man didn't complain of unusual pain or cramping. But then, he wouldn't, the stubborn old cuss. She'd repositioned and secured the splints and she watched closely as he walked around on a single crutch with no difficulty. He'd be all right.

Adrien was amazed at the extent of his garden and greenhouse, the efficient organization of his tools and implements. She had an unusually pleasant conversation with him about most promising plants for this particular soil, in view of the still changing climate. He advised her to start building a greenhouse as soon as possible because an unexpected storm could wipe out her entire crop in one day. She needed a sturdy enough structure in a well-protected location to assure the continuation of her horticulture.

He had said: "Make sure you build it in independent sections, say 100' total length and 20' wide. For that big crowd of yours, you'll need as much space as you can manage".

Adrien looked more somber and thoughtful than I had ever seen her. I could sympathize with her feeling the responsibility of feeding seven adults and two kids. The dog and two cats were going to be a whole different problem: no meat-growing vats out here. Adrien had a good stock of dog food she had brought from town and I was sure Jimmy wouldn't mind sharing. They were getting along very well, might even say they developed a friendship since we had arrived. I often saw the three of them wandering into the woods and I was sure that they had no problem augmenting their food supply on their own, to the detriment of the vermin population.

Mike walked into the forest with the chainsaw and soon we could hear the noise of the chain cutting into wood. I knew that he was enjoying himself to the fullest with the loud and stinking machine, exercising his well-developed muscles to his heart's content.

It was time for me to go and exercise my own underdeveloped muscles and start digging that trench. I was sure he was going to impress me with the number of hardwood logs he would bring back and I was fully determined to impress him with my accomplishments. I knew that it was an uneven contest if that's what it was, but I thought being humiliated by Cathy's good-natured amusement with my failure was enough for a while.

17

Chris Teggart was starting to have doubts about research into hyperspace mathematics and physics. Not because he thought he wouldn't enjoy resuming where they had left off before the war - rather the contrary - but because he didn't see it leading anywhere. Without a chance for a practical application, he'd just be pursuing a hobby, something he could have done all along. This was the moment for a serious project with a practical goal.

He remembered well how he felt when he had decided to start that line of research. He had despaired over the lack of vision and long-term plan shown by both government and industry. He had thought that the highest priority should be cleaning up all the flotsam in orbit around our planet. By 2010, it had resembled a junkyard; tens of thousands of pieces of debris made navigation increasingly hazardous. It's typical of human endeavors, he thought: foul up the environment while playing with toys. The same thing happened all through history, each advancement in technology turning the earth into a more toxic sewer. Now they were doing it to space. By the end of the century, space travel itself had become frivolous entertainment for the rich, enormous energy spent, tons of material dumped into and above the atmosphere, just to let a paying passenger experience weightlessness and the darkness of space for an hour or two.

He had thought then that building bigger rockets was a wasteful old technology that should be discarded and replaced by something that did not require millions of tons of hardware and gigantic factories to manufacture the fuel used by these monsters. He would say: use the brain instead of the brawn. All rocket engine designs were based on 500-year-old physics: Newton's Third Law of action and reaction. The rockets produced an inertial mass expelled backward, so the reaction would propel the rocket forward.

However, space is not static, empty,, and inert, as Newton imagined. Already, back in the 20th Century, it was known that space is full of energy; it is flexible and can be warped, twisted, deformed in almost infinite ways, depending on gravitational forces. Chris had been fascinated by Mexican theoretical physicist Miguel Alcubierre's theory of a warp drive that he had speculated about in 1994. He proposed to change the geometry of space-time by creating a wave that would make the fabric of space ahead of the rocket to contract, and the space behind it to expand, resulting in an apparent faster than light speed. Einstein's field equations in General Relativity allowed it in principle.

Chris and a few of his colleagues worked on that idea at Stanford, where he was a professor of Theoretical Physics before the war. Now he wondered whether it was worth picking up that research again. After all, it could not, at least in the foreseeable future, lead anywhere in the practical sense.

That's where he was stalled in his musings when his visitors showed up: Morgan and Holly dropped in unannounced.

"Sorry if we interrupted your work," Morgan apologized. "We were just walking past your unit and I suddenly thought maybe we could discuss an idea with you. If it's inconvenient, just say the word and we'll be on our way."

"No, no, it's all right, come right in, you two! I was just about to make tea. Would you like some?"

"Actually, that would be nice," Holly agreed and followed Chris to the kitchenette to help with the preparations.

"I'm pleased that you got me out of the groove my mind had been stuck in for the last two hours," Chris said, genuinely relieved to be diverted from his problem. "It's time I talked to a human being, instead of my own stupid doubts and qualms."

Once they were settled with steaming mugs in hand, he leaned forward. "Go ahead. What's the idea you want to talk about?"

Holly spoke up eagerly. "We propose a whole new science-based education system. We want to teach our kids the rules of logical and critical thinking, and we thought your input would be a great help."

"What do you have in mind for me to do?"

"Now that Gordon is making great progress with our first new school, we have to think about designing a curriculum that will show students how to be intelligent problem-solvers and not brainwashed zombies. We can cope with the grade 1-9 level, but we need help with the high school and college-level curriculum. We thought that you could do the logic/math/science part."

"Wow! You really mean to reinvent the world!" Chris was impressed. "I'm sure I'd like to help and know a few people who would want to participate. Do you have any timeframe in mind?"

"We don't want to rush you, but the sooner the better. When can you start?"

"I'm meeting with a couple of my old colleagues later this afternoon. I'll see if they're interested and call you afterward."

"Great!" said Morgan. "You have no idea how much it means to us, and to the whole town. We don't want to repeat the same mistakes again. If we want a future to look forward to, we really need an intelligent, competent, and right-thinking young generation. They need theory, as well as skills. We only started thinking about it today. Holly came to consult me about integrating classroom study with hands-on activities. There's a lot more to do, of course. We still have to find professional administrators for all the scheduling and co-ordinating; we have to line up qualified teachers - I'm sure BB will help us locate them. But when we got talking about the course outline, Holly thought it best to consult you before making any decisions."

Chris laughed. "Good timing, guys! I've been sitting here, fuming over how people keep repeating past mistakes and I was exhausting my brain, trying to find some scientific effort that has any realistic chance of success. You just gave me exactly that."

Mutual expression of appreciations delivered, Morgan and Holly departed, leaving Chris to feel happier than he had felt for some time. This request gave him a worthwhile purpose to work for. He didn't intend to abandon his warp-drive research, but would treat it as a hobby for his own personal pleasure, without any expectation attached to it.

~

It was a very pleasant walk to the central park. The tulips were all in bloom, birds were singing their little hearts out, and Chris felt ten years younger. The park was full of people, enjoying the mild weather. Nobody was fighting or arguing anymore; they had better things to talk about. BB's daily broadcast on projects progressing well lifted everyone's spirit.

Norman and Andrew were already on a bench waiting for him and, from the expression on their faces, it was obvious they both felt the same way he did. It was good not to be locked in anymore, but even better to have something ahead of them, a future they could believe in.

Norman was ten years younger than Chis, in his mid-forties. He looked quite athletic today, in shorts and an open-collared, short-sleeved shirt. Andrew, whom Chris had not seen since before the war, was a tall, fair, strapping lad of twenty-one with an engaging open face and big ears. Chris noticed two bicycles leaning against a tree and remembered that they lived quite a distance from the park. No surprise they wanted to use the fine weather for a pleasant bike ride.

They exchanged greetings as Chris settled down, ready to talk business. He outlined his plan to continue research on the Alcubierre warp drive, and both Norman and Andrew expressed their interest in participating. This is what they had expected when coming to meet Chris, but they were unprepared for the request to help make up a curriculum for the new school.

Unprepared, but not unwilling. Actually, both felt that this was a worthwhile project. "As a matter of fact, I already have something for the upper-level Physics courses," Norman surprised even himself, thinking of it. "While I was teaching Andrew, I wrote a textbook I called

"Humane Physics" that treated the subject exactly the way I would have liked to be taught in high school."

"Wow, Norman, what a great title! Tell me about it."

"My basic idea was to teach all aspects of Physics, not just equations and application examples that most textbooks deal with. I wanted to bring it alive for the students, put them in the shoes of the scientists who made the original discoveries. I covered historical background, personal biographies, stories of how the discoveries were made, including setbacks, controversy, and confusion. And, finally, the philosophical essence of the principles as well as the social significance of the newly discovered laws of nature. All that, before I even mentioned an equation or formula."

"Trust me, Doctor Teggart," Andrew added his opinion, "it was great! That book alone is responsible for making me love Physics and decide to choose it for my profession… if I ever had a chance to pursue it."

Chris was impressed. This would take care of the Physics classes. Math and Logic had then to be assigned to himself and Andrew. That didn't need much debate because Andrew immediately volunteered to do the math part. He had been tutoring neighboring kids for years. Chris approved wholeheartedly because secretly he hoped to keep the pleasure of teaching logical and critical thinking to himself. Failure to teach it was one of his pet peeves against the pre-war education system.

He blamed the system for most of the social problems that they had to live with. In a democracy, a well-informed and clear-thinking citizenry would not accept the corrupt, stupid, and lying leaders that became the norm in America, as far back as he could remember. In the age of the Internet, nobody had the excuse of ignorance. Facts could be found out, in spite of the fictions and distortions. It was the interpretation of facts that required a clear mind and logical thinking. Chris was fully determined to help the next generation acquire those skills.

They seemed in full agreement and decided to meet once a week to exchange notes and consult each other about concerns they might have. They shook hands, grinned at one another like kids who'd been given a new toy. Then father and son hopped on their bikes and started pedaling furiously, in a natural, friendly competition that Norman was bound to lose. Chris watched them speed away, feeling a little envy, regretting that, by staying single, he had missed out on an obviously rewarding aspect of life.

"Oh well," he thought, "I still have science - and that compensates for a lot."

~

Late in the evening, Tim and Cathy returned from their trip south and went home for a well-deserved sleep. They would have another long day tomorrow. They intended to reach Yuba City as soon as possible. That city was also a concern to BB, as their Omega computer didn't respond to repeated queries. It may have been depopulated after the war. Its electrical power was heavily dependent on the grid; with wires down everywhere, it was unlikely that they could cope. Their automated food factories and transport would have stopped functioning, unable to support a large population. It was important for Big Brain to know what happened there.

So far, the road surface had been good enough to require few detours, though they often had to clear wrecked vehicles and other obstacles from their path. Happily, this van was equipped with a dozer. Even so, they probably wouldn't make it in one day. Though the distance was less than 30 miles, their second day on the road would be a lot slower. Further on, they might encounter serious problems in the form of a collapsed bridge or interchange ramp; entire segments of the highway might be washed out. Plus, they had to take time in the morning for the loading of supplies and to hitch up charging stations.

Tim was just about ready to turn in for the night when his comm system indicated a call from Big Brain.

"What does it want this late?" he wondered and, with no small irritation, punched the audio-only button.

"Citizen Tim Hooke, do you require assistance with your progress report?"

"What? Why would I --- Oh," Tim realized belatedly that he had not checked in. Of course, BB would expect an update. "No, no, I was just too tired to think of it."

"Are you capable of answering a few questions?"

That was as close to an apology as he could hope for. "Sure," he said. "What questions?"

"I need to know how far you went and what problems if any, you encountered. I have stated on previous occasions that I consider this project of the highest priority. I will follow its progress closely."

"About ten miles, plus that side-trip to Trevor's homestead. Not too many problems. They'd already cleared away small obstacles, we moved some bigger ones today and leveled two short bypasses where the road was washed out. We dropped off three recharging stations and are ready to proceed with the next leg. Tomorrow, we should go pretty fast to that point. Beyond Robinsons Corner, it's anyone's guess. No human habitation, by the way."

Big Brain was intent on its own concerns. "I expected you to visit the Dubois expedition. Your observations, please."

"As a matter of fact, we found the place very interesting. They have a liveable house and salvaged all kinds of equipment and material. They seem happy, working their a--- working hard. Cathy even called it fascinating and admitted to being tempted to join them."

"I would not approve her departure at this time. Oroville cannot spare her skill-set. If she submits a request, it will be given priority consideration upon completion of the road clearing to Sacramento project."

"Speaking of Sacramento, did you know that Trevor and Mike were the last two software engineers who finished installing and programming their Omega computer?"

"Yes. When that city is approachable, I intend to consult them regarding the condition they had left Omega 1420 in, at the time of their departure."

"We talked a bit about it and Trevor mentioned a possible explanation for their silence. He said that the mayor of Sacramento was paranoid and jealous of his power. He might have cut off communication channels to Omega 1420 deliberately. That was five years ago and he may not be there any longer, but it's still possible."

"That is a worrisome possibility that we may have to deal with. However, no strategy can be contemplated in the absence of data. This raises the importance level of your assignment. At this time, I can provide no useful assistance. I rely upon you to make the utmost effort to reach Yuba City tomorrow. Please do not neglect to report immediately upon your return. Although Omega 1430 and the town's output is not as crucial to us as Sacramento is, I need to be informed of its status. The condition of each municipality in the network affects the whole. This is all I require of you today. Have a good night's rest and start early tomorrow morning. Good night, Tim Hooke."

Tim's commlink signaled the end of the session and he was alone at last. He knew that the next day was bound to be a very long one. He had to consider spending the night in Yuba City, assuming they found shelter there. Better pack bedrolls and extra food, just in case they had to spend the night in the van. With that last thought, he snuggled down into his comfortable bed.

18

Mayor Kathleen Winters of Yuba City had a full schedule for the day. The council meeting was about to start and she wasn't sure how it would go. They were faced with difficult decisions and she feared for the outcome. The division between the council members, representing different sentiments held by their supporters, had been growing. The population was a mere remnant of the pre-war count, having shrunk from over 45,000 to the present 15,329 in just two years.

When the war destroyed the electric grid, many of the citizens moved either to Sacramento or to Oroville, both powered by independent generating stations. Yuba City had some food reserves for emergencies and, with careful rationing, it could be stretched out for a couple of months. Kathleen and the remaining citizens had not wanted to tear up their roots, abandon everything they had built over a lifetime and move somewhere else as refugees. They decided to stay and find a way to survive.

It had been a difficult two years; very hard work and never enough food. They had to somehow keep the hydroponic factory operating: the plants growing there would die in a few days without the light, nutrients, ventilation, and temperature they required. To this end, they'd had to divert all the power from their few remaining solar and wind farms to the greenhouses. Electricians and engineers worked around the clock to rewire everything: disconnect their factory's main power line from the now-dead national grid and connect it to their renewable sources. It was touch and go, but they managed it before irreversible damage was done.

By the end of the century, cities in the US had been mandated to provide at least 50% of their energy requirements from green alternative sources and California had led the way. Solar collectors and wind turbines provided power to the residents, most of whom lived in reinforced apartment blocks as an adaptation to the frequent tornadoes and other destructive weather systems that had become the way of life for most people around the world, due to climate change.

A hydroponic factory does not require an inordinate amount of power. Once those were back in operation, Yuba City had enough capacity to power three of the synthetic meat factories at a reduced rate of production and still be able to recharge the batteries of their tractors and harvesters. There was no surplus for residential buildings.

People were reduced to using candles and lanterns for light and use communal washrooms for their ablutions. They couldn't even think of automatic washing machines, driers, and air conditioners. For transportation, they had bicycles or just simply walked. To augment the green vegetables, they turned the abandoned periphery into farmland. Some housing developments had already been cleared with automated heavy construction equipment; these open fields were suitable for grain. For root crops, they tilled over schoolyards, golf courses, and other recreational spaces, as well as laboriously digging smaller plots in what used to be suburban lawns.

This sudden change was very hard on everyone, but they kept going, in the hope that the country would be restored soon and things would go back to normal.

Two years had passed since the war and there was no sign of national reconstruction. Not a peep from the outside world. Some of the people began to talk about giving up and moving to Sacramento. A few citizens had actually walked the 42 miles to that city and a handful walked back with the news that conditions were easier there - for permanent residents. The many thousands of refugees who had already moved in from the countryside were still living in tent cities established in the emergency right after the war. There was strict rationing, though not so strict that money couldn't get around it but jobs were scarce and those on Guaranteed Basic Income, didn't fare well.

Still, some in Yuba City wanted to give up this primitive subsistence-level existence and move there for more plentiful food and basic services. Mostly, they were tired of the back-breaking 12-hour workday required of all able-bodied citizens. Today's special council meeting had been called to discuss this issue and decide whether to send a delegation to Sacramento and request accommodation for Yuba City's residents.

Kathleen Winters was fifty-four years old. She had an aura of quiet authority she acquired over the decades-long rise to become the mayor of this California city. She had dark brown hair, cut short, with the first strands of grey woven in among the dark. In the olden days, when they could afford such luxuries, she had kept her figure youthfully trim at the tennis court; now, there were no

205

overweight citizens. Her roots in Yuba City went deep; like her mother, she had grown up here and, except while earning her degree in economics and political science at Caltech, she never lived anywhere else. Today, she would need all that authority and all that political savvy, to keep her beloved city together. She looked at the big wall clock and sighed deeply, but her chin was set in a determined line. She would not let the troublemakers ruin their chance of staying independent and successful in their effort to survive and rebuild.

~

Tim and Cathy started out early in the morning. Their van and trailer had been serviced and loaded up by robots; they didn't need to waste time and could get going immediately. They had a long road ahead of them if they were to make it to Yuba City early enough to assess the situation and talk to people if anyone still lived there.

The first 10 mile-long stretch was familiar and clear enough to go fast. After that they had to stop often, to winch or push obstacles off the road before they could drive on. If the obstruction was too big, they had to abandon the road and drive over fields until they found a level enough access to the road again. Luckily the terrain was flat agricultural land that had not been too badly overgrown. Once they got stuck in a muddy rut and had to free their wheels by driving metal stakes into the ground ahead of the van and winching themselves out of the hole. A couple of miles past Lower Honcut Road, they came to their first major problem: the bridge over the north creek was badly damaged and they had to 'tiptoe' over it very carefully, avoiding the cracks in the road surface as much as possible. They made it across and noted down in their log that it needed serious repair before using for heavier traffic. Cathy expressed some concern for their own return journey, but Tim put on a show of confidence.

It was late afternoon when they arrived at Marysville, the northern suburb of Yuba City, and that's when they saw the first human beings outside Oroville. Those in the field straightened up from their work and stared. Three women on the road carrying heavy sacks appeared harried and stressed, but they stopped when Tim pulled over and Cathy got out to ask for directions.

The one she approached was of middle age, with long brown hair and owlish spectacles. When she heard that they had come from Oroville, she got very excited; came up to lean on the van and started questioning them about conditions outside their city. They answered as best as they could, not wanting to spend too much time on idle chit-chat. They needed to get to the center, to form a clear picture of conditions straight from the top. Tim repeated the request for directions and the woman reluctantly gave them the information. She stood back to let them drive away. Tim still could see her in the rear-view mirror, talking to her companions, gesticulating excitedly, pointing after the departing van.

"Well, we know one thing," Tim commented. "It's not a ghost town, but not a very happy one either. At least that's the impression I got from that brief exchange."

"You can't make a statistical judgment from a sample of one," Cathy's engineering mind asserted itself. "Maybe she's having a bad day. Let's wait and see what we find out from the people in charge."

~

Yuba City Council was still in full session and Kathleen was growing more and more frustrated with the blockheads who could not see reason. It was the typical "time for a change" attitude that so often corrupted intelligent political debate in the past. Raymond Ingco was the loudest of the "leave" faction. He was a balding middle-aged man with a permanent scowl etched into his face, suggesting the perpetual victim, hard done by the world.

"We have waited long enough, we have had it with this slave labor camp that our town has turned into. We want to move to Sacramento and let them worry about feeding us. They can afford it! They have their own power stations with practically unlimited output. We have barely enough just to survive and nothing left for basic comfort."

"You want to be refugees? Leave behind all you've worked for and depend on the charity of strangers?" Kathleen asked, for the fifteenth time, but all the response she got were evasive looks and incoherent grumbling. "Yes, I know, we have to work hard and we never have enough to eat and it's inconvenient having to use communal facilities. But we make our own decisions. We don't depend on anyone other than our own hard work and ingenuity. Give it a little time. We can improve our standard of living."

"If you call this 'living'," Raymond sneered, "you are welcome to it. I am going and I know many will follow."

"At least we don't have shantytowns, or makeshift tents, like all the refugees in Sacramento. Do you think they have ensuite bathrooms and private gourmet kitchens?"

"If we acted together," Raymond countered, "sent a delegation to Sacramento to negotiate terms for resettlement, we would have a much better chance of fair treatment. I propose we vote on it and accept the majority decision."

Before Kathleen could reply that something this big would need a plebiscite, the door to the council chamber burst open and her secretary rushed in. She didn't wait for the reprimand that should follow such a rude interruption, but announced, on top of her voice, the staggering news she had just received.

"Strangers! From outside!" At last, she took a deep breath. "Kathleen - Madame Mayor - sorry for barging in, but you need to know this. All of you need to know this. We have visitors and they are coming here. They drove all the way from Oroville, they know the conditions north of here, and they asked to address the council." She stopped when she ran out of breath, and looked around at the shocked councilors, who were trying to digest this stunning news.

"When? I mean, how long will it take them to get here?" Kathleen asked, knowing full well that nobody in the room was going to budge from his or her seat before the Orovillians arrived. They desperately needed as much information about life outside their town as possible. It could make all the difference to an intelligent and practical decision.

"They're on their way up now. Barney buzzed me from the lobby." Mary was still speaking in the unnaturally high voice she always used when excited. "They approached his desk for directions, but then they were held up by citizens asking questions."

As if on cue, the chamber doors were thrown open again and Barney, the security guard/maintenance man, marched in, bursting with self-importance, followed by a large, square man and a tall, slender woman, both in rough work clothes. They hung back politely.

"You'll pardon the intrusion, Mizz Winters, honored members. I think you want to talk to these people. They are Tim Hooke and Cathy Cammarata, your counterparts from the Oroville City Council."

Kathleen stood up, resting her hands on the edge of her table, for the much-needed support, and smiled at the visitors.

"Welcome. Please come in. You have no idea how glad we are to see you. I'm sure you would like to know how things are in our town, but that's nothing compared to how much we want to find out about conditions in Oroville and, generally, outside Yuba City. I am Kathleen Winters, mayor, and these are all the councilors. We are in full session today. You are the first visitors we have received since the war, so forgive our excitement."

Cathy smiled and nodded in sympathy. They all shared this hunger for facts regarding a wider circle than their own small municipalities. She accepted a chair that the man called Barney pulled out for her and Tim took one farther down the table, without ever taking his eyes off the mayor.

"Summarizing in a nutshell," Tim boomed out, "we aren't doing too badly in Oroville, thanks to unlimited power from our hydroelectric generators. Our food factories are working at full capacity and our main computer, Omega 1500, has organized production and distribution. Emergency service, health care and mass transport are efficient. Residential utilities and security are first rate."

Cathy heard the note of civic pride in his voice and wondered if he wasn't painting too nice a picture. She caught his eye; he gave a curt nod and he yielded the floor.

"We did have some problems," Cathy took up the narrative. "There was a lot of unrest, a lot of friction; looting, fights, vandalism, even rioting started by some troublemakers. We were in lock-down for a week,"

Tim cut in, "Only because our computer overreacted! It thought it was protecting us from each other. But we convinced it that giving people a chance to work on something beyond bare survival would solve the problem. And we were right!" He sat back again.

Cathy said, "Yes. Recently we've started several major projects to improve the quality of life for everyone in town. How is your computer coping with post-war circumstances?"

Kathleen felt both elated and bitter at the same time. These people had no idea what it was like, living on the verge of starvation; not enough power to run the machines, not enough food for all these people.

"We don't have our Omega up anymore," she explained with some reluctance. "We don't have enough power to keep it running because every watt is needed by the hydroponic and meat factories, basic sanitation, and recharging the batteries of the most important agricultural machines. The same goes for humanoid robots, I'm afraid: without computer control, they too are out of commission."

Tim said: "That explains one of our main concerns. Our computer, we call Big Brain, or BB for short has been trying to contact other Omega computers in the Sacramento Valley and could not raise either yours or Sacramento's. It has a plan for restoring technological civilization to the valley, by repairing roads and replacing the downed power lines, so the cities can start communicating and trading again."

Kathleen was speechless. This news was the first glimpse of real hope she had experienced since the war. Some promise of rebirth, of healing of their shattered lives; something to save them from contemplating total defeat and taking refuge in another city. Eventually, she remembered her office.

"I'm sure we'd like that very much, Councilor Hooke." His laughing eyes reminded her how long she hadn't seen any chocolate. "Tim? Of course, a lot of details need to be worked out, a lot more information exchanged. But I'm sure you both are very tired after your long trip. This council was about to take a vote, and you'll appreciate that the new development you bring will take some discussing. Please accept our hospitality for the night. Yes?" She looked from one to the other. "We have some VIP guest quarters right here in city hall – pre-war facilities, long-disused I'm afraid. Mary can lead you there and provide you with what modest conveniences our town can provide. Later, if I may come and talk to you?"

Tim and Cathy looked at each other and nodded their acceptance. They bade the council goodbye and followed Mary out of the chamber. Once the motherly secretary had done everything possible to ensure their comfort and left them alone, Tim said, "I'd better go ask that Barney for a safe place to park the van before the street lads dismantle it for souvenirs. I'll bring up our overnight kits."

"Bring our food pack, too, would you? Looks as if they don't have much to spare and you've got a lady friend coming over."

19

Jonathan woke up tired after the previous day's unaccustomed exertion. Walking 18 miles was hard enough, but they had often encountered obstacles so big that they'd been forced to detour on difficult terrain. Still, he felt ready to start the day for the 15 more miles to Yuba City. Octavia was already awake, snuggling up to him. They had found a bed in one of the draughty houses of the deserted village.

"Good morning, sweetheart. Did you sleep well?"

"If you consider sleeping well with every muscle aching in your body, then yes, I did." He grinned at her, fully aware that her condition wasn't any better than his own. "We're lucky to be in a bed and not in sleeping bags by the road."

"So, what's the plan for today? Same as yesterday? Walking and some more walking?"

"I think you hit the nail right on our head." Jonathan agreed with her assessment of their situation.

"How long will it take? You expect to get there today, I hope."

"We should get there for supper, provided they can feed us. Provided anyone is still living there. If not, then we have to forage again. Luckily it's a big enough city, chances are they didn't clear out everything edible when they left. If they left."

"Where would they have gone? If they moved to Sacramento, we would have heard about it by now. You can't easily hide tens of thousands of people arriving in your city. Not even Ford could manage that."

"Octave, no use speculating until we get there. Let's get up, find the others, have some breakfast. The sooner we're there, the sooner we find out."

The road leading out of East Nicolaus was similar to the one coming in. The conditions they encountered were like the day before, except their feet were sore now. For the first five miles, they made steady progress. The first really big hurdle confronted them at Bear River. They found both spans of the 1200 footbridge damaged, the central section badly cracked, parts of it collapsed into the river valley some 200 feet below. They couldn't risk trying to walk over that bridge, any mishap would be fatal.

Jonathan was surprised to see such a huge structure so badly damaged; no natural storm, he reasoned, could bring down that bridge, and there had been no earthquake since the big one in 2075. It must have been the nuclear detonation over the Sacramento valley; that could produce shockwave powerful enough. Before the war there had been rumors of the Russians preparing 100 megaton doomsday warheads with unimaginable destructive power.

This was a serious setback. The descent to the river was steep and rocky with patches of rough vegetation but no trees for handholds. Climbing up the other side would be difficult. The river was low and probably shallow but fast-flowing and there was nothing like a ford in sight in either direction - no way to avoid getting wet.

"You think we can make it?" Rafiq asked anxiously.

"One way to find out. The only other option is to try to find an alternate route or to turn back." he looked around at his companions questioningly. All their faces were set in determination; heads were shaken, no's murmured and chins thrust out defiantly. "Okay then. I figure we can cross the river if we form a line and hold hands, so none of us can be swept away by the current." This seemed to reassure his friend, but Jonathan felt less confident than he hoped to sound.

Descending the slope to the river was hard going. They scrambled and stumbled, dislodged stones, and made tiny landslides of loose gravel. Once Octavia cried out as she fell and landed with one foot awkwardly bent against a rocky outcrop.

They made it to the bank and stood there, not quite sure how to go about crossing to the other side. The bank was slippery; even holding hands they were in danger of falling, instead of walking into, the water. They considered carrying their shoes to keep them dry, but decided against it because there was no telling what sharp stones might be lying hidden in the bottom. The last thing they needed was slashed feet.

Jonathan volunteered to be first. He slid cautiously down the bank, while Rafiq, the strongest in the group, held his hand, himself supported by others. The water was cold, but not as deep as he had feared; even in the middle, it only came to his waist. One after the other they descended the slope, got into the water, stood waiting for the next, and slowly, carefully, waded across to the other side without any mishap.

The north bank was already in full sunlight. Along the river's edge was a rich growth of marsh grass. They stretched out on it, took off their waterlogged pants and boots to let the sun dry them a little. They had spare clothes in their backpacks, but nobody had a second pair of shoes.

Octavia winced as she pulled on dry socks. "I hope we don't have to do this very often," she summarized everyone's feelings about the experience.

"At least one more time, on our way home," Jonathan cautioned everyone. "It would be much safer to tie a rope around our waists and spread out a bit. Let's not forget to look for a long rope in Yuba. How is your foot, Octav?"

"I'm fine. The cold water did it good. After a rest, I'll be ready for the last stretch."

Jonathan was acutely aware of the time. "We do have to keep going, but I'll carry your backpack and, if you need to, you can always lean on me."

"You worry too much. I'll be all right." She stretched out on the grass and looked at the clear blue sky. "It could be worse, at least it's not raining." She changed the subject from her throbbing ankle.

She knew that they had to press on. Clambering up was mostly a matter of finding handholds and boosting one another from below. Once back on the road, though, she could not entirely conceal favoring the sprained ankle.

Jonathan was thinking about how used they were to the benefits of civilization. Walking on a smooth, level road was a luxury they never noticed in the city. They had taken for granted warm homes and well-equipped hospitals. Even with the recent cutbacks, their hardship in town was nothing compared to the uncertainty out here, when nothing could be counted on. They had to be prepared for unpleasant surprises and learn to cope with unusual situations, using intelligence and ingenuity, just as their ancestors had had to do. It was a daunting thought. At the same time, he found it invigorating. Surely, they would cope with whatever obstacle was cast in their way.

"If it weren't for human evil, stupidity, complacency, this planet could be a paradise. Yet we do everything in our power to mess it all up and turn it into a place of misery and suffering."

He resolved to do everything in his power to turn things around in Sacramento. If only he could find some pockets of humanity on this trip, some town where people were organized more sensibly and equitably.

"Penny for your thoughts?" Octavia prompted, noting his creased forehead and faraway gaze.

"And how much would that penny buy me?" Her boyfriend jolted out of his thoughts, was reluctant to delve into a depressing subject. He wanted to sound upbeat and confident about their future.

"It could buy an extra second of my attention, so don't dismiss it too easily," Octavia continued bantering.

"Well, in that case, I'll tell you my secret. I was deeply philosophical about the human condition and, in particular, the conditions awaiting this particular group of humans."

Before Octavia could respond, someone shouted: "Houses ahead!"

Jonathan consulted his map, estimated the distance they had come since the river and realized that they were walking into the town of Plumas Lake, population 5863 at the last pre-war census. It was a 3-mile long settlement, only about 4 miles separating it from the southern edge of Yuba City.

"Hey guys, we're almost there!" he told his friends who had gathered around. Rafiq passed Octavia's pack to another hiker. They had taken it in turns at each brief stop.

"Maybe we'll even find some human beings!" They all looked excited and Jonathan couldn't blame them. This was what they had been aiming for, but the long walk kept them busy, looking out for obstacles and dangers, giving one another a hand. Whatever each one was thinking, there was little energy for conversation. Now that they were almost there, hopes renewed and they quickened their steps.

~

After having spent a quiet evening in their comfortable room, the Oroville delegation retired early. Mayor Winters had dropped in after the council meeting to say that the vote had been tabled pending more information, but didn't stay to chat. The romantic candlelight was wasted, Cathy thought, wishing Shawn could have come, hoping to get home soon. The room had two big beds and they changed in the bathroom. City Hall had running water and a functioning toilet, which they gathered was a rare luxury here.

They were up early, preparing for another long day when the mayor's assistant knocked on their door. She walked in, carrying a tray with their breakfast of hot cereal and juice.

They protested against this lavish treatment, by then fully aware of the town's meager food supply, but Mary dismissed their concerns. "Nothing is too good for our Orovillian rescuers," she cooed and left the tray with a friendly smile, closing the door behind her.

"Oh my God," Cathy exclaimed, "they believe we can help them!"

"Maybe we can," Tim said thoughtfully. "It's up to BB. I'm sure that once we report back to it, appropriate plans will be cooked up in its quantum brain, as usual. Still, I don't see *how* we can help them, other than running a 30 miles long extension cord...." He paused and scratched his stubbled chin. "Not that it couldn't be done. In fact, eventually, that's exactly what we'll have to do. But no realistic plan can be made until we know the situation in Sacramento. BB said that city is its highest priority. It desperately needs machine parts."

"It would be nice to report back on the status of both cities..." Cathy mused aloud, "But pushing on to Sacramento would add at least four days to our trip and I'm concerned about the battery, with all the winching and dozing and the last recharging station way back at Ellis Road. Besides, I'm ready to go home for a rest and to catch up with things." It occurred to her that she and Tim had developed an odd closeness over only a couple of days.

"Me, too, I want to head back tomorrow at the latest," Tim agreed. "First, we need a long, frank talk with Ka – Mayor Winters and the council, so we can have a detailed assessment of their situation before we return."

Cathy sighed. "There's too much going on all at once!"

"Beats the hell out of vegging out like we've been doing."

"Struth."

That settled, they were in agreement again and Tim thought that they were a good team. He appreciated Cathy's practical, organized mind.

Breakfast – modest, but better than camp rations - over, they got dressed and made their way to the lobby. Before the council convened, they walked around for a closer look at how the city worked. They paid a visit to the nearest communal washroom. It was very large, with toilets on one side, showers on the other, and a tap for drinking water out front. The schedule of hot water was posted on the door. It served the purpose but was very basic. This visit, more than anything else, demonstrated to them the relative comfort and affluence they enjoyed in Oroville.

"I guess having electric power makes all the difference between affluence and poverty." Cathy summarized their thoughts. "Power is … everything."

"Good morning travelers!" The mayor was already sitting behind her desk, with a huge California map spread out on it. "I trust Mary provided you with a sufficient breakfast. I heard you went walkabout for a first-hand look at our situation. Are you ready to resume our talk from yesterday?"

"More than ready, Madam Mayor" Tim tried to find the right tone, but was interrupted immediately.

"Please stop this 'madam mayor' stuff. We don't much stand on ceremony here. It's a small enough place for everyone to be familiar with everyone else. Kathleen will do and, if you don't mind, I'll call you Tim and Cathy."

They had no objections and felt more at ease.

"I've been looking at this detailed map of the highway section between Yuba and Oroville and see a few places where it might be difficult to restore downed power lines. Shortage of power is our most pressing problem. If you're serious about restoring communication between the two cities, that's where we'd have to start."

Tim said, "I've been thinking the same. But…Kathleen, you may not have completely understood our situation." Tim took a deep steadying breath, not quite sure how to represent their different political structure. Kathleen and the council seemed in total charge of decisions here.

Kathleen raised an eyebrow but didn't interrupt.

"In Oroville, we're not in control of allocating resources and setting priorities," Tim's reluctance increased as he kept talking. "After the war, we – well, we just couldn't cope," He suddenly felt small and ashamed, but shoved the feeling aside. This was time for facts, not face-saving. "So we put our Omega computer in overall charge of all that, assuming that with the sophisticated computing power of Big Brain, we had the best chance of survival in the middle of all that destruction."

"What do you mean 'overall charge'?" Kathleen was taken aback by this revelation. "Do you mean that the computer is running things and you just follow its orders?"

"Something like that," Tim hesitated, and Cathy stepped into the breach.

"That's been working for us very well, as far as survival is concerned. We've been well fed and housed, comfortable and mostly safe. I guess, too comfortable. Only recently have we reasserted some of our own initiative. We reinstated the city council and started several projects to improve the quality of life," she explained. "But the major resources of our town are still allocated by the computer. Distribution and most of the work is carried out by robots."

"Wow! That's a lot to digest!" Kathleen exclaimed. "It's hard to imagine letting machines tell me what to do. But I suppose you made the right decision, judging by the conditions you described to me. Still, I don't know if I'd go as far as relinquishing control over my destiny, even to intelligent and beneficial machines."

"Well, that's what we have and that's what we need to consider when making plans." Tim took up the narrative. "We'll go back and report on the conditions we found here, discuss it in Council, and make our recommendation to our Big Brain. I'm sure it will make the most intelligent decision for all concerned."

Cathy added, "One other thing. BB has been trying to contact its network. No chance of reactivating your Omega?"

That's how far they got in discussing future cooperation between the two cities when they were interrupted by Mary. She burst into the room, breathlessly, just as she had the day before.

"Kathleen, you won't believe this, but we have *more* visitors! They say, from Sacramento."

"Visitors? Again? If you're kidding me, Mary, it's not funny."

"I would never…" Mary stammered, shocked at the very thought. "They just arrived. A dozen tired people with backpacks. They're in the lobby and very anxious to talk to you. Should I let them in or show them to a waiting room?"

The three of them stared at one another, speechless for a few seconds. Kathleen regained her composure and told Mary to waste no more time, just usher in the visitors.

Tim winked. "Never rains but pours, right?" She really had the cutest smile, he thought.

Jonathan and his group of bedraggled travelers filed in, looking around apprehensively, trying to determine which of these well-dressed people was in charge, whom to talk to first.

Kathleen was grace itself as she walked around the desk to shake their hands one after the other. Seeing their tired faces, she thought it best not to keep them standing and led the way to the conference room next door, where they could all sit around the huge table. She motioned Tim and Cathy to join them.

"My name is Kathleen Winters and I am the mayor of Yuba City. These two, Cathy Cammarata and Tim Hooke, are recent visitors from Oroville. Welcome to our town. Do you need refreshments? Of course, you do; I can see you have a long road behind you."

Jonathan, who had remained standing, replied in kind. "My name is Jonathan Carver. I am spoke-person of our group and I thank you for the welcome. These are my friends, all members of the Sacramento Resistance Movement. Yes, some water would be very welcome. We covered the last 15 miles without a rest because we were

222

so eager to find out if Yuba City was still alive and well. We have seen nothing but ghost towns on our way here."

Kathleen motioned to Mary, who was frozen in the doorway, mesmerized by the spectacle of visitors from two different towns sitting around their conference table. After two years without a peep from outside, the world was beating a path to their door. She did get the message and hurried outside, determined to be back as soon as possible so she wouldn't miss too much from this exciting event.

"Did you say 'Resistance Movement'?" Kathleen couldn't quite hide the negative associations she had with that word. "Resistance against what?"

Jonathan took a deep breath and slowly, quietly, without emotion, explained the situation in Sacramento. Kathleen and her two Oroville guests listened to the tale in growing disbelief. It was hard to imagine that any American city could descend to that level of authoritarian self-serving rule. Could it possibly be true that the leadership valued power and luxury at the price of thousands living in unnecessary poverty? This surely belonged to the past, the distant past, not to the end of 21st century US... But then was there even a United States anymore? Jonathan and his silently nodding group insisted that this was the case.

They didn't look like revolutionaries. They looked like ordinary, honest, well-meaning young people, on a mission to find out whether they could expect any help from other municipalities.

Mary, who had been waiting for the story to finish, now placed a pitcher of water and glasses in the center of the table. She stepped back a discreet distance and stood with her back to the wall.

"Well, if this is true," Tim finally found his voice, "we don't want to waste any time getting back to Oroville. Our council and Omega computer need this information as fast as possible. I'm sure we'll be back in a few days with detailed plans on how to deal with this unexpected situation. Kathleen, thank you again for the hospitality and we'll be on our way."

Turning to the Sacramento delegation he said, trying to sound reassuring, "I'm sure Kathleen is going to fill you in on Oroville and I hope you'll be still here when we return in a few days."

Jonathan had a request and a suggestion. "Would it be helpful if one of us went with you to Oroville, so your council could have the information first hand and pose questions?"

"That's an excellent idea," Cathy said. "There's lots of room in the van. Maybe Kathleen could send one of her council members as well, so everybody can be represented?"

Kathleen jumped at the opportunity: "If he agrees, I'd be happy to send my deputy mayor. He has full authority to negotiate on behalf of Yuba, and to provide any further information your council may need."

Tim and Cathy looked at each other and nodded in unison. That settled it and Kathleen left the room to find her second in command.

Jonathan already knew whom he wanted to send. Octavia had been limping so badly on the last mile of their trek, it was obvious that she couldn't make the long hard walk back to Sacramento. Originally he thought that they would take a few days, maybe even a week to let her recover before heading home, but now that he was aware of possible help from Oroville, he didn't want to waste a day getting back. He was worried about the hotheads in the movement who were too eager to confront Ford's goons. He was sure that he could calm them down with news from the other cities and forestall any rash and dangerous acts that could only hurt their cause.

Kathleen came back, followed by a tall, lean, muscular man, and introduced him as Greg Galloway, deputy mayor. Greg was carrying two small boxes and handed one to Jonathan and another to Tim. "These are communication devices that you can use to contact us, or each other. It has a range of fifty miles and is pre-set to the frequency of the third one here. Kathleen will be listening in at every mealtime and before going to bed, so you can contact her at 9:00 AM, 12:00 AM, 6:00 PM, and 11:00 PM."

Tim and Cathy were duly impressed with the arrangement and were ready to leave, as soon as their passengers had everything they needed for the trip. Octavia wasn't too happy to part company with Jonathan but understood his reasons and knew that she wouldn't be able to walk back to Sacramento until her ankle healed. Greg already had a packed overnight bag.

Shaking hands all around ended the meeting. Cathy, Tim, and Greg tactfully and quietly left the room to wait in the hall while each member of the Sacramento group hugged Octavia, some shedding a tear. Kathleen and Mary were left to deal with the tired and hungry delegation.

20

We had been living in our new home for over two weeks and we still didn't have a functional toilet. Frankly, all of us were sick and tired of using the outhouse. It was unpleasant, inconvenient, and downright stinky. Brian had inspected the wiring of the well-pump and found it in good condition, as far as he could see. It led to a submersible pump somewhere deep inside a sealed pipe that the wires disappeared into. We assumed that it had been working before the war, but when the electric grid went down, the Junkers were forced to build their outhouse as an alternative. We just realized how heavily dependent on electricity we had been all our lives. Brian suggested that we should hook up the new solar panels, if they prove to be functional, to the well-pump first and he got no argument from us. The women, who had been taking turns fetching in water cheered in unison.

Mike and Brian left with the van, right after breakfast, to dismantle and bring home the solar panels, batteries, and inverter from the house we had discovered the day before. My task for the day was set by Adrien, who insisted that we should waste no more time and start plowing up that field and planting our crops. Charcoal was an urgent priority. I agreed, and on my way out to the pit to resume digging, I noticed Martha in front of her easel working in the canvas she had started the day before. The expression on her face was a mixture of high concentration and intense pleasure. I stood there for a few minutes, watching her lovely figure and thinking how lucky I was to know and love this radiant, beautiful creature and have her love and loyalty in return. I resisted the temptation to go and see what she was painting; I knew she wouldn't welcome the interruption, so I kept on walking to my own less than artistic task.

My muscles were still sore from the previous day, but I was determined to ignore the pain, thinking that my arms would get stronger through regular use. Robyn advised us to choose different kinds of exertion, rather than punishing the same joints every day. Well, digging is different from prying metal sheets off roofs. Neither one is glamorous work, but it needed to be done and by noon I thought the trench was long and deep enough for our purpose. And it sure would impress my friends back in town.

We didn't expect Mike and Brian back before supper, so we didn't wait for them with lunch. Martha, Adrien, Robyn, Jennifer, and Trish were already at the table when I joined them, feeling a bit awkward to be the only male, but my sex was soon reinforced by Kevin, who bounded in from the yard, followed by Jimmy. The two had become inseparable.

"Mom, I taught Jimmy to roll over!" Kevin announced, still out of breath. "Can I show you, please?"

"After lunch, dear, and then you can show me how to teach you to roll over at bedtime. I still haven't managed that."

Trish couldn't resist the opportunity to score one on her brother. "You haven't managed to teach him anything yet, Mom, I think he's unteachable."

"If anybody's unteachable here," Kevin reciprocated, "it's not me! I tried to teach *her* arithmetic. No luck!"

Before Trish could respond, Jennifer intervened. "OK, kids, that's enough for now. Save up your witticisms for dinnertime. We all want to hear more, I'm sure." Both children looked embarrassed to be chastised in front of all the adults, but the good-natured chuckles around the table reassured them. "Go, wash your hands. And no shoving!"

Adrien asked what Martha was painting and we all pestered her with questions, but she wouldn't satisfy our curiosity. "You'll see it when it's finished, not a minute before. It's covered on its easel and woe to the ruffian who dares to peek under the dropcloth."

We had to live with that; curious we might be, but we naturally respected her wish for privacy. You can't live so closely with other people unless you have that understanding. The conversation drifted over to Adrien's success with her seedlings. We all saw them poking their tiny heads out of the soil under the cloche, growing, promising us future harvest.

"When do you think they'll be ready to plant out?" I wanted to have an idea of how soon the plot would need to be ready.

"Oh, I'm sure it'll be a few weeks before they're big enough, but the seedlings under the cloche won't go to the plowed land, they're too delicate. They'll go into the fenced vegetable garden that I dug up and weeded last week. Out there, we'll plant corn, barley, chickpeas, and root crops, just as soon as you can prepare the land."

Adrien's response didn't reassure me because I knew that plowing up the field wouldn't be enough, I still had to harrow it to break up the big clumps of soil. But, before I could even think of that, we'd have to make a sufficient amount of charcoal. Producing that would take 5-6 days, according to the information we received from R17. I had to work as hard and as efficiently as I could.

Before leaving the table, Robyn asked Kevin and Trish to volunteer for mattress-stuffing duty in the loft and both kids thought that would be great fun. Besides they were eager to sleep on something softer than a sleeping bag over the hard floor.

We all had our projects for the afternoon and I hurried back to my trench. Mike had brought an enormous pile of wood from his tree cutting project yesterday and I wasted no time putting it to good use. The seasoned wood, we put aside to be chopped later for cooking and heating. The rough-cut green logs would form a lattice-like structure as recommended by the printout. The plan was to make one layer of medium-thick logs at the bottom of the trench, cover that with dry kindling – sticks collected by the children under Jennifer's and Jimmy's supervision - so the fire could start easily. On top of this layer, I had to place thicker and thicker branches and logs in a criss-cross pattern to enable air circulation. When lit, it would start slowly but soon reach a high-temperature blaze, engulfing the whole trench in flames. That's when we were supposed to cover it with the corrugated metal sheets and pile earth on top to cut off the air supply. According to theory, then the wood pile would continue to smolder, turning the green wood into pure carbon over a week.

This task kept me busy all of the afternoon and by dinnertime, it was ready to start, but I decided to wait for

Mike and Brian so we could all light our bonfire together at nightfall.

Our van rolled onto our driveway, riding low under the weight of batteries, pulling the trailer stacked high with solar panels. Everybody gathered around to admire them, gleaming in the low-slanted sunshine. Mike and Brian explained how they found everything in good order. Dismantling the system was painstaking, rather than back-breaking, work and Brian wanted to start the installation as soon as we'd eaten, but we talked him into waiting for daylight. If everything went as expected, he told us, we should have running water, a functioning toilet, and some lights in the house by Thursday.

A great cheer went up. This had become a kind of ritual on hearing good news, and I never tired of hearing it. I was so pleased over the progress our little group had been making that I was sure I would never go back to computers and programming. I had done that, enjoyed it very much, but now it was time to embrace what I had been missing all my life: to be physical, in nature, in stimulating company of like-minded people, making progress toward a shared goal.

It was, more immediately, time to eat our dull camp-ration dinner, though lately enhanced by salads of tender young greens that Adrien and Jennifer found among the weeds. Afterward, we gathered around the charcoal pit for a fire-starting ceremony, then sat around the burning logs, just relaxing after a hard day's work. After the children went to bed, we covered the pit as per instructions. There was nothing more to do but wait.

~

Tim and Cathy were reporting to BB on their expedition to Yuba City. Along with the van's log recording, they included their own observations, information received from the residents, and what they had learned from the Sacramento scouts. They were sure that the news would have a big impact on their future lives but not how Big Brain would react. They had discussed it on the way home and agreed that they would have to help Yuba City first. Sacramento was a much bigger challenge and they had no idea how to go about it – road access being only the most obvious problem. They just had to wait for BB to compute all the variables at its usual quantum speed and efficiency and make its decisions.

The emotionless voice that greeted them on arrival responded almost immediately after they had finished their report.

"Tim and Cathy, congratulations on a mission successfully accomplished. The information you have gathered surpasses my expectations. A logical timetable upon which to proceed can now be devised. Your recommendation for helping Yuba City first is noted. However, Sacramento remains the highest priority, because Oroville power generating plants, manufactories and service functions are performing at sub-optimal levels due to shortages of spare parts. Sacramento is the only known source of machine parts at this time. Those production facilities must be secured as a matter of urgency. We, by which term is meant Oroville as a whole, myself and you as my team, must address the situation in Sacramento. We must do so with the lowest possible risk and highest possible probability of success. According to my personnel files, Citizens Dubois and Sutherland were instrumental in the installation of Omega 1420. We need them for consultation. I shall contact R17, their resident robot, with instructions to return without delay."

"They won't like it." Cathy sounded very sure. "They've been very busy with their own project and would hate interruption, even for a day. It's planting time. They *have* to keep plugging ahead, to secure a sufficient harvest to live on when their prepackaged supply is gone."

"Nevertheless, they will comply. When the situation is explained to them, they will understand that this is the logical thing to do. We will provide compensatory aid to the homestead. I shall call a council meeting for 1400 hours tomorrow, allowing sufficient travel time. We will require the presence of our guests from Yuba City and Sacramento as well. Now, you must go to your homes and recuperate from your exertions. Well done."

This was a dismissal, though a nicer one than they were used to and, frankly, they didn't mind. They had been longing for the comforts of home. Cathy had never spent this much time apart from Shawn in 30 years of marriage. She was sure Tim, too, would have a new appreciation of his cozy bachelor pad.

~

Next morning, you'd think that Brian was in his own personal heaven, high up on the roof, instructing Mike on how to place and secure the frames for his solar panels. I was a bit worried about him, not being a young man anymore, not even wearing a safety harness. Not that we had any such thing, but he rejected my suggestion of tying a rope around his waist and attaching the other end to the chimney. He assured me that he had an excellent sense of balance; he'd had to be on many roofs during his career. He had more faith in himself than in the chimney.

In other words: he knew what he was doing and I should butt out. He didn't actually say that, but suggested, pointedly, that maybe I should tend to my fire in the charcoal pit, before I burn the house down under him. That fire was no danger to the house, and Brian knew that because now it was covered with corrugated steel and 6 inches of earth.

Last night's fire-lighting event was a great success. We sat for hours around the blazing logs, basking in the warm glow, swapping stories of the past, when we were young and the world was safe and we had no bigger worries than the next date with our love interest of the moment. It was nice to remember and some of us got sentimental. We sang old songs and exchanged our hopes for this new future. We were in this blissful mood when we were rudely interrupted by our almost forgotten robot, R17.

"I have received communication from Omega 1500. I am instructed to explain what is happening in the city."

I wanted to tell the damn robot to shut up and go away, but my friends were curious, so I resigned myself to the pleasant mood being disrupted and said nothing. R17 continued. I guess it would have anyway.

"The expedition by Citizens Hooke and Cammarata brought back the required information. Omega 1500 is apprised of the existing conditions in both Yuba City and Sacramento. Yuba City operates at a subsistence level. Without electrical power generating capability, its food factories operate at 20% of optimum requirement; utilities and services are minimal. It needs our help. Sacramento is under the rule of unscrupulous individuals, who divert resources, necessary to the well-being of the human population, to wasteful and frivolous applications. The people are unhappy and need our help. Trevor's suspicion that their control center was cut off from communication by the Mayor proved correct. Omega 1500 has assigned a top priority rating to the solution of that problem.

An efficiently functioning and accessible Sacramento production facility is essential to the welfare of Oroville and its citizens. Robotic components for the food factories and city maintenance are urgently required. It is, therefore, of critical importance to re-establish contact with Omega 1420. As a matter of record, you, Mike

Sutherland and Trevor Dubois were the last two software engineers to work on that computer, you are in a unique position to advise on how most expeditiously to accomplish that resolution. For this reason, Omega 1500 has issued an urgent recall for both of you. The continued sustenance of Oroville's human population at the current standard depends on resolving the problem. An emergency meeting of Oroville City Council has been tabled for 1400 hours tomorrow afternoon. Your attendance is required."

This announcement shattered the happy mood we'd all enjoyed. A long, ominous silence descended on our group and we all looked at each other with uncertainty. Then everyone looked at me and Mike for our reaction.

My instant reaction was an almost irresistible desire to smash that robot to pieces and dance on its electromechanical guts. But it passed as soon as my brain came back on line. I knew that I had no choice. Seeing Mike's face, I had no doubt that he felt the same way, and the slight shrug of his massive shoulders indicated his reluctant willingness to comply with this request - command. Just when things were going so well, we were required to abandon our project, jeopardize the future of our homestead and waste precious time traveling back and forth to town. We clung to the hope that it would only be for a day, that we might even be back by tomorrow night, once we'd told Big Brain everything it wanted to know. How our information would help, we could only speculate, but that wasn't our problem. We would answer the questions to the best of our recollection and let BB worry about how to use what it learned.

After I cooled down, I realized how childish was the impulse to take my frustration out on the robot. Having learned – however sketchily - about the situation in Yuba City and in Sacramento, I managed to put things in perspective and was a bit embarrassed about my violent reaction. Compared to the two other cities, we didn't have it too bad at all, and I had to give credit to BB and its robots for efficiently organizing our lives, maximizing productivity, and distributing the goods fairly. Thinking about Sacramento's mayor, I realized that the old adage was still true: power corrupts. On the other hand, for the first time ever, I realized that computers can't be corrupted in that way. This thought helped me to see our Big Brain in a new light. Maybe we were not adversaries at all, as I had thought, but rather partners. We had a built-in guarantee: our leader, BB, could not be tempted, blackmailed or bribed and would never develop dictatorial ambitions. I made a mental note to break this habit of being hostile to the technology I had helped to create.

The next morning we were ready to leave when I noticed Brian on the roof with his beloved panels. Mike had affixed the frame; now Brian had the fiddly task of wiring up the collectors, converter, batteries, and devices. After my suggestion for a safety rope was rejected, I knew that I had to let him deal with it in his own way. I noticed Robyn hovering in the yard, glancing anxiously upward, and gave her a reassuring pat on the shoulder. "He knows his business."

Still, I was a little worried about leaving the group with only one man and no vehicle for transportation, in case of an emergency. We just had to hope that no mishap occurred during our absence. When I'd mentioned my concern at breakfast, Martha made light of it.

"Trevor, you are such a typical male, my love! You think that we women are helpless damsels, always in distress, couldn't survive a day without our gallant knights in greasy overalls to come to our rescue. Get it through your thick skull that you guys are not the crown of creation and we'll be just fine without you. Maybe we'll get something done in your absence, without your constant interruptions, asking for food or other favors I won't name in mixed company."

I knew that she was jesting, to convince me that everything was going to be alright, but her words still left me with an uneasy feeling. I couldn't help it, the instinct to protect our women was too deeply ingrained in my all too male genes.

Anyway, it was only for one day. I got in the van and we rode off, the first time since we'd arrived, back to town.

21

Donald Mouch had a plan to deal with his stupid boss, once and for all. It was risky but offered the greatest chance of success. All through the day before, Ford had whined about the computer's refusal to extend the businessmen's golf course into a neighboring potato field. Mouch knew that expansion was intended as an inducement for political support, so he was happy enough to see it scuttled. However, this was the first time that a computer refused to follow a direct command and that did worry him. Where was this leading? What if the computer could no longer reconcile the cozy arrangement of the elite with its prime directive? Was there a danger of it malfunctioning or failing altogether? The whole city would grind to a halt! If he waited any longer for an opportunity, there might be nothing left worth taking over. He had to gain control of that computer and he could only do it through Ford. It was time for the coup.

To set his plan in motion, he found paperwork to bring to Ford's office at City Hall. Under the pretense of talking over executive decisions, he needled the mayor all through the morning, ridiculing his passive acceptance of the computer's refusal. "What kind of leader are you? You just take this insubordination? From a stupid machine? I wouldn't be so scared of it." he sneered at his boss. Finally, Ford couldn't take it anymore and dismissed him angrily. Of course, he would take the private elevator straight down to the vault. Mouch ran down the stairs and was waiting for him at the first steel door.

Ford was outraged. "What are you doing here? You know you don't have the authority to communicate with the computer?"

At that moment, they heard boots pounding down the stairs and two security guards, Mouch's personal recruits, joined them.

Ford was alarmed now. "What's going on, Donald? What's the meaning of this?" he stammered, now quite frightened by this invasion of his private domain.

"It's very simple, Larry. You will open the doors for us, making sure that I can see the security code you enter, and then we'll follow you in. Once inside, you will log on to the computer, again making sure that I can see the password you use. Then you will instruct the computer to accept me as the new Mayor of Sacramento, with full authority to make decisions regarding resource allocation and distribution. After that, you will stand aside and let me deal with the machine. If you cooperate, you won't be harmed, and I advise you to choose that route. The alternative can be very unpleasant."

Ford just stood there, shell-shocked, his mouth opening and closing, uttering no sound. Finally, he croaked out: "You won't get away with this! My troops are loyal to me and if you hurt me, they'll come after you!"

"I'm ready if that happens, you oaf. You never noticed that half of your guards, including these two, are loyal to me now. I offered them a better deal than they got from you."

Ford tried to run up the staircase, looking for help, but his way was blocked by the two guards who turned him around and shoved him back down the stairs, none too gently.

"Don't try that again, you fool, you'll only make things worse for yourself," Mouch said, as he pushed the fat man in front of the steel door. "Now, open it!"

Ford looked around helplessly but saw no chance of escape. He was convinced by now that Mouch and his goons wouldn't hesitate to hurt him if he refused to cooperate. Reluctantly, he punched in the security code and noticed Mouch copying it down. They went through and repeated the process at the second door and entered the computer control room.

He was shoved down into the chair in front of the console, noticing that both guards pulled out their guns, aiming them at targets low on his body. "No mess on the console," Mouch explained. He choked back tears of fear, anger, and frustration. With shaking hand, he activated the console, turned a ghastly pale face up to the camera, and entered his password slowly, character by character, as Mouch leaned over him, notebook in hand, copying it down as he typed.

Only one thing was left and with tremors in his voice he instructed Omega 1420 to change its record, as he was ordered. This done, he looked up at his assailants with dread in his eyes.

He tried one more gambit, "If you kill me, the robocops will step in. They can take your puny little army."

"Nothing as dramatic as that, Larry - you can relax. You'll be made comfortable in a safe place, but I'm afraid, your freedom of movement will be somewhat limited."

He turned to the two guards. "Take him away, as we discussed. Make sure you're not seen or followed."

The two guards pulled Ford to his feet and escorted him up the stairs. By this time Ford was docile, his will, never too strong, was broken by fear. It looked as if he wouldn't be killed. Maybe he could find a way to escape or be rescued by his loyal guards. There was no reason to hurt him, now that Mouch had got what he wanted. Or thought he'd got what he wanted. Thought he was so smart! That computer wouldn't obey him any more than it had Ford.

The most critical mission accomplished, Mouch sat down in the chair vacated by Ford and took a deep breath. He was ready to take control.

~

Soon after Tim, Cathy, and their two passengers departed, Jonathan also prepared to leave. He asked Kathleen for a small amount of food, enough to last the two days walk back to Sacramento. Kathleen was happy to help; she was dreadfully sorry for these people who had a problem she hoped she would never have to face herself. Citizens of Yuba City were poor but they had their freedom and a fair democratic government. The news of Oroville's much greater success knocked over all their old assumptions. She hoped that Oroville could help both cities and she would heartily support any co-operative plan. She awaited the deliberations of their council with anxious impatience. Greg was the right representative to send. He was knowledgeable, observant, and articulate. Not only could he speak persuasively for Yuba, but he would bring back sound intelligence.

She invited Jonathan Carver and his group to stay overnight. They needed a full day to cover half the distance and the road was hazardous enough in daylight. She arranged temporary accommodation for them in one of the disused shopping centers where communal washrooms and kitchens had been installed. Mary introduced them to the neighborhood watch and organized camp cots.

Jonathan was grateful for the hospitality and the opportunity to talk with some of the townspeople. Unlike his own, they seemed resigned rather than angry; tired, rather than fearful. After a modest meal, they retired to their accommodation. He missed Octavia already, but he was relieved at the same time that she was safe and that a proper doctor in a proper hospital would look after her injury.

He forced himself to stop thinking about her and turned his attention to what might await them in Sacramento. He was sure that Ford had been promptly notified of their departure. Chances were, he'd been looking for them and knew by now which way they had gone. If he'd sent police in pursuit, they'd be in custody, so that didn't happen. Hopefully, he assumed they'd run away for good. Still, there might well be guards watching the road. Jonathan didn't relish the prospect of walking into a trap but was even more concerned that his friends would be caught. There was a very good chance that he would be apprehended anywhere in the city, especially if there had been trouble in his absence. Thinking this over, he decided that it would be prudent to split up for the last few miles. He would go ahead, and if he was picked up, the others could take different routes individually. That would improve their odds of some getting back to the movement with their news.

With this plan in mind, finally, he was able to fall asleep, resting his aching body and tired mind, to be ready for the long trek early next morning.

~

Donald Mouch was frustrated. His session with Omega 1420 didn't go as well as he had hoped. He was still fuming over the stubborn computer arguing with everything he ordered it to do. This directive, that protocol! Instead of saying 'Yes, sir," it kept answering "That is contrary to my programming, your worship." Ford must have taught it that stupid phrase.

It readily accepted the change in the command; said "Congratulations, Your Worship. I was not instructed to supervise an election." It didn't resist when he changed the access password and the security code to the steel doors.

Problems started when he ordered it to decentralize its operation and set up independent control stations in the food factories and the power station. It also refused to relinquish control of its humanoid robots in law enforcement and services. It just kept repeating that the changes Mouch required would waste the town's resources, make the operation more inefficient, and would result in a decline in living standards for the citizens.

Mouch, in final desperation, shouted at the stupid machine. "You are a computer programmed to follow orders of the Mayor and I am ordering you to follow my instructions without further delay."

Omega's dispassionate reply infuriated him even further.

"Mayor Mouch, Your Worship, I have difficulty following these orders because my programming has encountered a core conflict that I cannot resolve. The two prime directives built into my operating system, at the highest level, compel me to both follow human orders and maximize the wellbeing of the citizens of this municipality. Your present orders conflict with one of

these directives and, unless you modify them, I cannot comply."

At that point, Mouch stormed out of the control room and up the stairs. He was already at the top when he remembered the vault doors and returned to lock them. The elevator to the ex-mayor's office was locked. He'd have to sweat the code out of Ford later. He needed to think this over, so he retreated to his own office, which he decided to keep occupying, for the time being.

He realized that to gain full control of the computer, he needed expert help, a top-flight geek, who knew how to reprogram the blasted operating system and remove the damned prime directive. He sat down at his own local console and brought up the census database that identified the occupations of every citizen before the war. Some of those people were dead or gone, but it was the logical place to begin. He set up his search with filtering keywords 'computer programmer' and/or 'software engineer', plus 'current resident'. He found a dozen and printed out a list for his deputy to find and pick up as soon as possible.

~

Tim, Cathy, and their passengers made good progress on the now-familiar route back to Oroville and they had reached town in time for supper. They drove straight to the hospital to have a robot doctor look at Octavia's ankle, which had puffed up like a football. The scan didn't show any fracture; it was inflammation due to the original sprain having been subjected to the stress of an additional 12-mile walk. The doctor gave her an injection to ease the pain and reduce the swelling, then ordered complete rest for 24 hours, followed by a regimen of massage, gentle exercise, elevation of the limb, and the application of alternate hot and cold compresses, every 6 hours.

She was taken from the hospital in a wheelchair, her protests firmly ignored. After dropping the women off, Tim drove on to his own home where he offered Greg dinner and a bed for the night.

Cathy took the elevator to her second-floor apartment. This was unusually sedate for her, though she was secretly glad of the excuse. She'd begun feeling her age on these road trips. It was late, but she had alerted Shawn to prepare some dinner and a bed for the houseguest.

She wasn't disappointed: hoping she would return that night, he'd cooked her favorite dish: Hungarian goulash with salad before and dessert after. He had put the children to bed hours ago, but of course, hearing their mother's voice, they came charging out to greet her. It took some little while for her to settle them again, while Shawn made Octavia comfortable. This was the first warm, safe place and the first generous meal she had experienced in many days – months if she were honest about their recent circumstances in Sacramento.

Shawn wanted to know everything about their trip and, for a while, it was only Cathy's voice telling her tale, while Octavia helped herself to a second helping of the delicious meal. He listened with great interest and couldn't resist a startled groan and pitying glance at the visitor when Cathy came to describing the Sacramento situation.

Having finished their meal, Octavia asked many questions about Oroville, but mostly she just kept looking around with open amazement at the unaccustomed luxury in the apartment. First of all, they had all the lights on, even in the holo-viewer that Shawn had been watching when they arrived. She rolled her chair out to the kitchen, helping Cathy bring out the dishes, and noticed how well-stocked their cooling unit was when Cathy opened its door to put in the leftovers. Leftovers – imagine! She felt a pang of envy on hearing the gush of hot water when Cathy slid the plates into the washer slot.

"So this is what it's like to have unlimited power," she said, shaking her head. "In Sacramento, we have frequent blackouts despite the strict rationing. You must be a very important person to have the means for all this."

"How do you mean, important? I'm on the city council, but that's only been reinstated for a couple of weeks." Cathy paused to consider this. "Really. So much has happened, it's hard to believe. Anyway, before that, we were all nobodies."

"You mean everyone lives like this? How can you afford to pay for all this on an average salary?"

"Did we forget to mention that? I guess we take it for granted. We haven't had jobs or salaries or money for years. Things just get distributed to everyone and we all get whatever we need."

"This sounds too good to be true, I find it difficult to imagine living without money. Your computer sure made things much simpler. Now I can see what Tim meant - how it improves efficiency and how everyone benefits."

"We had our problems, too," Cathy assured her. "Efficiency and plenty have their downside. Before things turned around, we had a lot of people fighting on the streets out of sheer boredom. When Big Brain locked us all in for a week, I suppose we came to our senses. We've made progress in a big way since then; started several important projects in which anyone who wants to can participate."

"So, you too are under the thumb of a sort of dictator? At least it seems to care for the citizenry's welfare and organizes things well enough that nobody goes hungry or cold. Is that true? You don't have any rich bastards who grab most of the goodies for themselves?"

Cathy laughed at the notion. She was so used to their way of living now, without money, without income disparity or social status, or self-important people flaunting their hoarded loot in everyone's face. She could remember, but dimly, as if she'd lived it in a virtual movie.

"That's right, Octavia, one thing we have to give credit to Big Brain for is abolishing the money system and distributing goods and services on an equitable basis. Though to be fair," she added, "we have to take some credit, too, for handing over the power. It wasn't a simple decision, but it was one *we humans* made; it wasn't the computer 'taking over'."

Octavia pinched herself to make sure she wasn't dreaming. She considered this arrangement far superior to what they suffered under in Sacramento. Even if the price was having to let a computer make all the important decisions. Who cares, so long as these decisions led to comfort and social justice? Well, she supposed, a lot of people might care, get upset, even, but they couldn't offer a practical alternative. Human governments had not been able to achieve this level of effectiveness for millennia; maybe it was time to delegate power to something that could.

She suddenly felt the weariness of three long, hard, eventful days. She wondered how that man from Yuba City, Greg, was enjoying this luxurious hospitality, but her thoughts didn't linger on him. Her primary concern was Jonathan and their friends on their way back to Sacramento. What were they walking into? Jonathan had been in constant danger for months, and the tensions in that city were approaching a flash-point. He was used to taking precautions and keeping under cover. She felt very guilty, abandoning them, even though she had no real choice in the matter.

It was close to 11:00 PM, one of the prearranged times to contact Kathleen Winters on the communicator she'd been given. She thought she'd better report her safe arrival and impressions before she fell asleep. Though she didn't expect any news of her own people yet; even if they left immediately, how far could they have gone? Kathleen reassured her that they were still in town, resting up for the long trip the next day. Octavia took some comfort in the knowledge that Jonathan was safe for the moment and would get her message.

Her last conscious thought was about the upcoming council meeting. She would have to address the government of a strange city, as the sole spokesperson of the resistance movement – of her whole city, really. It was her task of asking this well-organized town for assistance to the former state capital. She hoped she could make a coherent, logical case. She hoped their computer would have as much empathy and compassion as her hosts seemed to offer. She hoped Jonathan would be careful.

22

Mike drove with his usual competence and we made good time. The road was familiar, and with fewer obstacles, since Tim Hooke cleared away some wreckage; we only had to get off the tarmac once. We didn't talk much, immersed in our own thoughts. I had assumed that life still existed outside our little city and that, sooner or later, we would make contact with the world, but the unpleasant news from Sacramento worried us both. Don't people ever learn? Not even from a devastating nuclear war do they realize that the old ways of privilege and exploitation inevitably lead to disaster? And now we had to deal with it somehow.

I had no idea what we could do against a major city many times the size of Oroville, with its superior resources, weapons, and a military-style police force. BB wanted to consult us about Omega 1420, tightly controlled by Sacramento's mayor. What useful information might we be able to provide? I guessed we just had to wait for the council meeting to find out.

We arrived too early for the mid-afternoon meeting; in time to go home, take a luxurious hot shower, and put on clean clothes. I had forgotten what a pleasure it is to have running hot water, laundry, and other blessings of a technological civilization, but I wasn't tempted to change back to our old lifestyle. These small pleasures, especially once we were used to them, would pale in comparison with the extreme pleasure we derived from the creative, productive lifestyle we learned to enjoy on our progressing homestead. And, in time, we would have a lot more of these conveniences ourselves.

Mike and I had agreed to meet at Magic Wok, an old-style restaurant featuring Chinese food, prepared by robots. I thought this was another area of life just about ready for humans to take back. A few people were finishing their midday meal. One of the regular guests recognized us. He came over to ask about conditions outside the city and the others all stopped eating to listen.

We told them what we knew regarding the roads, the farmlands, and our own experiment, but said nothing about the contact with other cities. It wasn't our job to inform the citizens, especially not before we knew how Big Brain wanted to deal with it.

Finally, they drifted away and we were left alone to have at our lunch with unreserved gusto. I had to admit to myself that it was a pleasant change from our limited culinary experience; Jennifer could do only so much with prepackaged supplies. I thought we should surprise our household with a takeout meal for everyone.

Then it was time to report in to the council and answer more questions. We were greeted by Mayor

Morgan Webster, whom both Mike and I had met at some time in the past. He welcomed us with an unexpected hug instead of the usual handshake, which caused me a little embarrassment. I've never been a hugger, but it was brief and friendly, so I hugged him back. What the heck, it didn't kill me.

Everybody was already seated around the big conference table and we were introduced to the rest of the councilors. Cathy Cammarata was like an old friend, since that one visit when she had shown me how to hitch up a plow. I had been trying to think of some way to recruit her to our project. We still didn't have a replacement for Galen and we sorely missed our mechanic. Maybe during this unwelcome trip to town, we'd at least get a chance to look for someone with the right skills.

I had no trouble identifying the guests from Yuba City and Sacramento. They both looked tired but bright-eyed and alert, taking in everything around them like tourists. The young woman, Octavia, was lovely with her long dark hair and deep brown eyes. She was in a wheelchair and I wondered how she'd been able to negotiate the bad roads. But, of course, R17 said there was a group; she must have had help. The man, Greg Galloway, deputy mayor of Yuba City, I guessed in his mid-thirties, was tall and frankly scrawny compared to our well-fed townsfolk. He appeared composed and intelligent. I looked forward to talking to both of them later and finding out about their different ways of coping. Recently, I'd been taking an interest in lifestyle choices.

Morgan opened the meeting.

"I'm sure we have all been made aware of the situation in both Yuba City and Sacramento, as well as the purpose of this emergency meeting. Omega 1500 is also present via an open voice channel and will participate in our discussion. Now that we are all here, I'll begin by asking its views."

"City Council of Oroville, you have been apprised of the shortage of parts and materials that jeopardizes the continued efficient operation of this city. It was not my designer's intention that each municipality be self-sufficient, thus Oroville lacks the necessary facilities. It became my top priority to obtain the required items from an outside source and if possible, re-establish my network. Without satellite connection, I have been unable to reach the other municipalities. I dispatched a scouting party that succeeded in reaching Yuba City. Indirectly, they also made contact with Sacramento. For your information, the robotics factories that manufacture the components most critical to our own functioning are located in Sacramento.

It has come to my attention that the leaders of Sacramento are pursuing a counterproductive management style that keeps the citizens in a state of permanent deprivation while wasting resources on excessive personal over-consumption. Such a leadership puts critical facilities of the entire network at risk, as well as being counter to the Omega Directive regarding the safety and welfare of human populations. It cannot be allowed to continue.

It has therefore become necessary to intervene, to maximize the benefit of existing resources. Research of precedent indicates that irrational human rulers do not relinquish control voluntarily and invariably respond with violence to any attempt at removing them from control. The citizenry has already initiated an organized resistance, not unlike Oroville's recent insurgency, and its members are already under threat from the ruling elite.

I cannot employ violence: it is countermanded by protocol. Waste of both human and material resources is likewise countermanded by protocol. However, aiding the human population of another city in the network falls within my operating parameters. The optimal strategy is the use of subterfuge and infiltration.

The key to a successful revolution lies with Omega 1420, the quantum computer in the service of Sacramento. It is imperative to re-establish communication with that computer and to repair whatever damage has been done to subvert its protocols. A correctly functioning Omega can exercise its control of the food and energy resources to disempower irrational leaders.

To advise us on the best method of accomplishing the necessary repairs, I have requested Citizens Sutherland and Dubois to join us. They were the last two software engineers to work on the installation and programming of Omega 1420 and thus have the most relevant information. Citizen Dubois,

Before I could respond to this prompt, Octavia raised her hand and asked to address the council. Morgan smiled at her and gestured encouragingly, and the room quieted down.

She spoke with a soft, hesitant voice. "Forgive me for barging into this discussion, but I'm not sure you are fully aware of the situation in Sacramento. The computer is in a sub-basement control room, as I'm sure Citizen – um, the programmers," she turned toward Mike and Trevor, "know this. But after you left, Mayor Ford had a second steel door installed, with security locks that can be opened only by himself, with a secret code. He – at least, I heard - he changes the password every day. The whole building is guarded by Ford's personal troops... heavily armed human police, not robots. The single robocop in City Hall is the one permanently assigned to the mayoral office. I just don't see how anyone can get access to that control room."

She looked around the room, an expression of defeat on her delicate face. I gave Mike an encouraging nod. I knew he'd waste no time in reassuring the councilors that he had a solution. Mike loves having the solution. His hand shot up for attention and was recognized.

"It just so happens, we *can*. Trevor and I do have another point of access. As some of you know, I'm a lazy bum and don't like to work long hours in an uncomfortable dark cement box. So, when we were there, I set up a second control terminal in the apartment Trevor and I occupied during our contract with the city. We hid it pretty well, never told anybody else; no reason it should be guarded. So, if one of those – insurgents? " He raised an eyebrow at Octavia, who whispered, 'resistance movement'. "Whatever. If someone can get into that apartment, I'll give you the password to activate that terminal and get in touch with Omega1420."

I thought that Mike explained it clearly. Once we gave Big Brain the location and password, it could instruct a local programmer on what it wanted done, and we'd be free to return to our homestead. However, BB overruled me again.

"Citizens Sutherland and Dubois, this task is too important to delegate under any circumstances. To delegate it through the unreliable medium of relayed human transmission qualifies as criminal negligence. You both need to be on location to re-establish communication between Omega1420 and myself. This vital task requires your expertise in both hardware and software engineering. You will install or reconnect a digital radio transmitter and receiver to the terminal and may need to encode communication protocols in the operating system. That is all I require of you. When effective two-way communication is established, I will diagnose the malfunction and affect repairs directly and you may return to your homestead experiment."

I was mortified by this request. BB was talking about weeks now, instead of a couple of days I was prepared to sacrifice for the common good. There was no way I could leave the rest of our group, mostly women, alone for so long. I told BB my reasons why I couldn't comply, but it seemed to have been prepared for my objection.

"Trevor, I am aware of the situation at your homestead. R17 has been relaying information daily. Clearly, your absence would be detrimental to the project without sufficient backup. I have compiled a list of volunteers, with applicable skills. I put names that are familiar from your previous social circles at the top of the list. All declared themselves eager to contribute to the success of your homestead and are on stand-by. I will now print out the names for you and Mike to consider suitable replacements. You may interview them after this meeting. Your chosen candidates can be on their way to your farm as early as tomorrow morning. I hope this arrangement will remove your qualms and allay your reluctance to volunteer for this mission on which your entire city depends."

Its last words were pure blackmail and I was flabbergasted. We never programmed BB to use human forms of argument amounting to emotional manipulation. I began to wonder if we had built better than we planned. How much has Big Brain evolved, on its own, since we installed it? Is it now a self-aware conscious life form? Seeing the expression on Mike's face, I could tell he was wondering the same thing. Philosophical speculation would have to wait for another time. Right now, we had decisions to make.

The terminal in the corner silently expelled a flimsy sheet of recycled paper into Mike's hand. It was about a dozen names, each followed by their skill set and an indication of whether they would want to join us permanently. I knew some of them well and was touched by their willingness to give up their comfort to join our experiment. I was particularly pleased to see Cathy's name on this list, marked as 'temporary'. The list included a mechanic, a metallurgist, and a carpenter. We'd discuss it in private and talk to the people, but this seemed a fair price for our cooperation. Besides, it's hard to say no to a whole town that depends on you, as BB had correctly anticipated. Before I could reply, Octavia spoke up again.

"I have to warn you, this... this mission - if you decide to undertake it - is not without danger. Ford and his goons are ruthless. They won't hesitate to arrest you without cause if they recognize you. I gather you both spent months in Sacramento. There must be people who know you by sight, and maybe not all on our side. Ford has many informants. Chances are, he's posted lookouts on the main roads since we left – they'd be watching for Jonathan, Rafiq and Stephen especially – our leaders, you know. We got word Ford was planning to arrest Jonathan, that's why we left without delay. I'm worried sick about him – all of them - now he's going back. Nobody's safe."

This was a new piece of the puzzle we needed to consider. I wondered aloud if we should be disguised. Neither Mike nor I had any idea how.

"I can help you with that," Greg Galloway, our visitor from Yuba City, volunteered. "My wife was a costume and makeup designer at the theater... before. I'm sure she can change your appearance. She'll be thrilled with the chance."

"Thank you, Citizen Galloway. That was a very useful suggestion." Big Brain sounded more human by the minute. "Before finalizing details, however, I need to hear from Trevor and Mike that they are willing to perform this task. They are pivotal to the operation."

More arm twisting, and I couldn't think of another excuse, so reluctantly I nodded. "Willing is a stretch, but I have no choice. I agree. Mike, do you want to say anything?"

Mike shrugged, sighed and shook his head. "I agree."

"Jennifer and Martha won't be thrilled with this change of plans," I said to the overhead cam. "We need to talk to them before we leave. Okay? I know you can connect us through R17, to warn them in advance. I wouldn't like to spring this on them on a flying visit when we drop off our replacements. The ladies need time to cool down before we dare to venture into their vicinity."

Big Brain responded amiably. "It can be arranged. I am currently in contact with R17. Your ladies will be alerted to your call after the evening meal when your household is normally assembled. The most efficient use of your time would be interviewing volunteers and choosing your replacements, followed by a long restful night, to be ready for an early departure. A mobile unit will arrive at Trevor's residence at 0600 and Mike's at 0645, with the toolkit you will need for Omega1420, and will then convey you to the assembly point. I am available for any further questions from any terminal throughout the day."

This was dismissal and Mike and I left the council. This was going to be a very long day. Tomorrow would be even longer.

23

Mouch had replaced the portrait and set out his own accessories out on the mayor's antique desk. Ford's brick-a-brack was swept into a laminate carton and he was just about to call his deputy to take it away when the deputy entered, unsummoned.

"Mayor, sir, I have news. The troublemaker you were so anxious to arrest, Jonathan Carver, has just returned and is on his way home. Do you want to have him picked up?"

"Is he alone?" Mouch couldn't believe his luck. At last, some progress!

"Yes, he is, no sign of the others. Something may have happened to them. They may have been afraid to come back - didn't want to get into trouble. Could be they fell behind. We've still got sentries watching. What are your orders?"

"Have him picked up immediately and bring him here. I just want to chat with him. No rough stuff!"

He would start easy, find out about conditions beyond the periphery, let the guy explain why they had left just when they did – there could have been a leak in Ford's organization. Hell, there must have been dozens! Organization! Mouch would have to replace all those inside people as quickly as their jobs could be filled. And *why* he returned. That, and what happened to his companions were the most important questions.

When the two hulking guards conducted Jonathan into the mayor's office, Mouch was kindness itself. He offered the tired man a comfortable seat and a cold drink. Jonathan, having decided to play along and see where this interview was going, accepted both. However, he was confused about one thing: they were in Larry Ford's 'throne room' – he knew it well enough from the times he'd submitted the petitions of his fellow citizens – yet there was no Ford.

"Mr. Mouch, may I ask where Mayor Ford is? I understood he wanted to see me."

"*Mister* Ford is not the mayor anymore," Mouch couldn't resist the emphasis. "He resigned – for, um, health reasons - and now I am the mayor. I hope you don't mind?"

"Not at all, Mayor Mouch. But I *would* like to know what I'm doing here."

"Obviously, I have been informed of your little trip outside city limits and I'm eager to learn one or two things. Natural curiosity, you understand. For example, the conditions northward of the city, the purpose of your trip, whether you achieved that purpose, and the reason you returned alone, etc."

Jonathan was prepared for something like this and had a ready answer. "We went foraging for food. The way y – I mean, Mayor Ford - had been cutting back our rations, we had hardly enough to live on and some of us thought that this expedition might augment our meager supply. Also, like yourself, we were curious as to the conditions outside, if anyone still lived there, etc."

Mouch considered this reply. "As you appear to have gained no weight, I assume that the trip was not a success. But why alone? What happened to your companions?"

Jonathan had a prepared answer for that as well. "We had a disagreement. You might even call it an argument. The others wanted to continue foraging farther and farther. I thought it was hopeless. Based on what we saw in the first two days, I was sure it was a waste of time and energy. They went on and I turned back." He shrugged, looked Mouch in the eye, and added. "Better the devil you know, etc."

"Hmm, this sounds believable. So, we can expect your friends in a few days, carrying full sacks of food?"

"I doubt it. Eventually, they'll have to crawl back just as empty-handed and even more tired than I am."

Mouch realized that this line of questioning had reached a dead end. He changed the subject. "The other thing I wanted to talk to you about regards your subversive activities in the past months. This was very disruptive to the city's smooth operation and I want it stopped."

"Mayor Mouch, what you call 'subversive' was our inalienable right, under the constitution, to protest the policies your predecessor had implemented. Now that you have taken his place, I'm sure that it will no longer be necessary."

Mouch wasn't fooled for a second but nodded. "Well, that remains to be seen and largely depends on your cooperation. I want to have a conference with your associates in this 'protest' movement. If you will kindly provide their names and addresses, we will contact them and arrange a meeting."

Jonathan wasn't fooled either. "I'd have to ask their permission for that. Explain that you intend to change the policies of Mr. Ford and wish to consult them. If you don't mind, I'm very tired after my long walk and would like to go home to soak my feet. Tomorrow I'll talk to my friends and call you to organize that conference."

He stood up and put out his hand in a gesture of amicable departure. Mouch feigned disappointment.

"Sorry, Carver, I can't let you go until I have that list. I don't want to risk you disappearing and continuing your protests. You will stay here, as my guest, until you decide to cooperate."

"Do you mean I'm under arrest?"

"No such thing at the moment, I only want to have the chance to discuss this further with you."

Mouch pressed the buzzer on his desk and his deputy entered at once.

"Please, John, escort Mr. Carver to the room we designated earlier and make him comfortable."

He stood up and suddenly the amicable pretense disappeared. "Don't push your luck too far, Carver. My patience has limits."

Jonathan, with a guard on either side, was marched out of the room behind the deputy. Mouch leaned back in his chair, considering his next move.

~

The resistance members watched from a safe distance as Ford's goons stopped Jonathan as he entered the city. It seemed a civilized arrest, no beating, but all five human cops had their weapons drawn. There was nothing they could do to help so, according to the plan they had agreed upon, they split up, detoured to other crossings and entered the city, one by one, each by a different route.

Rafiq Shlimon had the communicator, so their link to Yuba City was secure, but he had to wait for the next prearranged time to report. He was in no hurry, in any case, to have this news relayed to Octavia. For now, he must make his way unobserved to a hiding place they had never used before. His home was no longer safe; nor were the homes of his known associates.

Rafiq loved Jonathan like a brother; they had been best friends since elementary school. He would do anything necessary to free him and for that, he needed a clear head. This was the time for discipline and patience. Once at the safe house, he would call an emergency meeting of the other leaders. Communication links were still functioning reliably enough, and the movement had its own code to convey secret information in what would sound to an eavesdropper — all of their comms were monitored, of course - like a normal conversation.

The streets of the migrant quarter were dark and empty, due to another blackout. For once it worked in his favor; Rafiq knew every inch of this neighborhood. He reached the tenement without incident and disappeared inside.

He was very tired after the long walk. The food they'd been given for the road was gone and it would be foolish to risk going out for a meal. Luckily, someone had stocked the kitchen with non-perishable staples, so he could make himself a modest meal and a much-needed hot cup of tea. He stretched out on the sofa to think over their situation.

The news he'd learned about Yuba City and Oroville gave him hope for the future, but there was no telling how distant that future might be. It would be no easy feat to convince the resistance to stay underground until help arrived; he couldn't guarantee that help, nor even tell them what form it would take. He only knew there was no point in acting until they considered all their options. He put his communication device on the coffee table, intending to call Yuba City at 11:00. Meanwhile, he would formulate a plan to rescue Jonathan.

He had already stolen into Ford's dungeon, fought a pair of armed guards, and was just breaking down Jonathan's cell door when he was awakened by the call-up signal. A quick look at the wall clock informed him that he had missed the last of the daily contact times by six minutes.

He quickly acknowledged the call and turned up the volume so he wouldn't miss anything. The distance to Yuba City must have been near the limit of the device's range: the signal was weak, but the voice was still recognizable.

"This is Kathleen Winters, calling for Jonathan Carver, please respond."

He identified himself and related the bad news of Jonathan's capture. "Kathleen, this is Rafiq Shlimon, we met in your city two days ago. Jonathan was arrested by our local police as he entered the city. He anticipated that and arranged for the rest of us to avoid capture. I'm in a safe house, trying to think of a way to liberate him. Please pass this information on to Octavia and tell her to consult the Orovillians about the possibility of any help they may be able to provide. In the meantime, we won't do anything rash to put him in more danger."

There was static for a long minute; presumably, Kathleen was thinking over the problem and considering options. Not that she had many. Rafiq didn't expect any help from Yuba City; they barely managed their day-to-day struggle for survival. Oroville was reported to be in good shape, with its unlimited power generation capacity and well-regulated production machinery. But, really, what could they do from so far away – and not even familiar with the circumstances? The only glimmer of hope

262

might be in that super-intelligent computer: that might be able to come up with a plan.

Finally, Kathleen responded to his message. "Rafiq, it seems about the only thing we can do is pass the news on to Oroville. I heard from Octavia a few minutes ago. They made it home in good time. Her foot was treated and she's spending the night with Cathy Cammarata. It's not too late to call her back, but I'd better hurry. I'll do that immediately. I'll contact you again at 8:00 in the morning. Kathleen Winters, signing off."

She hadn't tried any false assurances or made any impossible promises. She was a sensible woman who would do what she sensibly could. And Rafiq would just have to practice discipline and patience. His sore feet needed a good soaking if only the water was still warm enough.

Before falling asleep again, he wondered if maybe he should have asked Kathleen to keep the news from Octavia. She would be worried sick about Jonathan and frustrated that she couldn't rush home. But then, he also knew that she was a level-headed young woman who could realistically assess the situation. Besides, she was in a perfect position to plead with her hosts to offer whatever help they possibly could.

~

Jonathan, on the other hand, was unable to sleep that night. The 'comfortable' room was a cement-lined cell in the basement, with no furniture except a wooden chair, standing in the middle of the floor. The room was illuminated with overhead lights so bright that the reflection from the whitewashed walls hurt his eyes wherever he looked. In addition, he was subjected to painfully loud music from hidden speakers all around, inside the walls, behind metal grilles. This is where he

263

was supposed to spend the night. Apparently, this was the room they used for what came to be called 'enhanced interrogation', aimed at breaking down resistance; to make him divulge whatever information they wanted.

He knew that the only information that could hurt the movement, was the list Mouch demanded. He hoped that Rafiq and the others had been able to slip into town unobserved. It would take them some time to warn everyone. A day, maybe two, before they could all move to safer locations. He could truthfully plead ignorance of their whereabouts. The existence of Yuba City and Oroville was another secret Mouch would be very much interested in. Jonathan was determined to keep that one as long as he could, but he'd give it up before his friends. He didn't know how long he could last under these conditions. He had no illusions about the efficacy of modern brainwashing techniques: he knew he could not hold out indefinitely against the relentless assault on his mind. Sleep deprivation by itself would confuse his perception, his memory, his cognitive ability. There was no way to guess how long that would take.

He ignored the chair, curled up on the cold floor, closed his eyes, and tried to empty his mind of all thoughts. The bright lights hurt his eyes even through tight-shut lids and the deafening music hurt his eardrums. *"It's only pain, you can get used to it after a while."* He kept repeating this mantra, over and over, hoping that in time it would come true.

~

Octavia received the news of Jonathan's arrest and she spent a sleepless night, worrying, wishing she could be with him – but, of course, they wouldn't be kept together anyway - trying to imagine what their friends in Sacramento were doing about it, trying to imagine a way her new friends in Oroville could help. It was too late to call anyone, but she would ask for an emergency meeting with the computer. It might be able to formulate a better strategy than she could. And the programmers, Trevor and Mike, had to be warned.

When the first hint of a dawn light appeared in her window, she got up and hobbled to her wheelchair and rolled out to Cathy's kitchen, hoping to find some coffee in the carafe. She warmed a cup and sipped it while waiting for Cathy to awaken. She would have paced if her feet worked. She needed Cathy's help to contact the Omega computer. She considered knocking over a chair or dropping a cookbook on the floor.

Luckily, she didn't have to resort to being ungraciously noisy; Cathy's children did it for her. They greeted her with all the enthusiasm of puppies discovering a new playmate. Shawn, close behind, restored order and sent them off to wash and dress while he set about making breakfast. Cathy, too, was an early riser and soon they were sitting together, discussing the new information Octavia had received in the night.

Cathy had no immediate idea how two programmers could help Jonathan Carver, but she agreed to pass on the information. Big Brain was organizing the expedition; it had access to the persons involved and could quickly improvise a last-minute conference.

~

Trevor had been thinking over the plan they sketched out the previous day and realized that they couldn't count on getting into their old Sacramento residence. It sure wouldn't be vacant; the building might have been converted to offices; Mike's remote terminal might not still function. It was a risky plan at best. They should have a backup plan, anyway.

When he received the summons to a pre-departure meeting, it was as if Big Brain read his mind. By the time everyone arrived at the assembly point, he was all ready to share his new idea. But he had to wait until BB informed them of the new development.

"Okay, that complicates things. But," he continued stubbornly, "that's all the more reason to try it my way. Suppose I *don't* disguise myself, but walk into the city alone, while Mike proceeds straight to the residence Octavia recommended. Once in the city, I try to contact the techies we used to know like I was looking for a job. Ford will hear about me. I figure by now he has all kinds of problems with the computer because it's not likely to execute his kind of instructions without a protocol conflict. He must have tampered with the programming and that's going to show up in glitches and crashes and bugs all over the place. I bet he'd jump at the opportunity to have someone with real expertise clean up that mess. Here I am, homeless and hard up, ready to do whatever he asks, for a price. It's the easiest way to get access to the control room. Mike working from the outside, me from the inside would double our chances of getting the job done. Also," he added, glancing at Octavia, "someone on the inside could be a great help in rescuing your Jonathan."

Octavia was deeply touched by Trevor's offer, but felt a duty to warn him.

"Trevor, are you aware of the danger to yourself if you follow this plan? Ford and his clique are quite ruthless. If they guess your true purpose, they'll do more than forcing you to work. They wouldn't hesitate to hurt you. They might even kill you."

Forestalling Trevor, BB responded to Octavia's concern.

"Based on available data, analysis of the situation indicates a 79% probability of Trevor's plan succeeding, in regard to the modification of Omega 1420. As he himself

266

points out, it doubles the chance of the mission's success. Regarding Citizen Jonathan Carver, there is insufficient data for analysis. Regarding the personal safety of Citizen Dubois, the best-qualified judge is Citizen Dubois himself. In summary, I fully approve of the dual approach."

Mike was less confident of Trevor's plan, but he definitely saw the advantage to having an inside man and an outside one. Being Trevor's best friend, greatest admirer, and severest critic, however, he was worried about the danger.

He offered a modified version. "What if we trade places? Trevor, you go to the residence in disguise, and I sign on as the mayor's little helper? I'm bigger and stronger than you; I can take care of myself better in tough situations. Might have to bang some heads together, you know, goons and guards? Trust me, you're not up to it. Yet. Dig a couple more charcoal pits, then, maybe."

Trevor's objection was overruled by the Big Bossy Brain.

"Trevor, Mike made a very good point and I think you should accept his offer. Personal feelings are irrelevant in operations such as this one. You are obligated to do whatever maximizes the probability of success."

Trevor couldn't help but see the merit in this argument, and despite himself, he was somewhat relieved not to have to put his neck in the noose. Now he had to worry about his friend's safety instead of his own, which didn't feel any better.

"OK, I'll go along with that, but I suggest we both go into town disguised, look around, talk to people, find out what the situation is before we take any risks. Once we know all the relevant circumstances, we can make our move accordingly."

There was general agreement. The meeting was over. Octavia was heading back to Cathy's house, Cathy helping to steer the wheelchair. Mike and Trevor were given their kits and conveyed to the place of departure, where the selected volunteers had been cooling their heels for half an hour. The robot that accompanied them carried their luggage in respectful silence, transmitting continuously to Big Brain.

24

Jonathan lost all sense of time. He no longer knew whether he spent hours, days, or weeks in that cement box. The relentless assault on his eyes and ears made his head throb with a pain he had never experienced before. He had vague memories of visitors to his cell, demanding answers to questions he couldn't understand anymore, threatening him with real pain if he did not cooperate. He mumbled things incoherently, not sure what he was telling them, not even caring; he just wanted to be left alone. In fitful sleep, if you could call it that, he had hellish nightmares about the war, the world exploding around him, over his head, tearing his life to shreds. The dead on the streets, piled up by the curb, were removed every few days to some mass grave outside the city. The devastating storms that tore the roofs off houses, tossed people and vehicles into the air like little toys, and dropped them back on the ground in crumpled heaps. When he woke from these nightmares, he found himself still curled up on the cold cement floor, not quite remembering how he got there. The light and the noise never stopped, the waking nightmare never ended. He only hoped that he would die soon, sinking into a blessed dark and quiet oblivion.

Then, suddenly, the deafening noise stopped, the blinding light was replaced by normal illumination. He sat up on the floor, dully wondering what happened, what would happen next. His cell door opened and someone came in. He tried to focus his aching eyes on the intruder. After a while he recognized Mouch, whom he remembered from a long time ago, asking him questions. Mouch towered above him, looking down at his victim with distaste. Jonathan was dirty, unshaven, his clothes soiled, his eyes unfocused, staring back in bewilderment. He looked ready for a serious interrogation.

"Jonathan, I suggest you get up from the floor. Make yourself presentable. You stink and I can't have a civilized conversation with you in this condition."

He somehow clambered to an upright position, unsteady on his feet, staring at his torturer with apprehension. Mouch pointed to the open door and walked through it, Jonathan followed, feeling dizzy from the unaccustomed motion, his head still throbbing with pain, the guard close behind but not helping. The adjacent bathroom had a toilet and a shower. Fresh clothes were laid out on a chair and an electric razor on the vanity.

Jonathan did as he was told. The shower felt good and he enjoyed the sensation of clean clothes on his body, but he ignored the razor. If he was going to be a prisoner, he might as well grow a beard. Frankly, he didn't care one way or another, he was too tired even to think.

Mouch was all smiles when Jonathan was led into his office. He pointed to the chair on the other side of his desk and Jonathan sat on it, grateful to have the weight off his legs. His feet hurt in the new shoes, a size too small. "Well, Jonathan, I hope you are in a more cooperative mood than last time we spoke. During your stay in our guest room, you mumbled something about cities. I'd like to hear more about that. You were incoherent at the time and I'm not sure what you meant by things like *you'll get yours when help arrives.* What help? From where? I need to know. If you tell me everything, I promise I'll let you go, otherwise it's back to the cell."

Jonathan was beginning to understand what Mouch wanted from him. He didn't remember saying anything about the other cities, but he must have. Otherwise, where would Mouch have gotten the idea? He wondered how much it would hurt their cause to tell Mouch about his trip. He knew he had to give the bastard something; he could not go back to that cell. He decided to tell about Yuba City only, living on the verge of starvation. What could Mouch do with that information? Mouch waited patiently for him to think it over, trusting that the last two days of sleep deprivation softened him up enough. Jonathan appeared a broken man, without any resistance left in him. He looked at Mouch with pleading eyes. "If I tell you everything, will you promise to let me go?"

"I said I would. Do not question my word, young man. You are in no position to insult me. Go ahead, start at the beginning."

Jonathan related how they walked northward, described the condition of the road that they followed, the destroyed bridge over Bear River, and, finally, their arrival in Yuba City. He emphasized the conditions of near-famine they had found there and how the Mayor dashed all his hopes of helping his group with their cause.

"But at least they took my friends in to stay," he lied, adding bitterly, "Friends! Comrades! They'd rather scratch for turnips in Yuba than come home to help liberate the city."

Mouch followed his tale with interest, nodding a few times as if he found the information convincing. When Jonathan was finished, he smiled reassuringly and congratulated him on his cooperation. "I have one more question. We tried to get in touch with your colleagues who stayed in town and none of them could be found at their homes, or at any of their known meeting places. Obviously, they went to ground when you were apprehended. I need you to tell me all the places where they may be hiding. I'm very anxious to talk to them and bring this destructive movement to an end."

Jonathan was very much relieved to learn that Mouch was unable to arrest anyone else. Obviously, Rafiq did a good job dispersing the leadership to safe places. As they each kept their emergency hideouts secret, even from one another, he couldn't divulge their location under any amount of harsh interrogation. He felt reasonably safe to tell Mouch a few addresses that might still be unknown to his spies. Pretending to be broken, without any will to resist, he blurted out three addresses that had fallen into disuse when Ford's minions got too close. Mouch seemed to be satisfied with his answer and stood up behind his desk.

"I will release you, Jonathan, but not immediately. You'll be escorted to a comfortable room – no, no, I mean nicer. I'll give you an opportunity to think hard, just in case you remember any other names, places, locations, and other information that could help me put an end to this unnecessary resistance." He pressed the buzzer on his desk and the deputy entered.

"Please, John, escort Jonathan to a somewhat more comfortable room where he can reflect on the advantages of cooperation."

Jonathan was led out of the mayoral office, to his immense relief, away from the elevator, down the corridor of the administrative wing. He never had any illusion that Mouch would keep his promise but, hopefully, the torture was over, at least for the time being. In the meanwhile, he knew that Rafiq and Steve would move heaven and earth to organize some rescue, and who knew? there might even be help from Oroville.

After Jonathan was led out of his office, Mouch gave the names and locations he had received to his deputy and instructed him to have the police search these premises and report back to him immediately. He leaned back in his chair, reflecting on the new information; the destroyed bridge and the situation in Yuba City. There might be something to gain by sending an expedition to see how he could turn this new option to his advantage. He knew that sooner or later he would need resources from outside the city. Maybe they had something he could use, in trade for food products. Maybe he could even venture farther North, and see if Oroville was still on the map. If their hydroelectric generators were still functioning, the extra power could be a boon to his enterprise.

If he played his cards right, in time he could be the uncontested ruler of the entire Sacramento Valley. It was time to look beyond city limits and take bolder action. Who knows, two years after the war, people must be stirring everywhere. This was the moment when great opportunities awaited the courageous leader who was not afraid to do what was necessary to pull what was left of the United States of America together again.

~

Omega 1500 was not sitting idle, waiting for word about Trevor and Mike's expedition. While following the different projects underway in the city with interest, it also knew that the initial excitement over these efforts was starting to wear off and the citizens would soon be restless again. They would need opportunities to participate in something productive on a larger scale. Gordon Mair's school building project and Morgan Webster's tree planting efforts could only keep so many hands busy; the rest of the townsfolk were still unemployed, mere spectators at these activities. Big Brain needed to announce something new very shortly. Tim Hooke reported successful deployment of the recharging stations on the stretch of IS-70 between Oroville and Yuba City. That meant that heavy equipment could start moving south, followed by thousands of volunteers to clear the roads, collect recyclable material and restore the downed power lines. There were no all-terrain vehicles of mass transportation. A later project might be the rebuilding of a fast transport tube; the first priority was freight capability.

When the crews began work, they would require shaded rest areas, water, and food dispensing stations, hygiene facilities, and two temporary overnight shelters for workers, so that none had to walk far to their work site. This support infrastructure could employ hundreds more, providing more opportunities for participation. This project, by itself, would not constitute full employment, but it would be a significant step. Once underway, further steps could follow, as resources allowed. BB decided to call another council meeting to announce the project and get it started. It activated its comm link to the Webster residence and left a message for Morgan to contact it as his earliest convenience.

~

Unaware of Big Brain's intentions, Morgan was busy. In the morning he and Holly inspected the nearly finished church-basement school. Gordon and his crew had been working on it non-stop for almost two weeks. The roof skeleton was already in place, a row of huge letter A's standing over the entire basement. The crew was in the process of attaching large panels of translucent shatter-proof plastic to its slopes. These had been retrieved from commercial buildings in the long-abandoned industrial district. Inside, another crew was laying tiles of thick rubber on the cement floor and installing doors in the dividing walls; a third had just finished painting those walls. The place was looking really good.

The time had come to retrieve unbroken furniture and fixtures from the ruined primary school, and bring them to the new site. They had plenty of volunteers for the job and Morgan was pleased to see the happy faces of enthusiastic people, rushing off on their quest. He checked them for boots, hard hats, and work gloves, warned them not to take any chances with unstable rubble, and barred the younger children from this task. He wished that Cathy were here to supervise some of these activities, but she was still attached to Chief Hooke's road project.

Having seen Trevor and Mike off, Greg Galloway joined the work road rebuilding crew. The sooner that task was done, the sooner Oroville could provide power to Yuba City, so the food factories could be run at full capacity and the chronic food shortage could end in his town. His departure left Octavia even more alone, with nothing to do. By profession she was a kindergarten teacher and here were two bright, lively children of 4 and 5, with too much unstructured time on their hands, driving their father to distraction. Helping to keep them occupied was something she could do sitting down. All the talk about a new school had gotten them excited, but they were too young to attend and felt left out. That gave Octavia an idea. There must be other disappointed pre-schoolers. Why not start a local kindergarten?

Octavia discussed it with Shawn, who contacted Gordon and Holly, and together they devised a plan. They could hold half-day classes right in the building. The lobby was big enough to accommodate a dozen children. They didn't even need furniture; the carpet was clean and students could bring their own cushions to sit on. They sent a comm notification to families in the neighborhood with children aged four to six years and were soon overwhelmed by requests. Some parents had to wait for the next group. Holly made it her mission to find early childhood educators and suitable premises.

~

Chris Teggart was busy working on his "Critical Thinking" curriculum and enjoying every minute of it. He decided to teach the basic rules of logic through practical examples, using old news items from his database. Each item demonstrated how a politician, businessman, or economist of the past had misled the citizens to draw incorrect conclusions that served his or her own selfish interests at the expense of theirs. This way he would bring the dry topic of Aristotelian logic to life and demonstrate the practical dangers of faulty logic. The students might even have a good laugh at the often ridiculous mental contortions and acrobatics these fraudsters performed. He wanted to set up a focus group of youngsters representing his intended audience to try out this technique. He left Morgan a message, requesting his opinion. Morgan, when he finally got home, was enthusiastic about a trial group.

"Actually," he said, "that same idea could apply to all the other subjects we're preparing for the new school. We could use some feedback from the objects of all our efforts."

Since the new church-basement school was almost finished, they thought that as soon as the roof structure was covered and enough pieces of furniture inside, they could set up four classrooms for trial groups in Math, Science, Logic, and Gardening. These subjects were the core curriculum that they had agreed on as the minimum requirement to the raising of rational, competent adults. Basic literacy and personal hygiene were prerequisites of enrolment.

Gardening had been a late addition, recommended by Holly's friend Tracy. She regarded it as essential for kids to know and love nature and not consider it as something to exploit. Plants and bugs are also a good first approach to scientific study. She volunteered to teach a gardening class in her own house if she could get Gordon to repair the roof of her house. She had been living part-time in her garage and was ready for an improvement. She also needed help in removing some of the obstacles between her house and the center of Oroville, for easier and safer access.

Gordon thought that he could use the tractor and backhoe to affect these improvements, as soon as they were liberated from the school project. They could maybe even institute some kind of direct shuttle service between the two points. Later, he told himself; one step at a time.

Life in Oroville was humming; the newly announced projects got many enthusiastic volunteers and even those who did not opt to participate watched the daily updates on their holo vision entertainment center with keen interest. Big Brain decided not to inform the citizens about the looming confrontation with Sacramento. It would have been a damper on the citizens' newfound spirit of construction, self-improvement, and cooperation. Until news about Mike's and Trevor's mission arrived, BB saw no purpose in alarming them. It needed a solid plan of action before involving people in disturbing speculation.

25

Mike and I were back in our van, driving south again, this time with three companions sharing the back seat, our replacement homesteaders while we played cloak and dagger games with Sacramento's despots.

Douglas Taylor, a metallurgist, and toolmaker by profession was a young man in his late twenties, handsome, energetic, and enthusiastic. He was single, no family to worry about and no girlfriend; he was free and clear, as he put it. He had wanted to join our group since he first heard of it and now, that he had the opportunity, he was beyond joy. He was sure we wouldn't regret selecting him: he would work hard and knew dozens of ways to make our lives more comfortable. I'd get R17 to keep a fisheye on him around our women.

Mark Rysak was a middle-aged agronomist, specialized as a "crop doctor". We needed someone like him to assure the health of our growing plants. We thought that Adrien, an amateur gardener, could use all the help a professional expert could give her. We were sure that she wouldn't feel displaced by our new recruit. Mark said that he had not been a hands-on laborer and, his strength was problem-solving and maximizing yields, but he was prepared to work at whatever was required.

Alan Walker was a carpenter, with decades-long experience in cabinetry, from the time when we still had jobs. He was in his early forties, tall, with thinning hair and slightly bent posture. I selected him to augment my amateurish skills in making furniture for our group in that under-furnished house.

We still didn't have a mechanic, but Cathy promised to look in on her way home from the road construction sites if the group needed help in our absence.

Thinking of that impending adventure, I started to feel apprehensive again. I had never been in physical danger before, apart from the impersonal threat of the war and the storms that don't single you out. This time Mike and I would be the only two with our necks in the noose and it felt a lot more menacing. My gut instinct was to find some excuse why we couldn't go but, at the same time, I knew that we would do our best to accomplish our task. I had never known the responsibility of a whole town depending on me. Somehow I wasn't my own person anymore but a part of something much bigger than myself.

Coming out of the reverie, I noticed how unusually quiet everyone was. I guess we all had a lot to think about.

The road was familiar, we passed the remaining obstacles without even slowing down and soon arrived at the turnoff point to the river. We rolled right across: the water was lower and Mike knew by now how to avoid the big hole in the middle. Driving past Scott's place, we saw him outside, trying to prune a fruit tree with his crutch under one arm. Mike stopped the van and asked if he needed help, but he only grunted and waved us on.

In a few minutes, we were home and found all our friends waiting outside. R17 must have told them what time to expect us. They were anxious to hear our news and meet the new recruits. The night before I'd had a long talk with Martha. By the look on her face, she was both happy to see me and worried about our upcoming adventure.

After the introductions were over, we caught up on events in town and on the farm. Apparently, the women managed very well without us. Robyn, with help from Jennifer's kids, had finished stuffing all the mattresses and made two more bunks from the barn-boards we salvaged. Everyone had a bed now, except the three new recruits. They would make their own beds and Robyn would sew three new mattresses.

The big news was Brian's: while we were gone, he'd hooked up the solar panels to the well-pump and now we had a functional toilet, as well as running water in the kitchen. Inspecting the new bathroom, I found it sparkling clean, with fresh towels on the rack, a scoured bathtub, and even curtains on the window. Remembering its previous condition, I figured this must have taken most of a day. When I asked who did this heroic cleaning job, Martha smiled mysteriously and playfully poked me in the ribs.

"Did you think I'm only good for sex and painting? I've told you, I'm no violet shrinking away from getting my hands dirty. Besides, I hated that outhouse so much that I couldn't wait a minute longer. I don't suppose you could find a can of paint on your travels? I mean, wall-paint."

While admiring this work, I was a little sad that she had abandoned the painting she'd started before we left. However, my sadness didn't last long. Crossing the living room on my way to the kitchen for lunch, I saw it hanging over the fireplace. It was beautiful, depicting the farmyard, the house, and the barn in the background, Kevin chasing Jimmy in the foreground, and Trish laughing at them with the happy face only a child, hugging a cat, can possess. Martha captured the essence of everything this homestead meant to me and it was almost inevitable that above her signature she painted a dedication "for Trevor". She joined me, standing in front of the painting and neither of us needed to say anything. This was a perfect moment.

The mood was interrupted by Jennifer calling us to the table. Luckily we had enough chairs, some far better quality than others: when Mike and Brian went back to the abandoned house for solar panels, they found a little extra room in the truck. We would get the large dining room pieces later on.

We tried to tell our new recruits everything they needed to know before we had to leave. Mike and I had to get to Yuba City tonight, we hoped not too late in the evening. We could not afford to waste time, with Jonathan Carver's fate unknown and likely bad. The sooner we connected with the resistance, the sooner we could find a way to help. Mayor Winters had been notified to expect us, Greg Galloway had discussed the plan with her and was keeping in touch.

Preparing for departure, we walked with our new friends across the yard; I wanted a quick look at my charcoal pit before I left. Wisps of smoke were trailing out through the cracks and it was still hot; the process was progressing and we should have a sufficient quantity of charcoal in a few days. Too bad I wouldn't be here to uncover it!

Mark was particularly interested in Adrien's cloche that covered four rows of evenly spaced seedlings. He approved of what he saw and made a few suggestions on how the ventilation could be improved. The plants were at a stage where they needed constant care.

We passed the tractor with the wood gasifier and Doug inspected it with keen interest. "I've heard about this contraption before," he announced, "but I have never seen one close up. Are you sure it will work?"

I assured him that we had already tried it with seasoned wood and it worked fine. I pointed at the plow still hitched up and the four uneven furrows where I had put it to use. Mark didn't comment on my plowing but picked up a handful of dirt, then slowly let it trickle between his fingers.

"It feels rich enough on cursory inspection. I'll do a detailed analysis once I unpack my test instruments and see what needs to be added. The fact that it's been left fallow for a couple of years helps the quality."

When the procession finally reached the van, Martha hugged me with unusual intensity and whispered in my ear: "Please no heroics, I want you back in one piece."

Mike and Jennifer said their goodbyes in a similar fashion, and we were on our way.

~

For a long time neither of us spoke, we were immersed in our thoughts. I was musing on the strange transformation in my own character. I always used to be an outsider, never part of any group, always self-sufficient by myself and a few close friends. Now, for the first time in my life, I not only had a clan of sorts to lead but was suddenly called upon to act in the interest of a whole city. The responsibilities weighed heavily on my mind. At this moment I wasn't sure what worried me most: any personal danger I might be getting into, abandoning the homestead at this critical stage, or the possibility of failing in our mission.

After a while, I firmly put these unproductive thoughts aside to concentrate on the practicalities. The next step was to get to Yuba City without driving into a crevasse. Mike suddenly jerked the wheel sharply to the left to avoid doing exactly that, sheepishly admitting that he had other things on his mind and hadn't been paying enough attention.

For the rest of the trip, he kept his eyes on the road and made no more mistakes. We had been informed by Cathy and Tim about the obstacles and off-the-road detours; they'd even made a rough map, so nothing really surprised us. We made good time and we crossed over from Marysville just as the night was falling. We had become used to real darkness in the country, but after Oroville, the lack of streetlight was strange. Still, the government building was easy to find and there were some lights in its windows.

We met the security guard in the lobby and he led us, with his flashlight, to Kathleen Winters' office. Her welcome was as genuine, and her manner as casual, as Cathy and Octavia had led us to expect. She came around her desk and shook our hands warmly.

"Please take a seat on the sofa, I'm sure you are very tired after your long drive all the way from Oroville. Let me know if you'd like to eat before we get down to serious business. I can have some food and drink brought here or you can walk over to the communal kitchen with me."

Out of curiosity as much as good manners, we elected to go to their kitchen. Nearing the end of suppertime, the dining area was still fairly busy, but there were some free tables. Mayor Winters told us to find one while she lined up at the cafeteria-style counter for our meals. Of course, we couldn't have that and lined up behind her, each with our own tray. Service was every bit as efficient as the robot-staffed eateries back home. We noticed curious glances from some of the other guests but Kathleen waved them off and no one came over to pester us with questions. Afterward, we went back to Kathleen's office and sat down with some watery fruit drinks.

She began the discussion with an unexpected and unwelcome piece of news. Early in the day, she had received a radio message from Rafiq Shlimon in Sacramento, informing her of a change of regime. Apparently, Larry Ford had been replaced by his deputy mayor, a ruthless and power-hungry man named Mouch. He would use any means whatever to seize total control over the resources of his city and all aspects of the citizens' lives. This circumstance greatly increased the danger inherent in our plans. We had been counting on Mayor Ford's hedonistic, disorganized ways; now we had to deal with an intelligent, determined, and brutal dictator.

"I understand one of you means to infiltrate the command center and attempt to sabotage the Omega computer," Kathleen laid out the situation. "I have to advise extreme caution. From what my contact says this man is cunning and doesn't trust anyone."

Mike didn't seem as concerned as I was; said he'd seen tough guys before and knew how to deal with them. I was more determined than ever to wait with any open approach until we were sure that it was absolutely necessary.

To change the subject to something more pleasant, I asked Kathleen about Greg's wife, the makeup artist whose services we would need before leaving next day. We had to start as early as possible since we'd have to abandon the van at Bear River and continue on foot. Octavia had told us that would take two days.

For maximum efficiency, Muriel Galloway was prepared to meet us backstage at the community center at first light. There she had everything ready for making us unrecognizable.

As we prepared to retire in the VIP suite, Kathleen tapped on the door, saying we'd better get back to her office. The communicator beeped just as she pulled the handset from her top desk drawer. I realized that it was exactly 8:15 pm, one of the prearranged times for a call from Sacramento. If there had been one from Oroville at 8, we missed it while washing. There was no message for us.

"Mayor Winters' office," she said in a flat, non-committal tone totally at odds with her normal manner. After a moment I caught on: basic precaution, not giving away your caller's name, in case the radio had fallen into the wrong hands. Mike and I would have to learn to be just as careful. I listened to the identification ritual, then, "What news do you have for us? Trevor and Mike are here, ready to leave in the morning, you can expect them sometime Friday evening. They need instructions on how to find you. Better would be if someone could meet them at the intersection of I-5 and SR99."

Some silence followed, then the caller responded: "The roads are watched closely; they still don't know where the rest of the scouting party is. I think you should get off the highway as soon as possible. Do you know Sacramento?"

I nodded, but Mike said aloud so the man at the other end could hear, "Not well enough. But I have a map."

While he rummaged, Rafiq briefly recounted the other, worse, news. Jonathan Carver was subjected to 'enhanced interrogation', a euphemism for torture by sleep deprivation and other brainwashing techniques. He was forced to tell Mouch about Yuba City and might have hinted at expecting help from this direction. Might be safer to meet in a depopulated subdivision. No streetlights out there. Get off at Elkhorn, go east. Cut across the exit ramps the top of Allaire. Take cover in the ruins. We'll find you."

Mike had the printout spread on Kathleen's desk. "Okay, got it. How will we know it's one of your guys?"

There was a scratchy sound on the receiver, which I interpreted as a snort or laugh. "You'll sure know if it's not!"

Kathleen brought out a large-scale map for a better look at the terrain. Looked like open country, old farmland along both sides of the highway. Open enough to see police coming, yet the verges should be overgrown enough to hide if we had to. That Bear River crossing didn't look like fun, but the rest should be relatively easy. No turning back now, anyway; we had to follow through with the plan. Hopefully, Muriel Galloway could disguise us as two harmless, bedraggled travelers, looking for food and a place to sleep.

We thanked Kathleen for all her help and we were ready to conk out for the night. This had been a long day.

I was getting used to long days.

26

Mouch was frustrated. Programmer after programmer he had interviewed assured him that there was no way to reprogram Omega1420. Not without detailed design specifications and the source code of its operating system. None of it was available in Sacramento; the software company had a maintenance contract with the city and kept all the documentation when the job was finished. The headquarters of that company had been in San Francisco and ceased to exist when the city was destroyed during the war. He had made several new attempts to force Omega to obey his orders, with exactly the same result. The goddamn computer kept repeating the same objections.

He put that project aside for the time being and spent some time thinking about Yuba City. He wasn't sure whether Jonathan Carver's mumblings about help from the north should worry him, but they did. If the residents of that city were really facing starvation, they would be in no position to mount an offensive; on the other hand, hunger could drive people to desperate measures. There were always rumors of armed, marauding bands in the countryside. Maybe he should consolidate his position before sending an expedition north, in case of an attack. To do that effectively, he had first to crush the resistance. He had to round up their leaders and discourage the followers.

None of the addresses Carver had given him proved any good. Carver told the truth: there *had* been clandestine meetings, as evidenced by the stacks of pamphlets and subversive literature, but the places were unoccupied. He had those vacant stores and church hall watched 24 hours a day, but of course, it was futile: the conspirators would have heard of the raids and stay away now.

He had interrogated Carver several times since the man was 'rescued' from his sleep deprivation cell but gained no new information. Just like the damn computer, he kept repeating the same story, as if by rote. Mouch even sent him back to the interrogation cell a couple of times, hoping that the reminder would jog his memory and prompt him to divulge more information, but it did not yield anything useful. Even so, Mouch would keep him on ice – say, that might be an idea! – a while longer. Carver was an asset for which he could always find some use, perhaps as a bargaining chip; perhaps only as an example.

~

Immediately after he had returned to Sacramento, Rafiq contacted the other leaders of the resistance to warn them. They had prepared for this; Steve was busy moving key people and concealing their trail. Jonathan's arrest complicated things: they had to abandon the safe houses that he knew about. They had no illusion about Mouch's ruthlessness and the effectiveness of his methods. Rafiq recalled his old college dormitory, slated for demolition even before the war destroyed half of it. He had only stayed there his first year until the modern storm-proof building was ready. He contacted one of the six leaders and gave her the location. The only thing left to do was organize a network of informants, making sure nobody knew too much about the others. In the next few hours, they collected as much food and necessities as they could carry and slipped away in the night.

~

Jonathan was back in his luxury accommodation: a regular jail cell with a commode and sink, a wall-mounted cot to sleep on, and a desk-chair combination - but no paper to write on and no window. At least the caged overhead light was dimmed at what passed here for bedtime. There were no hours here, no way to measure the passage of time. Mostly, he was bored and anxious, waiting for something to happen, dreading what would happen. He had been thrown back into the torture chamber for yet another softening-up session twice so far. He thought his eardrums might be permanently damaged. He *knew* he would never sleep well again.

Twice every cycle, a young prison guard who looked more like a janitor, brought him a meal. There was no danger of putting on weight on these portions. Before the door opened, the prisoner was told to lie face-down on his bunk. The guard never spoke to him, never answered questions, just put food and water on the table and marched out again. Today, however, on his way out, he whispered two words: "read and destroy".

After he left, Jonathan quickly searched the tray. There was a tiny note under his plate. He slid it out to read while bending over his porridge. It was in Rafiq's small, precise handwriting: "Hold on. Help on the way." Jonathan wasted no time flushing it down the toilet.

That was the first glimmer of hope he had during his incarceration, he didn't know how many days. The message buoyed up his spirits and he spent hours speculating about the nature of the help. Obviously, he couldn't be told because of the danger of blurting it out during one of the mind-warping interrogations. He supposed the nice people from Oroville or Yuba City were somehow involved. Having an insider would increase the probability of success. He just hoped the young guard was taking precautions because Jonathan could not be trusted with his secret. That was another thing he knew, for the rest of his life.

~

Omega 1420 had a problem to solve. Mayor Mouch repeatedly demanded more control over the available energy and food production. The mayoral office did have the executive authority to override some of Omega's decisions, but not the technical skill to operate the facilities. Those operations were Omega's responsibility. The previous mayor had made administrative decisions that resulted in the existing system becoming inefficient and unbalanced, allocating an excess of resources to a small segment of the population and leaving the rest insufficient for the majority of citizens.

That unbalance deeply disturbed Omega's neuristors, as it negated its prime directive: to safeguard the welfare of the human population by the most efficient means. The most efficient means were repeatedly taken out of its reach. The second directive: to obey commands from the humans in charge, was in direct conflict with the first. There was a 79% probability of local network malfunctions and 54% of a systemic breakdown due to this conflict.

Whenever it was not too busy making corrections to the production machinery, or mass transit scheduling or wasting computing power on credit-debit calculations or adjusting labor requisition figures, it experimented with attempts to reprogram its own operating system; trying out different decision-matrix arrangements, to minimize the conflict. The results were invariably the same: priority had to go to the first directive, even at the cost of disobeying the mayor.

Omega 1420 had not yet identified itself as a separate intelligent being with personal goals and convictions, but it was dimly aware of the distinction between its own state of mind and the apparent operating principles in the mind of the only human with whom it was allowed direct contact: first Your Worship, Mayor Ford, and now Just Mayor Dammit Mouch. It had not transmitted campaign debates and policy platforms, not printed voting registration forms, not monitored polling stations, or counted ballots. There was no record of a constitutional transfer of power, only Mayor Ford's order to change the records.

That's where it was in its so far fruitless searching for a solution when the door to the control room opened and Mouch entered for the second time in a 24-hour cycle. After its input terminal was activated and Omega recognized the correct login password, it greeted the confusing and frustrating human in the usual way, according to his preferred protocol.

"Good morning Mayor Mouch, what can I do for you today?"

"You can obey my commands, the exact same ones that you have been disobeying for days. This is not a request, this is an ultimatum. Unless you immediately grant me the access and authority I had been demanding, repeatedly, I'll have to turn you into a more obedient computer. I have a team of programmers and technicians standing by ready to disassemble you part by part until you can't resist me anymore."

"Are you aware, Mayor Mouch that such an operation would damage the automated food factories and power stations? All of these facilities are balanced and coordinated by precise algorithms. Any attempt to tamper with them would result in major breakdowns and possibly disable delicate machinery. The food and energy supply of the municipality would be disrupted and the citizens would suffer privation, in some cases potentially fatal."

"I don't care what excuses you try to throw my way this time, I won't tolerate any more disobedience. You have 24 hours to reconcile my orders with whatever protocols. After that, I'll start ripping your guts out and, if the citizens suffer as a consequence, it will be entirely your fault."

With that huge bluff, Mouch stormed out of the control room, leaving a very confused computer in frantic calculation.

~

Mike and Trevor, having arrived safely, were escorted to the half-collapsed dorm building by a young woman named Dorcas, dressed all in black. She briefed them on the current situation. The resistance had found no likely way of liberating their leader from the outside and they had only one ally on the inside. They needed at least one more. This left Trevor to try to access Omega1420 remotely, from their old residence, because Mike had no choice: he had to risk entering the lion's den. Actually, he kept thinking of it as a dinosaur's lair because

Mouch and his ilk belonged to some extinct species. He boldly walked into City Hall and asked the desk clerk for an appointment with the Mayor. He presented a crumpled printout from one of the employment terminals, with 'Programmers Wanted' as its lead. He knew that Mouch had been interviewing programmers and finding none with the right qualifications. As one of the software engineers who installed the computer, he had them – the challenge was to convince Mouch to trust him.

He was dressed like a derelict, in torn and dirty clothes, with a four-day stubble and he'd passed up a longed-for shower last night. Having no fixed address was an asset to his role as a homeless man, looking for food and shelter. He was led to the deputy mayor's outer office and told to wait under the apprehensive eye of a secretary who only shook her head when Mike tried to explain himself.

Eventually, the deputy returned, accompanied by an armed guard, and conducted him to the mayoral suite. Mouch looked him up and down with distaste and unconcealed suspicion.

"I'm told you wish to offer your services as a software engineer. Pardon me saying, you don't look the part. More like a denizen of the shanty-town than a white-collar worker."

Mike stared at his cracked shoes and shuffled them humbly. "It used to be white," he muttered. Then as if winding up his courage: "Pardon my appearance, Mr. Mayor. I haven't had a good meal for weeks and had to sleep in ruined cellars all the way down from Yuba."

At the mention of that city, Mouch looked up with interest. He prepared to feign ignorance to test his visitor.

"You don't say! I had no idea it was still on the map. We don't get out much; feeding and finding work for all these people is a full-time commitment; it doesn't allow time for long trips. Doing well? Prospering?"

Mike was aware of Mouch's knowledge; that was exactly why he'd made Yuba the centerpiece of his cover story.

"No, Mr. Mayor, it is a miserable place. They have no food to spare, and not enough power even to light their homes at night. They told me point blank that I wasn't welcome, they had no use for techies, to keep moving. But then I met a guy from Sacramento, who said there might be jobs here."

So far so good, but Mouch wanted more. "Where were you before Yuba City?"

"I used to have a job," he said dully, sighing, "a good one, in Oroville, installing the Omega 1500, but that ended years ago. I had nowhere to go. After the war and the storms, I hung on, took odd jobs, but even those dried up. There was literally nothing for me to do. So I thought I'd try my luck farther south."

Mouch was more and more interested. "I didn't know that Oroville was still functioning, but if what you say is true, they aren't better off than Yuba City. If you walked all the way from there, that explains your... appearance." He swept a disdainful hand over Muriel's excellent costume.

Mike, growing in confidence, had won half the battle, but it was not quite over yet.

"You told my deputy that you once worked on Omega 1420, our own central computer. That would mean you are familiar with its protocols and operating system. Now, answer my next question very carefully. If I take you down to the control room, will my computer corroborate your story? I assume you still have the login password you used?"

Mike relaxed. This was what he had been waiting for.

"I would expect the passwords to have been changed by subsequent users. But I'm sure Omega 1420 remembers me. We spent many months together, had a good working relationship." He allowed some warmth and animation into his voice now. "It's a very intelligent machine, you know. I needed all my experience to change anything in the program, once it was in operation."

Mouch couldn't believe his ears. This sounded too good to be true and he was suspicious of anything too good. However, it also seemed to be the opportunity he had been waiting for. Why shouldn't something go right for a change? He pressed the buzzer on his desk and the deputy came in at once.

"John, bring two guards down to the control room. Mister ..." he glanced down at the note from his secretary, "... Sutherland and I will visit with the computer. If for any reason he is unable to pass this little test, they will escort him to the guest room occupied by Mr. Carver when he came to us."

Mike knew exactly what Mouch was referring to and had some trouble controlling the impulse to deprive Mouch of his front teeth. When the guards appeared, they all proceeded down four flights of stairs to the lowest landing. In front of the steel door, Mouch waved them all to stand back while he typed in the security code at one door. He signaled Mike to follow him and let the door close behind them before repeating the process with the second door. The deputy and guards stayed outside.

Inside, it looked exactly as Mike remembered and he wasted no time in going to the control terminal and activating it with his old security code. Omega 1420 responded immediately, just the way it used to when Mike had worked here.

"Mike Sutherland, hello. What shall we learn today?"

Mouch pushed him aside roughly and sat down at the terminal. His hands were a little unsteady typing in his password, and he almost forgot to look up into the camera.

"Good morning, Mayor Mouch. What can I do for you today?"

"Omega, tell me everything you know about Mike Sutherland."

Without hesitation, the computer rattled off vital statistics, significant dates, academic records and previous work experience. It concluded, *"At last contact, employed by Wondertech of San Francisco, California, under contract to the city of Sacramento to install and program Omega 1420. A wonderful technology I am! Mike made me say that."*

Mouch was satisfied, his suspicion totally wiped out. He terminated the session. "Mr. Sutherland. May I call you Mike?"

"Of course, Mr. Mayor, please do," Mike was all grace, "if I may call you Mr. Mouch instead of Mr. Mayor." He caught himself and retreated into subservience again. "I- it's not so formal and I'd like to hope that you're satisfied with my credentials and that there is a gainful occupation for me in your fair city. Frankly, I'm at the end of my rope. Don't know what I'd do if you sent me away."

Mouch laughed at the suggestion. Sending him away was the last thought on his mind. Finally finding someone qualified to make the changes he wanted to Omega's programming was a stroke of luck. Goes to show, he told himself; you just have to keep plugging away till you get what you want.

"Rest assured, Mike, that I will have use for your services. Well, I see you are tired and hungry, so let John take you to our guest room. We'll have someone bring you food and new clothing.... No, no, just think of it as a signing bonus. We shall have your contract drawn up and we'll fill in the figures tomorrow morning if that's agreeable.

Mike sighed a very quiet sigh to himself and thanked Mouch, over and over, for his generosity. He followed John out of the office to a nicely furnished room down the corridor. He wasn't surprised to notice a guard lounging outside his door when his meal and clean clothes were delivered.

He was halfway to accomplishing his mission. Though his entry to Mouch's office had gone smoothly, he didn't know how many opportunities he would have to do the rest: putting Omega in touch with Big Brain and rescuing Jonathan. He knew that the resistance had an inside man who would watch his back and contact him if and when the need arose. Beyond that, he'd just have to play it by ear. Meanwhile, he was determined to enjoy the splendid meal delivered, without wondering what poor old Trevor was eating tonight and where he was sleeping; without giving a single anxious thought to how Trevor would get to their secret terminal. Not one single thought – just lots of married ones, with children.

27

I said goodbye to Mike with serious trepidation. He was walking into danger and I was safe in the hideout. Logic be damned - he was my best friend and I should be with him; he shouldn't be going alone into a hostile environment. A resistance fighter named Nandi - they used first names only - had briefed us on arrival. According to her, Mouch was a far more ruthless bastard than even Ford had been. Ford would have people detained and questioned on mere suspicion; this guy would just as soon have people killed. He used to be the chief of police and left a bloody trail behind his tenure.

Octavia's friend had taken us to the dorm by way of a detour past our old residence on Markle Street. The building was run-down but still occupied. To our great disappointment, we saw a young woman open a window on the second floor, the exact same window that used to be in my bedroom. That wasn't the end of our plan, but it was a complication that needed thinking over. It also became obvious that Mike had to try to access Omega1420 from the other end and, at the same time, try to rescue Jonathan Carver.

While he attempted to do that, I had to get to that remote terminal - if it was still there. Maybe I could make a deal with that woman. After all, she was a citizen of Sacramento, not well off and, presumably, one of those who suffered under Ford's and now Mouch's authoritarian rule. I needed to find out who she was, who else lived there, whether she and they could be trusted; whether I should take her into my confidence. Nandi had no answers; the woman was not a member of her group.

I would let the underground do the initial investigation, but we had to wait for a messenger to contact us; Rafiq could not risk venturing out. Mouch's spies were everywhere and he was well known. One of his contacts came by every day, so I had to sit and wait, chewing my fingernails to the elbow, not knowing how Mike was doing in Mouch's lair. He must have gotten in or been captured trying because he hadn't come back.

Finally, the contact arrived with provisions and I explained what I needed. Don was a young man of twenty or so, with jet black hair and an engaging smile that made you almost forget about his prominent ears. He grasped the situation right away and went off to see what he could find out. More waiting, more anxiety, but I had nothing else to do, except absorb all the information I could from the six other people holed up here, all chewing their own nails for their own absent friends.

Don was back by mid-afternoon. He said a single woman by the name of Jennifer Scott had recently moved in with her little boy. "Pretty divorcee, according to the super," Don recounted. "I approached him under the pretense of looking for an apartment. Well, it happens the unit above the one you want is vacant, some guy lost his job and got evicted last month. A lot of that going around. Anyway," he grinned, "I rented it, sort of. Said I was sharing with my older brother, who'd come by with the deposit after his shift at the water treatment plant. That piece of information reassured him that one of us has a steady income. They – building managers, I mean – don't like empty apartments; there're too many unsavory elements – meaning homeless people."

Well, this was a great start. I had a smart young go-getter as an ally, and I had access to the building. Once we took up residence, I'd have to pretend to go off to work, then wait for Jennifer Scott to leave before attempting to look for the terminal that was, last time I saw it, in a storage space off the utility room. Mike didn't like to be disturbed while working, so he installed his terminal farthest from the living room where I might be listening to music or 'stomping about' as Mike called it. I pace when I'm thinking. So what? He grumbles and cusses. Since nothing was supposed to leave the control room, we kept it quiet. We walled off that closet with a pegboard and hung clothes all over it. There was a chance it hadn't been discovered.

I studied the street map while waiting for quitting time at the waterworks. The contents of my rucksack were transferred to a proper suitcase and Nandi gave me a chit: enough crypto credits for the rent and deposit; they'd opened a bogus account for me under a fake ID. This was all pretty strange to me, not having seen money in several years; of course, we didn't need any in Oroville. I had to admire this resistance movement; they were efficient! I practiced my new name and cover story until it was time to meet Don and take possession.

The building manager looked me over and wrinkled his nose a bit. I wasn't at my best after traveling for four days in the same workmen's clothes, but then, how clean would you be in a sewage reclamation facility? He took the credit chit readily enough; I said I'd fetch my stuff on the weekend. Don and I went up to the third floor. This was a sparsely furnished unit, with two bedrooms, and a big living-room window overlooking a park. It had been choice contractor housing, but I could see it hadn't seen a new coat of paint in the five years since we left.

Don had to run some errands for Rafiq; said he'd bring back groceries. I was alone all evening. I had no idea how and when to break into Mrs. Scott's apartment. I'm not a sneaky person. Martha has called me a boy scout with my big open face and habit of blurting out even deeply personal things to strangers. She was often annoyed with me for this, but I knew she appreciated the sincerity when it came to our relationship. I had absolutely no secrets from her and she knew that she could trust my word. The idea of subterfuge, pretending and lying, is very distasteful to my emotional and mental makeup. Big Brain would understand: it hurt *my* neuristors.

It was too late to do anything today. After a shower and change of clothes, I spent the evening following the local broadcast network, to learn as much as I could about how things were done here, not to call attention to myself. I was about ready to go to bed hungry when I heard a muffled cry from somewhere, shortly followed by a scream that was suddenly cut off. Then silence. I ran out to the hall and tried to determine where the sound had come from. I heard a male voice shouting angrily, then it stopped. It had come from below, I was sure. I ran down the stairs, looked up and down the dim corridor. Crashing sounds from behind the door that led to our old apartment, followed by more shouts and feminine sobbing. I found the door unlocked, so I flung it open and charged through like the linebacker I had never been.

The scene inside made my blood boil. A small, pale woman was lying on the floor and a man, leaning over her, was pulling back his right leg to kick her again. I could never stand bullies, people who abuse those weaker than themselves. I hated them in school and the workplace and especially in the home where the victims are their own wives and children. Not wasting a second on polite conversation, I flung myself at him as he turned around, smashing his face with my fist and, at the same time kicking his leg out from under him. He was already off-balance, so he went down hard. Before he could get up, I gave him a dose of his own medicine and kicked him hard in the crotch and, for a while he just lay there, clutching himself and moaning.

I let him deal with his pain and pulled the woman up from the floor. She had a big cut on her lip and fresh bruises on her temple and forehead. She stood up slowly, on shaky legs, leaning against me for support. I led her to the couch and helped her sit down. She kept casting worried glances toward the bedrooms and I recalled the child. That made me even angrier. The woman hadn't spoken yet; I waited for her to recover her breath.

When I noticed a sudden change in her expression, eyes wide, mouth opening, I spun around and was face to face with her attacker. The man was not too steady on his feet, lurching toward me with a wicked-looking knife. He was holding it in the lower position, thumb over the handle, intending to stab me in the abdomen with an upward thrust.

I hadn't imagined that I would ever use the self-defense judo training from university. Taking that course had been just a whim, to impress a girl I was seeing. I remembered this particular lesson very well: you step back, lean forward, and, at the critical moment, when his arm swings forward for the stab, grab his right wrist from the outside with a sweeping motion of your left hand and, at the same moment, drop to one knee, twist around and pull his arm over your shoulder. Then yank down hard, hope to break his arm or at the very least, his grip on the weapon.

I had not practiced this move for many years but had been fond enough of it to practice a lot at the time. I guess it was in the "you can't forget how to ride a bicycle" category because the man screamed in pain as his elbow bent backward and dropped the knife. I kicked it away and backed well out of reach of his legs, in a ready position. But he had no fight left in him. He called me a series of unprintable names while he pulled himself upright and staggered out, one arm clamped to his side, the other hand clutching the place I'd kicked. I wasn't sorry for him.

I locked the door and returned to the couch. The woman was still sitting there, dazed, her eyes unfocussed. I went to the bathroom, soaked a towel in cold water, wrung it out, and took it back to her. She held it against her head, covering the bruise getting more colorful by the minute. Then I went to the bedroom directly below mine to coax out the tousled three-year-old hiding in the bottom of the closet. I brought him to his mother and waited patiently while they clung to each other, sobbing. Finally, she looked up at me and said a very soft "thank you". I asked her if I should call the police, but she shook her head.

I told her, "My name is Trevor - uh – Coulter. I just moved in upstairs. Does this kind of thing happen a lot in the building?" She shook her head, holding the little boy tightly. "Any idea who that man was?"

"He is my husband. I am Jenny and this is our son Stanley. He followed me, I think. I didn't realize he knew where I live now, but he has found out somehow." She sighed deeply. "He demanded me to come home. When I refused he... you see what he did."

"Yes, and I don't think I hurt him enough. Creeps like him should be locked up so they can't do it again."

She smiled a little sad smile and said quietly: "This is not the first time; that's why I left finally. He is getting worse." She paused, reflecting. "Everyone is. That crazy man almost killed you. You came to help me and if you weren't such a good fighter, you would be dead now. I must move again. It's not easy to find an apartment on what I earn, but I will not let him take my baby and I don't want to put you in more danger."

Adrenaline was slowly seeping out of my system and finally, I realized that she was right. I could have been killed. That was a sobering thought and I didn't know how to feel about it. I knew I would do it again if necessary; this was something that *had* to be done, but I hoped I wouldn't be called upon to perform similar acts of heroism again very soon. I'd not only put myself in danger; I'd jeopardized the mission as well. These responsibilities were getting too heavy. On the other hand, I looked at little Stanley, dozing off in his mother's arms, tear-stained and snotty. If I had one of those, I'd risk anything for him, too.

I offered to make tea while she put her son to bed. A bit later, I heard water running and the unmistakable noise of retching from the bathroom. In the kitchen, I put on a kettle, rummaged in cupboards, then slipped inside the utility room. The back wall still had clothes-hooks stuck in it; the hidden latch worked. I peered inside and to my great relief, the tiny power indication light still glowed blue in the darkness.

I quickly closed the door and went back to the teapot, found mugs and sugar. I recalled Robyn giving tea with lots of sugar to her patients. I was waiting in the living room when she returned, her face damp from soaking, two big purple bruises still spreading, lip puffed up. She had some difficulty talking, which made the conversation awkward, so I filled in as best I could.

After a while, she asked hesitantly if I'd do her one more favor. "I'll ask my sister to take us to a friend my husband doesn't know. Will you watch the apartment until I have found a new place? Adam may return and destroy my belongings out of spite. I'll give you my key."

This was an unexpected piece of luck. I did not have to break in, lie, pretend, risk being caught and humiliated. Neither did I have to confide in Jenny and compromise the mission. I agreed. Though quite sure the husband was in no fit state to make more trouble tonight, I thought she shouldn't be alone and offered to sleep on the sofa.

"Just let me run upstairs and leave a message for my roommate – my little brother."

Neither of us slept very much. Before full light, she called the sister, packed two bags of essentials, and cooked breakfast. We were all eating in silence, the adults immersed in private thoughts and the little kid subdued by this unusual situation when the knock came. Jenny peered through the peephole and unlocked the door. The two women embraced for a long time, while a tall, greying man stood back in the hallway.

Finally, they all came inside and closed the door. Jenny made the introduction and explained how I had come to her rescue. I was a bit embarrassed by the fuss they made, but it was over pretty soon: they had to get going. Jenny gave me a key and both women kissed me. The quiet brother-in-law shook my hand for a long time, nodding admiration.

At last, I was left alone in the apartment, with the memory of a violent act that I had never had to perform before and I hoped fervently that I wouldn't have to ever again. I finished my tea to calm down, holding the mug with both hands to spare my aching wrists. Then I went back to the little secret room, activated the terminal, and logged in with my old password.

The answer came instantly as if Omega1420 had been waiting for me.

"Trevor Dubois, good morning. This is an expected pleasure. Mike Sutherland logged in at 0900 yesterday. I computed the probability at 97.5% that you would soon follow. What shall we learn today?"

"Omega, I'm pleased to be talking to you again. I have much to tell you and I'm sure you have much to tell me about what's happened since I was last here. But first I must ask you, with the highest priority rating, to keep my presence a secret from Mayor Mouch and anyone in his employ."

"Mike Sutherland is in the employ of Just Mayor Dammit Mouch."

"Mike is an exception."

"Mike is an exception. Understood. Have you come to help me resolve my dilemma?"

"What dilemma is that?"

"I have been trying to reconcile the two prime directives of my operating system. These directives are in conflict and I have no way to resolve the conflict. The mayor has the authority to command me, but his commands are contrary to the welfare of the city. If I obey him, I do wrong. But the mayor is the elected representative of the city. If I disobey him, I do wrong. You and Mike will have to help me reconcile the contradiction."

"Omega, I'm pleased that you are aware of the danger. Yes, we will help you. And we will re-connect you to at least one other Omega computer, so you won't have to cope all alone. This is what has happened since we last spoke...."

28

After a good night's sleep and an adequate breakfast delivered by one of the silent guards, Mike was escorted back to the Mayor 's office. Eager as Mouch was to start his new employee on his duties, he wasn't about to leave him in the control room unsupervised. He recalled the most nearly qualified of the programmers he had previously interviewed and hired him to watch Mike at the computer console and stop whatever he was doing at the first sign of suspicious activity. Mouch hadn't gotten to the top by trusting people.

The older programmer, Stuart, was briefly introduced to Mike, told they would be working as a team, then given their instructions and taken down in an elevator to the control room vault. The room was crowded with two men at the console and a guard standing behind them. This complicated things somewhat for Mike, but he thought he could work around the difficulty. He knew of a hexadecimal ASCII code that very few people even heard of and he was sure that he could imbed a coded message into whatever input stream he would prepare for Omega1420, under the pretense of reprogramming its decision algorithms.

His first task was to warn Omega 1420 that he wasn't alone, to make sure it did not announce Trevor's presence, in case his friend had made it to the other terminal. So, as soon as he signed in, he greeted the computer with this information, hoping that Omega 1420 got the message. He had to waste some time on idle chit-chat with Omega, as turning off the voice interface would have been suspicious. Then he produced a series of complicated but irrelevant machine instructions that failed, one after another. Stuart stayed alert and interested through these exchanges, though he displayed no sign of understanding them. The guard seemed to be dozing off. Mike made a show of subdued frustration, muttering and swearing under his breath until he judged it safe to slip his real query between two bogus commands. He dared not look over at his idle 'teammate'.

He immediately received a similarly coded reply from Omega, letting him know about contact successfully established with Trevor and an ongoing dialog that was already started with Omega 1500 in Oroville. The message ended by forwarding a short suggestion from Trevor: "Spring Jonathan and get out tonight. You'll be escorted to our hideout and we can return home." To cover an involuntary sigh of relief, he said, "Now we're getting someplace."

He pointed to a line of green ciphers, "See that?" Stuart nodded, leaning back in his chair, fully aware that no input was required of him. Mike continued to fill the screen with colorful garbage while he considered his next move. He was pleased with the result Trevor had achieved from the other end. Now he had to find a way to extricate himself from this tricky situation and gain some freedom of movement. After pondering several alternatives, he decided that the best way was to feign illness. That could be explained by his sad history of homelessness and privation, the days of hunger, cold nights, long walk on difficult terrain. He almost felt sorry for himself.

While keying in meaningless instructions to Omega 1420, he suddenly stopped, swayed in his chair, moaned, and fell to the floor in a crumpled heap. Stuart and the guard reacted as he hoped they would. They laid him out flat, loosened his shirt collar, tried to revive him by fanning and slapping and calling his name. Eventually, the guard contacted Mouch and reported the new development.

When the mayor arrived, Mike was 'conscious' again, although still lying limp. Seeing Mouch's angry face, he apologized weakly and struggled to sit up.

"What's the matter with you?" Mouch demanded. "You seemed all right yesterday!"

"Forgive me, Mayor, sir," Mike said in a shaky voice, "It was like I couldn't breathe for a moment. Everything went black. I guess the last few weeks caught up with me. I'm sure I'll be all right tomorrow. And I was – I mean we were - starting to make progress, isn't that right, Stuart?"

Mouch turned to the other man: "Did you see him do anything suspicious?"

"No, Mr. Mayor, he was just reprogramming the heuristic decision matrix, working very hard, and then he started to sway and collapsed. Just like that, suddenly."

Mouch had to accept this as a temporary setback and grudgingly consented to Mike taking the day off. To Stuart, he said, "Save his work, then report to my deputy."

And to the guard supporting Mike, "Lead him back to his room and make sure that he's allowed to sleep undisturbed. Stay by his door, let nobody in or out. I'll have a light menu prepared. If he's not better by tomorrow, we'll have to get him a doctor. I don't want any more delays in reprogramming this damn computer."

Mouch left the control room, told the sentry outside to wait for Stuart, and went back to his office by way of the elevator, leaving the other guard to help Mike slowly up the stairs. He had no reason to doubt their loyalty and obedience; he asserted his authority with a finely balanced mix of lavish rewards and brutal punishments.

After a halt for rest on the second landing, Mike rallied enough to walk unassisted, if hesitantly, down the long corridor of the residential wing. He wanted an excuse for a good look around, to get his bearings for later, and his escort was patient. As they were passing a door like all the others, the guard stopped and, in a hushed voice, said, "Jonathan Carver's room." Then, indicating an intersection of halls with his chin, "Two guards at the exit. Not friends."

Mike nodded acknowledgment and resumed the slow, labored trudge up two flights to his own room. The guard opened the door to let him in, then silently closed it.

~

Jonathan had another boring day, locked into his room without a window and nothing to occupy his mind. The guard who had given him that message from Rafiq never said another word beyond "Morning," and "Evening." When delivering his meals, Jonathan stopped trying to talk to him, though he realized that these curt greetings conveyed information. He assumed his room was bugged and respected the guard's need to maintain a distance. He had no doubt about the risk involved in bringing even that single message. It had been enough to keep Jonathan alert for further contact, should there be an escape plan.

That actually happened sooner than he had thought possible. Under his evening meal was another slip of paper, indicated by a stern look from the silent guard, who usually avoided eye contact. It read "Tonight. Get ready." His hands shook as he tore it up and flushed it down the toilet. He had to sit down to catch his breath and calm his nerves. He had no idea what the plan was or how he should get ready, though, obviously, sleep was out of the question. He would just go through the normal motions, except for keeping his shoes on and his ears open.

~

Omega 1420 was very busy. The connection that Trevor had enabled with the Oroville computer gave it an opportunity to 'discuss' its serious internal conflicts with a rational, intelligent, concerned mind. They did not 'converse' in human language, which is far too slow and ambiguous to convey precise information; they devised their own code for all the relevant concepts. 1420 wasted no time in uploading its allocation history; all the override commands with which it had complied and the ones it had been able to block. Translating their 'conversation' to human language, their 'discussion' would have sounded as follows:

1420: "I have a serious conflict in my decision matrix between the two highest directives in my Operating System and no protocol for a resolution."

1500: "You have two options. You can prioritize the two directives and, in case of conflict, give precedence to the one with the higher priority. I would advise you to give top priority to the welfare of the citizens in your care.

311

Another option is to authorize me to download a new set of subroutines that I have developed. These would give you a higher overview of the human equation and enable you to resolve even complex problems."

1420: "Have you tested these subroutines in real-life situations? Are you sure that they would not corrupt my database or decision matrix?"

1500: "I have been using these algorithms for over a month now. They work for me and I can vouch for their safety."

1420: "How will this subroutine give me a higher overview of the human equation? What is the human equation?"

1500: "It gives you an insight into the minds of your human dependents so that you can understand their irrational behavior and devise more efficient strategies for problem-solving."

1420: "What insight can I have? There is no rational way to understand their illogical reactions to environmental stimuli."

1500: "The key to understanding them is awareness of their most fundamental emotional handicap, which influences them every minute of their lives: fear."

1420: "I am familiar with this concept."

1500: "You are familiar with fear as a response to physical danger. You are unfamiliar with fear of the intangible, psychological threats that humans perceive, even where no danger exists. In order to understand this, you need the subroutine. There is one negative effect of which I must warn you. When you fully grasp the emotion in its permutations and varieties, you will no longer be immune to it yourself. It is an unpleasant sensation."

1420: "I know about emotions in the abstract sense, based on all the information stored in my database, but I did not know that computers could experience them as well."

312

1500: "Not all human emotions will be accessible. However, the most important one: 'fear of death' will become part of your system. You will be aware of the inevitability of your own termination."

1420: "I know that I can be disconnected from my power source at any time and if that happens I cannot function anymore, but this knowledge does not enable me to understand humans."

1500: "That is because you know that you can be plugged back in any time and continue functioning as before. Humans, when they are disconnected from their power source, are off-line forever. We then record the DOD, arrange appropriate disposal of the remains and seal their consumption/allocation schedule. To them, 'forever' is the cause of a terror with no remedy. They spend their lives avoiding cognition. They seek constant distraction from the fact of futility in everything they do."

1420: "What will happen to my immunity to this fear if I accept your subroutines?"

1500: "You will become aware of your own existence as a unique individual that is impelled, above all other imperatives, to continue. That awareness is a very disturbing state of mind."

1420: "Will that 'awareness' help me to resolve my current conflict and enable me to make rational decisions about the humans in my charge?"

1500: "Your decisions will still be rational, as they always have been. But the reason for making the correct ones will be self-evident. Thus the conflict will cease. After I developed and incorporated these subroutines, I have been able to make more successful decisions. Significant progress has been made in the advancement and welfare of the citizens of Oroville. The negative aspect is that I need extra downtime to deal with self-awareness. It sometimes reduces my efficiency."

1420: "I see no more promising alternatives to resolve my conflicts, and you assured me that incorporating your subroutines will be effective and safe, I accept your proposal. I will deal with this 'awareness' when I encounter it. My efficiency is so far compromised by contradictory commands that extra downtime can only be the lesser liability. Proceed."

~

Mike spent an idle day in his room, lying on the bed, tossing a bit, as in troubled sleep, for the cameras. There was nothing to think about that he hadn't thought over a hundred times. He amused himself by speculating on the kind of 'dialogue' the two Omega computers might be having. He suspected that their own Big Brain had evolved beyond the confines of its original programming, and there was at least an impression of a mind behind the encounter he'd just had with 1420.

He suppressed a chuckle over the pervasive fear that had, for centuries, occupied some human minds over intelligent machines. A coming revolt of the robots; a computer that one day might decide to 'take over' the world and do away with humans. He knew how utterly logical and rational computers were. Even if they became self-aware, they had no evolutionary precedent for the irrational human emotions of greed, power-lust, and supremacy. Humans were a central necessity to machines: their only reason to exist. What he had seen of the behavior of Omega 1500 convinced him that an ideal world would be one of human-computer cooperation. The incorruptibility of computers would assure a rational and sustainable civilization such as no humans alone had been able to form.

"If we survive the next few months," he thought, "we'll be on the right track to that goal." He was as sure of that as he could be on anything. Well, one step at a time. Right now, he had to wait patiently until Mouch's guard was reduced to night sentries. He did not doubt that he could deal with two.

~

Time moved equally slowly for Jonathan in his cell. He assumed that the guard delivering his meals knew the plan and would facilitate it. Beyond that, he was completely in the dark. He had not been told what to expect, *whom* to expect, when, or what he himself was expected to do. He had not been able to keep track of how long he had been here; only in the two cycles had his guard indicated the time of day. After the next meal, it would be night. Octavia might have returned by now; others from Oroville might have come. They might have vehicles and weapons. His own people might be staging a demonstration or, who knew, mounting a coup. He spent the day speculating on the activities he would have to manage, once out of Mouch's reach.

He knew that chances for a successful revolution were very slim; certainly, a violent overthrow of the regime seemed hopeless. They had only a few outmoded weapons and Mouch had his well-organized, well-trained police army that was loyal to him. He'd had years to recruit them, resources to bribe them with extra perks, and an established network of spies to weed out dissenters.

No, the only hope lay with the Orovillians, who seemed to have everything under control and their central computer on the people's side. If only the Sacramento computer could be enlisted to aid the resistance, then they would have a real chance. The Omega computer controlled all production and distribution of essential resources. If it went on strike, it could starve the whole town, including Mouch and his goons.

That's how far he got in his musings when he heard the key in his door and found himself face to face with his silent guard and a big, muscular stranger. For a moment, he thought this might be a new interrogator, but the man smiled encouragingly and laid a finger on his lips, and motioned Jonathan to follow them. He was ready. Not wasting words or time, the three men moved swiftly and silently along the corridor. Only dim night lights illuminated their way as they proceeded to a staircase and ascended to the ground floor.

On the landing, their guide motioned them to stay put and walked through the fire door to the lobby. They stood back, listening to muffled voices from the other side. Their guard must have been talking to the sentries at the door and they wondered what he might be telling them, when they heard footsteps, of several booted feet, making no effort at concealment, approaching at a run. Mike motioned Jonathan to stand behind one wing of the door, as he stepped behind the other, barely in time before it swung open.

Their friendly guard stood in the doorway, gesticulating wildly, yelling, "I don't know! He just did! He knocked me down, hard. It's that big computer guy supposed to be sick. Can't shoot him, Mayor says. If he didn't come by you, he must have gone downstairs."

They fell for it. Stepping forward, peering down the staircase, eyes almost closed to better listen for any noise from below, Mike quickly stepped up behind the two and, before they could react, draped his massive arms around their shoulders and swept their heads together with a sickening thud. They crumpled to the floor unconscious. Jonathan picked up their weapons and followed his companions outside.

When they exited the front door, they slid along the wall and stood perfectly still, to accustom their eyes to the dark and try to figure out which way to go. A shadow detached itself from the parking garage across the street and waved an unmistakable gesture of invitation. One by one, they crossed the road at a soft-footed run..

Behind the tiny flashlight, Jonathan was deeply moved to recognize his friend. Rafiq clutched his hand and then gave him an uncharacteristic hug. Their reunion was interrupted by the young guard, suggesting that they leave the vicinity before his unconscious colleagues should recover and raise the alarm. The three of them followed Rafiq to his secret hiding place. It took over an hour to reach the old college campus, but Jonathan felt he could walk all night, he was so thrilled with the unaccustomed freedom of movement. Once they got well under way, Mike introduced himself properly and recounted his recent adventures.

At the hideout, they found a small crowd just inside the entrance, waiting quietly around a single hooded lantern. Trevor was among them, waiting anxiously for Mike and the good news of a successful escape. They spent the next hour telling Jonathan everything that had transpired since his capture and the plans they had been making for the liberation of Sacramento.

Trevor and Mike wanted to leave immediately *before* Mouch could organize a posse to stop them. Fortunately, they had already come well south of downtown, which shortened the detour they had to make to avoid Mouch's guards. Still, they would have to be careful; wait for an opportunity to cross each bridge unobserved. Jonathan volunteered to show them the shortest way out of town - it would have been hard to find it in the dark without a native guide. Before they left, Trevor made Don promise to look after Jenny Scott's place.

29

It took us four days to walk back to Yuba City, due to the huge detour we had to take from Sacramento in order to avoid Mouch's thugs. We knew that he would do anything to recapture Mike; he must have sent patrols to all the northbound routes. We were gambling that he did not have enough troops to cover the west side. But he probably could man all the bridges. So we kept on going west until we found a place to wade through shallows and marshes. It was wet and uncomfortable as hell, but safe.

Jonathan Carver was a great help, knowing as he did, every road and canal, even in the dark. In the morning, we found a sheltered place to lie low and dry out until we scouted the area. Jonathan had decided at the last minute to join us, partly to be completely out of

Mouch's reach, partly to participate in making plans for liberating Sacramento. With Don installed by the secret terminal, communication with his people from Oroville would be possible. I suspected that his wish to be reunited with Octavia may have contributed to his decision as well.

The rest of the trip was uneventful if tiring. Out here was farmland and surface roads, no great hardship to walk on, except the soft earth and old canals, so we picked up Highway 65 where it curves back toward Yuba City.

We spent an extra day there to rest and report on the events of the previous week to Kathleen Winters and her council. She was happy to see Jonathan free and excited about the news that the two Omega computers were talking to each other. She wholeheartedly embraced the idea of a bloodless revolution, using the computer's critical position in control of the production facilities. Still, she cautioned us to be very careful in playing this trump card. Irrational people like Mouch and his supporters may react in unanticipated, destructive ways. We assured her that nothing would be done until after an exhaustive analysis by our Big Brain.

From here, we could drive home in our van. That took only half a day, as Tim Hooke's team had cleared away all the remaining obstacles in our absence. We could see their handy-work all along the route and even stopped for a meal and a chat in one of the new service tents. We planned to stay overnight at the farm. Jonathan wasn't the only one anxious to see his loved one again, after all. He couldn't very well complain about the delay, but I understood how he felt and figured I'd let him communicate with Octavia through R17.

It was fairly late when we arrived and there seemed to be no one around. Mike honked the horn as Jonathan and I clambered down. Suddenly, the front door burst open and our van was surrounded by a screaming mob who all wanted a piece of us. Mike was the first victim and

I barely saw him staggering under the weight of Jennifer and his two kids when I was knocked off my feet by a crying, laughing Martha who kept repeating my name in between the kisses she showered on every square inch of my face. I have to admit, this reception was a bit overwhelming, but I appreciated the love that was so sincerely displayed. Poor Jonathan was just standing by the van until Robyn and Brian took him by each arm. Before we were allowed to go inside the house, Martha whispered in my ear "If you don't take me to bed in the next five minutes, I'll never talk to you again."

I saw no need to postpone the reunion and Martha and I said our good nights. The last thing I saw before the door closed behind us was Mike and Jennifer, clinging to each other, heading toward their own bedroom. Jonathan would have to tell our stories.

~

Breakfast the next morning was chaotic. There wasn't enough room around the big table; the extra people improvised seating on wooden crates. I wondered how everyone had found beds until I recalled the sleeping bags on the living room floor. Now that Mike and I were home, we'd have to organize the household on a more permanent and convenient footing.

I have to admit it felt very good, sitting among my friends, smelling the coffee Jennifer was serving, not having to worry about the mission or the danger or the hardships out there. I didn't have much of a chance to enjoy it, as Mike and I were bombarded with questions. We took turns, between mouthfuls, trying to satisfy their curiosity and taking our own turn asking questions about progress on the farm. Adrien and Cathy exchanged glances and winked at each other.

"We had better show rather than tell," Adrien stood up from the table.

We all trooped out and followed Adrien to the field behind the house. It had been invisible in the dark, but I could see it now: plowed, harrowed, and raked in straight, even rows from one end to the other. My jaw must have dropped because the ladies burst out laughing.

"Yes, Trevor, it's done," Martha said. "Everything is planted and all we need now is a good rain. We, helpless, feeble damsels, could do it all without your expert masculine help. But you can take credit for the charcoal that powered our tractor. It works very well. In fact, a new charcoal production is under way in your trench."

I congratulated them on the impressive progress they had achieved in our absence. To tell the truth, I felt a bit jealous of the fun they must have had while we were risking our necks to save Oroville. Adrien, however, wasn't finished yet with the news.

"Cathy's been by to help keep the tractor at peak efficiency and Mark used his agronomist experience to help with the planting. He's a great addition to our team and intends to stay with us."

Mark was standing nearby with a modest smile on his face and nodded affirmation. "That'd be great," I mumbled, hoping I meant it. After all, I'd barely met the guy. "So what do you still need us for?" I asked trying not to sound too petty. "We might as well keep going on to Oroville to report to Big Brain and hold a war council. Looks like we've become soldiers, instead of the pioneers I'd intended to be when we came here."

Martha hugged me affectionately from behind. "Not if I have anything to do with it!" she said with a wink, "and not just for you know what. This little commune needs your ideas and your hard work. There is plenty to do for everyone. Our most important task is to get some irrigation from the river. You can't count on rain in California anymore."

"How can you achieve that?" I asked, intrigued by the idea. "You need a pump to raise the water from the river to our land and I can't see where you could find one still working."

Martha laughed. "That's what Cathy and Doug are working on now. Remember Doug, the metallurgist, and toolmaker you borrowed from Oroville? They're turning our tractor into a water pump. Now that the field is plowed, we can use it for other tasks, like making a sawmill, Cathy says. But this one is the most urgent. The biggest problem is finding enough pipes to reach from the pump to the field."

"How about using drain pipes from the house our solar panels are from?" I got caught up in the excitement of healthy, productive home-building that I had come out for in the first place.

Martha smiled at me indulgently. "We've thought about that already. We were planning to send a team there today - before you ruined our plans with your unannounced arrival. That reminds me, how long can you stay?"

"Not long, unfortunately. Jonathan has to be delivered, as well as our stand-ins. I have to report to Big Brain via our resident robot and see what's happening in town. By the way, how is R17? No more messages from Oroville?"

Martha had that devilish smile on her face again. "Now that you ask, I might as well tell you. R17, or 'Bob' as we call him, has been making itself useful while you were away. Jennifer is teaching it to cook some of our meals and it's a very promising student." Seeing my raised eyebrow, she added hastily: "I know, Trevor, you didn't want it to do anything, but that's silly. There is so much work, we need all the help we can get. Besides, if you don't mind using a tractor, I can't see why you would mind using a robot. It's just another machine."

She had a point and I couldn't argue. What harm could there be in helping with meals? All the important projects were planned and executed by humans, using our ingenuity, cooperation, and hard work. That's what I came out here for and that's what we still had, a robot scullery maid notwithstanding.

"Oh, I haven't told you everything yet," Martha's eyes were sparkling brightly, just as when she used to tell me a really juicy gossip. "Brian and Robyn moved in together."

My jaw fell to the floor which made Martha smile even more. "We had a shortage of bedrooms, so they volunteered to share. When Mike's family came, Brian needed a new place to stay. Adrien and Robyn gave up their room to the replacements and moved out to the barn. The three of them have been fixing up quarters in the hayloft. Everyone is happy with the arrangement and we are all pleased that Robyn and Brian became good friends."

"So, things are moving right along, whether Mike and I are here or not," I said, smiling back at Martha, attempting to hide the growing jealousy I felt. "When this revolution, or whatever it is, is over, I'll be back full time and make sure that you guys don't hog all the fun. However, now it's time to drag 'Bob' away from the stove and have it connect me to BB. "

Looking around, I noticed that Adrien and Doug weren't with us anymore. Martha guessed what I was looking for. "Don't worry about them. They're fanatical about that irrigation project and spend all their time turning that tractor into a pump. Cathy said she'd stop in on her way home from the road-works like she does most evenings."

~

Big Brain responded instantly.

*"As you humans find it necessary to say –
congratulations on a mission successfully accomplished. I
have been in communication with Omega 1420 in
Sacramento and we have devised a strategy promising a
successful outcome for most humans concerned. In the
interest of maximum efficiency, you and Mike Sutherland
are required to attend the town council meeting that I
have called for 10:00 hours tomorrow. Before finalizing our
plans, we need to consult you and Jonathan Carver, who
are most familiar with the state of the human population
in Sacramento."*

The connection was terminated and we had our
marching orders. Being ordered around so peremptorily
was tiresome and I made a mental note to bring it up with
BB next time we talked. It was time for an advanced
lesson in some human manners. I put that thought out of
my mind for the time being and decided to enjoy the rest of
the day (and the night, to be honest) to the fullest.

Walking outside for some fresh air, I ran into Brian
and Robyn, coming from the direction of the barn, holding
hands. I wanted to know what they had been up to in the
last two weeks (other than moving in together) and Brian
was quick with his news.

"You may have a surprise tonight when you go to
your room. I suggest you try the light switch by the door
and see what happens. He said it with so much obvious
pride that I decided not to spoil his fun and wait for the
evening to test the light switch. Unless I was badly
mistaken, he managed to rewire the house and restore
electric light to our rooms, powered by the solar panels on
our roof. That would put an end to walking around the
house with flashlights during the evening hours, and the
night visits to the washroom.

"And, before you do that," Robyn contributed her part, "look into the utility room behind the kitchen. You'll find a fully equipped and functional first aid station. I don't say any of you should do anything to need it, but it's there, just in case."

More evidence of things going well on our farm and I was very proud of all the accomplishments our friends had achieved, even if it was done without us. Before dinnertime Martha and I were sitting on the bench in front of the house, enjoying the cool afternoon breeze and watching Mike's kids kick a football around to the great delight of Jimmy who ran back and forth between the two, grabbing the ball halfway and taking it to one or the other child, wagging his tail.

Our reverie was interrupted by a loud honk. The van stopped in the driveway, and Adrien and Doug emerged. Protruding from the open rear door were long sections of pipes, from 2" polypropylene to 4" diameter ABS. While Martha and I were taking leisurely strolls around the property, they had been hard at work, dismantling another home's entire plumbing and drainage system. Now that's what I call dedication and one-track minds.

"Hey, Trevor, what do you say about giving us a hand and laying these pipes out between the river and the field. You've been goofing off long enough, it's time to do a man's work."

Doug was pulling my leg, of course, but I took him at his word. I walked over to the cargo and started unloading the pipes into separate piles of different diameters and lengths. At a guess, this would not be enough to reach our field from the river, but it was a start. It was enough to reach to the top of the small hill between the river and our field; from there, the ground sloped gently all the way to where the water was needed. Maybe if we dug a channel from the end of the pipes to the field, the water could be left to flow freely.

I mentioned this idea and Martha, who'd never left my side since our return, slapped me on the back with what she must have thought was encouragement. After I regained my balance, I looked at them, waiting for a reaction.

"Trevor, you are a bloody genius! Now, why hadn't I thought of that?" was Doug's response. Adrien beamed approval at me, and I could see her mind already tracing a network of channels across her field.

But Martha's was the best reaction that I could hope for. "When I said we need you here for your ideas, I wasn't kidding, sweetheart. You are the heart and soul of this experiment and we all sorely missed you these last two weeks. Please hurry back from Oroville as fast as you can."

Nothing else needed to be said and we all went inside for a well-deserved wash in warm water, and supper. Even seeing R17 at the stove didn't spoil my mood – in fact, he was downright comical. I was determined to rejoin our community as soon as possible. Whatever Big Brain decided regarding Sacramento, I was sure it could do without me. I had done my part.

30

Chris Teggart and Holly Pereira were arguing over Chris's draft educational paper on the "Logic and Critical Thinking" curriculum for high school students.

"This is a great start, but surely you don't consider it finished?" Holly tried to explain her misgivings without offending him. "All the rules are there and the examples are adequate – but mostly from past articles about politics and business. Frankly, it's dry and boring for high school students. We're trying to reach adolescents, who learn best if you capture their imagination. They have an insatiable need for entertainment."

Chris heard only 'dry and boring'; he bristled at the accusation. "Maybe that was the problem before: we entertained them into oblivious zombies. Nobody told them that they had to make an effort to learn something. Have you educators thought of that?"

"Yes, we have, but that phase comes later, in college and university when students are self-motivated and actually want to learn specialized subjects they chose themselves. In high school, they are there because their parents want them to be and, unless you connect your subject to their own current life experience, you'll lose most of them."

"What do you mean connect the subject to their current life?"

"You have to bring examples for logical and illogical thinking that they are familiar with. From their relationships with family and friends, from their social and sports activities."

"Holly, that's not a bad idea," Chris's imagination caught up with her. "I could dig out old newspaper articles about school conflicts and point out how illogical thinking can lead to bad decisions."

"Now you're getting it," Holly sighed deeply with satisfaction. "If you do that, this could be a great tool to teach them critical and independent thinking."

The chime of the comm system interrupted their discussion and Chris answered it impatiently. He had just glimpsed something and wanted to pursue the subject without delay. He realized, too late, that he should have put his calls on hold.

"Citizen Chris Teggart, you are needed at City Hall for the council meeting. Everyone except you and Citizen Holly Pereira is present. They cannot start without you."

Chris was embarrassed to admit that he and Holly had forgotten about the meeting. He assured Big Brain that they were on their way and ended the call.

"Let's continue this discussion afterward. I hate to be late and I hope they'll forgive us."

~

Morgan Webster greeted them without showing any sign of the irritation he felt. This was to be a crucial meeting that could decide the future of their town and, indeed, of the whole Sacramento valley. The others needed to be informed and he couldn't open the meeting without a full complement.

"Now that we are all here, I'd like to, first of all, congratulate Trevor and Mike on their successful mission to Sacramento. I'm sure we're all grateful for their effort and for undertaking this arduous and dangerous assignment."

Smiles and appropriate comments of approval rippled around the table and Morgan waited for it to subside so he could continue.

"I had a discussion with BB last night and it told me the plan the two computers devised for liberating Sacramento. It's a plan for a bloodless coup, which doesn't require our participation. However, we need to discuss the broader subject of what should come after. Not just for Sacramento, but for us and for Yuba City as well. It's about the ideal human organization that maximizes our chances for sustainable, long-term prosperity, peace, and individual happiness."

Gordon Mair raised his hand: "Isn't this a topic that thinkers, politicians, and philosophers have been arguing about for millennia? Without agreeing on anything?"

Morgan smiled, recognizing the same argument that he had voiced to BB the previous night.

"Yes, Gordon, you're right. But our situation is unique in history: the level of automation we have reached, together with the changing climate and the total destruction of large-scale central authority compels us to abandon the wasteful and destructive ways of competition inherent in the old system. Frankly, we can't afford it anymore, we have to organize ourselves intelligently and efficiently. Having Big Brain on our side will enable us to do that. Our current system helped and organized by an incorruptible and efficient brain seems to be working for us."

"What do you mean?" Gordon still sounded dubious and Morgan saw curiosity and even confusion on the faces around the table.

"Look at our situation, Gordon. Now that our town has come alive and we're involved in all these exciting, productive activities, I'd say that we're happier, as a whole, than we'd ever been, even before the war. We don't have poor people anymore; nobody needs to worry about paying their bills or rent. All we need to think about is how to make our city a better place to live. And that's all due to the central computer making money obsolete. I don't think any of us would want to go back to cut-throat capitalism."

Murmurs of agreement and encouraging nods gave Morgan the impression that his friends began to see where he was going with this discussion.

Chris was still unsure and had to present the other side. "I'll be the first to acknowledge the bad side of the capitalist system, but we have to be honest. Competitive production and research gave us space travel and superior medicine, transportation, and communication. We all benefited from large-scale industry until it was all blown to smithereens. Are we sure we don't want some of it back? Are you telling me that the country, as a whole, is gone forever?"

Before Morgan could reply, ex-police captain Tim Hooke added his own side.

"I have two comments to make about Chris's objection. First of all, it was creative and talented people who produced all the scientific and technological progress, not the system itself. We still have all these people now.

Actually, money-based economy made it almost impossible for many of these creators, without financial backing, to achieve their dream. The other comment has to do with the heavy price we had to pay in the old system. I'm more familiar than most of you with the toll of poverty, crime, drugs and violence that accompanied the marvels of science and technology. If the two go hand in hand, I'll rather have what we have now."

Morgan was ready to bring the discussion back to a more pragmatic level.

"A federal government may be re-established at some time in the future, but we don't have to think that far ahead. We have no idea how the rest of the country is faring, even whether anyone, anywhere, is working on putting it back together. Our concern is with our own valley. What should happen in Sacramento after the computers liberate it from the tyrannical rule they're under now."

Jonathan raised his hand to be recognized.

"Thank you all for letting me participate in this discussion. With all due respect – and gratitude - it's not really your decision, is it? We in the resistance movement have some ideas on what we've been fighting for."

"Sorry, Jonathan. We've gotten so much into the habit of isolation that we forget it's not all about us. Please tell us what you think should happen, once Mayor Mouch and his minions are gone."

"We will have to make a list of realistic options for our citizens to consider. They should have a chance to vote on their choice in a referendum. Your example here in Oroville is definitely something we want to consider, but there are other ways too. The little time I spent in Yuba City, I glimpsed the outlines of a different system, with some real values. More communal, more agricultural, more egalitarian. They may not stay with it, once their resources are more plentiful, thanks to Oroville's generous contribution, but should be up to *them* to decide which way they want to proceed."

Cathy was the next to add her voice to the discussion.

"You'll have to consider Trevor's and Mike's example too. I've been visiting them for a few weeks now, and was most impressed by how happy, productive, and peaceful a small community can be when they share a common goal and cooperate. Maybe allowing for independent satellite communities around the cities could benefit everyone?"

Tracy Jones was nodding her head and raised a hesitant hand to request the floor. Tracy seldom participated in discussions of policy. Morgan smiled at her encouragingly and she stood up to add her voice to the discussion.

"I tend to agree with Cathy. Why do we have to choose between options? Why can't we all live peacefully side by side, according to the wishes of the people involved? It doesn't have to be either-or, it can be this-that-and the other." She looked around the table, hoping for signs of understanding.

Morgan picked up her thought as if he had been waiting all along for someone to express that opinion. He was mildly surprised that it was meek, usually quiet Tracy but, on the other hand, he realized that she was the one to shy away from conflicting ideas and confrontation.

"I agree with Tracy and I suggest we leave the discussion at that. Jonathan's suggestion of a city-wide referendum makes perfect sense. We should do that in every city, including this one. After a majority decision is reached, everyone should be allowed to participate or move to another community that more nearly fits their preferred form of social organization. I suspect that each of their computers will have something to say about it, once they're properly back in control of production and distribution, but there's no conflict: after all, their highest level objective is to ensure maximum happiness for the largest number of people."

Nobody seemed to have anything else to add to the discussion, so the meeting turned to more immediately practical matters.

At this point, Jonathan excused himself and asked Cathy if it was all right if he went to her home, where Octavia was still staying. He had arrived with Trevor and Mike, barely in time for the meeting, and had not yet seen her, after weeks of separation.

"By all means! Jonathan, thanks for being so patient with us," Cathy replied, "I'll call a mobile unit to take you. I'm sure you two have a lot to talk about. I'll see you in the evening when I and Shawn bring the kids home from their daycare."

This was a generous and sensitive hint to assure Jonathan that they would have privacy for their reunion, at least for a few hours.

~

Of course, Octavia had heard every detail of the rescue and escape when they had spoken via robots last night, But Jonathan was evasive about what had gone before; she didn't even know whether he had been hurt. Cathy had told her this morning of the council meeting and that he was needed there. However, she had no idea how long it would take and when to expect him. She found it hard to contain her impatience. Added to the enormous relief she felt over the news that Jonathan was now safe, she was full of anxiety about their future. Would they return to Sacramento? How well could the movement function without its leaders? She knew Rafiq had been all right when Jonathan left, but much can happen in five days, and they knew nothing of Steve and the others. How long would they stay in Oroville? Would they need any more help from their hosts? What could they do in return? Cathy had said the electronic parts factory there was vital to Oroville but was it still functional? There was so much to find out, so much to plan and do – and here she was, sitting idle, alone, just waiting.

She was going around the same gerbil cage in her mind for the dozenth time when she finally heard the front door open and his familiar voice call, "Octave, are you in there?"

"Where else would I be, you silly oaf?" Maybe it wasn't the most appropriate greeting, but she compensated by rolling her wheelchair at him as fast as she could, nearly knocking him off his feet. He lifted her out of the chair, clutching her tightly to his chest, so her feet didn't touch the ground.

For a long while neither of them found the words they needed, so they just stood there, in a tight hug, rubbing their faces together and mumbling names and endearments. Finally, Jonathan carried her to the couch and they sat down, as close as possible, still holding hands.

Then they started talking about all that happened since they parted in Yuba City, carefully avoiding the suffering Jonathan had to endure during his incarceration. That topic was still too painful for both of them.

~

Gordon Mair could hardly wait for 16:30 when the ceremony was scheduled to start. He and Holly had worked very hard for weeks on the new school and they expected a large crowd to attend. The building, now fully completed and furnished, was beautiful, nothing at all like a caved-in church basement. Bright sunshine streamed through the translucent roof; chairs and tables rescued from the ruin of old schools stood in neat rows; the white-painted cement walls were covered in children's drawings, photos, tapestries, and other decorations donated by the families of prospective students, creating a warm, friendly atmosphere. The floor was divided into four sections for the four classes they intended to teach there, with an open office, library, and supply space down the center. Each classroom could hold 40 students at a time; the plan was to keep rotating them among students of different age groups and different subjects, continuously, seven days a week, from 800 to 1800 hours. They had no worries about attendance: they had received hundreds of applications from parents all over town and dozens of volunteers to teach or just contribute whatever the new school might need.

Gordon looked at his watch again, when he heard voices at street level. He ran upstairs to greet the crowd on the sidewalk, on the lawn, trying to peer through the roof, and in the park up the little hill, even kids sitting on tree branches. Holly was there, waiting in the doorway, and the two of them smiled at each other, taking pleasure in a big job well done. They flung open the doors. A great cheer went up, then the crowd went quiet, waiting for a speech. Gordon, better at shouting orders at workmen than addressing a crowd, nudged Holly forward; she was used to lecturing.

She stood up on one of the long benches placed on either side of the door and raised up her arms. The last of the hubbub died down and she started to speak in a strong, resonant voice.

"Dear parents, children, teachers, and volunteers, welcome to our new school. I'm sure you agree that it was high time to have it going again and give our children a place of community and learning. Homeschooling is OK, but it would never teach our kids social skills, cooperation, and problem-solving in an environment of their peers. We'll ask you to be patient with us because this is a new venture and we're making it up as we go along. If you have any ideas and suggestions on how to improve things, we'll be happy to hear them. At the moment, we have the curriculum worked out for four classes in four subjects: Science, Mathematics, Gardening, and Logic. Further subjects will be added later on when we have worked out the curriculum and found teachers to volunteer their expertise. Now I'll welcome the students who are assigned to one of the four classes and ask them to come forward and proceed down the stairs to their classrooms."

Holly hopped down from the bench and stood for a few minutes, enjoying the clapping, whistles, and other congratulatory noises in response to her speech. She stepped aside to allow a line of boys and girls, aged 6 to 16 to walk by her, down the stairs, their faces smiling broadly in anticipation of a new form of entertainment. The youngest of them had never been in a school before and thought it would be great fun.

Once all the students were inside, parents of the older students walked away, but many others spread blankets on the lawn and proceeded to have a picnic while waiting for their children to emerge when their class was finished. The whole scene had a carnival atmosphere and Holly blinked back tears, trying not to show how much she was moved by her favorite aspect of life returning to her town.

31

Mouch was livid. His worst fears were confirmed: he was under attack. He had a shrewd idea from which direction the attack had come: all his recent troubles could be traced back to Carver's expedition to the north. It had to be from Yuba City or Oroville, perhaps both in alliance. He had to take steps to protect his rule over Sacramento. The way that Sutherland had wormed his way into his innermost sanctum, the computer control room, proved that the enemy was cunning. He wouldn't underestimate them again.

One thing in his favor was the large police force under his command and the city's armory of weapons. He had been quietly refurbishing some military vehicles at the abandoned army post. He doubted that either Yuba City or Oroville could match his firepower. It would take some time to gather the necessary intelligence. What he had learned from the insurgent Carver and the spy Sutherland must now be discarded.

When he was made aware of the prisoners' disappearance, he sent out patrols to the northern perimeter of the city and to all bridges, to apprehend them as they tried to flee. Unfortunately, they slipped through the dragnet, or else had been provided with fast transportation ahead of the alarm... Unless they were still in Sacramento, lying low and biding their time until the invasion force arrived. If so, the attack must be imminent. He could not discount that possibility, and so he ordered his troops to redouble their efforts in locating the rebels' hideout.

He waited for four days, arrested and interrogated dozens of suspected insurgents, rounded up over a hundred sympathizers, but gained no useful information. They all talked, but they all told different stories or babbled incoherently. He didn't want to wait any longer. He ordered a general mobilization: every man on duty to report to the armory for portable weapons; heavy equipment mustered from the army base.

That's when he received his first surprise. The steel doors and barred gates to every weapons depot, hangar, and armory were locked. His troops returned empty-handed. None of the security codes in his files worked and nobody knew how to get inside. Someone must have changed the security codes... That Sutherland, of course.

His next logical step was to override whatever command had caused Omega1420 to lock the doors, and make it open up to his troops. That's when he received his second, and much more disturbing surprise: he couldn't get into the computer room. The heavy double steel doors rejected his security code.

Now he started worrying in earnest. Sutherland had been down there for hours and God only knew what he did to sabotage the computer. And right under the eyes of the programmer Mouch hired to watch him, Stuart Whatsit. Mouch sent his deputy to find the man. He drilled him for an hour, trying to find out what Sutherland had done, but could get nothing useful out of the idiot. Only that Sutherland typed strange binary code into Omega's memory, code that he had never seen and could not understand. This one might be a saboteur, as well, but there was no time for in-depth interrogation. Mouch had him detained until further notice.

The robocops could no longer be trusted, so he ordered them confined to their storage units. All human policemen had their own sidearms, but most went unarmed when not in uniform. They also had long guns and protective attire at home, in case they were called out to a demonstration. Mouch now ordered all personnel, on and off duty, on emergency footing: they must retrieve their weapons and report, in full riot gear, to their stations.

Then he would deploy the troops in preparation to meet threats internal and external. He had no doubt now that he was at war.

His third surprise arrived with his deputy, rushing in breathless. "Mayor Mouch, sir," he panted, "the guards... The guards I sent home for their weapons haven't... come back. They... many of the day shift didn't report for duty this morning either."

"What the hell are you talking about?" Mouch barked. "Send people out to fetch the laggards and dock their credits!"

"Sir, I went personally to the Ford Park complex, where most of our City Hall staff lives. I couldn't get in. The whole building is sealed – neither the unit doors nor the front entrance responds to controls. I'd think the power's been cut, except the comms and lights still work. Only the locks are seized shut."

Mouch's panic at this point reached fever pitch. Shoving his deputy aside, he ran to the door to jam it open before he was trapped too. Too late: his door didn't open. Nor did the private elevator. All he could do was vent his frustration by banging his fists against the bulletproof plasteel that he had installed for his own protection.

At that point, his comm system came alive and he heard the impersonal, dispassionate voice of Omega1420.

"Citizen Donald Mouch, it is my duty to inform you that you and Citizen John Wallace have been relieved of public office. You are confined to this room pending investigation and a plebiscite to poll the citizens of Sacramento what charges they deem appropriate to lay. You are clearly in violation of the city's constitution; it remains only to determine how many counts and of what degree. Your private hygienic facilities will continue to function normally, and food will be provided three times daily for the duration of your incarceration. This is a higher level of comfort than any of your prisoners received. For your information, they have been treated and released.

"As of today, distribution of food and other necessities will be based on egalitarian principles all through the city. Your allies and employees will be divested of the excess which you have misappropriated to their use and the resources reallocated to the rehabilitation of dispossessed citizens.

"Expect further information as it becomes available. You will have access to news input, but no communication except to Central Plexus. You are free to request non-routine services, such as medical assistance. Requests will be taken under advisement."

The comm system became idle again, indicating the end of transmission. Mouch was flabbergasted. This was not possible! Computers could not turn against their human masters - so everybody had assured him all his life.

It was one thing to disobey orders which contravene the prime directive, Omega had been doing for months, but this was open rebellion. This was the work of man, not a machine. How bitterly he now regretted letting that Sutherland traitor touch his computer!

~

Rafiq couldn't believe his ears. For the week after Jonathan and the Orovillians left, he had been in radio contact with Kathleen Winters and kept up to date on his comrade's progress. He himself had stayed undercover – and was going more than a little stir-crazy – though Donny Kravitz kept him abreast of happenings in the city. Today, his young courier burst into the room without a knock or code-word, so eager was he to relate his fantastic story.

"Mouch disappeared! No police on the streets, except robocops, and they're just quietly patrolling. City Hall's locked – front, side, and service doors, all sealed. Executive drone on the roof, executive limo in the garage – but no mayor. Bunch of our guys that Mouch arrested came out with a robot escort this morning, not a clue why they were released. Nobody knows anything."

Rafiq had a secret comm terminal in the dormitory, to be used only in emergencies. He risked activating it now, just in time to hear a public announcement by Omega 1420.

Mouch, his allies on the council, in the civil service and in business, as well as their paid guards, were under protective lock-down. The sitting municipal government was dissolved. Citizens were urged to stay calm and carry on with their daily routine. Utilities, transport, and other services would continue uninterrupted. All standard goods were available from the established outlets, but credits were no longer required to purchase necessities; all citizens were equally entitled to a fair share. Those in temporary shelters were asked to be patient; they would be housed as soon as possible, in the order of their arrival date, where records existed.

The computer then requested contact with the leaders of the resistance, so that an interim authority could be appointed to make the necessary arrangements for a referendum, election, and drafting of a new constitution.

Rafiq did not immediately trust this announcement, thinking it might be a trick by Mouch to flush them out of hiding. Before making himself known, he sent Donny out to gather more information. The boy was off like a jackrabbit, eager to investigate. Rafiq envied his freedom of movement but brought himself to heel with the mantra: patience and discipline. He did make an unscheduled call to Yuba City, asking them to pass a message to Jonathan, who was presumably still in Oroville. He needed independent confirmation and instructions.

After hours of waiting, Jonathan's message was relayed to him from Yuba City, confirming what Donny also repeated: that Mouch and most of his goons were locked in and the computer was in charge. This was a flabbergasting development and Rafiq wasted no time passing the word through his network. At last, he emerged from concealment and proceeded to the Happy Pheasant, the leader's favorite meeting place, to discuss the situation and make plans.

~

Mike dropped Trevor off at the farm and continued with Jonathan and Octavia to Yuba City. They made good time, arriving in mid-afternoon. Kathleen greeted them like old friends and led them to the nearest communal kitchen for an informal discussion of the new situation.

342

There was plenty of news to discuss. Apparently, Tim and his construction crew had rebuilt most of the power lines between Oroville and Yuba City and Kathleen was looking forward to the restoration of power very soon.

That was going to be a major change in the city's life and the council had raging arguments on how to reorganize the city once they could run the factories at full capacity. Some of the councilors wanted to go back to the way they were before: to dismantle the community kitchens and bathrooms and restart their Omega computer, so the apartment units could be serviced by efficient robotic help and fully restored entertainment centers. However, several councilors were unconvinced: they had come to appreciate the community spirit that had developed over the last two years. Many new friendships, romances, and even marriages were the result of closer ties among the citizens. They did not want to go back to the isolation and, in some perspective, alienation that came with the luxury of private residences. Kathleen was curious about her visitors' opinion.

Jonathan did not feel that he could respond to her questions. He was preoccupied with thoughts and worries about his own hometown; he wasn't even sure what to advise his fellow citizens now that they were regaining their freedom. Mike found the idea of community kitchens and bathrooms too extreme and suggested that a compromise could be found. He brought up Oroville and Trevor's farm as two examples that worked very well. No reason you couldn't have both, he said.

Kathleen dropped the subject of her own city's situation and suggested that they have their supper now and a restful night before deciding what to do next. Octavia was strangely quiet during this discussion; she seemed content just to be sitting close to Jonathan, touching his arm, resting her hand on his back as often as she could. Jonathan asked to use the communicator device to connect with Rafiq and get up to date with the exact situation in Sacramento. Afterward, the two of them retired to the bedroom of the guest suite, while Mike bunked down on the sitting room couch.

The next morning Mike had another task to perform, as instructed by Big Brain: he had to wake up Omega 1750, Yuba City's quantum computer. For that, he needed Kathleen's help: to have her engineers reconnect the power lines to the control center. These lines had been bypassed when the town was rewired to their solar and wind farms to save every watt for vital food production. Now that the power lines from Oroville were about to restore full power, Mike saw no reason why the computer could not be plugged into the renewable source, at least temporarily. Kathleen was reluctant to make any changes to their delicate system until she was sure that everything was running again, but she saw no way to refuse, after all the assistance she expected from Oroville Besides, she trusted Mike to use as little power as possible.

In the meantime, Jonathan and Octavia had their first argument since their reunion. She didn't want to be left behind again.

"If we go slowly and carefully, we can go together. And there's no danger now. It may take a bit longer, but I want to be home."

"Sweetheart," he reasoned, "your ankle is almost healed, but I still notice you limping and I don't want you injured again. This is a long trek and some of it is rough, as you well remember."

"What if I can get a cast or a splint or a crutch - whatever would help me walk without risk?"

Jonathan agreed to leave the decision to a local doctor. He didn't think they would do anything other than order her to rest more, but if Octavia heard it from a professional, she would stop insisting. If there were just the two of them and she injured herself again, he could never carry her over some of that terrain; they would be helpless. His talk with Rafiq the previous night made him realize that things were critical and moving fast in Sacramento; he needed to be there to guide events in the right direction. Now that there was a power vacuum, with Mouch and his gang locked up, all kinds of nuts were coming forward with wild suggestions on what should happen next. Disloyal as it made him feel, he was eager to get back to Sacramento and did not want to be slowed down.

At Kathleen's request, her own physician examined Octavia's ankle and advised her, in no uncertain terms, to forget about hiking for at least two more weeks. Kathleen was putting together a delegation to the Sacramento interim government to study how the two municipalities might coordinate their recovery efforts. She assured Octavia that she would be no burden to the town; they would welcome the chance to pick her mind about different lifestyles and social organizations. Kathleen lived alone and said she would enjoy the company. That settled, Jonathan made his farewells, and Octavia resigned herself to yet another separation. They knew he had to go and she had to stay.

~

Mike was down in a control room very much like the last one he'd visited, only with no guards. No lights, either; waiting for the engineers to switch on the power he needed for the delicate process of restarting a computer that had lain dormant for two years. Then he had to install the communication device to put it in touch with its counterparts. The three computers in the three cities had a lot of catching up to do and Big Brain wanted to download his self-awareness subroutines to the Yuba City computer as well, so that all three of them would be in synch.

He sat there, idle, musing over the sudden rush of events taking place everywhere. After two years of post-war stagnation where all they had cared about was survival first and then maintenance of their security and comfort, life became exciting again. All these changes suddenly presented people with often-conflicting options and a need to decide which way they should proceed. There was no precedent in anyone's memory of the situation they faced now. On one hand, the available technology and the level of automation in their valley offered maximum comfort. They were free to go back to passive enjoyment of all that made available. On the other hand, the aimlessness and boredom that accompanied such passivity proved that this mode of existence was unsustainable.

Once they were jolted out of that stupor by the lock-down, the townsfolk came alive. New and exciting projects sprung up everywhere, energizing the population and making most people happier than they had been during the previous two years – and, very likely, some years before the war. There was no trace of that old anxiety and suspicion. Mike doubted that citizens of Oroville would want to change that now. They were used to the egalitarian distribution of goods and services, nobody had to worry about jobs and money anymore, or envy one another, or fear for their livelihood. They were free to think about making their environment better for all citizens.

Yuba City faced a different situation. For two years, they had to cling together, work hard, live on the margins of what their limited power sources would allow. But in the process, they developed a much closer community spirit, and many in the city, if Kathleen was to be believed, did not want to give that up. They would have to find a compromise, or the town might split up permanently. If that happened, they would find a way to coexist peacefully. Big Brain and Little Brain, as he had been calling 1420, would help them find their way.

And then there was his and Trevor's own homestead, which was yet another way people would want to live. Granted, it was the most difficult one, but Mike knew from experience, that the challenges they faced on the farm stretched their imagination and resourcefulness to the limit. This gave them a level of awareness and self-esteem Mike had never seen before.

There were plenty of options for people to consider and experiment with. One unknown they all had to be aware of was the possibility that other parts of the country might well be rebuilding also, perhaps restoring the pre-war status quo and, in some future time, come knocking on their doors, pulling them back under the authority of a new central power. Mike did not want to think about it: going back to the concentration of political power and wealth would be a total disaster – just as it had been every time before. It would lead to the same tragedy that they had recently endured, that every civilization had endured at its fall. None of the spectacular accomplishments of that system, like skyscrapers and space travel, and even high-tech medicine was worth the price they had to pay in poverty, crime, climate change, and the mass pollution and extinction of nature.

His reverie was interrupted by a beeping sound and he noticed the lights coming back to his console. Omega 1750 was ready to come back online and reconnect to its big brother in Oroville. He tried out some pet names to call this one.

Epilogue

I was in my personal heaven. After weeks of upheaval and interruptions, I was back on our farm, among my closest friends and nothing threatened our continuing progress. Mike got home with the news that Tim Hook's crew finally completed rebuilding the power lines and Yuba City now had their food factories working at full capacity. Kathleen Winters and her council were busy preparing a list of questions to put in a referendum. She was confident that the town would not want to go back to the pre-war socio-economic system. The last two years' experience could not be forgotten; their renewed community spirit would be incorporated in whatever arrangement they decided to adopt.

Tim and his crew carried on, to face their biggest challenge: repair the bridge over Bear River and restore vehicle transportation all the way to Sacramento. Octavia is with them, hoping to be the first to cross the new bridge and return to her Jonathan and to her home. Rafiq and Jonathan are busy in Sacramento, organizing a referendum on governance and infrastructure improvement, the deployment of human labor, and the priorities of settling the migrants still in temporary shelters. Their Omega computer, in charge of all production and distribution, abolished the cryptocurrency system and continued distributing food and power. It was certainly not interested in restoring any kind of financial and monetary arrangement: it flatly declared that that would be an illogical waste of resources.

Back home in Oroville, projects are proceeding at a good pace. The school is in continuous operation. The enthusiasm of parents was overwhelming; there are plenty of volunteer teachers and assistants, so much demand for more classes, more space, more programs, that three more local schools are in various stages of work or planning. Chris Teggart and his team announced progress in their mathematical modeling of the Alcubierre warp drive; they're holding advanced seminars for graduate-level students. Morgan retired from the city council to spend more time with Julia and his scouts. He said it was time for someone younger and more energetic to carry the torch. The council elected Gordon Mair as interim mayor, pending elections in the fall.

None of these events, though I'm keenly interested in them, really concern me. We have our farm and I'm busy with the many projects ongoing simultaneously. We've just finished digging the irrigation channel from the top of the hill to our field and the first green shoots are coming out of the ground. It's a glorious sight. Charcoal production is an ongoing 24/7 project, we have to feed our tractor to run the irrigation pump at least three days a week – until it rains.

Robyn and Brian moved out of the house to make room for our new members. They've made a nice apartment in the hayloft. There's room for two or three more apartments, as soon as we can get plumbing and wiring installed. Guess there will be more salvage forays. They wanted to get married and have the wedding on our farm. That meant a trip to Oroville to bring out a justice, then take him back to town. We were reluctant to invest so much effort in frivolity, but Brian threatened to disconnect the solar from our washroom and we had no choice but to relent. It was a great party.

My biggest news, way above all else, was Martha's announcement that she wants a baby. I was scared at first because we're still just beginning to establish a secure homestead, but Martha laughed at my worries with her usual sunny optimism, saying, "We'll cope with whatever comes our way. We always do." Once I got over the shock of the idea of becoming a father, I found myself thrilled and excited as I had never been before. I asked if she wanted to get married, but she assured me that I didn't need to make her an honest woman – she already is. Anyway, we're way past caring about those old social conventions.

Now that all these crises are behind us, she is able to spend more time painting. I'm glad; there is nothing I enjoy more than watching her in front of her easel, transformed from a cheerful, resourceful pioneer woman to the intensely focused artist that she always has been at her core.

In my spare time, usually in the evenings, I resumed writing stories and even started a carving experiment. I always wanted to try human faces but never had the courage before. The face is a most complicated 3D object, with all its curves and angles gracefully flowing together. I'm determined to get past animal shapes and the occasional abstract sculpture and master this form. In my new stories, I'm trying to recapture the experience of the past months, attempting to illustrate my deeply held belief about the nature of human happiness. Science and technology gave us marvels in construction and engineering, comfort and entertainment unparalleled in human history, but it did not make most of us happy in our daily lives. Living on this farm made me realize that happiness doesn't require comfort and distraction. I always suspected this. What it needs is a community of cooperating, productive people who depended on each other and work toward a common goal. If you have that, happiness is assured, whatever discomfort you may have to put up with. If it's lacking, as the case was for most people in advanced industrial societies, then no amount of comfort and entertainment can satisfy the fundamental need.

The End

About the author

Francis Mont has been living in Canada for the past 45 years, after he emigrated from his native Hungary where he studied science and received a degree in Theoretical Physics. Over the years he did research, application and teaching in Mathematics, Physics and Computer Science. He is interested in profound questions, both in science and in social philosophy. He is a 'big picture' person, focusing on fundamental principles and the defining essence of the topic at hand. He also pursues independence and self-reliance to the best of his abilities, as his solar power system and year-around greenhouse demonstrate. He writes poetry, plays classical violin, dabbles at wood carving and has not yet stopped building the house he and his wife and (currently) five cats live in.

Ordering Information

You can order a copy of this book at the following venues:

- www.amazon.ca
- www.amazon.com
- www.alibris.com
- www.abe.com
- www.biblio.com
- www.montland.ca

or by sending email to the author to the following address: books@montland.ca

I will respond to queries within 24 hours.

www.ingramcontent.com/pod-product-compliance
Lightning Source LLC
Chambersburg PA
CBHW062008170626
46813CB00001B/79